THE STRANGER

About the Author

Simon Conway is a former British Army officer and international aid worker. He has cleared landmines and the other debris of war across the world. As Co-Chair of the Cluster Munition Coalition he successfully campaigned to achieve an international ban on cluster bombs.

He is currently working as Director of Capability for The HALO Trust, coordinating the charity's response to the urbanisation of warfare and growing use of improvised explosive devices.

He lives in Glasgow with his wife, the journalist and broadcaster Sarah Smith. He has two daughters.

A LOYAL SPY, his third novel, won the 2010 CWA Steel Dagger Award for Best Thriller of the Year.

Visit Simon Conway's website at www.simonconwaybooks.com and follow Simon on Twitter @simongconway and Instagram @simongconway

Also by Simon Conway

Damaged
Rage
A Loyal Spy
Rock Creek Park

THE STRANGER

SIMON CONWAY

HODDER &
STOUGHTON

First published in Great Britain in 2020 by Hodder & Stoughton
An Hachette UK company

1

Copyright © Simon Conway 2020

Extract from *The Hollow Men* from *Collected Poems 1909–1962*
by T.S.Eliot published by Faber and Faber Ltd

A CIP catalogue record for this title is available from the British Library

Hardback ISBN 9781529324280
Trade Paperback ISBN 9781529324310
eBook ISBN 9781529324297

Typeset in Plantin Light by Hewer Text UK Ltd, Edinburgh
Printed and bound in Great Britain by Clays Ltd, Elcograf S.p.A.

Hodder & Stoughton policy is to use papers that are natural, renewable
and recyclable products and made from wood grown in sustainable
forests. The logging and manufacturing processes are expected to
conform to the environmental regulations of the country of origin.

Hodder & Stoughton Ltd
Carmelite House
50 Victoria Embankment
London EC4Y 0DZ

www.hodder.co.uk

For Stan

Thanks to Nick Sayers, Paddy Nicoll, Sapna Malik, Simon Morton, Jason Arancon, Audrey Gillan, John Robb, Rob Williams, Alana Eissa, David McKie, Joe Hall, Rachel Brock, Peter Bouckaert, John Montgomery, Tom Meredith, Phil Robertson and Sarah Smith.

Let me also wear
Such deliberate disguises
Rat's coat, crowskin, crossed staves

T. S. Eliot, *The Hollow Men*

Mar 30 ███ 2.05AM

Dear Minister,

Our friends in the east have informed us that they have taken custody of the terrorist known as the Engineer and his pregnant (seven months) wife.

We have arranged to take control of the pair and place them on our aircraft for a flight to your country. It is vital that one of your officers accompany the Engineer on our flight in order to provide legal custody of his wife.

Thank you and best regards

███████

London
SE1
5 April

FOR THE URGENT ATTENTION OF THE MINISTER OF FOREIGN AFFAIRS, ████████████████████

Following message from ████████ in London

1. I congratulate you on the safe arrival of the Engineer. This was the least we could do for you and for your country to demonstrate the relationship we have built in recent years.

2. The intelligence that resulted in the capture of the Engineer was British. I know we did not pay for the air cargo but we are eager to work with you in the questioning of him.

3. I would like to send one of my officers who is familiar with this case and speaks Arabic. I would appreciate it if you could give him direct access to question the Engineer. I will call to confirm this.

PART ONE
HUBRIS

How are we going to wage war anymore, with everyone watching?

David Brooks

I

The make-up artist

There is nothing to suggest that this day is different to any other.

The prisoner strikes a match, the light spilling across a dead man's face, revealing bruised eye sockets and a livid burn that runs from the temple across the man's cheek and down the side of his jaw. The match goes out. The prisoner strikes another, his hands trembling slightly. It takes several to light enough candles to work by.

He fills a plastic bowl with tepid water from the jerrycan that sits by the door and sprinkles a few soap flakes from a plastic bag on the surface. He reaches up for one of the rags hanging, like bat wings, from the clothesline that runs the length of the ceiling. The cloth is stiff as cardboard and he has to dip it into the soapy water several times before it is pliable enough to fit in the bowl. He stirs it in the water with his fingers and wrings it out several times. When he is ready he kneels on the floor by the body and says a short prayer before he begins, whispering so that the guards on the other side of the door do not hear him. He tries to approach each new body with care and tenderness, but there is little time and once he has started he works with unhesitating speed. He uses the damp cloth to wipe the grime and soot and crusts of dried blood from the man's face and then his neck. He sees that the mouldy blue patina of livor mortis is beginning to creep up the sides of the man's neck and over the roll of his shoulders.

He wrings out the cloth several times and the water in the bowl gradually turns black. He changes it once, pouring the wastewater into a drain in the nearest corner of the room, and refills the bowl from the jerrycan. While the power is out he tries to stay close to the door and the candles. He does not know what else is in the room.

He uses another rag to dry the man's face, pressing the stiff, leathery cloth against the cold wet flesh until it softens and becomes absorbent. Preparations complete, he reaches for the plastic bag hanging from a nail on the wall that contains the tools of his craft: the cosmetics and the chopped-up pieces of sponge; the brushes and spatulas; the swabs, second-hand dentures and glass eyes. He begins with concealer. It comes in thick plastic tubes in two different colours. He squeezes it on to the man's skin like paint and then uses small squares of sponge to distribute it evenly: yellow over the bruises and in the dark cups of the man's eyes and green over the raw wound on the side of his face. Then he applies a layer of pancake, mixing it from a palette to match the man's skin tone, spreading it on his cheeks, and then rubbing it into the eyes, the nose, the chin and throat. Over this he lays more make-up, using cotton swabs to add a touch of colour about the eyes and on the cheeks.

The electricity comes back on. He feels it first as an insect hum in the overhead strip lights that is followed by a sense of dreadful foreboding, and then the room is brutally illuminated.

The prisoner was an actor, a performer on stage and screen. He was, by profession, a storyteller. But the words in his vocabulary are insufficient to describe the horror of what he has seen.

There are twelve of them lying naked, with caved-in chests and shrivelled limbs, in a row on the concrete floor: nine men and three women. The women are the worst because he lives with the constant fear that one of them will be his wife.

Not today.

He sees that each one of them will be a challenge. One of the men has had his face skinned off, which will require a thick layer of the prison's dwindling supplies of make-up. The guards will grumble and accuse him of being wasteful. Another man's head is separated from his shoulders, but the decapitation was done with a minimum of sawing and he knows with the confidence of an expert that it's just a question of fitting the parts back together.

6

He sees that a woman's eye has been gouged out. Since he first saw such a thing he has been regularly visited in his dreams by a childhood toy, a teddy bear that was missing an eye, that he refused to let his mother replace. The teddy speaks to him with a chorus of voices. They are eager to share their secrets with him and he tries to listen but he can never remember them when he wakes.

He lives and works in a former Ottoman administrative building that is used for interrogation. When he first started this work there had only been one or two bodies a week and he had more time to disguise the wounds but now it feels like he is toiling on a gruesome factory line, forced to work at reckless speed, like an acrobat on a trapeze, always in danger of a spill. So many bodies, so much work – he often wonders what carnage must be going on outside to merit such a regular supply.

When he has finished all twelve the prisoner puts the tubes and the wooden palette box and his sponges and brushes back in the canvas bag and he knocks on the door.

The photographer is a large man who smells of cigarettes. He has a drooping moustache and a sallow, pockmarked face and he wears the same leather jacket every day. He carries an elderly Polaroid camera on a braided strap on his shoulder. His mood is much better when the electricity is working and he doesn't have to use any of the precious supply of flashbulbs that he keeps loose in his pockets. He surveys the line. If the photographer is dissatisfied with some aspect of the prisoner's work, he grunts without speaking and points at the area and the prisoner applies more make-up. When he is content the photographer takes a head-and-shoulders photo of each corpse in turn. It is the prisoner's job to collect the photos as they spool out of the camera and wave them in the air until they dry.

He places them on the chest of each victim.

When they are done the photographer knocks on the door and they wait together for the medical examiner. They do not speak or make eye contact. The photographer lights a cigarette. He seems unnaturally agitated, frightened even.

The prisoner closes his eyes and attempts to inhale some small portion of the smoke as the photographer exhales.

The medical examiner is a small man in a white laboratory coat with an ink stain on his breast pocket. He hurries in with the usual preoccupied expression, carrying a handful of brown manila folders that he hands to the prisoner, one for each victim. The medical examiner stops beside each body, matches the photo to the face and hands it to the prisoner who paperclips it to the front page of the file. By the door, the photographer lights another cigarette.

When he is done checking, the medical examiner takes the folders back one by one, signs his name on the death certificates and in each case records: *death by natural causes.*

They are at the end of the line when the medical examiner starts to tremble. He looks up. Their eyes lock.

In a faltering voice he whispers, 'Are you the Engineer?'

The prisoner is startled. He has not heard that name for years, not since he was last interrogated.

The medical examiner is shaking with fear. The prisoner glances at the photographer who is at the far end of the room and does not appear to have heard. Back when they used to torture him, it was the answer that they most wanted, first the Arabs (Egyptians, Iranians, Iraqis) and then a queue of other nations; the Americans, the Russians, the British: *Yes, I am the Engineer!*

And so, mostly for that reason, because the truth would be too difficult to explain, the prisoner turns back to the medical examiner and nods his head.

The guards escort the prisoner back to his cell in one of the sub-basements.

Occasionally a voice will call out to him as he is passing one of the other cells but he learned long ago not to answer. No one who is brought here lasts for long. Apart from the guards, he believes that he is the only long-term inhabitant of the building and even the guards don't last for long.

Entering his cell, he is relieved to see that his bucket has been emptied of waste and there is a mug with black tea, and a bowl with boiled potatoes, olives and a crust of hard bread waiting for him on the stone shelf that serves as his bed. The door is bolted behind him.

He eats the potatoes and with his fingers, sucks on the bitter flesh of the olives and spits the stones on the floor. Afterwards he scrupulously wipes the bowl clean with the bread, which he has made easier to chew by dipping it in the tea. His teeth have loosened since he has been in prison. When he is finished, he puts the bowl on the floor and unfolds the rough blanket that he placed that morning under the kapok-filled pillow.

He blows out the candle, stretches out on the shelf and considers the strangeness of his day. He assumes that it was day rather than night though he cannot be sure. There are no clocks in the prison and no natural light. No one, not even the medical examiner, wears a watch. He just assumes that his work is conducted during the day. It makes sense to him that the interrogators are nocturnal beings; that they do their best work at night. The days are his to conceal their crimes. He equates the sound of the guards' boots approaching in the corridor and the turning of the key in the lock with morning. It's the routine that makes up his life. It's astonishing really, he thinks: the human capacity to establish a sense of rhythm in the worst of circumstances. It is easier now than it was at the beginning. When he first came here he was in a cell closer to the surface and it was difficult to sleep. He was interrogated daily. And then they seemed to forget about him. Eventually, when they decided that he could be useful to them in a different way, they moved him down to the deepest underground level, where the walls are so thick that he does not have to listen to the screams or smell the burning flesh.

He has no idea how long he has been imprisoned. He does not know how many birthdays have passed, how many gatherings of uncles and aunts, nieces and nephews. He does not think he is wrong that he will not see any further such days. They are likely to take place in his absence. Only a fool would cling on to hope.

There will come a time that he is not able to do anything to disguise a particular wound or the supplies of concealer will run out. Or someone, somewhere, will give up the ludicrous pretence that the victims of torture have died of natural causes. His usefulness will come to an end. He has accepted that he is as expendable as the corpses that queue each day for his attention. He has long assumed that his former identity has been forgotten. And so, he is utterly confounded by the medical examiner's question.

Is there someone out there who remembers you? Is someone looking for you?

Then he feels the deep rumble of an earthquake shaking the walls and a rain of grit on his face. The outside world has come knocking.

It's a turbulent revival. One moment the prisoner is staring into darkness and then the next his whole world is shaken on its axis and he is thrust, raw and new born, into blinding light.

The earthquake is followed by the sound of gunfire, clanging doors and boots in the corridor.

He sits up on the bed.

Someone is calling out. 'Who is there? Who is there?'

'I am a prisoner!' he yells back. He lurches forward.

The door crashes open and hands grasp his elbows, bodies press against his. Someone is speaking but he cannot hear the words. He is dragged out of the cell and along the corridor and into startling daylight. He is confused for a moment, not just by the sunlight but because it seems like the air is filled with confetti and then he realises what he is seeing and feels a sudden rush of exultation.

Death certificates! All those death certificates turned to ash!

He is carried up a steep rubble slope past the twisted hulk of a truck chassis and bundled into the back of a pick-up that races out through the entrance into the ruined city beyond.

He sits sandwiched between two men and for the first time in more than a decade he catches sight of his reflection in the rear-view mirror and immediately looks away, preferring to witness the devastation of the world around.

They pass burned-out cars and festering rubbish, piles of bricks and rubble that clog the streets, centuries-old buildings that have been destroyed.

They drive past the ruin of the mosque where he worshipped at as child, past the empty bazaar with its ancient passageways now choked with fractured masonry, and past the shattered carcass of his elementary school with its abandoned playground.

He has returned to the stage and the chorus are chanting 'Not to be born is best'.

2

The Atlantic Council dinner

Frank Booth, a former Secretary of State for Foreign and Commonwealth Affairs, now exiled to the backbenches of Parliament, stands in the bathroom of a suite in the Hay Adams hotel, with his elbows out and two ends of black silk ribbon hanging limply in his ruddy fingers. He is staring at himself in the mirror and his wife of nearly thirty years, Margaret, is banging on the door.

'Frank. How much longer are you going to be?'

'Just a minute.'

He considers another attempt: over and under or under and over? It's not as if the Americans give a damn. But the British Ambassador will be wearing a proper one and he can imagine the air of condescension that will greet him if he resorts to a ready-made bow tie.

Fuck.

His hands are broad and heavily veined, too large for such delicate work; not the hands of a man whose occupation is cerebral, but of a born blue-collar worker, a lathe or a loom operator, bred for Britain's industrial revolution. Some carefully concealed part of him has always felt like an impostor in Whitehall. Even now. But he could always fix a smile, no matter who the audience. 'Your naff look' is what his caustic, too caustic, youngest daughter Emily calls it. For him it is a necessary carapace, an essential tool for any successful political career. Along with the certainty of being right, the flow of power that rises in the groin.

'It's my turn,' Margaret chides him from behind the door.

At least they'd been given a decent room.

He unlocks the door and his wife bustles in wearing bra and tights. He feels lucky that she has kept herself trim with Pilates and careful dieting and that he still feels attracted to her when required.

'Here let me help you with that.' She takes the ends from him. 'Don't slouch. Stand up straight. What have you been doing all this time?'

'I was on the phone.'

Some of the most momentous conversations of his period in office took place in the cramped privacy of toilets, often on trains to and from his parliamentary constituency, talking to the Americans with a close protection officer standing guard outside the door.

'Hold still. Who was it?'

'Bridget.'

While Margaret had been blow-drying her hair in the bedroom he had taken a call from Bridget, his literary agent, who was breakfasting in Dubai.

'What does she want?'

He sighs. He doesn't want to be asked what the conversation was about. *Just another bloody indignity in a life jammed full of them.* 'She says they want me to jazz it up. Thirty years in British politics and a front row seat on the world stage at a time of global crisis are apparently not enough for my publisher.'

'Well that's ridiculous.'

Bridget had been at her most emollient, practically purring down the phone as he perched on the side of the bath. He imagined that she was in a hotel bed with a tray and on it a boiled egg and a folded white cloth napkin. Silk pyjamas. 'What about your colleagues, sex, drugs, drink, you know. That's all they want. Some headline copy for the memoir. They really do want to give it a push, Frank. I promise. They want people to hear from you just as much you do. It's just that from a certain point of view it's a teeny bit humdrum. A bit flat. Their words not mine. We've got to try and get it into the supermarkets, Frank.'

'And my analysis?'

'Of course! That's important. Of course, it is. And they'd like more of that as well. I mean what about Iraq, what was going on in the prime minister's head?'

'So, what did you tell her?' his wife asks, pushing the folded end of the bow through the back of the knot, and then standing back to sharply tug both ends and tighten the bow into shape. 'I hope you told her to stuff it.'

'They want to give it a push, that's what she said.'

'In exchange for gossip?'

'Not exactly gossip. Insider knowledge. I mean that's sort of the point. I was there when the crucial decisions were made.'

His wife rolls her eyes and shoos him out of the bathroom. Now is not the time for another fight over the rights or wrongs of the Iraq war and besides he doesn't care for the plaintive undercurrent in his own voice.

He goes to stand beside the nearest of the bedroom's two windows and faces the night. Their suite looks out across the landscaped symmetry of Lafayette Square, with its vacant benches and martial statues, at the floodlit portico of the northern facade of the White House. The President's residence and principal work place: the centre of global power.

The first time it really struck home that he wasn't in government any more Frank was in a lift. It refused to move. He looked around, vaguely irritated and then realised with some embarrassment that there was no one else there to push the button.

No one to carry his coat or the red boxes that came with a cabinet position, no one to steer him through the pitfalls of his diary or offer pithy analysis in the back of his ministerial Jaguar, no one to keep watch on his movements, no one to stand guard outside the door of the train carriage toilet while he talked in private to the US secretary of state.

A former cabinet colleague, now in the Lords, had taken to introducing himself with 'I used to be someone.' It might have been sad but his former colleague was so transparently pleased with his lot – which as far as Booth could tell, consisted of several paid non-executive posts on the boards of defence contractors – that it was difficult to feel any sympathy. They were the same defence contractors that were headquartered in gleaming high-rises across the Potomac River, just a couple of miles from where he was now standing.

I used to be someone. It wasn't the sort of thing Frank imagined himself saying.

He was who he was: an MP struggling along on a backbencher's salary; a boy who had grown up with a bruiser of a father in a back-to-back terrace; the first in his family to reach university. He had met his wife at an anti-nuclear rally. He was a politician who'd served in one of the highest positions in the land and someone who had been forced by circumstances to make some tough, and at times ruthless, choices. He had set out to do some good but along the way had come to understand the murkiness of the world.

Another colleague, now a grande dame of the party, had once said of him that he possessed 'Rat-like cunning, a plausible manner and a modicum of natural ability.'

He glances back at his wife as she comes out of the bathroom and goes over to the bed where her dress is laid out, still in the plastic sleeve provided by the dry cleaners.

'Have you thought about what you're going to say to him?'

The last time he'd seen the former prime minister – his prime minister – it had been in the south transept of St Paul's at the service of commemoration for Afghanistan. They had hardly spoken. Throughout the service Frank had found himself distracted by the sight of the prime minister's short-lived successor, a former chancellor of the exchequer, bending and folding his order of service in ham-fisted origami, trying to read the words. He pitied him, though for primitive reasons he also thought him faintly ludicrous.

'Not really,' he admits. 'I don't suppose we'll get much chance to talk.'

He might be toxic back in the UK but over here in America the ex-PM was still a lion.

'He owes you,' Margaret says, stepping into her dress.

'Does he?' Frank muses. He has certainly been loyal.

'Here do me up.'

She turns her back to him and, as she pulls in her stomach, he pulls the zip from the base of her spine to the base of her neck.

'There,' he says and smiles.

His phone vibrates in his pocket. He takes it out and stares at the caller ID on the screen – Unknown.

'Frank Booth,' he says.

'Hello, Mr Booth, you don't know me but I'm Kirsty McIntyre. I'm a journalist with *The Guardian*.'

Scottish: the lower pitch of a Glasgow accent. He recognises the name from her byline – Diplomatic Correspondent? Foreign? Security? But he can't put a face to her. He has a difficult relationship with *The Guardian*. He doesn't much like the leftist metropolitan elite and they don't much like him. 'What can I do for you Ms McIntyre?'

'I have some questions about your time as Foreign Secretary.'

He turns back and moves closer to the window again to face the night. He stares at a massive oak at the entrance to the park.

'I'm always happy to answer questions,' he says. It's what he always says. It goes with the naff smile.

'The questions relate to a number of documents that have come into our possession.'

'Go on.'

From the corner of his eye he sees sudden movement in the darkness behind the parapet on the roof of the White House: the dark outline of a man moving. For a moment, he wonders if an intruder has gained access to the roof but then he realises that it must be one of the snipers changing position.

'They include two faxes.'

'I'm sorry?'

'Two faxes.'

'Please, I have an engagement. Can you get to the point?'

'Yes. I know, the Atlantic Council dinner. That's quite a guest list. You'll be feeling right at home there, I'm thinking?'

He sighs. 'Ms McIntyre.'

'It's just that these faxes were found in a compound used by the Syrian intelligence service in Damascus, I mean the sort of place where they torture people, and they relate to the rendition and subsequent questioning of a man known as the Engineer. Do you remember that name?'

It suddenly feels very cold in the air conditioning.

'Go on.'

'There's a fax that we believe is from the CIA and it refers to them flying the Engineer and his pregnant wife on one of their own planes to Syria.'

'Have you spoken to the CIA?'

'No. Not yet. But we will, of course. You can be sure of that.'

'It sounds to me that the CIA are the people you need to be talking to.'

'Here's the thing, Mr Booth. I'm being straight with you here. There's another fax. This one is from London. It's to the Syrian foreign minister and we believe it's from a senior MI6 officer named Samantha Burns.'

'I see.'

'Mr Booth, was the British government in which you were foreign secretary complicit in the capture, rendition to Syria and subsequent questioning of the Engineer?'

'Ms McIntyre, I really couldn't tell you. As I've said before, as foreign secretary, you can't know everything that the intelligence services are up to.'

'Yes, Mr Booth, you have said that before, I'm aware of that, on a number of occasions. The thing is I'm asking you about this specific case.'

'I really don't know what you're talking about.'

'Did you authorise MI6 participation in the questioning of the Engineer?'

'I refer you to my previous response.'

'Come on, Mr Booth, this isn't a courtroom. I'm just trying to find out the truth. We have a source in Whitehall who claims that this was authorised by you.'

'I think I've said enough.'

'Did you authorise MI6 participation in the torture of the Engineer?'

He cuts the connection.

'Frank?'

He turns back to his wife.

'You look terrible,' she says.

'It's nothing to worry about.'

She is watching him with the wearily familiar expression of someone who has been asked to live with more disappointment than she deserves. 'What have you done?'

'It's just a stupid journalist digging for dirt.' He summons the smile. 'You look beautiful. Come one, let's go see the Americans.'

3

Kompromat

Jude Lyon, an officer of the British Secret Intelligence Service, more commonly known as MI6, stands, straight-backed and martial, before an expanse of raw canvas at least four metres on each side, in a high-ceilinged room in the National Gallery of Scotland. He is holding a rolled exhibition brochure in his right hand that he taps unselfconsciously against his thigh. The brochure has a quote from Robert Louis Stevenson's honeymoon memoir *The Silverado Squatters* on the first page: 'There are no foreign lands. It is the traveller only who is foreign.'

Jude finds the paintings strangely unsettling: they have the foreboding quality of a dream or a memory. The artist is internationally famous but, if you believe the brochure, notoriously difficult to pin down – a man without borders. He was born in Edinburgh but his childhood was in the USA, Jamaica and India. His family moved frequently. He went to nine different schools. Now he divides his time between Jamaica and Canada, where he has a teaching post. There is a quote from him that says: 'I'm always foreign. But then who's from anywhere?'

Jude's immigrant provenance is equally exotic and fragmentary, shot through with competing veins of conformity and criminality, from a cigar-chomping bank robber for a grandfather to a general given to eccentricity and dark moods for a father.

For all that he is clubbable and well groomed, his curriculum vitae a whistle-stop tour of the establishment, there is something solitary and non-conformist about Jude. His desire for service is tempered by an increasing distrust of those in authority. And he carries within himself a reckless desire for truth that operates regardless of a quieter voice that struggles to plead caution.

The painting that he has been standing in front of for the last ten minutes is the most disturbing and, because Jude has reached a crossroads in his life and has an unquiet mind, he has been struggling to understand why.

It's a huge oil painting with, according to the blurb, the power of an ancient symbol. It shows a spindly-legged man with raised, almost transparent wings standing on a darkened foreshore with untold depths behind him. The receding tide is lambent with foam and the sky is a deep mauve with only a narrow strip of lighter blue on the horizon, hinting at the approach of dawn.

Abruptly Jude realises what it is that the painting reminds him of. Abu Ghraib. It's as if the painting is a negative, or an X-ray, of the infamous image of a hooded figure-on-a-box in a black poncho with his arms raised like bat wings. One of the cache of amateur digital snapshots of anonymous hooded prisoners, and US military policemen mugging and grinning for the camera, that marked the moment when the ideals of eighteenth-century America foundered in the sand. When the public began to accept what they already knew, that all the pretty talk of freedom and modernisation in Iraq disguised naked aggression and deep-seated cultural contempt. The realisation that the West was now mired in a hellish conflict with no end in sight; a conflict that, more than a decade later, continues to grow and mutate, infecting entire regions of the globe.

A leather-gloved hand cups Jude's right buttock and gently squeezes.

'A penny for your thoughts?'

Yulia is a head shorter than him, even in her beloved Louboutins, but her copper-flecked eyes are lit with fire, her smile is voracious and her voice is husky and low.

'Daydreaming,' he says.

'Let's go back to bed.'

★   ★   ★

Back in the Balmoral hotel, on silky sheets with a ludicrously high thread count, they fuck. She is straddling him with her spine bowed forward and the fingers of one hand between her thighs. He guesses from the glaze of sweat on her brow and her flushed cheeks, and the hypnotic rhythm of her hips racking against his thighs, that she is close, and he realises that he is not far behind.

'Fuck me, Jew-boy!'

She is in black stockings and a wasp-waisted corset and her Louboutins. He believes that between the shoes and the custom-made corset, she's wearing at least three thousand pounds sterling to bed. And that doesn't include the jewellery, notably the rock on her finger, that he thinks must be worth three or four times that. It's impossible to reconcile with her husband's government salary and more likely attributable to his alleged links to PMC Valkyrie Group, a shadowy Panamanian-registered private military company that acts as a front for Russian intelligence.

The corset is to hide the stretch marks that are the only things that she appears to be self-conscious about. On the face of it, the fifteen-year difference in age between them doesn't seem to faze her at all. *And why should it?* She's getting what she set out to find when she posted her profile on an infidelity site on the web. She was very specific in her requirements: a handsome, well-mannered and virile man with martial posture, an art history degree, and a full head of hair. And although the upper echelons of the intelligence services may not be prepared to openly acknowledge the method by which it has been achieved, they are getting what they want: namely, proximity to her husband, a diplomat in the military attaché's office at the Russian Embassy.

As for Jude, on the face of it he has nothing to complain about. She is as energetic a lover as she promised on the site. She gives every part of herself and exults in his taking her. As poised as she is in public, she is equally uninhibited in the bedroom. But, inevitably, given his questioning nature, there is a voice that is asking: *Is this what you signed up for when you vowed to defend the realm – playing the honey in a trap?*

She comes with her mouth wide open and her lush, expensively dyed hair tumbling across her shoulders. He follows soon after.

She tumbles off him and they lie beside each other, arms and legs akimbo, panting. He gazes without seeing at the flawless white expanse of the ceiling, and the image of the winged man on the dark foreshore returns unbidden to his mind.

'You're not here, are you?' she says.

'Of course, I am.'

'You are such a beautiful boy.'

She has a way of speaking English that makes any endearment, no matter how innocuous, sound derisory.

The final scene is unexpectedly deferred. The jaws of the trap remain un-sprung. There's no late-night knock at the door, no humiliating exposé of several weeks of diligently saved pornographic messages and graphic selfies, nor any tears or recriminations. There is no suggestion by a world-weary fellow spy that, if Yulia is prepared to cooperate, her brutish husband will remain none the wiser. Instead they sleep, rolling in and out of each other's arms, and wake feeling refreshed and good about the world.

Something has happened.

They are sitting at either ends of the bath in a mountain of foam when the call comes. It's Totty pretending to be his brother.

'Grandma's taken a turn for the worse. She's asking for you.'

'I'll be there as soon as I can.'

He ends the call and treats Yulia to an apologetic grimace.

'I'm really sorry.'

She pouts and for the first time, he senses a deep well of anger in her. She does not like or expect to be let down, let alone abandoned on the one occasion they have managed to carve out more than a few hours alone together. Perhaps it does not help that she's an only child whose parents are dead and, for the purposes of this operation, Jude has a large and fictitious family, which allows for multiple means of communication. Grandma on her last legs is code for 'get your arse back to Vauxhall Cross pronto'.

He wonders what must have happened to prompt such a message. Is he compromised? Yulia is not showing any signs of suspicion, but it stands to reason that a woman who can success-fully conduct an affair under the nose of a tyrannous and violent husband who works for the GRU, Russia's military intelligence unit, must be a truly accomplished liar. Of course, there is another possible explanation. Her husband knows that she has allowed herself to be snared in a trap but she does not. In which case, she is the one most likely to face her husband's wrath.

He gets out of the bath, grabs a towel, and pads across the room while the voice in his head scolds him. *What has she done to deserve this? How can you have fallen so low?*

The questions rise like bubbles of gas.

4

The gibbet

Roland Totty meets Jude at arrivals but instead of driving into London they head west along the motorway before taking the turn-off to Hungerford.

'Queen Bee is in a fury,' Totty confides in him as they are crossing the common. Totty always gives the impression that he has special insight into Queen Bee's moods but Jude guesses that the opposite is true. That's why she keeps him close. He is a useful idiot.

'Why?' Jude asks.

'*The Guardian* has got hold of a story. They're threatening to print tomorrow.'

'What is it?'

'She's not saying.'

Samantha Burns, otherwise known as Control, but more commonly Queen Bee, lives in a farmhouse in a secluded village in west Berkshire that, according to the grapevine, is exclusively populated by retired Whitehall mandarins and espiocrats. The village is in a coomb, a narrow steep-sided valley through which a river does not run, and they drop down into it from a chalk escarpment that is dominated by a 20-foot wooden gibbet, a medieval gallows-like structure.

Totty recklessly navigates the narrow steep-sided lanes, hemmed in by hedgerows thick with dog rose and buckthorn, and eventually pulls into a gravel drive and halts against the eaves of a brick and flint farmhouse with a thatched roof. They get out of the car. For all that she recruited him from the army, and has carefully cultivated his career, this is Jude's first visit to Queen Bee's home. It feels like he has been let into a jealously guarded secret. It must be very damaging, whatever it is *The Guardian* has uncovered, to merit such a break with protocol.

Totty uses the cast iron knocker on a substantial-looking oak door and clicks his fingers impatiently.

Camilla Church opens the door. *Oh no*, he thinks helplessly, *not here, not now*. She looks Jude up and down without making eye contact. He sees, with a sudden stab of mourning, that she is wearing her wedding ring again.

'Go through,' she says, in a steely tone, 'she's waiting.' She glances at Totty, 'Not you. You can wait in the car.'

Queen Bee is standing in her kitchen, artfully casual in pressed jeans and a flawless navy cashmere sweater with a string of pearls. Her hair is blow-dried and there is a hint of make-up about her eyes. With her is a stranger, unmistakably American, with lush, well-groomed hair, a button-down tattersall shirt, pleated chinos and sockless loafers.

'Welcome, Jude,' Queen Bee says. 'Thank you for coming at such short notice.' She is looking straight at him with palpable sincerity and if she is furious she has it well hidden. She is as self-contained as she was on their first encounter in a flattened town in Afghanistan.

'What's happening?' he responds, aware of his former lover striding across the kitchen in the direction of the coffee maker. There is nothing soft or consolatory about Camilla's beauty. She is all hard angles and disdainful polish: from her newly styled razor-cut platinum bob to her cocked elbow and knee-high leather boots.

'Nasruddin al-Raqqah has resurfaced,' Camilla says.

The full enormity of that takes a few moments to sink in. The last time that Jude had heard that name was on the tarmac at an air force base in Pakistan. A sleek, dart-shaped Gulfstream was waiting on the runway and tall black-suited Americans, unworldly as Tolkien's elves, were standing waiting while the Pakistanis and the Syrians exchanged paperwork relating to Nasruddin's pregnant wife.

The plane was on the ground for less than thirty minutes

and when it was gone Jude never expected to hear that name again.

'Come on,' Queen Bee says, 'let's clear our heads and go for a walk.'

They choose from amongst a selection of muddy wellington boots of varying sizes in the boot room and the American accepts woollen socks to go with a pair. They follow a footpath up the hill with Totty trailing behind. They pass a sloping field filled with sheep and another with pheasant pens, before entering a tunnel of interlocking hawthorn, and finally emerging at the top.

'We're on the highest point of the Berkshire Downs here,' Queen Bee explains. 'In fact, the highest point in south-east England.'

'I've always wondered, why do they call them downs when they're up?' the American asks.

'It's an old Celtic word for hill,' Queen Bee explains.

Gazing at the natural hollow with the village and a Saxon church at its heart, Jude reflects on how typical it is of Queen Bee to hide in plain sight. Her very own hideout just a stone's throw from London. It is as if she has bent the landscape around her to deflect unwanted attention.

'What's that?' the American asks, pointing at the large wooden pole topped by a cross bar on the far side of the hollow. 'I saw it on the way in.'

'A gibbet,' Queen Bee replies. 'It was only used once back in the seventeenth century. They hung the bodies of an adulterous wife and her lover for all to see.' Jude looks at it and imagines black crows wheeling around it. Beside him, Camilla is stone faced. There are no secrets here. 'It's served as a warning ever since.'

'Al-Raqqah,' the American says.

Queen Bee touches Jude's forearm lightly and he takes it as his cue to speak. 'Nasruddin al-Raqqah, also known as the Engineer, was an al-Qaeda bomb-maker responsible for the death of twenty-five British soldiers in a complex ambush in 2004 in Iraq,' he explains. 'He fled the country following the attack and we tracked him to Pakistan where, two years later, as a result of intelligence that we provided, he was apprehended by the Pakistani intelligence services.'

'You assured us that he was a potential source of actionable intelligence,' the American says.

Queen Bee sighs. 'Given his history and the constraints that we were operating under we concluded that we were unlikely to be able to place him under sufficient pressure to reveal anything of significant value.'

'So, at your request, we gave him to the Syrians,' says the American.

Queen Bee looks at him in the manner of a schoolmistress challenged by an unfathomably dense pupil. 'At the time, it was thought we could do business with the regime.'

'Sure,' the American shrugs. 'It was *glasnost* in Damascus.'

'So, what's happened?' Jude asks.

'Somebody busted him out of jail,' the American replies.

'We don't know that for sure,' Camilla retorts.

'It's on YouTube.'

Queen Bee raises a hand to still them. 'We know that an armed group affiliated to Islamic State assaulted a Syrian government facility on the outskirts of Damascus at the end of last week and released a video of the attack. They retrieved a prisoner from the basement. It may be Nasruddin al-Raqqah.'

'Totty told me in the car that *The Guardian* has got hold of something?' Jude says.

'Unfortunately, the Syrians have proven to be assiduous in their record keeping,' Queen Bee replies. 'Two documents, faxes, have come to light, one from our friends here and one from us. They were recovered from the facility after the assault by an underground group of local activists. The faxes refer to Nasruddin's rendition by the CIA and his subsequent questioning in Syria by a member of the British Secret Intelligence Service.'

The American sighs. 'Vouchsafe, O Lord, to keep us this day without being found out.'

'We have been found out,' Queen Bee acknowledges. 'There's nothing we can do about that. For the press, it's like an aching tooth. They won't leave it alone. The prime minister has made it clear that there will have to be an investigation. An audit committee has been established.'

The American shakes his head. 'We told you to leave it to us but you insisted on sending your boy down there.'

'It was our intelligence that found him,' Queen Bee says, 'I had every right.'

'We've got no dog in this fight, Sam,' the American tells her.

'I completely understand,' Queen Bee says, briskly. She turns to Camilla. 'Could you escort our friend back to the house? I need to have a quiet chat with Jude.'

'Of course.'

Jude half-expects Camilla to click her jackboot heels.

'I hope you make it through this, Sam,' the American says.

'Don't you worry,' she says. 'There's life in me yet.'

They stand in silence while Camilla and the American descend through the sloping tunnel of hawthorn towards the village.

'We can no longer rely on our closest allies,' Queen Bee says, when they are out of earshot. 'They have become erratic and inconsistent. Their politics and policies are a malicious circus.' She sighs and looks at him. 'Syria is a terrible mess. We don't need someone like Nasruddin running around making things worse.'

'Understood.'

'You look tired. It must be difficult to make believe you care. Emotionally, I mean.'

He stares at her without understanding her meaning.

'Yulia,' Queen Bee explains.

'I've never claimed to care for Yulia,' he replies, unnerved by the question.

'Does she have feelings for you?'

He hesitates. 'She's used to getting what she wants. I'm not sure how she'll cope with rejection.'

'Nevertheless, you're off the op.'

Jude nods. It's not unexpected. *Why bring him here unless they have other plans for him?* But he is uneasy about the consequences.

He has been working on Yulia for months now. And, *Dammit*, he likes her. She's helped him to see beyond Camilla.

'You'll have to give evidence to the audit committee,' Queen Bee explains. 'The prime minister has given it to Chuka Odechukwu.'

'I don't know the name,' Jude says.

'He's a lawyer from the Cabinet Office attached to the National Security Council. Very ambitious. He'll be thorough. I expect you to be frank and honest. Have you got that? Frank and honest.'

'Of course.'

A flash of movement catches his attention, an acid yellow butterfly trembling on the ground. Looking closer he realises that a swarm of tiny black ants have surrounded it and are beginning to tear it to pieces.

'There's something else I need you to do. Something not for the committee.'

'Okay.'

'I want you to find him.'

'Nasruddin?'

'Yes.'

So that's what they are doing here on the top of the hill.

'Camilla has found you a researcher,' she says. 'You'll have your own discreet premises off-site, but with access to up-to-date intelligence and surveillance assets.'

'And if I find him?'

She looks out across south-east England towards the English Channel. 'We'll use a missile. After 9/11 the Americans got in the detention and interrogation business. I don't need to tell you what a mess that was. After that, they had to find somewhere else to put enemy combatants. So, they gave them away to third parties with more experience at extracting information, but that has been equally problematic. Frankly it's easier to deal with them by drone.' She returns her attention to him. 'Camilla will sign off on your travel expenses and she'll be your point of contact if you need to reach me. Can you work with her?'

'Do I have any choice?'

She is looking at him in a manner that suggests that the answer is self-evident. 'I want Nasruddin found and I want it done quickly. Is that clear?'

'Yes.'

'I know I can trust you, Jude.'

'Yes.'

'Come on let's get home. My husband has baked a cake.'

He looks for the butterfly on the ground but not a speck of it remains.

Back in the kitchen there is no sign of the American. Camilla steers him to a seat at the table and gives him a cup of tea, a slice of Victoria sponge and a new, hardened laptop with a fingertip reader. She talks him through the access procedures. As she leans over him he realises that she is wearing Chanel No. 5, a distinctive scent that he has always considered both provocatively sexy and as impenetrable as a suit of armour; a perfume that he has never known her to wear before.

'I've sent you a link to the film of the jailbreak,' she says. 'Make sure you look at it before tomorrow.'

He doesn't reply. The effort to maintain control in her presence is costing him more than he cares to admit.

'Chuka is expecting you at 9 a.m. sharp, at Vauxhall Cross,' she tells him.

'Okay.'

'Totty will run you home.'

'Okay.'

'Are you still in Shoreditch?'

'Yes.'

She shakes her head. 'When are you going to find your own place?'

He can't help himself. 'You know me, anyone's bed but my own.'

'I don't want a fight with you,' she says.

She walks him out to the car and raps on the window with her knuckles to wake Totty. She turns to Jude.

'Just remember who you're working for and concentrate on the task you've been given.' Her expression softens a little. He detects a hint of compassion. She knows how he feels about Queen Bee. 'Don't go off on one, Jude.'

5

Breaking the Walls

Jude comes up out of the depths of Old Street Station and heads east towards Shoreditch. As he walks down Rivington Street the mass of people starts to thicken: drinkers and vapers spilling out on to the cobbles from the pubs and restaurants. He stops off for a pint of semi-skimmed from a Bengali corner shop and then a pot of Vietnamese beef pho from Boat People. He queues for the counter alongside a floor-to-ceiling photomontage of visa applications for the owner's extended family.

His friend Sanjay's loft is in a cul-de-sac just off Shoreditch High Street. It's on the top floor of a former bonded warehouse turned garment sweatshop, now populated on its lower floors by start-ups peddling newly minted algorithms. On the pavement outside there are what Sanjay likes to call a 'vintage of hipsters': skinny, tattooed simulacra of Edwardian explorers and Norwegian fishermen necking artisanal beers.

'Excuse me,' Jude murmurs, sliding between them and reaching for his keys.

Sanjay's obsession with security may verge on the paranoid but there is something reassuringly bulky about the keys to his flat. They are of the patented kind that can only be copied with letters of authorisation and there are four of them, one for the hardwood street door, and three for the steel door into the flat. Jude rides the freight elevator to the top, nods to the CCTV camera watching from inside a black sphere above Sanjay's door and disables the alarm as he enters. He throws all three bolts behind him and crosses the waxed floorboards to the kitchen.

He puts the milk in Sanjay's large stainless-steel German fridge, which has nothing but steel cans of esoterically-sourced coffee in it, and sits on one of the stools at the mottled zinc-topped island to eat his pho while it's still hot. He stares through the wall of glass at the cluster of faux-skyscrapers in the City with their nursery-school nicknames: The Gherkin, The Walkie-talkie, The Cheese Grater, The Can of Ham.

When he is finished he goes through into the master bedroom and opens the closet. He parts the rows of Sanjay's identical suits and kneels down. There is an electronic safe bolted to the solid brick interior wall. He enters the code and it clicks open. Inside there is a bundle of three burner phones, each one marked with different coloured electrical tape; four further burners still in their packaging; a pile of sim cards; an unregistered Glock 17 9 mm pistol with two fully charged magazines; a radio-frequency detector with a 10 MHz to 25 GHz range; and two zip-lock bags, one containing cash of various currencies and the other a variety of passports, some of which are unknown to his employers. He takes the phones and lays them out on the kitchen counter, and adds the one marked with yellow tape that he has brought with him from Edinburgh to the collection.

He switches them all on.

Three vibrate. Red, yellow and green: two missed calls from his sister Hannah; a message from Yulia that says *Call Me*; and a voicemail from his therapist reminding him that if he fails to attend a session she will have to report it to his employers.

There is nothing from Camilla on any of his phones.

He doesn't understand why Queen Bee has forced them to work together. Surely Camilla doesn't want this any more than he does. He contemplates calling her but uncomfortable memories of post-split monomania delay his hand. In the months after she went back to her husband he had often messaged her in the dark hours when no one should press send.

Be calm, he thinks. Be reasonable. Don't call. He fills the kettle.

The red phone vibrates. It is his sister Hannah again. He hesitates, reluctant to engage, but as much as he tells himself he can live without his family, he does not like the idea of losing her. For her sake, he should make the effort. He accepts the call.

'Jude?'

'I'm here.'

Her voice wavers, takes on a slightly petulant tone.

'We haven't seen you for ages.'

'It's been difficult,' he says. His occupation is neither acknowledged nor discussed and she knows better than to ask him where he's been. There is a privileged status to being the oldest and only male child in a family where dysfunction reigns.

'Come over on Thursday,' she says. 'I'm cooking dinner.'

His sister wants a happy family and he's an ingredient she can't do without.

'That's very kind of you but . . .'

'Come on make the effort.'

'I don't know.'

'What's the matter with you?'

He can't tell her that he's been knocked sideways by a double blow: the first punch a face-to-face with a former lover who he has been expressly forbidden to have any contact with; and the second, an all-too-vivid recollection of his role in a questionable operation in the so-called 'War on Terror'.

'Just a work thing,' he says. 'I'm fine, really.'

'Come over. Get away from it all. The girls will be really disappointed if you don't come and see them soon. You're their favourite uncle.'

'I'm their only uncle.'

'Say you'll come.'

He sighs. 'I'll come.'

'That's brilliant.' Her voice alters, she sounds happy, excited even. 'We'll see you at seven-thirty.'

'See you then.'

'Looking forward to it.'

They hang up. He feels better. He makes coffee and carries it over to the island where his new laptop is waiting. It looks sinister enough to launch intercontinental ballistic missiles. He fires it up, opens the shield icon and logs on to the secure server with his right index finger. There is no text with Camilla's email, just an attachment that contains a video clip. It is labelled *Breaking the Walls #24.* The file icon is a video grab of a man's head and shoulders. The martyr. He is a bear of a man with a thick bushy beard and he is wearing a black scarf bearing the insignia of Islamic State.

Jude lifts his black unsweetened coffee to his lips and presses play.

The martyr is standing beside a truck with his shoulders hunched and his hands in his pockets. He is wearing a dirty white shalwar kameez that is several sizes too small for him. He looks up from his feet and squints uncertainly at something or someone unseen.

'It's time for you to make your peace with God,' the cameraman tells the man in Arabic but it appears that he does not understand. He looks crestfallen.

'I'm sorry,' he says in English with a recognisable Yorkshire accent. 'I can't speak it. I wish I could. Everyone expects it. I'm just not a very good speaker.' He takes his hands out of his pockets. They are surprisingly small given his size and they flutter at his throat. 'My tongue has got like . . . a knot in it. I wish I could make you understand. The words I'm supposed to say . . . it should come from the heart. I just can't do it.'

He shakes his head sorrowfully.

'Speak English!' the cameraman urges him.

The martyr looks surprised. 'Okay . . .'

'Jihad!'

The martyr nods slowly. 'Okay.'

He inhales and exhales.

'Okay.'

Finally, he looks straight into the lens and Jude gets a glimpse of animal fear, the desperate mental struggle of a man to keep himself together in the face of imminent death. 'I'm doing this for Allah, for his glory. I am happy to give up my life. Truly I am. So that my brothers may be freed from the dungeon of Assad where they have been like . . . tortured and maimed. I am here today to give my last breath for them. I have no regrets. I'm not a bit sorry . . .'

A fighter in a balaclava with a Kalashnikov strides into the picture and throws his arm around the martyr's shoulders. He points at the camera with his index finger, either mimicking a handgun or brandishing the *shahadad*, the finger of God, it's not clear which. The martyr looks embarrassed at the interruption but then he joins in. Another fighter steps in. They are all pointing: the condemned aping for the camera.

The camera pans from left to right. A convoy of vehicles are queued in a narrow bomb-damaged street with rubble pushed into piles at the sides. At the head of the convoy is a bulldozer reinforced with homemade armour plates with only a slit for the driver to see through. Behind it is the martyr's truck and after that a line of pick-ups full of armed men.

'In! In!'

The cameraman films the martyr climb into the cab of the truck to the accompanying roar of a diesel engine and the clatter of tracks as the bulldozer starts to move. The camera pans left and films the bulldozer as it advances to the end of the road and pivots right. The sound of gunfire is almost immediate. Rounds ricochet off the armour as the bulldozer advances on its target.

The cameraman is lifted into the bed of a pick-up, which follows the truck as it drives down the street. Jude can see a pyramid of aircraft bombs lashed together and connected with bundles of bright pink detonating cord in the bed of the truck. As they turn the corner the cameraman catches the bulldozer smashing through the front gates of a high-walled compound with its blade raised. It pivots again, creating a path for those behind to follow.

When it comes to it the martyr does not hesitate.

The truck accelerates through the gate, crosses a dusty parade ground and collides with the entrance to a low bunker-like stone building. Time seems to stand still for a moment. Then the bomb explodes. A massive detonation – the camera angle spins crazily, debris thumps the ground and a thick cloud of rolling smoke engulfs them in an instant. Someone is screaming and someone else is whooping for joy. The cameraman rolls out of the back of the pick-up and on to the ground.

Men run past, firing randomly into the smoke. The cameraman climbs unsteadily to his feet and follows. Unrecognisable shapes loom out of filthy grey cumulus. He takes cover briefly beneath two fighters who are firing from the top of a pile of rubble. They slide back down beside him and a sudden, jerky tightening of the shot reveals them exchange a few barely discernible words in a language that Jude does not recognise. He hits pause, rewinds and watches the exchange again. It's definitely not Arabic.

He presses play again.

The cameraman runs forward across the compound and reaches the lip of a massive crater. The explosion has broken open the cellars under the building and the fighters slide down the crater's smoking slope between lumps of torn concrete and twisted and tangled fingers of rebar, and scatter into the tunnels beneath. The cameraman follows two of them into the jagged mouth of a stone corridor that slants down steeply. The walls are rough blocks without mortar. The corridor levels out. Rows of steel doors are set at regular intervals into deep recesses either side of the corridor. Many of them are buckled and open, revealing empty cells. A fighter is calling out to anyone still living.

'Who is there? Who is there?'

A voice is heard, someone crying out: 'I am a prisoner!'

The fighters are jubilant – offering thanks to God. At the end of the corridor they throw open the bolts on a door that is still intact. A man in ragged overalls is staggering towards them from the back of the cell.

'We are here to rescue you, brother,' one of the fighters says.

They lift him up and drag him with his arms across their shoulders up the corridor towards the sunlight. The video ends.

Jude slides the cursor back a few seconds and freezes on the face of the prisoner in the cell. He puts his coffee cup down.

A decade has passed. In the video, the man's face is hollowed out by starvation, masked by a ragged beard and matted hair, and cast in shadow. It's impossible to be sure.

But it could be the Engineer: a bomb-maker of unusual sophistication responsible for the deaths of twenty-five British soldiers, perhaps now at large somewhere in the chaos that is Syria.

Nasruddin al-Raqqah.

Jude crosses to the glass and stands watching the City. Given that the film is already on YouTube it's only a matter of time before the suicide bomber's family are identified. The security service will be scouring their databases to try and match his voice with those of persons known to have left the UK for jihad. A family somewhere is about to have to come to terms with a very public death. Perhaps the families and their friends and neighbours already know. Soon the tabloids will be tipped off. The nation's self-righteous fury will descend up on them.

His yellow burner throbs. Another message from Yulia:

My dear vanishing, rather neglectful Houdini . . . you have disappeared into the ether!

It's an absurd situation. A prize asset in the Russian Embassy carefully snared and then casually abandoned. He wonders for how long Yulia will retain her sense of humour and what form her anger will take when it comes.

In the guest bedroom, he undresses, brushes his teeth, turns off the lights and climbs beneath the covers. After a time, he dozes into a dream where he laughs and kills and makes love at the commands of a ruthless puppeteer.

6

The audit

Jude shelters from the rain beneath the distinctive ski-jump roof of the bus terminal on the drab island at the centre of Vauxhall Cross roundabout, with traffic on the multi-lane highway swirling around him.

He is wearing a navy single-breasted suit with a crisp white shirt, a plain blue silk tie and silver-plated cufflinks.

A face to face the world.

A train rattles by on the raised tracks behind him heading in the direction of Clapham and on the other side of the traffic is the hideous Inca pyramid that is MI6's headquarters. He contemplates a sodden copy of *The Guardian*. The two faxes, one from the Americans and one from the British, are side by side on the front page. Certain details have been redacted, including the address of the less-than-discreet building opposite. He turns the page. There is an image on the inside of a filing cabinet in the midst of the rubble of a demolished building and beside it an image of a windowless room with twelve dead bodies lying in a row on the floor. They are naked with their genitals pixelated and their limbs are as spindly as sticks. The source of the images, according to the paper, is an intrepid activist group that operates behind enemy lines and call themselves We Are Being Slaughtered. They discovered the faxes in a metal filing cabinet found in the bomb-damaged ruins of the interrogation centre.

The Guardian has given the story to Kirsty McIntyre. He recognises the name. She's a friend and former colleague of his sister, Hannah, and Jude recalls meeting her at a raucous party in Clerkenwell to celebrate Hannah's leaving *The Guardian* for *Channel 4 News*. It was not long after he returned from an army tour in Afghanistan and he remembers defending the British Army's mission in Helmand in the face of considerable scepticism.

He'd like to talk to her again.

He crosses the highway by the raised footbridge and approaches the armed policeman at the pedestrian entrance to the building. He checks in his pass at the armoured glass reception booth and places his black work phone in a locker and his keys in a plastic tray before stepping into the scanner with his arms raised in surrender.

Beyond it a woman wearing blue surgical gloves frisks him and points him to a waiting area with taupe armchairs and a coffee table stacked with aging magazines. He flicks through a copy of *The Field*.

Totty arrives five minutes later clad in a fluorescent jacket and bicycle clips.

'You're early,' he says, plaintively.

They step through the air-lock entry system and Totty escorts Jude to an unmarked glass lift that propels him smoothly to the top floor.

Chuka Odechukwu QC of the Investigatory Powers Tribunal is standing under a recessed downlight in the middle of the corridor with a phone pressed to his ear. He is tall, as lean and lithe as a long-distance runner, and his shaved head shines like polished walnut. He is impeccably dressed in a single-breasted chalk-stripe suit, a pale blue shirt and a navy blue tie with a full Windsor knot. He smiles with perfect white teeth at Jude as he approaches and says, 'I'll call you later.'

He shakes Jude's hand firmly.

'Thank you for coming, Mr Lyon.'

'Please call me Jude.'

Chuka turns to Totty. 'I believe that you have a room for us?'

'Of course,' Totty replies. He leads them to a conference room with opaque glass walls on all sides and a blond wood table surrounded by leather backed tubular steel chairs. Chuka hands Jude his phone, saying 'Hold that for me will you.'

He sweeps off his jacket and hangs it on a coat stand in one corner.

'Thank you,' he says, taking back his phone.

'Can I get you anything?' Totty asks, hovering expectantly.

'Black coffee,' says Chuka in a manner that suggests that he's used to giving orders. 'Okay with you?'

Jude nods.

Chuka waits for Totty to leave, closes the door and turns around. He scowls at the black sphere with its red pin light in one of the top corners of the room and returns his attention to Jude.

'Samantha Burns tells me that you're a loyal servant of the nation,' he says, in his expensively schooled accent, with a hint of sarcasm that suggests that loyalty is not in and of itself a virtue. 'She couldn't speak more highly of you. Good in a crisis, apparently, and the soul of discretion. Ten years of exemplary work in the service and before that the army. Is that about it?'

'She's very kind,' Jude counters.

'Take a seat.'

It appears that the 'get-to-know-you' element of the interview is over. They sit opposite each other at the table. Jude watches while Chuka removes his cufflinks, weighty silver scarab beetles, and places them neatly side by side on the table before rolling up his sleeves.

'Shall we get started?' he says.

'I'm ready when you are,' Jude replies.

'I have been tasked with investigating whether the UK government acted in accordance with domestic and international law in relation to its involvement in the detention and alleged rendition of the Syrian national Nasruddin al-Raqqah,' Chuka explains. 'To begin with I'd like to hear from you, in your own words, about Nasruddin al-Raqqah and your involvement in his detention in 2006. Try not to leave anything out.'

He starts talking and Chuka listens to him without taking notes, with the same degree of professional scepticism as his psychiatrist. Jude is cautious and careful. He gives Chuka the bare bones: that he was a spectator not a participant; that his main contribution was to hand over the address of the Karachi safe house and confirm the identity of the target – Nasruddin al-Raqqah – the killer of twenty-five British soldiers. How he'd tagged along with the Pakistani Army Commandos on the raid to confirm that they got the right man. He'd seen Nasruddin taken into custody and visited him once in his cell. He had travelled with the police detail that delivered Nasruddin to the airport. He had been there on the tarmac when the handover to the Americans took place. He explains that at the time he was stationed in Karachi, the teeming seaside metropolis that is Pakistan's largest city, and his every move was monitored by the ISI, Pakistan's nefarious intelligence agency. He did what he was told and had no influence on the outcome. When he is done telling his tale he sits back in the chair and moments later, as if on cue, there is a knock on the door.

'Get that will you,' Chuka says.

Jude opens the door and Totty sets a tray between them. They've clearly pushed the boat out for Chuka: a cafetière, ceramic mugs and a plate of biscuits.

'Everything okay?' Totty asks.

'You can leave now,' Chuka tells him.

Jude closes the door behind Totty and resumes his seat. Chuka pours them both a coffee and slides a mug across the table. Jude watches while Chuka snaps a Hobnob in two and sets one half aside on the tray.

'What was the purpose of your deployment in Karachi?' he asks.

It's clear the bare bones will not suffice.

'I was part of a small unit that was tasked with cultivating assets inside the Afghan Taliban,' Jude explains. 'At the time, they were using the city as a bolthole for wounded and burned-out fighters.'

'Were you successful?'

'Is that relevant?'

'You tell me.'

'The ISI were not happy with our presence. They obstructed us at every turn. We got hardly any actionable intelligence.'

'So where did the intelligence come from that led to Nasruddin's arrest?'

'London,' Jude tells him.

'Not from one of your regular sources?'

He shakes his head. 'No. I got a call on the secure line in the embassy.'

'And the caller?'

He pauses. What had Queen Bee said to him? Be frank and honest. 'Samantha Burns.'

He watches Chuka put the uneaten half-biscuit carefully down. 'Samantha Burns called you in person and gave you the address of the safe house?'

'Yes.'

'Did she tell you where she got it from?'

'No. I assumed that it came from a GCHQ intercept. If it was a human source, I think I'd have known about it, given that I was the man on the ground.'

'And if there was no record of such an intercept?'

Jude smiles helplessly. 'Pass.'

'Somebody must have told Samantha Burns that Nasruddin was there.'

'Yes.'

'But you don't know who?'

'That's correct.'

'So, a mystery source unknown to you provides a key piece of information and Samantha Burns issues you with a set of instructions.'

'Yes.'

'Which were?'

'She told me to inform my counterparts in the ISI and assist with the arrest.'

'How did they react?'

'As expected, disbelief followed by angry denial. Then, after twenty-four hours, an about-face.' He remembers a bear of a Pakistani ISI officer, with startlingly blue eyes, cursing him across the table in a restaurant on Hawke's Bay. He had really hated the idea that Jude knew something that the ISI did not and on his own patch, too. Jude had ridden in a jeep with him at dawn the next day when they went to make the arrest. It was a frosty journey. Jude had been waiting in the stairwell when the Commando unit brought Nasruddin out of the apartment with a sandbag over his head. The ISI officer had lifted it up long enough for Jude to identify him and then they'd dragged him out into the sunlight.

'I understand that the raid was trumpeted as an outstanding example of inter-agency cooperation,' Chuka says.

'If you say so.'

'And they let you visit the prisoner in custody?'

'That's right. Later that afternoon, I had fifteen minutes with him in his cell.'

'Alone?'

'No, I was escorted at all times.' Jude remembers Nasruddin cowering in the corner, trying to put as much distance as possible between himself and the monster of an ISI officer.

'What did he say to you?' Chuka asks.

'He was distraught. He kept saying that he was not the Engineer.'

I'm not the Engineer! I'm not the Engineer!

'The Engineer?'

'The Engineer was the *nom de guerre* that he used in Iraq when he was behind a complex ambush that resulted in the death of twenty-five British servicemen.'

'Including the Butcher twins?'

'That's right.'

The death of so many British soldiers, in a series of interconnected explosions in a booby-trapped compound north of Basra, had dominated the news cycle for several weeks and caused considerable embarrassment to the then foreign secretary, who'd been splashed across the front pages with a weighty gobbet of spit on his face after an altercation with the Butcher matriarch at her twin sons' graveside.

'And what made you believe that he was the Engineer?'

'His fingerprints were found on the mobile phone that initiated the bomb that demolished the house.'

He knows as soon as he's said it that he's been played.

'You've just handled my phone.'

'He claimed responsibility,' Jude protests.

'Yes, I've seen the video. It was quite a performance. I enjoyed the Shakespearean flair. The tabloids loved it. He's quite a literary chap, Nasruddin al-Raqqah. I imagine that is the sort of thing that would show up in his file?'

'I can't comment on that.'

His answer subtly changes the atmosphere in the room.

Chuka frowns. 'Why not?'

'I haven't seen his file.'

'So how do you know his fingerprints were on the phone?'

'Samantha Burns told me.'

'Here's the thing, Jude,' Chuka says. 'There is no file. There was a file once, or so I'm told. And then, not long after an Arabic-speaking member of the Secret Intelligence Service visited Nasruddin in Damascus, the file was shredded. Someone, using an administrator password reserved for the software designers and believed to be long defunct, deliberately overwrote the encryption keys rendering the data "cryptographically inaccessible" for now and evermore.'

Chuka's chin is thrust aggressively forward.

'You speak Arabic, don't you?'

7

On the ropes

In the silence that follows the question, Jude realises that Chuka is trying out a theory that he has been complicit in some kind of conspiracy and cover-up. It's the kind of theory that has a habit of wrecking a man's career.

'I've never been to Damascus,' he says, with some satisfaction.

'I know,' Chuka tells him, leaning back in his chair. 'Samantha Burns sent Edward Malik to Damascus. We both know that.'

So, Edward Malik, former MI6 agent runner, was the Arabic-speaking officer whose name was redacted on the cover of this morning's *Guardian*.

'Actually, that's news to me,' Jude replies.

'I'm surprised,' Chuka says. 'I thought you two knew each other?'

Jude answers with care and accuracy. 'It's true that we were both attached to the Af-Pak Controllerate but we served on different sides of the border. I saw his name now and then in footnotes on reports coming out of Afghanistan but we never met.'

'I'm still surprised.'

'Malik was deliberately firewalled. He was reputed to be running an agent high up in the Taliban.'

'And if I told you that the agent was in fact high up in the Pakistani ISI and provided the information that led to Nasruddin's arrest?'

Chuka's question fills him with a deep sense of disappointment. What was the point of him being in Karachi, doing his best to gather actionable intelligence while at the same time dodging the ISI if there was a source there all along that could have provided him with the information he needed?

'Again, that's news to me,' he says.

Abruptly, Chuka changes tack. 'Was Nasruddin's wife with him in the cell when you went to visit?'

And so, to the part that haunts him still. 'No. They were kept separately.'

'You didn't see her at the apartment during the raid?'

'No. I didn't see her until the handover at the airport.'

'But you travelled with her to the airport?'

'There were several vehicles in the convoy including an ambulance.'

'But you saw her delivered to the plane?'

He feels the anger rising in him like indigestion. 'They had her restrained.'

The Pakistanis had wheeled her out across the tarmac to the plane on a hospital gurney, where a Syrian government official, who had arrived with the Americans, signed for her in triplicate.

'Did you know she was pregnant?'

She had been bound head to foot with black gaffer tape so that she resembled an Egyptian mummy and the worst of it was that the bulge of her pregnancy was visible in outline.

'Yes. It was obvious.'

'And that didn't bother you?'

'Of course it bothered me!'

'There's no need to raise your voice,' Chuka says, calmly. 'I can imagine how upsetting it must have been. After all, there's no suggestion that she was implicated in any terrorist activities. Unless Samantha Burns told you otherwise?'

'I didn't even know Nasruddin was married.'

'And did you protest afterwards?'

His answer shames him. 'No.'

'Did you speak to the representative of the Syrian government who signed for her?'

'No.'

'Can you confirm whether Nasruddin was, at any point, in British custody?'

'He was not,' Jude replies. 'I was there as a witness only. I watched the handover and I watched the plane take off.'

'And then what happened?'

Samantha Burns' words come back to him again: *I expect you to be frank and honest. Have you got that? Frank and honest.* And while he has been as assiduously honest as instructed, her full intention has not been clear to him until now.

'I received a call.'

'Who from?'

He pauses, aware that what he's about to say is, by any measure, explosive. 'The foreign secretary.'

Chuka is visibly astonished. 'Frank Booth called you, in person, and spoke to you?'

'Yes.'

'What did he say to you?'

'He said that he wanted to congratulate me personally. He said that he was very grateful for what I had done and that the world was a safer place.'

Across the table, Chuka is massaging his forehead as if afflicted by a sudden migraine.

'I think you'd better leave now,' he says.

Camilla is waiting for him outside the interview room, wearing an expression of stern rebuke. He follows her to the bank of elevators.

'You think she didn't know what her husband was doing?' she says, as they descend to the basement.

So, she was listening to the interview, no doubt reporting back to Queen Bee on the quality of his performance. 'I don't know.'

'Don't be a fool. Couples don't keep those kinds of secrets from each other, even if they try.'

'Don't they?'

She shakes her head in irritation. It seems that they are trapped in roles as ancient as warfare. He can tell what she wants to say: *why do you have to make everything about us?* But of course, she won't, not here where the walls have ears.

'I'd like to speak to Edward Malik,' Jude says.

'Forget it,' she tells him. 'It's not pertinent to the task you have been given. Malik was dismissed from the service in 2011.'

'Why was he dismissed?'

'Stay away from him, Jude. I'm warning you as someone who cares about you. Queen Bee would say the same. Concentrate on finding Nasruddin and don't step outside the parameters of the job you've been given.'

'Why do you care?'

She looks exasperated. 'Stop it.'

'Is that why Queen Bee brought you in on this? To keep me on a short leash?'

The elevator stops and the doors open on the underground car park.

'Don't be so bloody paranoid,' she says. She won't meet his eye. 'Come on.'

He falls into step beside her. They are heading towards an unmarked black car with its engine running. It's a four-door saloon sitting low on its axles – discreetly armoured. As they approach a burly driver gets out and opens the rear door for her.

'Where are we going?' Jude asks, crossing around the back of the car to the other door.

'Yorkshire,' she tells him, across the car roof. 'We've identified the suicide bomber.' Yorkshire is where three of the four suicide bombers who had killed themselves and fifty-two others in coordinated attacks in London on 7 July 2005 had originated from – they were clean skins, totally off the radar and the security services had been terrified of a similar event ever since.

Jude's black-taped work phone is waiting for him on the seat. It occurs to him that Camilla has had plenty of time to clone it.

'The family have been detained?' he asks.

She nods again. 'The home secretary has signed an interception warrant and GCHQ are already scouring their data.'

The car drives them a short distance west to the London heliport at Battersea where a Metropolitan Police helicopter is waiting for them. They climb in the back and buckle the safety harnesses.

The helicopter lifts with a jolt, turns and puts its nose down and the city rapidly falls behind them. They head north along the A1. It's too noisy to be heard above the sound of the rotor blades and if they use the headphones there is a risk that the pilot will listen in.

In the army he learned to nap anywhere, anytime, and so Jude closes his eyes and soon he is sleeping.

8

An orphan of Islam

The detective chief inspector from the North East Counter Terrorism Unit sprawls with his hands locked behind his head and contemplates the live video feeds from three adjacent interview rooms. Built like a prop forward, with a flattened nose beneath a mop of wheat-coloured hair and thighs like over-sized hams, he is forthright and casually confident.

'Fourteen young men and women from this town have gone missing in the last twelve months,' he tells them. His accent is posh northern English, with a rugby-field boom, an effortless ability to be heard across open spaces. 'They're presumed either dead or serving with what's left of Islamic State.'

In Room One, a distraught mother clutches the dog-eared photo that she has kept with her in her bag since her eldest son Hamid first went missing.

'He was not a bad man,' she says, struggling to hold back the tears.

The photo is of a smiling Hamid surrounded by boisterous children in a Turkish refugee camp and she treats it as if it is incontrovertible evidence of her son's saintliness. It's certainly hard to reconcile with the tongue-tied, downcast figure from the martyrdom video.

'He was a kind and gentle boy,' she says. 'He wouldn't hurt a fly.'

In Room Two her husband is saying nothing. He is sitting ramrod straight on one of the uncomfortable plastic chairs, his whole body bristling with humiliation.

In Room Three the brother has his mouth open and a forensic technician is taking a swab from the inside of his cheek. Unlike his parents, he has been strip-searched and his clothes and jewellery bagged. He is skinny and hollow eyed, clothed in police-issue blue coveralls that are several sizes too large for him. The contrast with his bulky elder brother could not be greater.

'The kids that go astray are invariably from patriarchal families within marginalised communities and are vulnerable to alternative authority figures. They are usually emasculated in some form and there is often a strong sexual flavour to their rejection.'

'Spare us your cod psychology, Paddy,' says a young Asian woman from the back of the room. She is wearing a pale blue Turkish-style hijab with bright pink lipstick.

With no legal authority on home turf, Jude and Camilla have been escorted to the station's situation room where they are gathered around a workstation watching via live video feeds. It's first names only. The DCI introduces himself as Patrick and with him there is an officer from 'Box' – MI5. When she hops down off the desk, Jude does a double take at her height. She is tiny.

'I'm Asha,' she says, with an amused look on her face.

'Jude.'

They shake hands.

'So, what do you know?' Camilla asks, with her customary abruptness.

'The parents are unremarkable,' Asha explains. 'Regular mosque-goers but no history of extremism. He is a tax adviser with a local accountancy firm. He stood for a seat in the last round of local council elections. He came close to winning. She is a homemaker, a doting mother apparently.'

'And the brother?'

'Yusuf, the spoiled, priapic younger son. He claims he's a community worker at the Tempest Centre in town but no one there has ever seen him lift a finger for anyone else. He's a drug dealer. Until about four months ago he could be found hanging around the Tempest gates selling pills to teenagers. Rumour has it that he came into money and moved from retail to wholesale, distributing pills across the county.'

The technicians have left and the younger brother is contorted on one of the chairs and protesting his ignorance. *The liar's lean.*

'And what do we know about Hamid, the suicide bomber?'

'He was training as a primary school teacher,' Asha says. 'He left for Turkey over a year ago to help deliver medical supplies to Syrian refugees. He volunteered for a while at a school in one of the camps on the border. There's no shortage of social media material showing him mobbed by happy children. Then about four months ago he ceased all communication with the parents and he disappeared from the camp. After two weeks, they reported his absence to the local police. He was added to the watch list.'

'Have the two brothers been talking to each other?' Camilla says.

'If they have, Yusuf's been diligent about erasing his conversations,' Patrick says.

'Anybody notice that Hamid's disappearance coincides with an uplift in his brother's fortunes?' Jude asks.

Everybody is looking at him suddenly.

'Just saying . . .'

'What options do we have?' Camilla asks.

'We're not going to get anything out of the parents,' Asha says.

'Which leaves Yusuf,' Patrick says. 'We either leave him in the cells or we let him go and see where he goes.'

'What surveillance assets have you got?' Jude asks.

'A red team on standby,' Patrick replies. 'Five surveillance operatives.'

'Gets my vote,' Jude says.

Patrick looks at Camilla who nods in assent.

'Let me have a go at him first,' Asha says. 'I'll get him riled up before we let him go.'

Patrick shrugs. 'Be my guest.'

Yusuf looks up and sneers as Asha enters the room. She politely thanks the uniformed officer who is holding the door for her and crosses the room to sit at the table. She studies Yusuf with a neutral expression on her face.

'When did you last speak to your brother?' she asks.

'Don't remember.'

'Was it before or after he left the camp in Turkey?'

'Dunno.'

Asha sighs. 'When did he cross into Syria?'

'Dunno.'

Asha sits back. 'You know what they say?'

'No, got no clue.'

'They say the devil would be powerless if he didn't entice people to his work.'

'Dunno what you're talking about.'

'Somebody persuaded your brother to leave the camp he was working in, Yusuf, to turn his back on the children he cared about and travel to the worst place in the world where he blew himself into smithereens. And for what? Did he even know why? You've seen the video. He couldn't speak Arabic so how did he even know what he was dying for? You've seen how distressed he looked. Was he drugged? Who drugged him? Who was it, Yusuf? Who persuaded your brother to blow himself up? Whoever did that, killed him.'

Yusuf shakes his head. 'The way I see it, you're the one that's working for the devil. Look around you, sister. You're a puppet for the oppressor, a mirage in the desert. You've lost your way. You obviously don't understand jihad. Why shouldn't my brother blow himself up for Allah?'

'The Koran says God does not love aggressors,' she replies, calmly; 'that you should not harm innocent people.'

Yusuf sneers. 'Who told you that? What Koran was that? Now you be saying that jihad is about getting up for prayers and that sort of thing. That's not jihad. That's the Western mind's way. The true Muslim mind knows that this life means nothing unless it is sacrificed for Allah.'

'What do you know about sacrifice, Yusuf? Your mother pays your rent and alimony and your speeding fines while you dog around town, addled as fuck, selling ecky and harassing women that are too good for you.'

'Fuck off!'

Asha softens her voice. 'Your mother's heartbroken, Yusuf. She's in the next room bawling her eyes out because her beloved eldest son's blown himself up. What do you have to say to that?'

His lower lip has begun to wobble. 'Leave her out of this!'

'How can we? Your brother played a starring role in a terrorist video. If we find out your parents have been sending money to him they'll have to go to prison.'

'You bastards! Let us go!'

'You don't get it do you, Yusuf? You've got the nation's press camped outside your front door. The tabloids are baying for your blood. You reckon you're going back to something that resembles an ordinary life? I don't think so. Your parents can say goodbye to their jobs. Prison may be the safest place for them.'

He's weeping, with his head in his hands.

'Tell me who sent Hamid to Syria.'

'I can't.'

She leans forward. 'You can't or you won't?'

Yusuf jumps to his feet and the policeman on the door moves to block his way. He is red-faced and furious, the tears streaming down his cheeks.

'Fuck off, bitch!'

Asha gets up and walks out. Back in the situation room, she grins at Jude: 'That should do it.'

9

In the Griphouse

They cross the underground car park to the white surveillance van and climb in the back. Inside it smells of fast food and stale sweat and it makes them look like over-sized children crammed into a toy.

'Shuft up,' Asha tells Jude. He slides further along to make room on the bench that is wedged between the battery chargers and the eyepiece of the periscope, and opposite floor-to-ceiling racks of electronics. Every surface not taken up with equipment is covered in industrial grey carpet designed to absorb sound. Patrick and a technician named Barry, who is sitting in front of a bank of side-by-side monitors, occupy the only two seats.

Camilla has returned to London, which is something to be grateful for.

The speaker on the radio receiver crackles into life as the first operative checks in on the protected frequency. 'Silver this is Red One, the target's exited the building and he's heading into town on foot.'

'Red Three, seen,' a woman replies, gunning the engine on her motorbike.

'Let's go,' Patrick says.

Barry speaks to the driver via the intercom and they head for the city centre while the operatives keep up a running commentary of Yusuf's movements.

'This is Red Two, he's static at the pedestrian crossing. He's crossed and he's heading south on Commercial Street. Speeding up now and he's taken his hands out of his pocket. He's got something in his hand. He's dumped it in the litterbin. He's crossing the road again.'

'His phone is not moving,' Barry says.

'He's ditched his phone.'

'We're on,' Patrick, says. 'Red One this is Silver, recover the phone.'

'Roger,' Red One replies, before groaning, 'Ah man, the bin's full of dog shit and takeaways.'

'Confirm you've got his phone,' Patrick replies, grinning.

'Roger.'

'This is Red Two, the target's static. He's eyeing up the vegetables outside a corner shop. Now he's looking both ways. He thinks he's fucking Jason Bourne. He's off again. He's turned down a one-way street and he's checking out the traffic.'

'This is Red Three, I'm going to have to take the bike round the long way.'

'Ditto the car,' Red Four adds.

Red Two cuts in. 'Fuck! He's running for a bus!'

'Come on,' Asha breathed.

They wait as the seconds tick by.

'This is Red Two, don't worry I'm on the bus with him. He's fidgeting like a toddler.'

'Red Three this is Silver, send locstat?'

'I'm stuck at lights. I'll be with him pronto.'

'This is Red Four, I'm also at the lights. I've just picked up Red One.'

'Give me the bus route,' Patrick demands.

Barry calls it up on the screen.

Patrick studies it for a few minutes while the car driven by Red Four overtakes the bus and drops Red One at the next stop. When the bus arrives, Red One gets on and Red Two gets off.

The bus resumes its journey.

'Silver this is Red One. He's up out of his seat.'

'Shit,' Asha breathes, 'he's heading for the mosque. It's almost prayer time.'

The target has entered a narrow street full of Asian shops with the mosque's minaret visible in the distance.

'This is Red Two, it's like Piccadilly Circus out here. The streets are full of people heading to the mosque.'

'This is Red One, my suntan's not going to pass muster in this crowd.'

'This is Red Two, we're going to lose him.'

'Red One, this is Silver, fall back. That goes for you too Red Four. Reds Two and Five, Birdcage.'

'Birdcage?' Jude asks.

'Get in close to the target without breaking cover,' Asha explains. 'If they don't get in close they'll lose him.'

'Red Three, this is Silver, get around to the rear entrance,' Patrick says.

'Roger.'

'This is Red Five, he's going inside. Shall we follow?'

'Yes, follow.'

'He's taken off his shoes but he's carrying them. He's not going in the prayer room. He's heading down a side corridor. I'm stepping back.'

'This is Red Two, I'm right behind him. He's following the emergency exit signs. He's exited the mosque.'

'This is Red Three, I've just seen him come out the back. He's heading up Mill Road.'

'Red Four this is Silver. Head for the junction of Mill Road and Strawberry Grove.'

'Roger.'

'This is Red Two, he's entering the industrial estate and heading for the mill. He's making for the Griphouse Gym. He's going inside. What do you want us to do, Boss? Shall we follow him in?'

Patrick glances at Asha who is shaking her head.

'All callsigns, do not go inside,' Patrick says. 'Take up static positions observing all exits and await further instructions.'

Built in the nineteenth century, the redbrick mill is set back fifty metres from the road and separated by a stretch of littered ground that offers little cover for a frontal assault. To the casual observer it looks abandoned but there is a painted sign for the Griphouse Gym at the foot of the stairs that lead up to the double doors at the main entrance.

Asha and Jude are standing outside the van in a car park just out of sight of the mill. The road that runs past it, which was busy with traffic minutes before, has just been sealed off. Patrick is standing on the opposite side of the car park talking to the gold commander, while beside him waits the specialist firearms officer who will lead the assault. His black fatigues are bristling with CS canisters and stun grenades, and there's a Glock 17 pistol in a holster strapped to his thigh.

Inside the mill, a technician is lying prone on the floor directly above the gym, preparing to drill a hole and insert a fibre-optic cable.

'The Griphouse Gym is owned and managed by Mohammed Chaudhary, also known as Little Mo on account of his vast size,' Asha explains, between drags on a cigarette. 'He's an ex-offender who used to work at the Tempest. He set up a gym there so the local boys could use up some of their energy but the staff objected to the racket and he moved it out here.'

'You think he's the one stove piping kids from this town to Syria?'

'Maybe.'

'Why do they do it?' Jude asks.

'Run off to Syria? Better to ask why anyone stays. The Muslim community here has been unravelling since the collapse of the textile and coal industries. It's a breeding ground for nihilism. The kids around here have low education achievement, high unemployment and one of the largest prison populations for any ethnic group. It's so claustrophobic, they'll tell you they feel like it's a crime to breathe. That makes them particularly vulnerable to persuasion.'

'And Hamid?'

'I've seen the video. He was a big, slow-witted kid who thought he was going out there to help. I don't think he knew what's-what about anything that was happening to him. Do you?'

'No.'

'I'll tell you something that does rile people up around here, Jude. Secret planes flying Muslims to black prisons to be tortured.

What were the Intelligence Service thinking, handing Nasruddin al-Raqqah over to the Syrians?'

'He killed twenty-five British servicemen.'

'Not everyone believes that here.'

'Why not?'

'Because they don't believe the things the government says. And if the man was guilty, why wasn't he put on trial?'

'I don't know,' Jude concedes. He's been punishing himself with the same question for more than a decade, ever since he stood on the runway in Pakistan and watched Nasruddin being escorted in shackles on to a plane with his pregnant wife lashed to a stretcher beside him. 'I wish I did.' He watches as Patrick climbs back in the van and the assault team leader heads across the car park to the back of the mill. 'I wonder if I could ask you a favour?'

She cocks her head to one side. 'Go on?'

'Can I borrow your phone?'

Her eyes narrow. 'Why?'

'I don't want to use my work phone. It's a private call.' He delivers his most winning smile. 'To my sister.'

Reluctantly, she hands him her phone. 'Go on. Don't get me in any trouble.'

He walks some way off to call Hannah.

She answers on the second ring. 'Hello?'

'It's Jude.'

'You never call from the same number twice. What is it?' He can already detect a hint of disappointment in her voice. She is expecting him to cancel dinner.

'You are friends with Kirsty McIntyre, aren't you?' he asks. He knows that they spent two years together at *The Guardian* before his sister moved into television news.

'Yes. Sure. Why?'

'I'd like to meet her.'

'Okay . . .'

'I was wondering if you could invite her to dinner?'

Momentary silence at the end of the line. 'This is about the rendition story, isn't it?'

'She's single, isn't she?'

When it comes to Jude, it's his sister's greatest wish that she finds someone for him. To that end, she is prepared to set aside all misgivings. 'Kirsty's between men at the moment.'

'So?'

'I'll call her.'

'Thanks.'

He cuts the connection and walks back to Asha who is standing watching him. Across the car park, Patrick opens the back of the van and shouts, 'We're in! We have audio and video.'

In the back of the van Patrick, Asha and Jude huddle around the monitor while outside the assault team approaches the building.

'There are four males in the room,' Patrick says. 'Your man Yusuf is on the floor getting the shit kicked out of him.'

'Little Mo's going to kill him if he keeps that up,' Asha says.

Yusuf is curled up on the floor protecting his head while a large, heavy-set man stands over him.

'The road's dead quiet, Mo,' one of the other men shouts from a window. 'No buses or nothing.'

'You stupid bloody fool!' Mo yells. 'I told you not to come back here.'

He kicks Yusuf who curls up tighter.

'What we gonna do Mo?' the man by the window shouts.

The assault team has assembled silently outside the door to the gym.

'Paddy?' Asha demands.

Patrick leans forward and speaks softly into the microphone. 'Bronze this is Silver: go . . .'

'I told them he was no good for fighting. Anyone could see that. He didn't know how to stand up for himself.' Yusuf is pleading for forgiveness and understanding. He's back in Room Three in a white paper suit. 'I thought they was gonna use him as a medic or a storeman or something.'

Asha is sitting stone-faced opposite him. 'Are you really that stupid?'

'Little Mo promised me.'

Yusuf had sold his brother out of the relative safety of a Turkish refugee camp and into the hands of a Syrian people trafficker for a stake in Mohammed Chaudhary's distribution business. The raid had yielded five thousand ecstasy tablets, a sawn-off shotgun and two young men with packed bags. Amongst their belongings the forensic teams found freshly issued passports along with print-outs of Turkish e-Visas. Under questioning the young men have revealed that they had been instructed to travel by air to Istanbul and then overland by bus to the Turkish city of Gaziantep, near the Syrian border. They had been given the address of an apartment owned by an elderly couple who would offer them food and shelter. They had been told to wait for a man known as Stork.

Back at Sanjay's loft, after an uneventful train ride to London that he mostly dozed through, Jude recovers his phones from the safe and lines them up on the zinc countertop. There is a lengthy message from Yulia on his yellow burner. He hesitates, tempted to swipe delete without reading it, but it seems cowardly and disrespectful. She deserves better. And so he opens it instead and scrolls down as he reads:

First and foremost, what I would have preferred to have happened after our truncated weekend, (and hopefully every time), is something a bit more engaged/engaging than silence. I cannot deny that you have neglected me somewhat.

So, if you would like us to continue to explore our darker, more carnal selves, then we need to have more regular communications BETWEEN trysts.

Communication is what he has been expressly forbidden to offer. There's nothing he can do about it. He can't reply. His employers are across her phones and will know about it if he tries. Instead he opens up the Toughbook. He logs on to the secure server with his index finger and checks his messages. There is one from Camilla telling him to be at one of the entrances to Vauxhall underground station at 9 a.m. the following day and she'll walk him over to the Situational Awareness Group's office.

Another message informs him that the Turkish police have raided the address in Gaziantep given to the two young men arrested in the Griphouse Gym. They have taken an elderly Syrian couple into custody and are questioning them on suspicion of aiding the journey of foreign jihadis into Syria. Of the mysterious Stork, there is no information as yet.

Since his interview with Chuka Odechukwu that morning he's been itching to access the human resources database and call up the personnel file of Edward Malik, the MI6 officer who travelled to Syria to question Nasruddin al-Raqqah. He thinks that if anyone knows Nasruddin and where he might find shelter it ought to be Edward Malik. But Jude is not sure if his permissions will extend that far and besides, as soon as he looks they will know about it. Camilla has already warned him to stay away from Malik. He feels stymied.

His red burner pings. It's a text message from his sister about Kirsty McIntyre:

She'll be there Thursday night

The Mountain of Languages

The Situational Awareness Group is located in an unlovely, utilitarian office block on the Albert Embankment that was built in the thirties and is mostly inhabited by non-governmental organisations and pressure groups. Jude has heard rumours before that it is occasionally used as spill-over capacity for Vauxhall Cross but this is the first confirmation.

Camilla is waiting for him at the entrance to the tube station, looking fierce and poised.

'You're late.'

He doesn't tell her that's he's spent the last few minutes watching her from the raised walkway that leads to the traffic island or that, as much as it hurts, he loves the very sight of her. Neither does he share with her that, while he was watching, his yellow burner pinged. Another message from Yulia:

I must say, of the people I have encountered via that website, your behaviour is by far the most unpolished and un-gentlemanly

She's right, of course. He feels tarnished and rude.

'They've seconded a rain man from GCHQ to work with you,' Camilla tells him as they cross Albert Embankment and pass rows of bicycle racks. They enter the building side by side and ride a lift in silence to the fifth floor. He follows her from the elevator bank along a corridor to a brushed steel door. She presses her thumb to the reader on the wall and the red light turns to green.

'Nobody will disturb you here,' she says, pushing the heavy door inward and holding it for him to enter. In the hallway beyond, there is scaffolding where someone has been inspecting ductwork, and rolls of new carpeting that are stacked like plastic-wrapped timber from a forestry block. He's tempted to ask her why the secrecy is necessary but he can tell what kind of response that will yield.

He follows her through another door and into the brightly lit interior of an open-plan incident room. There are two women sitting in a partitioned workstation who turn to stare at him. The young woman is tattooed, her bare arms fully sleeved with geometric shapes – lightning flashes, mandalas, stars – and her blonde hair is slicked back and flares into a mullet behind her ears. She gets to her feet but seems at a loss as to what to do next. 'I'm Gretchen,' she says, glancing back and forth between Jude and Camilla without making eye contact or offering to shake hands.

'Hello Gretchen.'

It seems that Camilla's rain man is a woman. The rumour mill tells a story that GCHQ recruited several gifted analysts by means of a fiendishly complicated mathematical puzzle that was chalked out on selected pavements in Shoreditch over a series of weeks.

'And this is Dr Falchikov,' Gretchen tells them.

Sitting beside her is a small round woman with steel-grey hair drawn back in a bun. She has a great shelf of a bosom that is barely contained by a tweed suit jacket, and her tights are as dark as well-brewed tea.

'Hello Dr Falchikov.'

She stares at Jude with eyes that sparkle with amusement in a face that is etched with wrinkles.

The whole of one office wall is taken up with tiled flatscreen monitors showing a single screengrab from the film of the prison break that is frozen like a shoot-'em-up game paused between levels. And in the far corner of the room, Jude sees that there is a gently humming Echelon database server in a steel cage, a proxy of the central server inside MI6, which is linked to databases at MI5, GCHQ and New Scotland Yard.

'Take a seat.' Gretchen points at a chair in front of the video wall. 'You've seen the film?'

'I have.'

'This is not the first,' Gretchen explains, and with the push of a button the wall displays a mosaic of screengrabs from different videos. 'The videos have stylistic characteristics that suggest the same amateur filmmaker. Twenty-three others like this one have been posted on the extremist website Al-Amaq in the last seven years. The group making them call themselves 'Breaking the Walls' and we believe that they are a freelance unit who make their living by breaking jihadis out of prisons and selling them. They're technically competent in their use of explosives and they have access to a ready supply of suicide bombers, including British nationals. Their weapons are typical of the types we see in the conflict: Eastern European Kalashnikov copies and Chinese RPGs. Geo-location data embedded in the videos means that we can plot their progress across Iraq and Syria. On that basis, we calculate that they have released more than a thousand imprisoned fighters who have gone on to swell the ranks of Islamic State.'

'So, who are they?'

'We don't know,' Gretchen tells him. 'They deliberately disguise their faces and they rarely speak. We do know that they are not native Arabic speakers.'

Jude feels Camilla's presence at his shoulder like a draught of cold air.

'Go on,' she says.

Gretchen taps on the keyboard and once again the entire wall is filled with smoke and debris.

She presses play.

Jude watches as the camera plunges into the smoking crater, following two of the fighters as they slide down its collapsing sides and advance into the ruptured tunnels. The film is near its end. Even after several viewings it is hard to distinguish any details because of the swirling dust and the shaky camerawork but again he catches the occasional glimpse of buckled cell doors and damp, glistening walls. The fighters call out for survivors and then, just when it seems that no one can be left alive, there's a voice in the darkness.

'Voice recognition?' Jude asks.

Gretchen shakes her head. 'The sound quality is not good enough.'

Then a glimpse of filthy matted hair and a holy man's beard.

'Facial recognition?'

'Not a chance.'

She presses pause.

'According to the members of the activist group who gained access to the site after Breaking the Walls had left, the fighters did not stay long, not more than thirty or forty minutes,' Gretchen explains. 'They came, they grabbed the surviving prisoner and they left.'

'And what about the activists? Apart from the embarrassing faxes, what else did they find?'

'Hundreds, possibly thousands, of death certificates – many more were probably destroyed in the explosion. They also found twelve recently deceased prisoners showing visible signs of torture. It will be difficult to calculate how many people died there. We Are Being Slaughtered have turned the papers they recovered over to Human Rights Watch who are posting them in batches online.'

'Is Nasruddin's amongst them?' Camilla asks.

Gretchen shakes her head. 'Not so far.'

'So, we have to assume that he's alive and they got him out,' Camilla says.

Jude knows they wouldn't be here if Queen Bee was convinced that Nasruddin was dead.

'They were looking for a high-value target,' Gretchen says.

'How do you know that?' Jude asks.

She scrolls back through the video.

'There.'

The truck has just exploded at the entrance to the prison, killing Hamid.

She presses play.

The camera lunges forwards through drifting, yellowish smoke in which dark and menacing shapes loom and veer away. A sudden rent in the smoke reveals a rampart of rubble made from lumps of concrete and twisted steel. There are two men with Kalashnikovs crouching above, taking it in turns to rise up out of cover and fire their rifles. In a brief hiatus, they slide down towards the camera. In the tightening of the shot, the younger of the two leans in to the other and speaks to him. Gretchen presses pause, rewinds and plays the exchange again. It's the point at which Jude paused on first viewing the video. It's a short, sharp comment in a guttural language that he does not recognise.

'This is the bit that is interesting. I've cleaned up the sound and cut out some of the background noise. Even so, it's difficult to hear what they are saying.'

'Voice analysis?' Jude asks.

'The language they are speaking is not recognised by the computer.'

'What about the wolf's head patch on their shoulders?'

Gretchen nods. 'You're on the right track. It's an insignia of Chechen separatists,' she explains. 'But they are not speaking Chechen. The computer would have picked that up.'

'So?'

'It's not the only language spoken in the Caucasus,' Gretchen replies.

'It is said that when god was distributing languages he tripped and spilled his basket in the Caucasus,' Dr Falchikov says. 'There are as many different languages as there are rocks.'

She has been so quiet that Jude had forgotten that she is sitting there.

'Dr Falchikov is an ethnographer,' Gretchen explains. 'She's a research fellow at SOAS.'

'Okay,' Jude replies, glancing at Camilla.

'The Doctor is a specialist in the languages of the North Caucasus,' Gretchen explains. 'She has clearance to be here.'

'The North Caucasus is the most ethno-linguistically diverse region in the world,' Dr Falchikov says.

'She has identified the language,' Gretchen adds.

'They are speaking a most complex language in the noun category,' Dr Falchikov says, with satisfaction.

'She says that it is spoken by just a few thousand people in a high-altitude ethnic group in the west of Dagestan,' Gretchen says.

'Nowhere is the North Caucasus more complex than in the autonomous Russian republic of Dagestan,' Dr Falchikov says. 'The Arabs called it the Mountain of Languages. The Greeks, the Mongols, the Persians all invaded at one time or another. Invasions, repulsions, migrations, each one gave birth to a new language.'

Jude and Camilla are staring at her expectantly.

Jude sighs. 'Do you know what they are saying?'

Dr Falchikov smiles. 'Of course. The younger one addresses the older one as "Colonel". He tells him that the "Mighty Men" will make them both rich.'

'The "Mighty Men"?'

'As far as I can tell, it's a reference to the Hadith,' Gretchen tells them. 'It goes: "The black flags will come from the East led by mighty men, with long hair and beards."'

'Someone inside Islamic State is willing to pay for him,' Jude says.

'Thank you, Dr Falchikov, you have been most helpful,' Camilla says, briskly. 'Gretchen, please escort the Doctor back to reception and arrange for her to return to wherever she came from.'

'I could do that,' Gretchen replies, as if the request is both unexpected and somehow unfamiliar.

Dr Falchikov insists on shaking Jude's hand before she leaves. She uses both hands, gripping his palm tightly with one hand and stroking the skin on the back of his hand with the other.

'You should speak to Valery at the Russian Embassy,' she tells him, frowning with concentration, as if she is reading something unexpected in his grip. 'He is not an easy or likeable man. He is too quick to anger. But perhaps you know that? I'm sure that he will know more about Breaking the Walls. And the so-called "Mighty Men". Perhaps also the man you are looking for.' She looks across at Camilla. 'Please send my regards to Samantha Burns.'

Camilla bristles with indignation. 'Of course.'

They wait in silence while Gretchen accompanies the Doctor out the door.

'She's right, of course,' Camilla says, when the door clicks shut. 'You should definitely speak to Valery.' He watches her lip curl. 'You can compare notes on fucking his wife.'

II

The Basra Ambush

Jude sits at a scratched laminated desk in a glass-walled office off the incident room and watches as another train rattles by. In the arches beneath the raised railway tracks there is a Portuguese deli, a deserted gay sauna, and a motorbike shop displaying rows of shiny bikes on the pavement. Camilla has gone but she has left him feeling ill at ease, buffeted by events that seem increasingly out of his control.

He opens the laptop and logs on. Once again, he resists the urge to give in to his curiosity and go searching for more information on Nasruddin's rendition and the man sent to question him, Edward Malik. Instead he decides to seek reassurance in what he knows. To read the Basra Ambush file and remind himself why, despite his anger over the treatment of Nasruddin's wife, he felt such a sense of satisfaction at his capture.

The Basra Ambush had caused the biggest single loss of life to the British Army in Iraq and sparked a massive manhunt for an elusive and erudite bomb-maker known only as the Engineer.

At that time in Iraq there were more than two thousand bomb attacks a month, using every means of initiation imaginable to set them off, including car alarms, wireless door bells, mobile phones, pagers and encrypted GMRS radios. Global jihadists from Chechnya, Afghanistan, the Balkans and the Middle East were sharing technologies, tactics and procedures at a dizzying pace, via the internet, clandestine training camps and CD-ROMs. What distinguished the Engineer was the complexity of his ambush, the multiple devices and means of initiation, his deftness at channelling and canalising coalition forces into a pre-prepared kill zone, and his unnerving ability to predict the location that would be used for the control point in the aftermath of incident.

Soon Jude has twenty tabs open on his screen, each one an item of evidence: the original warning order, the radio-logs and phone transcripts, helmet-cam footage, Red-Amber-Green assessments, NOTAMs and after-action reports including the forensic investigation by the Weapons Intelligence Section of 11 EOD Regiment. Carefully he reviews the sequence of events that led to the death of so many British soldiers.

The ambush was sprung with a night-time call to one of the Coalition confidential tip lines. The phone lines were a British innovation in Iraq, based on experience in Northern Ireland and set up in the face of considerable American scepticism. In the call centre, which was located in one of Saddam's former palaces, police officers from Britain and Northern Ireland acted as mentors to the phone operators. An unidentified Iraqi caller gave information pointing to the whereabouts of a former senior regional official in Saddam's Ba'ath Party. He wasn't one of the top officials on the infamous deck of cards but there was a two-thousand-dollar price on his head.

A British policeman monitoring the call alerted the US Special Counterintelligence Directorate, a joint CIA and Department of Defense clearing house for informant data. They were overwhelmed and unwilling to respond to what they regarded as a low priority target. Next, he turned to Task Force 14, also known as Task Force Black, a British special forces unit who received immediate authorisation to launch an op. At the time, the British were keen to prove their worth to the better-resourced Americans.

Jude imagines them scrambling to get ready. Shrugging on their body armour and helmets. Loading weapons, checking the functionality of radios and electronic counter measures. Goggles fitted, engines fired. Everyone running through their last-minute mental lists, triple checking weapons, rehearsing 'actions on'.

The target was north of Basra, an isolated farm compound in a bend of the Euphrates river with only one road to it that cut through a plantation of date palms. It was a large two-storey farmhouse surrounded by an expanse of sand, with the only cover a copse of king palms situated just inside the perimeter wall. Jude clicks on a video file and views the target through the green-and-black contrast of the night vision goggles worn by a helicopter pilot straining every sinew to avoid collision.

According to the records the airspace was crowded. There were ten air assets stacked up on each other: a group of Puma helicopters carrying the SAS troopers and their supporting Paras; and, below them, closest to the ground, Lynxes orbiting the target, each with a sniper looking out through the open side door. Flying at the top of the stack, a lumbering Hercules command aircraft banking in a figure-of-eight pattern was coordinating the air assets with the assault on the ground.

Ground forces from the Special Reconnaissance Regiment were approaching on the road from the south in a convoy of Humvees and souped-up Land Rovers.

As the Pumas put down and the assault teams disembarked, events began to run rapidly out of control. A child carrying what looked a baby wrapped in a blanket ran out of the farmhouse at the centre of the compound towards the approaching SAS troopers. He detonated the bomb too early to kill any of the soldiers but one of the Pumas was so low – about fifty feet – that the explosion caused the helicopter to lose control: it was blown upwards on a cushion of blast and then, for a split second, it dropped like a stone. Against the odds, the pilot managed to recover control briefly enough to perform a hard landing that resulted in a concussion and several fractures but no fatalities.

The explosion acted as a lure and an accelerant. Caught in the open between the helicopters and the building, the soldiers responded as expected.

They charged.

Jude is hunched against the monitor, watching a feed from one of the Lynxes, listening to the agitated commentary of the pilot and the shouts and barked commands of the soldiers as they break into the building and begin clearing the ground floor rooms.

The explosion whites out the screen.

Four SAS soldiers died in the blast.

Jude pauses the video feed and enlarges the post-blast analysis report. It was conducted by an ammunition technical officer named Franklin who recorded the events in clipped sentences packed with acronyms: he concluded that the bomb was at least a thousand kilograms in weight and, based on swabs recovered from the scene, made of a plasticised mixture of ammonium nitrate and aluminium paste. The bomb was located under the main stairwell and connected by means of an insulated copper wire to a radio-controlled firing switch situated in a sandy hollow about eighty metres north-east of the building, just outside the range of the Task Force's electronic counter measures – the jammers that provided a bubble of safety, overwhelming any signal being transmitted.

An attached sketch map shows a second wire running from the firing point to the grove of king palms just south of the farmhouse adjacent to where the helicopters landed. Jude switches back to the video feeds. Three explosions in quick succession like popcorn puffing up on the video screen: improvised directional fragmentation mines packed full of shipyard confetti that, on detonation, eject overlapping cones of thousands of shards of molten metal. The nearest Puma was shredded. The pilot and loadmaster died instantly. The co-pilot was blinded. Another Puma was too damaged to take off again.

The next bombs went off as the convoy approached the farm compound through the date plantation. They were initiated by a passive infrared switch that detected the heat of the lead vehicle's engine and fired shaped charges, concave copper discs packed with explosives, buried one hundred and fifty metres apart under the road. The explosives transformed the discs into fist-sized projectiles of molten copper, travelling at well over a kilometre a second. They punched straight through the tarmac. The first penetrated the underbelly of a Humvee, killing the driver and one of the passengers in the back, and slicing off the legs of the commander in the front passenger seat. The second went off just behind the rear vehicle in the convoy, flipping it over and dumping it in the ditch beside the road.

After that, the assault came to a sudden halt. Everybody was frozen in place. Denied permission to land and extract casualties, the helicopters soon ran out of flight-time and were recalled. The surviving soldiers did their best to keep their wounded comrades alive and hunkered down in the dust to wait.

It was dawn before a High-Risk Search Team from Joint Forces EOD group began to breach into the compound. Their work was painstakingly slow: their first discovery was a bomb made of a stack of six artillery rounds in a culvert just outside the compound gates; the second a fragmentation mine that had failed to detonate in the palm grove beside the hulks of the three downed Puma helicopters. An X-ray of the charge revealed that it was booby-trapped. The mine was linked by means of fishing wire and a Soviet-era MUV tripwire switch to a second more deeply buried mine. In each case the searchers called forward an IED technician to render the devices safe and then moved on. They opened up a route to the smoking ruin of the main house and around it until they found the command wire that led from the back of the house to the sandy hollow.

Rather than follow it, they bounced along the wire, coming in at it from right angles at irregular intervals. Five pressure-plate improvised devices with crush-bead necklaces, designed to explode when stepped on, were discovered beside the path. As soon as they were rendered safe the team began to gather forensic evidence from the firing point in the hollow, including the circuit board that acted as the bomb's firing circuit and an Indian copy of a Nokia phone used as the receiver. Next was the point of initiation, a recently dug trench beside a small jetty alongside the Euphrates, another hundred metres beyond the firing point. In the bottom of the trench they found another phone, the transmitter, and several cigarette butts.

By this time, it was noon and the air was hot enough to strip paint. The commanding officer of 2 Para had arrived by Lynx and established an incident command point two kilometres south of the compound, at a crossroads. From there, he had coordinated the deployment of a cordon: two platoons of reinforcements in a rough semicircle on the outer edge of the plantation and a third on the far bank of the Euphrates, a wasteland of dried mud banks and deserted Marsh Arab villages that had been the bomber's escape route. Once the cordon was secured he began the extraction of casualties through the safe lanes opened up by the searchers.

The final bomb went off beneath the centre of the crossroads just as a Puma was lifting off, carrying six casualties on stretchers and four of the walking wounded. It was as large as the bomb in the farmhouse and contained almost no metallic components. Forensics recovered fragments of a plastic casing and a barometric pressure switch from the crater. The explosion killed fifteen soldiers: two from the Parachute Regiment including their commanding officer, two pilots, a loadmaster from the Army Air Corps and the ten wounded passengers. Jude reads the transcript of the testimony of a major from 2 Para who was on the scene soon after the explosion. He described body parts scattered over the road and hanging from the rotor blades of the helicopter. A photo shows the entire area as a mass of twisted, dust-covered metal, shattered glass and debris. All that was recovered of the commanding officer was a single epaulet that was taken from the scene by the commander of British Forces in Iraq and shown to the cabinet a few days later at a security briefing in 10 Downing Street.

The bomber had known that the downdraft created by a fully-laden helicopter taking off was greater than that of an empty one landing and had set the pressure switch accordingly. He had correctly predicted the location of the command point and placed the bomb in such a way as to maximise casualties and disrupt their evacuation.

It was another five hours before the remaining casualties were extracted. In that time two others had died of their wounds.

The video claiming responsibility was released on a jihadi website on the night following the attack.

Jude checks on the server and Chuka is right, there is no personal file for Nasruddin al-Raqqah, not even a deletion report.

There is no record of his place of birth or his early life, no birth certificate or school diploma or university degree, no clue as to the identity of his parents and siblings, no hint at the formative experiences that led him to embrace a virulent credo that threatens to destroy everything achieved in five hundred years of human progress.

But the video is available for all to see.

Jude clicks full screen and then play. He has seen this video before, more than once.

Nasruddin's head and shoulders fill the screen as they did the cover of every British newspaper the day after the ambush. He is staring at the camera, his dark eyes blazing holes. He claims a great victory over the crusaders in unaccented English and it doesn't take long for someone to notice that, in his final statement, he is paraphrasing Shakespeare's Henry VI:

'I will not pause, I will never stand still, until death has closed my eyes or I have had my revenge.'

12

The lion's den

A polite young man escorts Jude from the reception at Chelsea Harbour to the marina at the centre of the development. They walk down a floating wooden jetty between burnished white yachts beneath a reddish evening sky. All around them is the sound of water lapping against hulls and the soft slap of loosening halyards against masts.

A heavily muscled man in a tracksuit is standing waiting at the prow of the largest yacht with his legs stoutly apart. He walks the length of the boat as they approach and waits for them at the top of the gangway.

'The Counsellor is waiting for you on board,' the young man says. He nods and departs.

Jude stands at the bottom of the gangway and reflects on the series of events that have propelled him into a late-night encounter with a man he has so recently cuckolded.

'You want to know about the Colonel and the Mighty Men,' Camilla had told him by phone. 'That's it. Just that and what it might tell us about Nasruddin's whereabouts.'

And of his personal safety, given that the man he is due to meet is neither easy nor likeable, and has reasonable grounds for murderous rage, not a word. He has never felt more expendable.

Fuck it, he thinks and advances up the gangway.

The muscle pats him down before he boards and relieves him of the fresh-from-the-packet burner phone that is the only means of communication that he is carrying. He leads Jude below deck to where the Counsellor is sitting at a table surrounded by a horse-shoe-shaped cream leather banquette.

Valery Ermolaev is a large, round-shouldered man with a hanging gut, thick limbs and blunt extremities including a misshapen head. On the other side of the table, with his head between two gleaming brass portholes, there is a heavy-set Arab with sallow skin and a bushy salt-and-pepper moustache. Both of them have shot glasses in front of them. The Arab is wearing a white monogrammed bathrobe with navy blue piping and there are three bottles of triple-distilled Moskovskaya vodka midway between them.

'Jude. You are very welcome here,' Valery says. He speaks slowly and deliberately and Jude concludes that he is very drunk. 'Come and sit with me.'

He pats the bench beside him.

As soon as he sits, Valery fills a glass and slides it across to him. 'Drink that.'

Valery turns back to the Arab in the bathrobe. They speak in Russian while Jude sips the vodka and waits patiently for them to finish. The Arab considers Jude with bloodshot eyes and a couple of times Valery glances at him in a manner that suggests that they are talking about him. Eventually the Arab shrugs and waves at Jude.

'Go on,' he says, in English.

Valery rests a meaty hand on the back of Jude's neck. 'How is Queen Bee? I don't think she likes to see her name so prominently displayed in newsprint.'

'I think that's a fair assumption,' he replies.

'Do you think that she will survive this?'

'Why shouldn't she?'

Valery smiles, as if at a private joke. He reaches for one of the bottles with his other hand and refills his glass. 'You feed a crocodile, you run the risk of losing a hand. You should know that.'

'Should I?' Jude wonders.

Valery looks him in the eye. 'You know what it says about you in your file, Jude?'

'I've no idea.'

'That they failed to neuter you at English boarding school and, as a consequence, you fuck other men's wives.'

79

Jude feels the heft and span of Valery's hand on his neck, the knuckles as large as walnuts, and imagines it tightening, crushing the life out of him. The Arab is watching him very closely.

'How is Mrs Camilla Church?' Valery asks.

'She's fine,' he says, carefully.

Valery's face creases in sudden laughter. 'You should see your face.' He lifts his hand from Jude's neck and drains his glass of vodka. 'So, Queen Bee has tasked you with finding the Engineer, am I right?'

'That's right.'

'She doesn't want him running around telling tales, I think.'

Jude doesn't reply.

'The question in my mind, Jude, is why she has chosen you? Of course, you are one of the few people to have met Nasruddin. Have I surprised you? I know that you were there on the tarmac in Karachi. I am thinking it's more than that. I think maybe you have a reputation for discretion and for tackling jobs that others find unsavoury. I also think perhaps it is easy for her to disown you if this all goes wrong?'

'I guess I better get it right then,' Jude replies, deadpan.

And then, without fanfare, Yulia is standing by his side.

'My darling,' Valery greets her. 'This is the handsome young man that Queen Bee has sent to us. Jude, this is my wife Yulia.'

'Hello, handsome young man,' she says. There are mischievous lights dancing in her eyes. 'Budge up.'

Valery shifts his bulk further along the bench and Jude follows. He is now sitting wedged between Yulia on one side and her husband on the other.

'You know the way I usually conduct business?' Valery says with a dismissive wave of the hand. 'Not with Russians you understand, but with foreigners. I promise a favour for a favour. Documents for documents, that kind of thing, but when I get the documents I tell them to go fuck themselves.'

'Please, darling,' Yulia says.

'All right, all right, you are in luck, Jude. On this occasion, I'm not going to tell you to go fuck yourself. It is in neither of our interests for chaos to succeed. Islamic terrorism is as much, if not more, of a threat to Russia as it is to you. And for Freddie here it is a matter of national survival. Isn't that right, Freddie?'

The Arab in the bathrobe nods ponderously without speaking.

'What my husband means to say is that we're going to help you out, Jude,' Yulia tells him. This is not the Yulia of restaurants and hotels, of expensive lunches followed by carnal afternoons, who expressed nothing but disdain for her brutish husband's tedious occupation: 'whisper whisper here, whisper whisper there. It's all so tedious, darling.' His sense of jeopardy is increasing exponentially.

'My superiors will be pleased to hear that,' Jude replies, willing Valery not to look down at his lap where Yulia's hand is now resting on his thigh.

'You have no idea, Jude, how happy Queen Bee will be,' Yulia says.

There is something about the ambiguity of that statement, the inference that Yulia knows Queen Bee's state of mind better than he does, that further alarms him.

'I have been told to find out what you expect in return?' Jude says. He's been warned to expect an outrageous list of demands, and right now would not be surprised if it included his body dumped in a canal, but when it comes the price is surprisingly low. At least on face value it is. 'We simply want regular updates on your progress,' Valery tells him.

'Okay.'

'But you will bring these to us in person,' Yulia tells him. 'Only you. Nobody else. You must tell Queen Bee that.'

Jude hesitates. Under the table, Yulia's fingers are caressing his inner thigh. 'Why me?'

Valery shrugs his shoulders and stares moodily into his vodka glass. 'That's the price, Jude.'

'I'll tell her.'

'Good man,' Yulia says with a smile for everyone at the table. 'So, to business, what can we do for you?'

'What can you tell me about the armed group that call themselves Breaking the Walls?

'For that, I regret to admit, you have come to the right place, Jude,' Yulia says, running a finger up the central seam of his trousers, tracing his cock. 'These bandits are undoubtedly from Russia. They are not true Russians, of course. They are mountain people, unruly and criminal in nature. Nonetheless they were born within the borders of our federal state.'

'Their leader is referred to as "the Colonel",' Jude says. 'We speculate that he may have served in the Soviet Army?'

'No. I can tell you for sure that he was not a colonel in the Soviet Army,' Valery replies, shaking his head. 'He was not a product of the Soviet Union but rather a product of its collapse. Of course, he completed his compulsory military service but as a firefighter in Siberia. His kind was not allowed to serve in active combat. Even then he had a certain talent for enriching himself at others' expense. His unit extorted money from local businesses in return for not setting fires. He honed his skills in the turmoil that followed. He fought in the wars in Karabakh and Abkhazia. He made himself and those around him rich by looting abandoned homes and he rose to be a senior commander in the Confederation of Mountain Peoples of the Caucasus. He fought against Russia in the first and second Chechen wars and we put a price on his head. In 1999, he led a thousand fighters into Dagestan, the place of his birth, in a failed attempt to ignite an uprising and seize control of the republic. We came very close to capturing him. After that he fled the region.'

There are times, when having sex, that Jude has envisioned a brick wall in an effort to prolong the act. He's doing something similar now with the grain of the table while Yulia squeezes and strokes, and Valery continues talking. 'We have reports that suggest that he fought with al-Qaeda's 055 Brigade alongside the Taliban against the Northern Alliance in Afghanistan. Then he turned his ire against the American occupiers in Afghanistan and then Iraq. For the last seven years he has been leading a ragtag army of fellow outlaws from the Caucasus, breaking prisoners out of prisons in Iraq and Syria, and selling them on to al-Qaeda affiliates and latterly Islamic State and its offshoots. I do not know whether

Nasruddin was snatched to order or whether it was an opportunistic move. Either way I do not think it will be long before the Mighty Men seek to acquire him.'

'And what do you know of the Mighty Men?' Jude manages.

Valery and Freddie exchange a look that he cannot interpret.

'Rumours,' Valery says with a shrug, 'tall tales. Unverifiable evidence. Some say that they are a myth, an ogre to frighten us.'

'They were as real as you and me,' Freddie says.

'Their name certainly features in one of the founding myths of Islamic State in Syria,' Valery explains. 'We've heard it from a hundred different sources. In 2012, one year into the Syrian revolution, twelve men carrying black flags were sent into Syria to establish Islamic State. It is said that only one of them is still alive.'

'The *Sheikh al-Jabal*,' Freddie adds.

Yulia abruptly stops stroking and Jude stifles a gasp.

'It means "the Old Man of the Mountain",' Valery explains, apparently oblivious. 'There are no photos of him. He is mentioned in intercepts but there is no voice track to identify him. He is said to have been a mentor to al-Zarqawi, the psychopath who ran al-Qaeda in Iraq. He is an Arab. It is said that he is a leader of one of their murderous tribes. Isn't that right, Freddie?'

Freddie nods.

'Some say that he believes that he is a prophet. He surrounds himself with brutalised orphans, extreme fanatics and the zealous remnants of Saddam's intelligence apparatus. He commands fierce loyalty amongst those who serve him.' He glances at Freddie. 'Our friends in the Syrian intelligence services have not been able to penetrate his inner circle.'

'You think that chasing Nasruddin is going to lead to the Old Man?' Jude asks.

'Perhaps.'

'And your friends in Syria want to be rid of the Old Man?'

'As you and Queen Bee want to be rid of Nasruddin. In this, all our interests coincide. Yes? Freddie here doesn't care if it is a Russian bomb or a Syrian bullet or an American missile. He seeks only an end to his enemies and those who harbour them.'

Freddie nods.

'So where do I start?' Jude asks.

'Leave the Colonel and his gang to us,' Valery says. Jude is pretty sure that Queen Bee isn't going to be happy to hear that. Nasruddin in the hands of the Russians isn't likely to be any more appealing to her than having him in the hands of the Old Man.

'In that case, what do you want from me?' he asks.

'We cannot be sure that we will succeed,' Valery says.

'There are other avenues,' Yulia adds, squeezing and stroking again. 'Nasruddin's wife, for instance. It is possible that he will reach out to her. She was released from prison not long after the Americans flew her to Syria and shortly before her child was born. She returned to her family home near Dar'a in the south of Syria. We understand that she stayed there through the early years of the conflict, however we have information that she has recently crossed into Jordan and is now in one of the camps, beyond our reach and that of our friends.'

'We know that you have good friends in Amman.' Valery says. 'They are your allies not ours. Perhaps they can help you find her? That is good cooperation, yes? Tell Queen Bee that is the best course of action. It is good that we work together now?'

'Yes,' Jude replies.

'But we are odd bedfellows nonetheless?'

'Yes.'

Across the table Freddie is gently snoring.

'I'm just surprised that we have not met before.' Valery leans in close and whispers in his ear just as Yulia withdraws her hand and Jude barely contains a climactic shudder. 'It may interest you to learn that you are on a list that we have of potential recruits.'

'Thanks, but no thanks.'

'Please,' Yulia says. 'We're in no hurry for an answer.'

'I'm not interested.'

'Of course not,' Valery says. And for a fleeting moment the mask slips, and Jude gets a sense of the hatred lurking beneath. 'You are a man of loyalty.'

'Is that everything?' Jude asks.

Valery smiles, but his eyes are cold. 'For now, yes, Jude. Isn't that right, my darling?'

'Yes,' she replies. 'But don't be a stranger.'

Camilla calls him on the burner as he is hurrying past the auction houses on the Lots Road, feeling rattled and unnerved.

'You better tell Queen Bee that the Russians are also hunting for Nasruddin,' he tells her.

'What?' she demands.

'They say he's going to lead them to a member of Islamic State called the *Sheikh al-Jabal*, the Old Man of the Mountain. Have you heard that name?'

There is silence at the end of the line.

'Apparently, he was one of the Mighty Men, the founders of Islamic State in Syria.' He ought to tell her that Yulia was there and in more than a supporting role, that Yulia must be aware of the sting operation against her, that Yulia and Valery are clearly working together as a team, but he can imagine the crisis that it will provoke at Vauxhall Cross. Besides he doesn't yet know what it means. *Fuck!* Can it be possible that, however close their working relationship may be, Valery doesn't know about his wife's affair?

'They've made it clear that they are only prepared to deal with me,' he adds.

Camilla is immediately suspicious. 'Why?'

'I think Valery wants to recruit me.'

'Are you being sarcastic?'

'He gave me one piece of potentially useful information,' Jude tells her. 'They think Nasruddin's wife has crossed into Jordan. She's from the very south of Syria and according to Valery she went back there after she was released from prison. The town's been under attack by government forces since the start of the revolution. There's nowhere to escape to but Jordan. That's the place to start looking.'

'There are a million Syrian refugees in Jordan, Jude.'

'Obviously it's not going to be easy.'

'But you have your friend in Jordanian intelligence.'

'Yes.'

'So, you want me to go to Queen Bee and tell her you need authorisation to travel to Jordan?'

'That's about it.'

She cuts the connection.

He's in the back of a cab heading for Shoreditch when the burner vibrates. A text message from an unfamiliar number:

Imagine my surprise! By rights, I should be FURIOUS, there's no denying that you have deceived me, but I can't help but be intrigued and excited by the prospect of working together. Bravo!

He immediately instructs the driver to pull over. He gets out and stamps on the burner before dumping it in a pavement waste bin. The last thing he needs is for Russian intelligence to know where he lives.

Back in Sanjay's apartment he throws his coat over the back of the sofa and fills a tumbler with cold water from the fridge. He drinks it in one go and then refills the tumbler. He walks over to the window and presses his forehead to the cold glass. He can still feel Valery's massive hand tightening on the back of his neck.

Five minutes later, a black Range Rover pulls up at the end of the cul-de-sac and Yulia gets out of the back wearing a black mink coat that he'd wager she's naked beneath.

You're an idiot. Of course her husband knows.

He watches as she slips out of her Louboutins and sashays towards him on the cobbles, shiny as a fishing fly concealing a hook.

13

Out of the frying pan

After prayers, Nasruddin climbs the ramparts of the ancient fort to watch the sunrise. Cross-legged on the top of the wall, he is struck by the sheer stubborn survivability of life. Ten years in a hole without the sun. His limbs have been starved to the point of emaciation and his whole body is covered in the pimple-like rash caused by crusted scabies, but it's hard not to feel some shade of hope watching the tide of light glide swiftly westwards across the desert floor. He had not expected to see the outside world ever again; to watch a sunrise or feel the wind on his face, to walk the world's stage or deliver a monologue. He had resigned himself to execution when the make-up ran out.

It is as if he has been re-animated: a revenant risen from the dead in violent upheaval and gifted a sacred task. That task is clear. He must find his wife and the child that he has never seen or cradled in his arms.

He is not naive. He understands the obstacles that now stand in his way. There's no such thing as Free Syria, though there might have been once. A brief flowering of compassion and collaborative thinking, but it has long since been bombed back into the Dark Ages. The handcuffs that he is wearing and the cell that he is kept locked inside during daylight hours show that he has merely swapped one form of imprisonment with another. His new captors operate in a market place that places a cash value on human life. And they seem to think that he is valuable.

They were on the move for several days after the prison break, driving by night and laying up under camouflage netting during the daylight hours, only stopping briefly at night for meals and to fill the car with petrol from the bowser truck that trundles along at the back of the convoy. Now they have set up camp beside a cross-roads on the plains that Nasruddin believes are somewhere south of the Euphrates river. There is no habitation for miles around and no vegetation except for a stand of wasted date palms leaning like drunks against each other and no water other than a rusty trickle in a narrow defile midway up a solitary hill.

At the top of the hill Roman ruins overlook the crossroads, and the crumbling gypsum ramparts provide shelter from the sun and the enemy planes that occasionally fly overhead, etching contrails in the deep blue sky.

Soon they will come for him and take him back down to the cell that is his new place of confinement in the bowels of the fort.

There are twenty or so of them and their expressions are coloured by every hue of grimness and fatigue and determination. They are dressed in frayed camouflage with a distinctive wolf's head badge on the left shoulder, and a motley collection of tennis shoes, army boots and flip-flops on their feet. They wear black or chequered headscarves and balaclavas and carry burnished Kalashnikovs with the bluing rubbed off. By day they sleep in tents in the ruins of the fort or service the vehicles that are disguised under desert camouflage netting at the base of the hill. Each night they set up a checkpoint on the road and escort him down off the hill to wait with them.

On the first night, while searching a bus, they singled out a man in plain clothes, who they suspected of belonging to the Syrian military. They tied his hands, and the bandit that the others call Magomed filmed him on his phone.

'Bashar al-Assad, this is your government,' Magomed said, before the big one with the scar on his face shot the man in the head.

They dragged his body to the side of the road and rolled him into a ditch while the occupants of the bus formed an orderly line, desperate to avoid eye contact as they waited to re-board.

As far as Nasruddin can tell from the snippets of conversation that he has overheard, they have been criss-crossing the desert for several years, building vehicle-borne bombs from scavenged steel plate and breaking into prisons and ammunition stores spread across the territory of Iraq and Syria, or what was once known as Iraq and Syria. They buy in suicide bombers from cross-border traffickers. The men, and the occasional woman, are mostly hate-filled orphans or softheaded strays, stovepiped through Turkey from grim European ghettos.

They take a great deal of satisfaction in the up-armouring of the trucks and bulldozers that they use to bludgeon their way into prisons and stores, and they take equal satisfaction in the width and depth of their bomb craters. They are fortunate that the Soviet Union provided so many aircraft bombs to the Syrian regime, and that they are so easily stolen and re-purposed.

'Thank you, Russia!' Magomed yells.

They make their living by selling the prisoners on for profit and their client base includes a menu of armed groups foraging on the corpse of what was once Syria. Many of the prisoners are hardened jihadists who are only too willing to return to the fight.

Their leader is a veteran of wars in the Caucasus, Afghanistan and Iraq, and Libya, a fugitive known only as the Colonel. His deputies are also fugitives: Magomed is a nervy, talkative twenty-something who films everything on his phone and Arkady is in his early fifties with the build of a Soviet-era weightlifter and a caved-in right cheek bone that marks a bullet's passing.

Nasruddin is finally introduced to the Colonel at the end of the second day after their arrival at the fort, while the bandits are settling in for the evening wait. A cluster of umber-coloured tents, open on all sides, are pegged down inside the ruin and the smoke from the fires is swirling up into the folds of canvas and drifting away with the evening breeze.

Magomed escorts him to the Colonel's tent and removes his handcuffs. Entering, Nasruddin takes off the ill-fitting plimsolls that he has been given and leaves them at the edge of the rug. One of the Colonel's companions gets up, creating a space for him in front of the fire. He sits and Magomed brings him a bowl with soft, leathery dates and pale cubes of cheese. Nasruddin places a piece of cheese in his mouth and spends a moment savouring its sharp taste. Then he chews on the exquisitely sweet flesh of a date.

The Colonel is staring into the flames, frowning with concentration and every now and then stirring the embers with a stick.

'Ah, Nasruddin, it used to be easier I can tell you that.' He has a look of quiet sorrow on his face as he speaks. A look which his companions share: Arkady gravely and Magomed with a hint of ferocity. 'The prisons were full and even though we lived a hard life, always moving and never resting, we feasted every night. We made good money. Sometimes we got fifty or a hundred men, even three hundred. Good quality too. Islamic State paid a decent price for them. But now it is no good any more. The butcher Assad kills them in his prisons faster than we can free them. The ones we do get are damaged goods. And who is there to buy them? It's hard to find a market. Islamic State is diminished. Its finest captains are spread to the desert wind. Now we don't just have to search harder but we must also seek out the best value people. People like you Nasruddin.'

Nasruddin finds his hands trembling slightly as he listens and the bowl feels fragile between his fingers. Fearing that it might break, he places it in his lap and folds his hands around it.

'What is this story that I hear about you?' the Colonel asks him. 'That you were a gift from the crusaders to al-Assad?'

'It is true that my wife and I were flown here on an American plane,' he concedes.

'Why did the Americans spend money to bring you here?'

He shrugs. 'Because they are squeamish about torture and Assad is not.'

'Show him your hands,' Magomed says.

The Colonel reaches out and takes them in his. He considers the nude and stubby ends of Nasruddin's fingers. The fingernails were pulled out at the root with a pair of needlepoint pliers, one by one over a couple of excruciating days, soon after Nasruddin's arrival in Damascus. They never grew back.

'What did you tell them?'

They had beaten him with a thick black cable all over his body, especially on his palms, his back and his hips. They would beat him three or four times and then ask him a question. If he hesitated or garbled his answer they beat him again.

'Everything. Anything. Whatever they wanted to hear.'

In between sessions he was put in a room where he could hear the screams of other prisoners being tortured. At the end of each day they told him the next day would be worse and often it was. They had inserted rods into his anus. They had swung him by his feet from cords and from his hands by iron trammels.

The Colonel nods as if this is not unexpected.

'Are you ready to fight again?'

For a moment, Nasruddin doesn't understand the question. Why direct it at him? He's not a fighter. He never was. Besides, who would he fight and how?

'I have to find my wife,' he says. 'We were separated after we landed. She was pregnant with our child.'

'There is nothing left of the world you remember,' the Colonel tells him, sternly.

'I have to try.'

'That is not your fate, Nasruddin.'

The Colonel rises from the carpet and goes out into the night.

Nasruddin remains seated and watches as the Colonel tours the encampment, stopping at each tent in turn. He eats more cheese and dates.

'Has God in his bounty provided you to us?' Magomed asks with a smile on his face. 'Will you make us rich?'

'I don't think so,' Nasruddin replies.

There is a shout from down by the checkpoint.

'Time to go to work,' Magomed says. 'Come on.'

The bandits grab their weapons and douse the fires. They hurry as a group out of the fort. With his hand on Nasruddin's upper arm, Magomed steers him down a rough-hewn stair alongside the stream into a crooked defile between sheer rock walls, and then along a crevice that descends at right angles to the defile. The crevice is narrow and crude, difficult going in the dark, but it levels after a while and begins to slope downward until it reaches the road.

A vehicle is approaching: a battered dump-truck with a cargo of gravel that comes rumbling along the road and eases to a halt in front of the line of bandits standing in its path.

The driver dismounts and flees, urged on with a couple of warning shots.

'We will use this to deliver a mighty bomb,' Magomed tells Nasruddin, kicking the truck's tyres.

They drive the truck off the road, conceal it and return to their tents.

As they climb the hill through the narrow crevice, Nasruddin finds himself walking alongside the Colonel.

'What's going to happen to me?' he asks.

'You are the Engineer. Your destiny is for others to decide.'

Sitting watching the sunrise, Nasruddin contemplates his task. He knows that if he is to see his wife again he must seek to impose his will on events, but he has only ever played roles written for him by others. He needs to learn to trust his judgement but it seems almost impossible.

He is a bare, forked animal.

As the sun rises further in the sky, Magomed joins him on the stone rampart and offers him a cigarette.

'Are you ready to prove that you are alive?' he asks.

Under the circumstances, Nasruddin is unsure of the answer to that. Who's to say this is not hell, or at least some halfway stage, and there is a long way yet to go before he re-joins the living?

Magomed holds up his phone. 'When you're ready.'

Nasruddin finishes his cigarette and flicks the butt over the ramparts. If enjoying the sunrise and a cigarette is a measure of existence, then perhaps he is alive after all.

'Go ahead.'

He stares into the lens and begins speaking.

14

The personal history, adventures, experience and observation of . . .

They are about midway through the session, after yet another forty-five minutes of facetious deflection, sly flirtation and flippant half-truth admissions, when Helena surprises Jude by opening a drawer in her Danish rosewood desk and taking out a packet of cigarettes, a bronze Zippo lighter and a wooden ashtray inlaid with mother-of-pearl.

'We both know you don't want to be here.' She lights up without offering him one. He watches as she inhales with her eyes closed and softly exhales. There's something intentionally shocking about it. No one smokes inside any more. He looks at the wall behind her head, the framed diplomas and citations, and asks himself why he is here in his psychiatrist's office and not somewhere else, anywhere else, frankly. 'As you have no choice wouldn't it be better to try and benefit from the experience?'

Helena is staring at him as if she is expecting an answer.

'Okay,' he says, not sure where he's going with this. Where else is there to go? They've been through all the usual David Copperfield stuff. How Jude's father, the general, silenced his demons six months after his twin daughters were born with a 9 mm calibre bullet to the temple. He remembers his mother as depressed and in mourning, overwhelmed by back-to-back feeding and surrounded by piles of laundry. The solution was clear. Jude must be sent away to boarding school. His first was an idiosyncratic place run by a Falklands veteran horrifically burned when his ship went down in San Carlos Water. He was a sadist who used a leather belt to administer punishment to the boys. Before a beating he'd remove the belt slowly, folding it in half and yanking at the ends so that the two sides met one another in a snap. Even now, whenever Jude hears that sound it stops him cold. The headmaster's wife was the school's piano teacher. She shared her husband's sadistic tendencies, rapping knuckles with a ruler like she was swatting wasps. A herd of cows roamed the school grounds, grazing the playing fields and occasionally nosing their way into class. Jude remembers a recurring dream about his father, in which it turned out he was not dead but in fact engaged on some secret mission for the Crown, and returned to rescue Jude and take him to live in a secluded cottage in the Scottish Highlands. He was bullied for a time and in response developed defensiveness, and a readiness to swing his fists that got him in trouble and almost expelled.

When he was twelve, his mother died of acute myelogenous leukaemia, a virulent cancer of the blood and bone marrow, and Jude's stepfather of two years, also a soldier, who saw more promise in Jude's rugby playing than his mediocre academic achievements, sent him to a fee-paying secondary school established in the nineteenth century to educate the orphans of military officers. Its proudest achievement was counting amongst its alumni fifteen holders of the Victoria Cross, Britain's highest award for courage. Jude defied his stepfather by getting A grades and at the age of seventeen was at the centre of a school scandal after losing his virginity to an adulterous schoolmistress, ten years his senior. He completed his final year of schooling at a local community college and from there went to Edinburgh to study history of art. He dropped out after a year and took off on an around-the-globe meander with the strong-willed daughter of a Tory peer who, in his heyday, had served in Margaret Thatcher's cabinet. Jude eventually returned and after a couple of years of indifferent study he'd secured a mediocre degree.

Two months after graduation, Jude's stepfather bought him lunch at the Special Forces Club in Knightsbridge, and told him that while he fully recognised that it was now for Jude to find his own path through life, and equally Jude must recognise that he was no longer going to receive any financial support, as a parting gift he would pay for him to study a martial art, any martial art, but it must be full time and for a minimum of six months. Jude's immediate response was to refuse but after several weeks of truculent resistance he finally asked himself, *why not?* He chose the ancient martial art of *pencak silat*: a full-body fighting form incorporating strikes, grappling and throwing. There followed a punishing six-month stint in an Indonesian jungle camp that proved to be one of the most rewarding experiences of his life.

He's not one hundred per cent sure if it was his stepfather's intention, and the old man airily dismisses the idea to this day, but a few months after his return from the camp Jude passed the Regular Commissions Board and joined the army. He served for five years, first in the infantry and then the Parachute Regiment. He completed a tour in Iraq as a platoon commander and subsequently, after passing P-Company, as the battalion intelligence officer when the Paras deployed to Helmand in Afghanistan. It was while in Helmand that he found himself in the ruins of an Afghan town, in the immediate aftermath of a vicious and sustained firefight, delivering a briefing to a remarkably composed senior intelligence officer in a pale blue silk shalwar kameez. She had the gift of making you think that you had her undivided attention and her voice had a soft and beguiling Scottish lilt. Jude surprised himself and enraged his commanding officer by delivering a damning verdict on the Paras' policy of deliberately picking fights with the Taliban in built-up areas which, to his mind, was achieving nothing other than reducing towns to rubble and depriving local people of their homes. Afterwards, she gave him her card. There was nothing about the card that identified her position or employer, simply *Samantha* and a telephone number in felt-tip pen.

'When you're ready, why don't you give me a call.'

Six months later he called her. She didn't require reminding who he was and appeared unsurprised at hearing from him. On her instruction, he sat the civil service exams and was thereafter guided into the secret world of MI6.

Helena sighs. 'Let's try and concentrate, shall we?'

'What else do you want me to say?'

Helena stubs out the cigarette and waves away the smoke with immaculately manicured fingers.

'I think it's time we talked about women.'

Again, she catches him off guard. 'Women?'

'You've been avoiding the subject.'

'Have I?'

'Yes.'

'I like women,' he says.

'I'm not talking about sex,' she says. Which is a shame, because if he's honest with himself, it's the only kind of therapy that he really enjoys: the annihilation of orgasm. 'I want to know whether you trust women?'

When he smiles, Helena gives him a familiar look, not exactly disapproving, but unwilling to indulge his attempt at deflection. 'What's so funny?'

The night before, Yulia had only stayed long enough in his apartment to have sex bent over the sofa. He hadn't taken his eyes off her throughout the act and after she had gone he had swept the apartment for listening devices with his handheld RF detector, just in case. Holding the detector, he had never felt so lonely in his life.

How to explain?

'I'm having an affair with a married woman,' he confesses.

'*Plus ça change*,' she replies. 'We both know you're unwilling to commit.'

'And I'm back working with Camilla.'

She frowns. Helena knows all about Camilla. 'Under what extraordinary circumstances was that deemed a good idea?'

'As far as I can tell, Queen Bee has her keeping an eye on me.'

Helena knows better than to delve too far into operational details but he can tell by the light in her eyes that he has sparked her interest. 'Why would Queen Bee do that?'

'I'm not sure,' he says. 'I think she's worried about what I might find out.'

'Are you saying that she doesn't trust you?'

'No,' he says, too emphatically, followed by a painful admission, 'I don't know.'

'Are you concerned that she may become disillusioned with you?'

It's so obviously Helena's greatest wish that he acknowledges his orphan fixation on Queen Bee.

'Why should she become disillusioned with me?' he retorts.

Helen gives him a sympathetic look. 'And how are you finding it, working with Camilla?'

'Difficult,' he admits.

'Does her husband know?'

Roger Church, Camilla's husband, is the reason that he's in therapy. Jude had almost crippled him in a fight.

'I've no idea,' Jude replies.

Roger Church had confronted them in a darkened alleyway in Soho. It was 2 a.m. on a work night, and they had stumbled out of Soho House, roaring drunk, their hands roving all over each other. The fight was over in seconds but, even so, it was almost calamitous. Roger stormed into the alley after them and threw a punch at Jude's face, which he countered without thinking with his left forearm. Thinking played no part in any of it. It was all speed and aggression after that. Jude launched a double inward palm strike followed by a kick to the solar plexus with his right knee. Roger stumbled backwards on to the street and a crowd of revellers crowd formed an arena. Jude should have paused. Instead he jabbed Roger in the eye with his fingers Next, he grabbed him by the legs and threw him to the ground. He spun round, astride Roger's legs, and pulled.

'Stop!' Camilla yelled, loud enough to break through his gin-fuelled fury.

It's hard to say whether he would have finished the move. In competition, this was the point at which you always stopped; either way he is grateful to Camilla for not letting him find out if he has what it takes to break a man's back.

It wasn't the kind of thing his employers were prepared to overlook. There were too many witnesses. And the cuckolded husband wasn't happy. Samantha Burns offered him a choice: either he ceased all contact with Camilla and attended monthly therapy, or the matter was referred to the police. The latter would, in all likelihood, result in a court appearance on an assault charge, possibly a jail sentence and almost certainly the revocation of his security clearance.

Once a month, Jude wonders whether he should have taken the jail sentence. Anything would be better than having to ride the Jubilee line to the north London suburb of Dollis Hill – otherwise known as 'dull-as-hell' – to listen to the scalpel-like insight of Dr Helena Van der Leij, dedicated shrink to the intelligence services.

'Something has got you riled,' Helena observes. 'Who is she, this married woman?'

'A rival.'

'In what sense a rival?'

'She works for the other side.'

'The other side?'

'She's Russian.'

'I see. Do your employers know?'

'Yes.'

'Including Camilla?'

'Yes.'

'What is it you're not telling me?'

Should he admit that the Russians appear to have turned the tables on him and snared him in his own trap?

15

Headpiece filled with straw

'My name is Nasruddin al-Raqqah.'

His ravaged face fills the video wall. It's the stuff of childhood nightmares. It is clear that his 'liberators' have made little effort to tidy Nasruddin up for the proof-of-life video. The skin around his eyes is greyish-white and seamed with dirt, his eyes have a yellowish tinge and his teeth have retreated from his gums giving him a skull-like appearance. He may look twenty years older than he should but, under the matted hair and filthy beard, it is undoubtedly Nasruddin, the Engineer. To Jude, it seems a gruesome demonstration of the endurance of human suffering.

Nasruddin's voice is flat, without inflection or emotion, as if the suffering he describes happened to someone else. A world away from the fierce denunciation of the video released after the Basra Ambush.

'I was kidnapped by the British for a crime I did not commit and they sent me to Damascus. I was questioned and tortured. I spent more than ten years in a tiny cell deep under the ground without sunlight, without speaking. Every day I washed the bodies of those killed by Assad. Thousands of bodies, men and women. I thought I was dead and in hell.'

He lowers his head for a moment and then looks up again at the lens.

'But now I am free.'

Jude leans back in his chair. *Kidnapped by the British for a crime I did not commit* – Queen Bee wasn't going to like that. The very idea of it made him feel uncomfortable.

Beside him, Gretchen says, 'The video was uploaded to a Tor service with an "onion" address on the dark web at 0500 hours

GMT this morning. The service uses a network of volunteer computers to route users' web traffic through a series of other users' computers so that the traffic cannot be traced to the original user. And it was distributed via Telegram, an encrypted communication application often used by Islamic State for sending multimedia messages on Android, iOS, and Windows devices. In addition to the video, the message linked to a dark web page called "Funding Breaking the Walls without leaving a trace", with a Zcash address for payment via an anonymous vendor acting as an escrow officer.'

'How much do they want for him?' Jude asks.

'There is a reserve price of five hundred thousand dollars.'

It seems like a lot of money for someone who has been out of action for more than a decade and looks like he is at death's door.

'Any bidders?'

'We don't know. We haven't cracked the code yet.'

'But as long as the link is up, there's a chance he's still alive and available for sale?'

Gretchen nods. 'That's right. And there's plenty of speculative chatter about him.'

He imagines that the virtual caves of the dark web, where conventional search engines cannot reach, must already be awash with rumours about who might buy Nasruddin and what revenge he might seek. And it is only a matter of time before the news spreads to the surface web and the British public becomes aware of it.

'We should warn Camilla,' he says.

Gretchen has the good manners to look embarrassed. 'I've already briefed her.'

Nobody is in any doubt about who really runs his team. 'Thanks Gretchen.'

He calls Camilla from his office.

'Where have you been?' she demands.

'I was seeing my therapist.'

An awkward silence follows. His youngest sister, Tamar, is the only one, apart from Camilla and, of course, Queen Bee, that knows that he is in therapy, and she tends to respond equally uncomfortably.

'I'm glad you're getting help,' Camilla says.

'She thinks I'm making progress,' Jude says, more cheerfully than he feels.

'That's good.' He can tell from her voice that she isn't sure whether to believe him. She's nobody's fool. 'You've spoken to Gretchen?'

'Yes.'

'What next?'

'We wait and see if someone buys him.'

'And if Queen Bee doesn't want to wait?' she says.

'It depends how much she wants to spend. She could put in a bid.'

'Is that some kind of stupid joke?'

There's something about the vehemence of her response that doesn't feel quite right. Of course, making a payment to a terrorist organisation would be illegal but there were quite a few steps between where they are now and making an actual cryptocurrency payment.

'It's probably what the Russians are going to do,' he says.

'How do you know that?'

The message had arrived as he was leaving his psychiatrist's office:

> Darling, you've left me positively sore. I have retired to
> bed. Thank God for the internet. Such bargains available in
> its darkest corners . . .

'It's what they do,' Jude says.

'We're not the Russians,' she snaps and cuts the connection.

He's not the only one that's rattled. Something is up with Camilla too.

An hour later, Gretchen knocks and sticks her head around the door. 'Boss?'

'What is it?'

'We've heard back from the Turkish Police,' she explains, entering his office. She's holding a glass jam jar in one hand and her phone in the other. 'They've sent through a transcript of the questioning of the man and woman arrested in Gaziantep.'

'Forward them to me.'

'Of course.'

She puts the jam jar and the phone on the table between them. He watches as she adjusts the volume on the phone and swipes right across several screens before tapping a white noise app. The room is filled with the dissonant clatter of a tumble dryer.

She leans forward and whispers, 'I swept the office for listening devices and found several.'

He nods.

'They're not Russian. They're ours.'

He nods again. So, Queen Bee is listening. He should be outraged or at the very least disappointed, but as Helena accurately predicted, his response is to wonder what he has done to lose her confidence.

Not even the woman who hired you for your honesty and willingness to speak truth to power seems to trust you any more.

'Should I remove them?' Gretchen asks. 'I don't like being listened to.'

He shakes his head. There's no point. Either Gretchen will have missed some or they will be swiftly replaced. Better not to alert those listening.

Gretchen pauses the app and the room is silent again.

She turns the jam jar around. It has a handwritten label that says: *Rhubarb jam.*

'This is for you,' she explains. 'I grew the rhubarb on my allotment.'

He imagines how lonely it will look beside the cans of coffee in Sanjay's fridge. He can't remember the last time someone gave him a present.

'Thank you,' he says, unexpectedly humbled.

She walks out of his room and a minute later his inbox pings. Before he clicks on it he pauses, understanding that if Queen Bee is listening then she is probably also reading everything that he does. It's like having a stranger in your skull, looking through your eyes. Nevertheless, he opens the file and starts to read.

It is easy to understand their plight: an elderly Syrian couple from Aleppo whose only son had died in the fighting. Their two daughters had gone missing in the chaotic exodus of hundreds of thousands of people within and across their country's borders. They lost all their belongings and were forced to flee their home when it was flattened by one of Assad's barrel bombs. After a journey lasting several days that included walking through a minefield on the border, they had ended up in a Turkish refugee camp. Not long after their arrival, a friendly man in the camp who introduced himself as Stork approached them – no one used their real name in the camps because of the fear of Assad spies masquerading as refugees. He gave them tea and jam. Over the course of several weeks Stork befriended them, bringing them small gifts that made life a little easier and sitting with them to chat about the world. He seemed well known to the administrators in the camp and switched effortlessly between Arabic and Turkish. And then one day, out of the blue, he offered to set them up in their own apartment in the nearest town provided that they acted as hosts for occasional visitors. They were cautious at first, of course; after all what did they really know about this man, Stork? But he was patient and answered their questions. He explained that the visitors would be volunteers from England who were here to help the people of Syria. It was his job to find work for them with the various charities that worked on the border helping the refugees. Sometimes they might go on into Syria. He warned them that the visitors might be nervous at first and it was up to the old man and his wife to make them feel at home just as they had made him feel at home sitting at the entrance to their tent.

What was the old man to do? Winter was coming and there was no one to look after them. Gladly, he accepted the offer.

They moved into the apartment and gave their identity papers to Stork who had kindly offered to secure them official residents' permits. For two weeks, they lived happily just the two of them in the apartment and then one evening the man came to the door with three weary, dust-covered young travellers with backpacks. After that there was a steady stream of young men and women from English cities that the old man only knew for their football teams. Most of them could hardly speak Arabic. There were bedrooms with bunk beds, one for the women and one for the men. The man's wife cooked meals and made tea. She did laundry and cleaned the apartment. She tried to care for the travellers as if they were her own children. It wasn't easy. Some were scared and others were angry. Sometimes they were rude. They were not used to the food. Occasionally, Stork would come with McDonald's in a big brown paper bag and this seemed to make the travellers happy for a short time.

When did they realise that the men and women in their apartment were there to fight?

They were not supposed to have phones. Stork was clear about that but one of them had smuggled one in. When the old man found him with it the young man showed him a video of an attack on one of Assad's military camps. The old man recognised the martyr who drove the truck. He was a jittery one who had stayed in the house three months before.

'We're all going to heaven,' the young man with the phone told him.

That night he confided in his wife and they lay trembling beside each other in their bed. They realised that they would never see their identity papers again. If they gave themselves up they would be treated like terrorists. They were trapped. And so, deprived of a choice, they continued to look after the travellers until the Turkish Police smashed in the door and arrested them.

They are shown the martyrdom video and positively identify the suicide bomber who drove the truck that blew open the interrogation centre where Nasruddin was imprisoned. The martyr was a large, quiet man who spoke very little and only stayed a few days before Stork came to collect him.

They are sifting through photos from Interpol identifying the dozens of missing British citizens who stayed at the apartment on their way to martyrdom.

16

Habeas corpus

Jude's sister Hannah and her family live in a redbrick Victorian semi in a row of near-identical houses in a leafy quarter of Stoke Newington, which, judging by her friends and neighbours, is where all liberal-leaning people of similar professions gravitate once they have children. Jude arrives with a bunch of flowers, a dessert in a box from a nearby patisserie, a gift-wrapped children's book and, because his brother-in-law is a wine snob and Jude likes to keep him wrong footed, a bottle of Lebanese Chateau Musar.

He opens the gate and walks up to the door past a pastel blue hydrangea. He can hear the girls chattering inside.

He presses the doorbell and listens as they shriek with excitement. He does not know what he has done to earn such devotion.

The eldest, Olivia, opens the door. A dandelion of blonde hair surrounds her head. She is wearing pyjamas and is missing her front teeth. The side table behind her is a mess of bicycle helmets and satchels.

'It's Uncle Jude,' she calls.

The younger one, Abigail, has her mother's dark soulful eyes and lush hair. She is huddled midway up the stairs clutching a floppy-eared toy rabbit.

Hannah joins them in the hallway, kisses him on the cheek and relieves him of the bottle, the flowers, the *tarte tatin* and the book, which he promptly takes back and waves at the children.

'Just that and no more,' Hannah tells them.

Olivia grips him by the hand leads him up the stairs past Abi who gets up and follows.

In their bedroom, they sit in a row on Olivia's bed and in recompense Abi gets to rip the wrapping paper into shreds. It's *Where The Wild Things Are* by Maurice Sendak and tells the story of a fierce little boy – who, Jude reassures them, can be just as fierce as little girls – and how he has been sent to bed with no supper and how he sails away to where the wild things live and becomes the wildest thing of all. He's reached the part with the Wild Rumpus – and the girls are choosing their favourite Wild Things – when the doorbell chimes and he hears female voices in the hall. The girls are too rapt to pay it any attention.

He closes the book with the boy back in his room and his supper still warm.

'That's it. Your mother said one story.'

The girls climb obediently under the covers and he kisses them on their foreheads. They smell of soap and all things nice.

'Night, night, Uncle Jude.'

'Night, night.'

He pauses at the top of the stairs, briefly struck by guilt and shame. *What do you think you are doing bringing your work into this hallowed space?*

Research, that's all it is, he tells himself. But deep down he knows that this is no longer just work. It's become personal. He doesn't just want to find Nasruddin, he wants to know the truth about him too. *Is it any wonder that Queen Bee is watching and listening so carefully?*

Hannah is filling courgette flowers with ricotta on a wooden board in the kitchen. The French windows leading to the garden are open and he can see smoke rising from a barbecue on the deck.

An attractive, dark haired woman is sitting at a table set for six with a half-finished glass of rosé wine. Kirsty McIntyre: single, thirty-four years old, mortgaged with an ex-council flat in Spitalfields, enthusiastic cook, rarely misses her weekly yoga lesson, 642 friends on Facebook and 5,436 Twitter followers as of just before Jude pressed the doorbell.

'You remember Kirsty,' his sister says.

Her smile is as sassy and the gleam in her eye is as provocative and questioning in real life as they are in the many images of her on the web. Her hair has changed since her newspaper byline was last refreshed – no longer a bob, it now tumbles to her shoulders. Clearly, she doesn't remember him at all.

'We met once,' Jude explains. 'It was ten years ago. Hannah's leaving party at the *Guardian*.'

'You'd just come back from Afghanistan,' Hannah tells him.

'Sorry,' Kirsty says, her smile widening. 'I guess I must have been off my tits.'

'Girl, you were,' his sister adds.

Kirsty is wearing a white top with a deep V that seems to wrap around and tie at the back. It shows off her arms and a skin tone that is almost Middle Eastern despite her Glasgow heritage. Skinny jeans and open toed sandals with a heel. Toenails a coral pink colour.

He's half in love with her already. Again, the warning voice in his head: *Be careful. She's your sister's friend. Do not knowingly deceive her.*

Hannah fills Kirsty's glass and turns to him. 'Pink wine?'

Jude grimaces.

'All man, my big brother,' Hannah says. She nods in the direction of the cupboard where Ben keeps his malt. 'Did I tell you he is single?'

'Aye, you did, several times.'

'I am in the room,' Jude says, holding the cupboard doors open and inspecting his brother-in-law's treasured collection of spirits inside.

'Did the girls go to bed okay?'

'Tucked in, lights off,' he replies, pouring a generous glug of Lagavulin in a tumbler.

'You know they'll be down later on, wanting to meet everyone,' Hannah says, whisking batter in a glass bowl. 'You can bet on it.'

'Who else is coming?' Jude asks, eyeing the place settings warily.

'Ben insisted on inviting Jonathan. I don't know why. They can't agree on anything.'

Ben shares the same unfathomable family-shepherding gene as Hannah – some human variant of collie dog. Ben's brother Jonathan is never short of an opinion. He was one of the Young Turks in the No. 10 Policy Unit at Downing Street in the early nineties. Unlike some of his colleagues, he hadn't managed to win a seat and harbours a certain degree of resentment that he isn't running the country, largely ameliorated by earning colossal sums of money working as a management consultant for McKinsey. His wife Elizabeth is the chief designer for a high street retail chain that sells fashion accessories.

'They feel safe coming this far east?' Jude asks, sitting beside Kirsty.

'It's like going on safari,' Hannah says. 'Vicarious excitement viewed from the protective height of a Range Rover.'

Kirsty and Jude clink glasses.

'*Slainte*,' he says.

The front door opens and Ben, Jude's brother-in-law, enters carrying his briefcase and a brown paper bag from the off licence. He is wearing a pinstripe suit, which suggests that he has spent the day in court practising his trade. He goes straight to the kitchen counter, puts down his things and kisses his wife. Jude envies their evident and, it seems, uncomplicated happiness. Ben waves to their guests, casts a surreptitious glance at Jude's bottle, and announces that he is going up to change.

'Tamar might even come,' Hannah says out of the blue.

'Seriously?'

Their sister Tamar is the true prodigal. Jude is an amateur by comparison.

'Obviously I'm not going to lay a place setting for her.'

Kirsty raises her eyebrows. 'So, this really is a family gathering?'

'I know, now you're wondering "to what do I owe the honour?".'

'Hannah likes to have at least one civilian at her gatherings,' Jude adds, quickly. 'It reduces the chances of it turning into a fistfight.'

'And you're quite the celebrity after your scoop,' Hannah adds. 'Revealing wrongdoing at the highest levels of government.'

The doorbell rings. Jonathan and Elizabeth sweep in looking glossy and bearing gifts – chocolates and champagne. Kirsty is introduced to Elizabeth who looks her over carefully as if to assess whether she will be an agreeable addition to the family. Ben reappears in a spectacularly crumpled pink shirt and fills their glasses.

Hannah takes charge of the seating plan. 'You stay where you are beside Kirsty,' she tells Jude. She sits Jonathan and Elizabeth opposite them.

'What were you doing in Afghanistan?' Kirsty asks.

'I was there with Op Herrick,' Jude replies.

'You're a soldier?'

'No,' he laughs. 'Not any more.'

'What's so funny?'

'I couldn't get out of the army quick enough.'

'How come?'

'Not very good at taking orders, I suppose.'

'So why did you join?'

Now is not the time to explain what Helena, his elegant shrink, has coaxed him into admitting: not only that he is a commitment-phobe but that he has spent his life embracing public institutions and then fighting his way out of them.

Lifting his nose from his glass, Jonathan says, 'I've always thought a Chablis can be a bit of a pig in a poke.'

At the head of the table, Ben bridles.

'And what do you do now?' Kirsty asks Jude.

'I'm a risk analyst. I advise investors about emerging markets.'

'Jude is the patron saint of the Hail Mary pass,' Jonathan explains. He is not a member of the inner circle trusted with the knowledge of Jude's true profession. 'He advises gamblers on how to rid themselves of their money.'

Hannah serves the courgette flowers in the centre of the table on a large, oval platter and invites them to eat them with their fingers. They are deep fried with a sheer coating of silky tempura batter, crunchy and creamy at the same time, and for five minutes or so the table is silent as they eat.

*   *   *

Conversation ranges from the mix of credulity and gullibility that makes the present incumbent singularly unfit to be the US president to the latest humiliation heaped on the UK government by Brussels. Hannah rails against the feebleness of the official opposition and the rising tide of xenophobia across the country. Jonathan feigns interest in local house prices and the quality of nearby schooling. Kirsty exchanges sidelong glances with Jude who pulls his best 'what do I know?' face.

Ben goes out on to the deck and grills a stack of thick sirloin steaks that he brushes with golden rapeseed oil and rubs with a coating of salt as thick as road grit. When they're done he carves them into slices, crusty on the outside and rare in the centre.

Kirsty retains her sense of humour throughout.

'What is it that you do?' Elizabeth asks Kirsty as they are eating.

'I'm a journalist.'

'Kirsty broke the Frank Booth rendition story,' Hannah says.

'I heard Booth on the radio this morning,' Jonathan says. 'Personally, I don't see what all the fuss is about. Nasruddin al-Raqqah was a terrorist.'

'He was denied the normal judicial process,' Ben responds. 'Speaking as a lawyer, I'm against rendition on principle.'

'He killed twenty-five British soldiers and injured many more.'

'How do you know that's true? You've thrown out habeas corpus and a thousand years of legal precedent. Let me remind you what the Magna Carta says: "No Freeman shall be taken or imprisoned, or be disseized of his Freehold, or Liberties, or free Customs, or be outlawed, or exiled, or any other wise destroyed; nor will We not pass upon him, nor condemn him, but by lawful judgment of his Peers, or by the Law of the land." Nasruddin should have been tried in a court and the state should have provided the evidence against him.'

'And if to do so would have compromised the identity of a source?'

'Come on!' Hannah retorts. 'That's the kind of excuse that got us into trouble in Iraq in the first place. It's the defence of scoundrels. And what about the wife? What did she do wrong? She was seven months pregnant.'

When Kirsty explains the circumstances of Nasruddin's wife's rendition, being bound up like an Egyptian mummy, Elizabeth looks visibly upset. 'That's barbaric.'

'What happened to her?' Hannah asks.

'According to the people I'm talking to inside Syria she was released just before her daughter was born,' Kirsty replies. 'She went back to live with her parents in the south of the country.'

'And now?' Jude asks.

She shrugs and stares into the bottom of her glass. 'We think she may have fled the country.'

'If you can find her you've got a good chance you can go to court,' Ben says. 'Maybe you can even pin it on Frank Booth.'

Kirsty knows more than she's letting on, Jude's suddenly sure of that.

'Do you think he knew?' Hannah asks. 'Did Frank Booth know she was on that plane?'

'He denies it,' Kirsty replies. 'But yes, I do.'

'Your Whitehall sources?' Jonathan asks, sceptically.

'I don't think anyone is going to fall on their sword for him at Vauxhall Cross.'

'You have sources inside Six that are actively briefing against him?'

She shrugs, refuses to answer with an apologetic smile.

'Booth's defence seems to be based on the argument that as foreign secretary he couldn't know everything that was going on,' Ben explains. 'The counter argument is that as the minister, he was the only person who could sign off on the offer of indemnity to the UK intelligence officer who went to Syria to question al-Raqqah. And given the way things were in 2006, it is extremely unlikely that MI6 would have sent someone down there without obtaining that indemnity first.'

Hannah is forthright. Of the three siblings, she's the preacher – the one that sees the world in black and white. 'If Booth signed off on sending an intelligence officer down to Syria to interrogate al-Raqqah then he should come clean. His performance on the *Today* programme this morning was evasive and mealy mouthed.'

'Don't you hold back girl,' Kirsty says.

The doorbell rings.

Hannah and Jude exchange a look.

'Are you expecting someone?' Jonathan asks.

'Tamar,' Ben replies.

'I'll go.' Jude rises, lays his napkin down on his seat and heads for the door. The doorbell goes twice more while he's approaching.

17

The prodigal sister

'What took you so long?' Tamar demands when he opens the door. She has the temperament of their father, the general – moody, imperious and secretly fragile – and although she was just a baby when he died, she has always taken his life lessons to heart. Embrace your role as a giver of commands. Keep those around you in their place at all times: it's for their own good and they will love you for it.

'It's nice to see you,' he tells her.

Tamar was modelling the Jessica Jones look back before Netflix turned the comic book into a TV series: purloined black leather jacket, black T-shirt, boyfriend jeans and scuffed paratrooper boots. Kohl-rimmed eyes and the pallor of a heroin addict. She pecks him on the cheek as she passes, dumps her motorcycle helmet on the hall table and leaves him to follow in her wake.

'I came,' she announces to the room. She throws herself down in Jude's chair and contemplates the half-finished meals on their plates. 'You slayed the fatted calf for the elder brother, does Ottolenghi have a recipe for that too?'

'You don't have to eat,' Hannah retorts.

'I'll eat.'

Jude pulls up another chair while Ben fills a plate for her.

They watch as she wolfs down the contents in a manner that suggests that she does not know where the next meal is coming from.

'So, what have I missed?' she says, between mouthfuls.

'We were arguing the merits or otherwise of rendition and torture,' Ben says.

'Our enemies are barbaric,' Tamar says, matter-of-factly.

'So, we should sink to their level?' Ben says.

'Absolutely not,' Hannah responds, firmly.

Tamar shrugs. 'If you knew what I know.'

Hannah points an accusatory finger at Tamar. 'That's lazy and unverifiable!'

'Mummy?'

Abi is standing in the doorway holding her floppy-eared rabbit.

'Come here, sweetie,' Hannah says. Abi scurries over and her mother scoops her up and folds her into her arms. Abi watches them with her thumb in her mouth.

'Which one's that?' Tamar asks.

'Abigail,' Hannah tells her in an exasperated voice. 'I wish you'd make more effort.'

'Not my bag.' A phone is ringing. Tamar takes it out of her jacket pocket and holds it to her ear. 'Speak.'

She listens and nods while reaching for the nearest bottle.

Hannah rolls her eyes.

'On my way.' Tamar drains the glass and looks around her. 'Duty calls,' she says. 'Thanks for dinner. Don't get up.'

'I'll walk you out,' Jude says, getting up from the table. He follows her down the hallway and they pause in a pool of light outside the front door.

'What is it?' Tamar asks.

'I need your help to find someone,' Jude replies. 'I can't use the normal channels.'

'Who?'

'A former MI6 officer called Edward Malik. He was dismissed in 2011.'

Now he has her attention. She has that pissed off look she saves for those who have only themselves to blame. 'And why can't you use the normal channels?'

'Strictly speaking, it's outside the parameters of my investigation.'

'The parameters of your investigation?'

He sighs. 'They want me to find Nasruddin al-Raqqah.'

'And how does finding Edward Malik help you with that?'

'He's the last person to have spoken to him. He's the one they sent down to Syria to question him.'

'Is that why Kirsty McIntyre is at the dinner table?'

He shrugs. 'She knows Hannah.'

'You should be more careful about mixing personal and professional,' Tamar warns him. 'Is this little event sanctioned?'

'No.'

'Who do you answer to these days?'

'Camilla Church.'

She shakes her head. 'Are you serious?'

'I'm not sure I can trust her.'

'So why did you have an affair with her?'

She puts on her motorcycle helmet and crosses to her vintage Triumph, which is parked in the shadow of a plane tree.

'Will you help me?' Jude asks, following her.

She mounts the bike and turns the handlebars towards him. 'No promises but I'll see what I can do, Jude.' She switches on the engine, guns the accelerator, and he steps aside as she roars off up the street, decelerating suddenly as she approaches the first of the speed bumps.

'She's an acquired taste, your sister,' Jonathan says, when he returns to the room.

'Shut up,' Elizabeth tells him.

'Jude's brought pudding,' Hannah says.

'I'll get it.' Jude crosses to the kitchen island. Kirsty joins him and searches for plates and forks while he divides the tart into six. He glances at her surreptitiously while she's bending over a drawer.

'There's cream in the fridge,' Hannah calls out.

'Right.'

She brushes past him in the space between the island and the cooker on her way to the fridge. He wonders if it's deliberate.

They eat pudding at the table and afterwards Elizabeth announces that the children have an early start and it is time to leave. Jonathan casts a longing look at the bottle of Lagavulin that Ben has placed on the table but does not disagree with his wife.

'I should really head off too,' Kirsty says.

'Why don't you two share a cab?' Hannah says, to Jude and Kirsty. 'You're both going in the same direction.'

Kirsty smiles at him, 'Sure, why not? We can Uber it.'

Five minutes later, they spill out into the street and watch as Jonathan and Elizabeth drive off in their Range Rover. Soon after, a Prius approaches, rising and falling every twenty metres as it crosses the speed bumps.

Hannah hugs him and then Kirsty. 'Thank you so much for coming.' She gives Kirsty a conspiratorial look and says, 'I'll call you tomorrow.'

They sit beside each other in the back of the car with their thighs almost touching.

'That was quite an evening,' Kirsty says.

'Yes. I'm sorry that you were thrown in at the deep end.'

'It was interesting.'

'That's one way of describing it.'

'So, what's the story with your sister, Tamar?'

It's a question that places him on difficult ground. How to acknowledge his sister's profession without suggesting that there is in it some vein of secrecy that is not confined to her alone?

'She's a police officer.'

Kirsty looks astonished. 'Wow. You really are an unusual family.'

The car pulls up outside Sanjay's loft and Jude wishes that the journey had lasted longer.

'Do you have a card?' he asks.

'No. I'm sorry. I didn't come out with any.'

On impulse, he tells her the number of his red burner and watches while she saves it on hers. When she looks up, she is wearing an amused smile that might mean she likes him but probably just means she's humouring him.

'If you want a drink or something give me a call,' he says, wincing inside.

'I'll do that.'

He opens the door, gets out and waves as the car departs. He had not expected to like her as much as he did. He should not pursue this further. He should not see her again. He knows that but he is already looking forward to it.

The buzzer goes five minutes after he lets himself in the apartment. It's Camilla, demanding to come up.

'That's quite a stunt you pulled tonight,' she tells him as she strides ahead of him into the living space. She's wearing skin-tight black Lycra leggings and buckled boots.

'Kirsty is friends with my sister Hannah,' Jude offers as explanation as he trails behind her. She turns to face him with her back to the glass. Her grey eyes have a luminous sheen.

'You can't help yourself, can you?' she says. Her voice is unemotional, watchful even.

'What does that mean?'

'You think seducing someone is the solution to every problem.'

'Is this about Yulia or Kirsty?'

Or you, he thinks.

'What did you find out?'

'That Nasruddin's wife gave birth to a daughter. That Kirsty is looking for her and she may already know where to find her.'

'Why are the press so obsessed with this?'

'They can smell a cover-up,' he tells her. 'They're not the only ones.'

'I didn't ask for this job any more than you did,' she says. She goes over to the freezer and retrieves a bottle of vodka that he had forgotten was there. She pours herself a shot and downs it. She pours another. 'There's a vacancy for permanent secretary coming up at the Department of Work and Pensions. Roger is in the frame for it. Queen Bee has made it pretty clear that she'll block his application if this . . . thing . . . goes badly.'

She downs a second shot. She doesn't normally do fragility, her beauty is too alarming for that, but there's evidence of strain in the slope of her shoulders and the set of her jaw. Not so much that someone who doesn't know her well would spot it but Jude, a fellow veteran of sleepless nights, can see she's in trouble. He realises with sudden clarity that she's carrying a secret that's too heavy for her to bear.

'I'm sorry,' he tells her.

'Queen Bee is protecting her own interests,' she says simply. Her eyes meet his, candidly.

'What do you mean?' Jude asks her.

She ignores the question. 'She says you can go to Jordan.'

'You could have called me and told me that.'

'I wanted to see you.'

'Why?'

She walks over to him and puts her hands on either side of his face and looks at him. He can feel the pull of it like a rip tide, the fierce and almost irresistible desire to kiss her, on the mouth, on the eyelids, on the pale softness of her throat.

They look at each other for a long time. She's willing him to do it.

'You think it was easy for me,' she says, 'being told I couldn't see you again?'

It's a moment before he finds his voice. 'I think you should leave.'

She gasps and releases him.

'Why are you so angry with me, Jude?'

He hadn't even realised that he was trembling with rage. He looks away. 'Just go.'

'All right,' she says.

He listens to the sound of her boots on the floorboards and the door slamming behind her.

18

The Mighty Men

It is shortly before dawn and Fig struggles through the dusty streets of the town towards the ancient amphitheatre where the Old Man is waiting. There is a sand storm brewing and Fig has a white turban wrapped around his head with the tail pulled across his face to cover his mouth and nose from the swirling dust. It is a blessing of sorts that may have bought a few hours respite from their enemies.

The town appears deserted apart from a stolen Humvee with a turret-mounted machine gun parked at the crossroads at the end of his street. The rest of the fighters are in the network of bunkers and trenches on the outskirts of town that they have been digging since they captured the town fourteen days ago. The Humvee's interior light is on, the windscreen wipers scudding back and forth to dislodge the sand. It is close enough for him to be able to make out the exhausted face of the driver and the turret gunner who is huddled beside him. Fig raps on the window with his knuckles and barks a command in a voice sharpened on the parade ground of the Rustamiyah Military Academy in Baghdad. The startled gunner jumps up to man the gun.

Turning on to Main Street, Fig is battered by the force of the wind. There is garbage everywhere. Plastic bags billow out of the gloom like airborne jellyfish and stick to him. Several times he is forced to stop and shake himself to dislodge them. He struggles past the charred ruin of the museum, crossing the street to avoid the half-buried corpses outside the entrance where they had beheaded a dozen spies the day before.

The dogs will have to dig for them after the storm.

He leaves the road and immediately the force of the wind subsides. He follows a rope line that marks a safe path through the

Roman ruins, past ancient colonnades and collapsed lintels and the recently pulverised remains of a temple to an idolatrous god of storms and lightning. He sticks to the path. Since blowing up the temple, the Old Man's demolition teams have been working without rest to prepare and lay booby traps in preparation for the coming battle.

As he approaches the amphitheatre, Fig encounters the head of the Old Man's bodyguard, the familiar bulk of Jomaa, a giant of a man in camouflage and a black turban who has been with the Old Man since the very beginning. Jomaa acknowledges his presence with a curt nod. It disturbs Fig to know that the giant would kill him without hesitation and there is nothing he can do about it. You had to hand it to the Old Man; he knew how to pick his acolytes. Fig had dug around in Jomaa's past hoping to uncover the sort of dirty secrets that everyone hides. Anything for leverage: he had sent spies to the man's home village only to find that it had been razed to the ground and the population slaughtered. No family, no dependants, no friends. Reluctantly, Fig had concluded that the man was not normal. He is an ascetic dedicated solely to the security of his master.

Jomaa frisks him and waves him on. Another of the bodyguards, a woman in a black hijab that he does not recognise, escorts him up the ramp that the Romans had once used for sacrificial animals. More recently it had been used to herd prisoners who were captured during the fight for the town into the arena. Inside it is quiet despite the coming storm and Fig sees that he is the last to arrive.

Fig remembers how he felt the first time he met the Old Man in the aftermath of the American invasion of Iraq – the mixture of awe and fear – unsure of whether he was about to be beheaded. A man whose given name even then had been long abandoned, and whose age and guile had earned him the nickname *Sheikh al-Jabal*.

The Old Man is leaning on his staff at the centre of the arena. Before him there is a semicircle of advisers from his high council. There is Namir, the Tiger, who commands more than a thousand veteran soldiers: Chechens, Kashmiris, Afghans, Pakistanis,

Kuwaitis and Qataris, who have each sworn a *bamiyat*, an individual oath of allegiance to the Old Man. There is Abu Shahid, with a cadaverous face that is pale and mottled, who runs the youth wing of the Brigade with end-of-the-world zeal and is responsible for the Rorschach of dark stains in the sand where they had lined up prisoners after the fall of the town and executed them. For each one a bullet to the back of the head delivered by Islamic State's youngest recruits, boys ranging from eight to eleven years old. There is the Afghan Rahmatullah, the Old Man's taciturn personal physician, who it is said once treated Osama bin Laden. There is Wahab Mutairi, the Kuwaiti who manages the group's multiple revenue streams, cash and crypto-currency savings. There is Hamid Alhabali, who commands the engineering units that have been digging tunnels and trenches, bulldozing rubble into ramparts and punching rat-runs through rows of houses. There is Wahid al-Dib, whose men have laid an intricate and interlocking maze of booby traps and command- and victim-operated improvised explosive devices across the town.

And there is Fig, who was once an intelligence officer in the tyrant Saddam's army. Acknowledging his arrival with a nod, the Old Man turns to face in the direction of Mecca and leads them in the dawn prayer. In unison, they raise their hands to their ears and then fold them on their chests, bow and drop to the ground, pressing their foreheads to the dirt in obeisance.

At the end of the prayer, Fig turns his head to the right and says, 'The angel who records your good deeds is to this side.' Then he turns his head to the left and says, 'The angel who records your wrongful deeds is to this side.' He says the words by rote because they have no meaning for him. He long ago abandoned the distinction between good deeds and wrongful ones. He believes that God is dead and only exists as a shadow in the cave-dweller minds of his companions.

When they are finished they stand and the Old Man surveys them. He looks both exultant and exhausted. Fig wonders if he has been here in the arena all night and has been granted another of his apocalyptic 3 a.m. visions. They are all thinking it and he can sense the nervousness in the others. It is never easy to judge the Old Man's moods.

'Tiger?'

With his reputation for ferocity in battle, his massive brow and swept-back hair, it is not for nothing that their military commander is known as Namir, 'the Tiger'.

'Sheikh.'

'How are the preparations?'

'The defensive works are complete. The explosives are armed.'

'Are the men in position?'

It is a form of liturgy with familiar questions and prescribed responses.

'Yes, Sheikh,' Tiger replies, 'they await your orders.'

The final question is addressed to them all. 'Are they ready to die?'

'They are!'

Satisfied, the Old Man looks his way. 'Fig?'

Fig licks his lips and bows his head. He is always careful to project a supplicant's respectful expression: a mode of behaviour acquired and honed over years of service in the Ba'ath Party, working for Saddam and his murderous sons. Speaking truth to power is a risky business – after all, Jomaa only waits for a command from his master to end Fig's life – but it is the role that is expected of him. 'If that is your wish . . .'

The note of caution in his voice is enough to provoke a murmur of dissent from his fellow council members. Abu Shahid steps forward to protest. The Old Man's response is almost impercepti-ble, a narrowing of the eyes and a tightening of his fist on the staff. Abu Shahid stops in his tracks.

'Go on, Fig, say what's on your mind.'

'The enemy are bringing tanks forward and when the storm lifts they will control the skies again,' he explains. 'Our trucks will find it difficult to manoeuvre because of the shifting sand.'

'Tiger?'

Tiger nods. 'He's right.'

The town was full of martyrs ready to sacrifice themselves by driving vehicles packed with explosives at the advancing enemy, but without manoeuvrability they were next to useless.

'Sheikh, the vehicles are only one element of our defence,' Abu Shahid says, indignantly.

'An important element, nonetheless,' Fig replies with barely disguised irritation.

There is a tension between the advice given by Fig and his fellow former members of Saddam's intelligence apparatus, who constitute the operational core of Islamic State's fighting force and advocate staying on the move and avoiding set piece battles, and the messianic vigour of those of the Old Man's followers like Abu Shahid who believe that they should fight and die for Islamic State.

Fig doesn't want to die here in this ghostly ruin surrounded by endless grey sand. But the Old Man appears not to be listening. He is staring at the far wall of the amphitheatre where the clouds have parted and the light of the rising sun has created a band of burnished gold. It is fleeting, a few moments only, then the clouds close again and darkness returns.

'I have been considering our future and our end,' he says.

They wait to hear more.

'I have been weighing the struggle between the near enemy and the far enemy.'

And so, to the other great tension in the movement, the rivalry between those who believe that the corrupt monarchies of the Gulf and the military dictatorships of the Maghreb and Egypt, and the idolatrous Shiites, are the enemy, and those who choose to believe that the true enemy are the Crusader nations of Europe and North America. Fig calls them the isolationists and the internationalists. The internationalists believe that the final great battle of mankind will only be had when the crusaders are goaded into total warfare. And the only thing that will cause the Western nations to react on that scale is a truly transformative act of destruction, something more than the symbolism of jets scything into skyscrapers. The Old Man knows Fig's views on this.

'We are hard pressed on all sides,' the Old Man says. 'We cannot go on fighting and losing. We face extinction.'

Fig sees that Abu Shahid's face is shining as if extinction is everything he has ever dreamed of.

'Fig?'

'Sheikh?'

The Old Man beckons him and he steps forward.

'Come closer.'

The Old Man reaches out with a hand as ragged as a claw and places it on his shoulder. He is aware of the female bodyguard who escorted him into the amphitheatre standing at the Old Man's shoulder, watching him with eyes that are the colour of polished walnut.

'What news of Nasruddin?'

'He has been found and freed from one of the tyrant's prisons.'

The Old Man shakes his head, almost imperceptibly. 'You're sure?'

'A group claiming to hold him have reached out to us with video evidence. I have seen it and I can confirm that it is him. They want money.'

The Old Man looks as if he has reached a decision. He looks beyond Fig to his semicircle of advisers. 'Is there anything else?'

'Nothing,' Abu Shahid replies.

'Then go.'

Fig waits with the Old Man's hand on his shoulder as they begin to leave the arena.

'Tiger,' the Old Man says. 'Wait.'

Tiger approaches.

'Sheikh?'

'It is time to strike back.'

Tiger nods his head in acknowledgment.

The Old Man looks up at the roiling sky as if it is his to command. Then he looks at Fig. There is such intensity in his eyes that Fig begins to tremble.

'You will bring me Nasruddin but first you will bring me the Stranger.'

Many years have passed and many different personas worn and discarded since Fig last heard that name. *Al-Gharib*. The Stranger.

'He is alive?' Fig asks.

'Yes.'

It's even more surprising than the news that Nasruddin is still alive.

'You know where he is?'

'Yes.'

Fig gets his first inkling of what the Old Man is planning.

'Then I will bring him to you.'

The Old Man squeezes his shoulder in gratitude.

'Tiger?'

'Yes, Sheikh.'

'Be ready to depart at dusk.'

'And the defence of the city?'

'The men will stay and fight. Abu Shahid will lead the defence. He begged for martyrdom. Let him have it. Only a small group of us can continue.'

Fig is squatting by the camping stove on the floor, heating a pot of coffee, when the rug that he has hung against the door is pushed to one side and a woman enters the room. It is the bodyguard from earlier. She has exchanged her camouflage for a clean white shalwar kameez.

She scans the room, taking in the bottle of whisky on the ledge of the bricked-up window and the Yezidi girl who is curled up on the bed in the corner. If she disapproves she does not show it.

'Coffee?'

She nods.

He pours the syrupy liquid into two small cups and they sit cross-legged opposite each other. She is remarkably calm and self-possessed.

'I am Zeina,' she says. 'I will take you to the Stranger.'

Fig had always assumed that the man known as the Stranger was executed long ago, in the cauldron of Iraq. His transgressions were too numerous and too egregious to be tolerated, even by the standards of the time. The news of him alive is startling, like finding an atomic bomb at the back of a cupboard, and the idea of him unleashed is exhilarating and horrifying, in equal measure.

19

The red queen

Frank knew that he represented an active constituency, his first parliamentary campaign had taught him that, but he hadn't realised how active until he found he was invited to everything imaginable. He'd spent almost every Friday for the best part of twenty years holding surgeries and attending events. Weekends too, back when they still had a house in the constituency.

He had always regarded Members of Parliament as being divided into two camps: those who loved their constituents and those who secretly despaired of them and longed to return to the safety of Westminster. For much of his career he had counted himself amongst the former. As a newly elected member there was nothing he had relished more than the cut and thrust of debate – he'd even carried his own soapbox around and taken on all comers on a Saturday morning in the unlovely concrete shopping centres that pass for the civic heart of his constituency. But, if he is honest with himself, the years have ground him down and his heart is no longer in it. There is only so much you can do. His constituency surgeries are filled with people with miserable and gruelling problems that lie outside his power to solve. He steers them in the direction of the Borough Council and suffers the expressions of disappointment and reproach on their faces. If he can see their faces, that is. More and more of them seem to be in full veil. It makes him feel uncomfortable. You can hear what they have to say but you often can't see what they mean.

He is so tired of it all. He thirsts for the anonymity of London and the comfortable tenure of a peerage.

★   ★   ★

The end of his last surgery of the day is fast approaching and Frank is sitting in the back room of his stuffy utilitarian office, half-listening to a pensioner who is complaining about the increasingly noxious smell from the local sewerage plant, when he hears a commotion in the waiting room: the unmistakably strident voice of Cathy Butcher demanding to speak to him. His first instinct is to bolt but he's tried that before and the Butchers have experience of blocking his exit routes. One of the more painful episodes of the last twenty years involves a shaming *Daily Mail* front cover with a photo of him dangling out the back window of his office with a dog attached to his trouser leg and the caption *Set the Dogs on Him!* It was in the aftermath of the Butcher twins' funeral debacle and he was desperate to avoid another public tongue-lashing. He was halfway out the narrow window into the alleyway behind when Jonno Butcher, one of Cathy's seemingly inexhaustible supply of meat-faced nephews, had dropped the leash on Elsie, an English bull terrier with a wedge-shaped head that would not have looked out of place on a shark, and provided the lurking paparazzi with the 'gotcha!' photo of the year.

He has no choice but to face the music.

The door is propelled open and Cathy tracks mud and straw into the room on her wellington boots. Amongst those constituents who have caused him a disproportionate amount of grief, Cathy Butcher stands head and shoulders above the rest. She is every MP's nightmare.

'I want a word with you, Frank Booth,' she says, accusingly.

Frank watches enviously as the pensioner, who has been clutching her handbag to her chest since Cathy's explosive entrance, practically jumps out of her chair and scurries out.

Cathy sits and glares at him from under her shaggy mess of ginger hair. Her piggy little eyes shine like black pearls.

'Why is he even still alive?' she demands.

Frank's problems with Cathy Butcher date back more than a decade to when he'd described her as 'dishevelled' in an email exchange with the Borough Council, in which he'd strongly backed the council's attempt to strip the Butcher family of a network of interconnected allotments on the west side of the town.

Cathy had proven to be a formidable adversary. The evening of the leaked email, she had made an appearance on BBC local news sitting on a bench outside the wooden shed that she called her office with a defiant expression on her face. Standing beside her in the allotment, with mud on his polished brogues was her posh-boy shyster lawyer who'd announced that Mrs Butcher was of Irish origin and that the references made against her within the email were racist and that the email contained personal insults of a grossly offensive nature.

The next salvo had come in the form of Cathy's niece, Tiffany, who'd appeared topless in the allotment on Page Three of *The Sun* under the title *Very Tidy*. But the real shocker came when her twin sons, Carl and Kurt Butcher, appeared with their faces pixelated under the headline *The Clean Up Crew*. The two SAS troopers were stripped to the waist and lean as whippets, lounging on the steps of the 'Big Brother House', the SAS villa in Baghdad, with guns in their hands. Kurt was quoted as saying: 'We may not be the tidiest soldiers but we've got guts.' How the hell was Frank supposed to know Cathy's sons were war heroes? After a week of relentless pummelling in the tabloid press and an announcement by the local police that they were launching a racism investigation, Frank had capitulated and made the humiliating pilgrimage through the maze of canes and bird netting to Cathy's 'office' in a live news encounter that was christened 'the allotment summit'. After forty minutes the foreign secretary had emerged from the shed like a penitent sinner and told the waiting press pack: 'I am mortified by what has happened. I have given her my sincere apologies. She has accepted that there was a misunderstanding and has accepted my apology.'

Victorious, Cathy was untouchable: the undisputed ruler of a fiefdom of allotments that, according to local rumour, were used to stash hundreds of thousands of pounds worth of cocaine, amphetamines and ecstasy destined for the run-down housing estates of his constituency.

His next and even more brutal encounter with the Butcher clan had come in the wake of the Basra Ambush and the death of her beloved Kurt and Carl. As a loyal supporter of the Iraq War and their constituency MP, Frank had little choice but to attend the funeral. He remembers the unruly crowd in the graveyard that had closed around him and the rattled look in the eyes of his close protection officers as they were jostled forward. Suddenly he'd found himself at the edge of the graveside directly across from Cathy Butcher, who was being held up by several of her nephews. Panicked, he tried to push back through the crowd but it was impossible. Cathy looked up from the coffin. Their eyes met and he saw the unbridled fury in them.

'You bastard!'

She hawked and spat in his face.

A cameraman caught the expression of horror on his face and the gob of spit on cheeks. Again, he was shamed on the cover of the tabloids. He remembers his first encounter with the prime minister after the graveside debacle, the look of embarrassment with a hint of distaste on the PM's face. He'd wanted to yell at him ... *this is your fault! Why the hell did we have to go to war in Iraq? Why? It's not as if it was a campaign pledge written on a fucking mug! It was your stupid, bloody choice!*

But he hadn't of course. He'd chosen his course and he was not one to give up just because the going was tough. He was a dogged survivor, the sort of person that could be relied upon.

'You told me that it was dealt with once and for all,' Cathy snarls across his desk. 'You promised me that murdering bastard Nasruddin would die.'

There were times when he had indulged in the occasional bout of conspiracy thinking, sensing a malevolent hand at work (Tory Central Office, a local Lib Dem councillor with a grudge, even the kamikaze left of his own party) but ultimately, he knows that Cathy Butcher is vehemently her own woman – a one-woman nemesis.

'Cathy, it's as much of a surprise to me as it is to you,' he says.

'You lied to me!'

'I thought he was dead. Just like you did!'

'Where is he?' she demands.

'Cathy, please.'

'He's running around free as a daisy while my boys are six feet under!'

'We don't know that.'

'My question is what are you, Frank Booth, going to do about it? You own this mess. You need to sort it. So, tell me. Go on?'

Frank shows her his empty palms. 'What can I do?'

'I want a fucking missile landed on that bastard's head within a week.'

'I'm not in government any more,' he protests.

'You don't fool me, Frank, with your "it's out of my hands" line. Get on the phone to your chums in high places. Get a bloody drone in the air! Find him. I want this dealt with. And if it's not I'll be going public and you really don't want me doing that.'

His heart sinks. 'Going public?'

The last thing he needs is Cathy spouting off to the media again.

'You told me that the little fuck was going to die.'

For two years after the twins' death his constituency home had been picketed by a revolving community of placard-waving Butchers and their unruly dogs that occupied a tented encampment at the entrance to his driveway. The pressure on Frank had been almost unbearable. He vividly remembers shouting across his desk at Samantha Burns, 'Find me the Engineer!' and he remembers the overwhelming feeling of relief when she told him that they had finally tracked Nasruddin down in Pakistan. He'd been so overjoyed that he'd called up the agent responsible and thanked him personally. After that he was on a roll. Of course it was a secret, but telling Cathy was the only way that he could get her and her ghastly family to leave him alone. Once again, he had made the pilgrimage to her 'office' in the allotment but this time he had promised her that vengeance was at hand.

'I really don't think talking to the press is a good idea,' he says.

Her face takes on a sly cast, which fills him with sudden trepidation.

'I heard you on the radio denying all knowledge,' she says. 'Which is odd, mightily odd in fact. Because you told me that he would suffer every bit as much as my sons did.'

His mouth dropped open. 'You wouldn't,' he protested.

'You've seen nothing yet Frank,' she says, standing and thumping her fist on the table. 'I promise you this, if you don't get this sorted, you can kiss goodbye to a comfortable retirement!'

She stomps out, slamming the door behind her.

Frank slumps in his chair, filled with self-pity. What has he done to deserve this? It is all so damn unfair.

20

The white queen

'I've decided to call it a day,' Frank explains to Usma, his constituency secretary. 'Can you cancel my remaining surgery? I'm going to get the train back to London, the next train. I don't want you to think it's your fault. It's not because of Cathy. You couldn't have stopped her. It's because I'm sick. I mean I'm just not feeling well. A touch of jet lag perhaps. So, it's time to go.'

Frank rarely finds himself alone in a room with Usma and when he does he often finds himself saying whatever comes into his head to fill the silences. There is something unsettling about the way she looks at him with her large doe eyes. You could lose yourself in them forever. He has often wondered what she would look like if she removed her hijab and let her hair down. He imagines it spilling over her shoulders in lustrous, inky-black glory. She is chubby in a way that veers between teenage puppy fat and full-grown voluptuousness.

She hands him an envelope.

'What's this?'

He opens the envelope and removes the folded sheet of typewritten paper inside. He glances at the contents and is taken aback.

'You're resigning?'

She nods but does not speak. It seems very sudden. He wonders what kind of trouble she's got herself into. It occurs to him that she's got herself pregnant. She is looking very rosy cheeked. Her family will be furious.

'I can't go on, Mr Booth.'

'I'm very sorry to hear it, Usma.'

'I'm so disappointed.'

Of course, she is. An educated girl like her, what was she thinking? Don't these kids know how to take precautions?

'Torture is wrong, Frank. Everybody is asking me about it. I can't go on!'

She bursts into tears and runs out of the room.

'Just bloody great,' he says.

The Syrian president Bashar al-Assad was a mild-mannered, liberal-leaning ophthalmologist with a consensual manner and a pretty English wife. Of course, he came from an awful family – his father was a mass murderer – but back when they handed over Nasruddin to him for questioning, it seemed that Bashar was exactly the sort of man to modernise the family business and lead the country into the twenty-first century. How was Frank supposed to know the man would outdo his predecessors and end up plunging Syria back into the Stone Ages? He could only rely on the advice he was given.

'Name?'

'Frank.'

'Don't I know you?'

'No.'

'You're that MP.'

'No.'

The man in brown behind the counter shrugs and scrawls his name on the side of a paper cup. It's another ten minutes before Frank's train is due. It's been a pig of a day and he can't wait to get back to London. He never wants to see or speak to a constituent again. Sometimes he wished they'd all just die in a monstrous gas explosion.

He smells her just before she speaks, a silky waft of a perfume that he will never forget and then her voice, soft as honey and clear as a bell, 'grande cappuccino'.

'Name?'

'Tracy.'

He remembers vividly once finding his wife standing over the laundry basket in the bedroom of their London home. She was sniffing his shirt collars suspiciously, hunting for traces of that same perfume. The dreadful anxiety of being caught that even now sends a shiver down his spine.

'Tracy?'

'Force of habit,' she replies. Then he remembers that it's her real name. After Tracy Samantha Lord in *High Society*, her father's favourite film.

With a self-deprecating shrug, Queen Bee re-enters Frank's orbit: he hasn't seen her in the flesh for almost a decade, not since soon after he left government and, as he later realised, he ceased to be of any practical use to her.

Their cups are placed side by side on the countertop. Tracy and Frank in black felt-tip like a sitcom couple from seventies television. She is the only woman that he has ever carried across a hotel room to a bed. She'd made him feel young and virile.

'Shall we?' she says, in a voice that will brook no protest.

Dutifully he follows her across the concourse to a row of aluminium seats beneath the departures board. She still has fantastic legs. There is a part of him that is sufficiently detached to admire how carefully choreographed this is: a chance encounter, two old acquaintances about to share a train back to London.

He sits and removes the lid from his cup, staring morosely at the milky scum on the surface of his tea. 'I take it this isn't a social call?'

'This can't be a surprise,' she says.

'Are you going to push me under a train?'

'We don't do that sort of thing,' she says, pointedly.

'Not on home soil,' he responds. 'Not with our own hands.'

'This isn't Russia.'

'Not yet.'

She sips her tea.

'I heard you on the *Today* programme.'

'I thought I did rather well under the circumstances.'

She sighs. 'The thing is, Frank, we both know what happened. It's not correct to say that you were unaware of the details of Nasruddin's capture and questioning.'

'You told me he was the killer.'

'Stop feeling sorry for yourself, Frank. You saw the intelligence. We acted on the best information that was available at the time.'

'The wrong bloody information!' It was the same story for the entire war. There were no WMDs. Nobody wanted democracy or freedom. They just wanted to kill each other over whichever version of Islam was the correct one. 'It was a fucking shambles!'

'Pull yourself together. Difficult decisions were made in the heat of the moment. You know that.'

'I believed you!'

'You wanted someone to suffer for what happened in Basra and we delivered.'

His agent Bridget had phoned him, after the *Guardian* piece came out, from yet another literary festival, this one in a stately home somewhere in the wilds of Scotland. She'd warned him that his publishers were threatening to cancel publication of his memoir unless he came clean on the rendition and torture.

'I should just tell the bloody truth,' he says.

'I don't think so,' Samantha tells him. 'Not if you want to survive this.'

He is indignant. 'Are you threatening me?'

'We have documents with your signature on them. Everything we did was authorised by you. For Christ's sake Frank! You phoned up the officer involved to congratulate him. I was in bed with you when you did it.'

He sighs, defeated. 'What do you want me to do?'

'Hold your nerve. Be the man I know you for. Don't panic.'

'And what are you going to do?'

'I'm going to sort it out.'

'What does that mean?'

'Do you really want to know?'

'No.' He stares at his shoes. 'I want a peerage.'

He doesn't mean to say it and he hates the hint of pleading in his voice but he just can't help himself.

'Oh, Frank. Now is not the time. Be patient. When this is over, I'm sure they will find something for you.'

'Why is Annabel Fowle allowed to keep her peerage?' he demands.

The London train is announced on the tannoy. He stands but she remains seated.

'Don't speak that name,' Samantha says, coldly. He doesn't think he's ever seen her look so angry. 'Do you hear me?'

'That's our train,' he says, meekly.

'I've got a car waiting.'

It is only later, sitting in the over-lit first class carriage with his face pressed to the glass and only his troubles and a quarter-bottle of wine from the trolley for company, that he realises that she could have given him a lift back to London in her official car if she'd wanted to.

He orders another bottle as the trolley passes and then changes his mind and pays for two. No one who hasn't held high office can understand the pressure that he was under. Who the hell are they to judge? He kept his beloved country safe and that is all they deserve to know. By the time he reaches Euston he has drunk two more quarter-bottles, and in wine-fuelled outrage he tweets:

I have never been complicit in torture!

21

The *Übermensch*

Zeina drives all night. She avoids the bombed cities and the regime checkpoints, following dirt roads that have been long forgotten. A few hours before dawn, the road begins to climb. It leads upward over the slopes of an ancient mountain where broken boulders are piled on each other's backs. In the gloom, the great rocks look like the heads and shoulders of giants.

The further they travel into this ravaged landscape the more she is filled with a sense of purpose. She has not felt like this since she was first recruited into the Old Man's bodyguard and he told her that he had great plans for her.

The man in the car beside her, the one they call Fig, seems oblivious to her excitement.

As the sun's first light flares on distant peaks they reach the high point of the pass and then the road plunges down, switch-back after switchback, into a hidden valley. She sees the silhouette of pine trees on the slopes that shimmer with gold as the sun follows them down.

Abruptly they are driving between tents on a street of sorts, at the base of a cliff. There are people amongst the tents: a group of women and children in gaily embroidered clothing with uncovered heads.

'Who are they?' Fig asks.

'They are nomads,' she explains. 'They live by their own rules.'

The road ends by the hulks of two burned-out pickup trucks. Zeina parks and switches off the engine. They see that there are camels and goats grazing amongst the trees.

'We need an escort to go further,' Zeina tells him.

A man approaches the car window on the driver's side. He leans in to look at them both. He has a face as weathered as the cliff behind him. His eyes are bloodshot and there are brass hoops in his ears.

'We are here to see *al-Gharib*,' Zeina says. 'The Old Man sent us.'

She hands him the ancient-looking coin that the Old Man had pressed into her palm before she left. The man studies it carefully before putting it away in the folds of his robe.

'Is he expecting you?'

'No.'

'Wait here.'

The man returns a few minutes later carrying a goatskin filled with water.

'I'll take you there,' he says.

Zeina winds up the windows and locks the doors. There is something about this that the man finds amusing.

'We are not thieves,' he says.

They walk along the dirt road, past the burned-out pick-ups, and follow a narrow trail through pine trees to the cliff. The man lifts aside a pile of brush to reveal a passage that ascends between walls of sheer red rock.

'Follow me.'

It is a hard climb and the only comfort is the shade. In places, the passage becomes a ledge that zigzags back and forth as it climbs the sheer face of the cliff. After an hour, they stop to rest in the partial shade of a rock at the cliff-edge. Sitting down, Zeina looks into the valley below and upwards at the peak.

The nomad rolls a cigarette from a scrap of newspaper with hard-smelling tobacco mixed with crumbs of hashish.

'How long has he been here?' Fig asks.

The man smokes thoughtfully, waiting until the cigarette is half-finished before replying.

'Since the Old Man brought him here.'

'When was that?'

The man just shrugs, as if time means nothing to him. He flicks the stub of his cigarette over the cliff and stands up. 'Come on.'

The final stretch is even steeper and the path less defined. At times, they are forced to scramble upwards on all fours. It ends abruptly at a barred steel gate with a dark tunnel beyond it.

The nomad produces a key from his pocket and unlocks the gate. The tunnel is perhaps twenty metres long and so narrow that they have to walk in single file. It opens up on to a high vantage point that overlooks a grassy meadow that seems suspended in the air.

On the far side of the meadow, close to the precipice and beside a stand of pines, there is a stone building with a domed roof and a tower. It is of severe and simple construction with whitewashed walls and barred windows.

There are two sentries sitting in a shallow scrape a few feet from the tunnel opening. One of them has an antique bolt-action Mosin-Nagant sniper rifle in his hands and there are two VHF radios propped on a rock beside him. A path leads down through a jumble of rocks to the meadow below.

Out of breath again, Fig sits on a rock.

Zeina notices that there are hundreds of empty brass cartridges in the dust around his feet. When Fig has recovered sufficiently, he digs amongst them with the toes of his boot and says, 'What happened?'

'He tried to escape,' one of the sentries says.

'How often does he do that?' Fig asks.

'Only when we don't have any drugs to give him.'

Zeina is swaying on her feet, feeling light headed from the climb, the heat and the overnight drive. Her feet are sore and she is struggling to think straight.

The nomad hands her a plastic tub that looks like it might once have contained ice cream. 'Put your things in that. Belt, watch, gun . . .'

She fills the tub with her belongings and then passes it to Fig to do the same.

'We lock him in at night but let him out in the morning,' the nomad tells them and hands Fig a VHF radio. 'Stay on the path until you reach the bottom. There are tripwires in the rocks either side. When you get down there, try not to surprise him. He doesn't like to be surprised.' He pauses and looks her up and down. 'He hasn't seen a woman for many years.'

'Come on,' Fig says, suddenly impatient, and she follows him down the path towards the meadow, leaving the nomad and two sentries behind. She keeps her eyes open for tripwires and several times spots the distinctive curved shape of claymore fragmentation mines. She sees that one of them has *Front Towards Enemy* written on it. It occurs to her that it is pointing in the wrong direction.

They reach the grass at the bottom of the hill and follow a path towards the stone building. About midway there, they pass a boulder with a stack of dirty plates on it.

Fig calls out ahead of him. '*Al-Gharib!*'

There is no reply but as they approach the building, a man walks down the steps from the doorway towards them. He is tall and barechested with a mop of dark hair and there are stag's horns tattooed on his chest, the tips of the antlers the span of his shoulders.

'Well,' Fig says, 'I never expected to see you again.'

The Stranger nods to him with a smile that seems both affectionate and contemptuous. 'I'm surprised you survived this long.'

Fig acknowledges this with a wry smile. The Stranger looks over Fig's shoulder at Zeina and a shiver of pure atavism travels down her spine. As a child, she'd read tales about jungle predators transfixing their prey with a stare. Only now does she know how it feels.

'You look tired,' the Stranger says. The pupil of his eyes are almost black, shining with reflected light.

He's right. She's exhausted. It takes all her reserves of strength to reply. 'I'm fine.'

'You're English?'

It feels like he is toying with her. Her feet are heavy and her legs are trembling. 'So are you.'

'No.' He laughs and waves them in to the building. His voice is filled with irony. 'Please, my home is your home.'

It's cool inside and as severe as a hermit's cell. There is a wooden table and two wooden chairs, and a cot bed beside a simple wooden dresser. There is a well-thumbed copy of *Thus Spoke Zarathustra* on the dresser and beside it a copy of *The Bacchae* by Euripides.

'You can sit down there,' the Stranger tells her.

'Go ahead,' Fig tells her, in a reassuring voice.

Too tired to resist, she sits down on the edge of the cot and unlaces her boots. She kicks them off and leans back against the wall. Her eyelids are heavy as manhole covers and she struggles to keep them open.

'Don't fight it,' the Stranger says, in a soft, hypnotic voice. She knows how much danger she is in but she can't help herself. She slides down the wall until she is lying with her head on the pillow. It has a sour and earthy but not unpleasant odour. Within moments she is asleep.

When she wakes up it is still light. The Stranger is sitting at the table with his works spread out in front of him and the VHF radio beside them. She watches as he cooks up with a silver tablespoon and then, with his tongue in the corner of his mouth, he ties off his arm and slides the needle in a vein. When he is done he leans back in the chair, tips back his head and closes his eyes. She knows that now is her chance and she should run but something holds her in place.

Eventually he opens his eyes again.

'Where is Fig?' she asks.

'He's gone back down the hill. But don't worry. You're safe with me. You want to get high?'

She meets his gaze and shakes her head.

'You should try it,' he says. 'It cures almost everything.'

'You're making fun of me.'

He smiles. It's all teeth. The smile is hollow somehow. The muscles stretch his lips in the usual way, but the gesture is imprisoned in the lower half of his face. Above it, his eyes are stone cold.

'You've been here before, haven't you?' he says.

'Yes.'

It was not long after she had joined the Old Man's protection detail, perhaps three months ago; it was hard to remember exactly when so much had happened since then. She had waited with the sentries at the top of the hill while the Old Man and Jomaa went inside the building to speak to the mysterious prisoner who it was said had once been a scourge of the enemy invaders.

'Did he tell you not to look me in the eye?' the Stranger asks.

'Yes.'

'But you decided to ignore him?'

'Yes.'

He smiles to himself. 'What else did he say?'

'He said that you don't feel pain.'

'He's wrong about that. I do feel pain. I just don't feel anything about it.'

'He also said that you are lonely.'

'The Old Man? He said that?' He shakes his head. 'I don't do well in company.'

'That doesn't mean you're not lonely,' she replies. The Old Man had described him as a lone wolf surrounded by sheep. 'It just means you can't fix it.'

She does not tell him that her brother was a junkie in whom intellect and aggression vied for control. That he disappeared in Karachi when she was a teenager and is presumed dead.

'I can see why the Old Man sent you,' he says, as if he can read her mind.

He rolls up his works in a leather pouch and stows it in the lid of a backpack that he pulls from under the cot. 'Are you hungry?'

From a stone ledge set in a recess he produces a wooden bowl with olives in and some flat bread. He fills a cup with water from a stone pitcher. She takes a seat and begins to eat the olives while he watches. The bread is soft and smells freshly baked as she tears it apart. She thinks someone must have carried it up the hill from the tented encampment below.

'You're not hungry?' she asks.

He shakes his head. 'Excuse me.'

She watches while he kneels in front of the dresser and begins to fill the backpack, pulling clothes off the shelves.

'Why are you here?' she asks.

He pauses. 'You mean imprisoned?'

'Yes.'

'I frighten people.' He puts the backpack on and looks about him. 'I learned to like it here, eventually.' He glances in her direction. 'Are you finished eating?'

'Yes.'

'Come on.'

He hands her the radio. Leaving the remains of the food on the table, she gets up and follows him out of the building. They are about halfway across the meadow when he steps away from the path and approaches the boulder standing alone on the grass. He kneels in the shadow of the rock and motions Zeina to get down and join him. She watches as he scrapes at the dirt with his hands. Eventually he uncovers two lengths of wire bound in black electrical tape. He strips away the tape and exposes the cut ends, careful not to let them touch.

'Give me the battery from your radio.' She pops the back of the radio and passes the battery to him. The Stranger presses an exposed wire to one of the two circular steel connectors.

He presses the other wire to the second connector.

The hillside explodes.

Zeina cowers as rock chips whizz overhead.

Eventually, the Stranger stands up and surveys the devastation: the smoking craters, broken boulders and the blood spatter coating the vantage point where the guards once sat. She realises that he must have changed the way that several of the directional fragmentation mines were facing.

'I've been wanting to do that for a while,' he says. He smiles at her. 'Let's go and find my old friend Nasruddin. It's time for him to play his part again.'

22

Friends reunited

They come for him in the middle of the night. 'It's time to leave,' Magomed says. He kneels beside Nasruddin and unlocks his hand-cuffs while another of the bandits points a gun at him. It's the first time they've done that. They seem jittery and nervous. 'Get up. Follow me.'

Nasruddin climbs shakily to his feet and staggers out of the cell into the moonlight.

'Faster,' hisses one of the bandits prodding him with his gun. As they are crossing between the tents, Magomed's phone rings and he listens and nods.

'What's happening?' Nasruddin asks.

'Change of plan,' Magomed replies.

They follow the narrow defile down to the road where a car is waiting with Arkady at the wheel. They put Nasruddin in the back between two bandits with Kalashnikovs between their knees. Magomed gets in the front and leans back, between the gap in the seats, to speak to him.

'We've found a new buyer,' he says. 'Someone prepared to pay more than anyone else.'

They drive into the darkness.

'Do you trust the buyer?' Nasruddin asks.

'We don't trust anyone,' Magomed replies.

Just before dawn they stop and Magomed tells him that he has to get in the trunk. It seems that he is destined to occupy ever-smaller spaces.

'Don't make any noise,' Magomed tells him, slamming the lid closed on him.

The car starts again and they drive for an hour or so before slowing to a halt. For a while they advance in fits and starts as if lined up in a queue. The trunk steadily fills up with a fine mist of dust. Nasruddin covers his mouth and nose with his headscarf. He hears voices, Magomed's and one other, and he imagines that money changes hands. Seconds later there is a burst of laughter. There is no attempt to search the vehicle. The car starts again and once they are moving, Nasruddin attempts painfully to shift position. His legs are entirely numb.

Abruptly they veer off the road and rattle along the verge for a while before stopping. The engine is switched off. There are more voices this time. They are louder and in a foreign language. Soon they surround the car. Though he can't understand the words he can detect an element of desperate bravado in Magomed's voice.

The gunshots when they come are startlingly loud. There are four of them in quick succession.

Nasruddin listens to the sound of someone's footsteps on gravel and then the trunk is opened.

'You are Nasruddin?'

'I am.'

The man is wearing a black turban and his smile gives the set of his jaws a starved and hungry look.

'You are welcome.'

'Nasruddin!'

He wakes with a shudder. The man in the black turban is squatting on the floor, just out of reach. Nasruddin's latest cell is a storeroom in a low breezeblock building in an isolated compound surrounded by a floodlit earth berm. They arrived in darkness and that's as much as he saw. Beyond that he has no idea where he is; if anything, his latest captors look more desperate and ill-kempt than the previous lot.

'Is it true that you killed many crusaders?' the man asks.

Nasruddin shakes his head. 'All I did was speak the words. All I've ever done is say the words.'

A phone is ringing. The man takes it from his pocket and answers in a language that Nasruddin does not understand but thinks must be Russian. He does not believe that his captors are from Islamic State. When the call ends the man turns his attention to Nasruddin again.

'You will make us all rich,' he says.

Nasruddin doubts that. It's what Magomed told him and Magomed is dead.

His next visitor is an actual Russian. He is large and bulky, wearing a camouflage jacket and body armour over a black-and-white striped T-shirt and he carries a rifle across his back. He compares a picture on his phone with Nasruddin and announces that he is satisfied.

'What's happening?' Nasruddin asks.

'You're the bait in a trap,' the Russian tells him with a smile.

He is woken by the sound of gunfire. Someone is shouting that the building is under attack. Instinctively, Nasruddin rolls off the bed and crawls underneath it. He lies on his stomach and listens to the clatter of boots running in the corridor outside and then the sharp staccato of automatic weapons fire. An explosion shakes the room and dislodges dust from the ceiling. It's become a familiar experience.

He hears laughter.

Abruptly, the door is kicked open.

'Nasruddin?'

He looks out from under the bed and sees a man squatting there with his face obscured by a white turban and a bloody machete in his hand. The man gestures for him to come out and helps him to his feet.

'Follow me,' he says, in a voice that is horribly familiar.

The corridor is thick with brown smoke and the acrid smell of propellant and the walls are smeared with blood spatter. Halfway to the end they catch up with the Russian. He is crawling painfully towards the door leaving a trail of blood behind him. Nasruddin sees that his Achilles tendons have been cut. The man in the white turban stands astride him.

'Where are you going, *devushka*?' he asks, tenderly.

'Help me,' the Russian pleads.

The man raises the machete and slashes downwards, burying it into the back of the Russian's head. Then he puts a foot between the Russian's shoulder blades and tugs the blade free.

'Come on.'

He pulls Nasruddin after him along the rest of the corridor and out into the sunlight.

A crashed drone and several military vehicles are burning and a dense plume of black smoke is rising into the sky. There are bodies spread across the sand. A beaten-up Land Cruiser is parked at the entrance to the compound and men disguised with headscarves are moving amongst the bodies executing the wounded.

'Time to go!' yells the man in the white turban.

They all turn and run for the Land Cruiser.

Nasruddin gets in the front and the man slides along the bench seat after him. The driver turns the key in the ignition and the vehicle starts with a throaty growl. The rest of them pile in the back amongst stacks of wooden ammunition boxes. As they drive out the entrance, the man unwraps his turban. It is, as Nasruddin suspected, *al-Gharib*, the Stranger.

'Hello, Nasruddin,' he says.

It is as if there is something behind his eyes, ancient and capricious, and only recently awakened.

They are racing south across the desert on a narrow strip of black-top. Nasruddin is sitting between the driver and the Stranger. The cab is filled with the chatter and adrenalin-filled buzz of those who have survived a battle.

'I can't believe that we just did that.'

Nasruddin realises that the driver in the seat beside him is a woman. Her cheeks are flushed with fear or excitement, he can't tell which.

'We are small and agile,' the Stranger says. 'They were static and slow.'

'You brought down a drone!'

'Shotgun filled with No. 10 birdshot,' the Stranger replies. 'The best drone killer there is.'

A phone on the dashboard starts to vibrate. The Stranger snatches it up and listens for a few moments before cutting the connection.

'Where are we going?' Nasruddin asks.

The Stranger throws his arm around Nasruddin's shoulder and turns to him. He is smiling. Nasruddin think it's the evilest look that he has ever seen in a human face.

'Get this, buddy. I'm putting the old team back together. We're going to find your wife.'

23

Leaning together

They camp that night under an overhanging rock at the entrance to a sandstone wadi. Zeina stands with Nasruddin as the fighters sent by the Old Man disguise the Land Cruiser with camouflage netting and scavenge for dried wood to build a fire. She watches the Stranger climb until he disappears behind a rock. It occurs to her that he has gone somewhere private to shoot up. He wasn't shy of doing it in front of her but perhaps he feels differently about the men now under his command. The notion comes to her that they share a secret. She shivers but is secretly pleased.

'Does he really know where my wife is?' Nasruddin asks, with a pair of scissors in his hand.

She looks at him and sees the hope and fear written on his face.

'He says so.'

Nasruddin gives her a resigned look and resumes cutting away the matted clumps of his hair and beard.

The Stranger appears at the top of the rock and stands with his feet apart, scanning the horizon with a pair of binoculars. She wonders what he is searching for. They haven't seen a single sign of human habitation for a hundred miles, not a fence or a building.

'He doesn't need to threaten my wife to make me do what he wants,' Nasruddin tells her. When she doesn't respond he says, 'But he will do it anyway, for no other reason than it pleases him.'

Later, after they have eaten and the moon has risen over the crest of the hills, the Stranger squats down beside Zeina in front of the bonfire. So close that she can smell him. Even motionless, he appears about to pounce.

At first, he ignores her. He stares across the fire at Nasruddin who seems to shrink inside himself, and the rest of them fall silent. Then his eyes flick to her feet.

'The Old Man told me that you were a cop?'

'I've left all that behind,' she says.

'Have you?'

Inside Zeina goes very still. On the outside, nothing changes.

If he thinks she's a spy then now is the time to kill her. He doesn't need a weapon. She imagines his hands on her throat, squeezing. It terrifies her and excites her in equal measure. She's never felt so instantly and absolutely attracted to someone. She pictures her naked, violated corpse abandoned in the wadi and the vultures circling above.

Instead he says, 'I hear that you don't like to be touched.'

'We have something in common then,' she says. Though she wants him to touch her more than anything.

He laughs. There is a teasing quality in his voice. 'What are you doing here? Tell me the truth. I'll know if you're lying.'

She has the option of repeating the careful lie, mundane but believable, that she has told all the others: that there was no road to Damascus moment. It was more the steady drip-drip of racism and bigotry against her community, the promiscuity and Godlessness all around. But she knows that he will see right through that. She doesn't believe in God any more than he does.

'I didn't have anywhere else to go.'

'Why?'

She takes her time, nudges a branch towards the centre of the fire with her foot and looks into its fiery heart while he watches her.

'I killed someone.'

He nods to himself as if he has had a suspicion confirmed. 'Of course you did. Was it someone close to you?'

'Yes.'

'You've always run towards danger,' he says, moving even closer to her. 'I can see the hunger in you. You can't live without it.'

She remembers the first time a man punched her when she was in her police uniform, the coppery satisfaction of blood in her mouth and the rush of adrenalin as she swung her telescoping police baton – a regular Saturday night on the high street. She loved that baton. It was halfway between a whip and a cudgel. Without it the world was an empty place.

'I bet you got started early. When you were just a child. I'm right aren't I?'

She wants to shout at him. *You don't know me at all!*

He smiles as if he can tell what she's thinking. 'Is that how it started for you? Who was it that abused you? An uncle? Your father?'

'No!'

Her mother had told her that her father was dead. But that wasn't true. She knew from that letter that she found amongst her mother's private things that he had left her.

Once a whore always a whore, he had written.

'Your mother?'

She flinches.

The Stranger is staring at her intently. His stare excites her beyond measure. It is utterly without shame or pity.

'You killed your mother?'

It was Zeina's curse to bear her mother's shame: to be an unloved girl and to have the same unclean place between her legs.

'How?'

He's expecting her to say that she poisoned her mother because that's what women do but it wasn't like that, not at all. She can't help herself. She's kept it hidden for so long but it opens up like a sudden crevasse: the secret that she has never shared.

She had been a police constable for a year.

It was the end of her shift and she was sitting in her uniform at the kitchen table with a mug of tea in front of her. But it didn't seem to make any difference. Her mother was swaying over her, flexing her fist and about to strike.

'You whore!'

Zeina didn't cry, then or now. Not one tear. Her mother had stolen that from her too. A hard knot of anger had formed where her heart should be. It didn't stop her mother from blubbing. She was as free with her self-pity as she was with her fists.

'You filthy disgusting whore!'

Zeina just sat with her hands in her lap and when her mother was finished she bent her head as if she agreed with the verdict. As if the years of drunken rages were Zeina's fault, as if all those bruises on her teenage arms and torso were richly deserved. As if she had asked to be raped, on those nights when her mother rolled in from the street with a man and passed out before she could satisfy him. And then she looked up and said, 'Everything I know, I learned from you.'

She said it softly and it took a moment for her words to sink in. Then her mother gasped and struck her, an open-handed slap to the side of her face that left her head ringing.

Never again.

She reacted without thinking. One moment she was sitting and the next she was standing and the baton was raised above her head, ready to strike.

'I beat her to death with my baton,' she tells the Stranger. She can remember the exultation of each and every blow.

'You'll do,' the Stranger says, after a pause, one killer to another.

She thinks, at that moment, that she would do anything for him.

Just before dawn, he wakes her. He is carrying a Dragunov sniper rifle slung across his back and his mismatched eyes are shining. She unzips her sleeping bag and shakes her head to dislodge sleep. He up-ends her boots, taps them together to dislodge anything inside, and hands them to her. Otherwise she is fully dressed.

'Come on,' he says. She quickly laces her boots.

Together they climb the rock, moving at a crouch so that they are not visible against the lightening sky. They take cover in a hollow and watch the headlights out on the plain.

A convoy of four vehicles is approaching from the north.

'Who are they?' she says.

'We don't have any friends,' he explains.

He eases himself forward to the lip of the hollow and stares down the optical sight of the Dragunov. She listens to the steady beat of his breath as he takes aim.

He squeezes the trigger and the crack of the shot echoes the length of the wadi.

The vehicles veer off the road and come to a halt in a protective circle. Dark figures spill out on to the sand. Returning fire strikes the rocks off to their left, well wide of the mark.

Beside her, the Stranger rolls out of the hollow and she follows. They sprint down into the wadi where the fighters have stripped the Land Cruiser of its camouflage and started the engine. They climb in the vehicle and drive out of the wadi.

They turn south, racing for the border.

24

The Knights of Justice

It is after midnight when Jude emerges from the arrivals hall in Amman. He carries his black duffel bag out across the broad esplanade beneath the massive concrete sand-dune canopy to where his old friend is waiting. Talal is wearing jeans and flip-flops, and a baseball cap on his head, and he is standing beside a black Land Rover pickup with his Alsatian, Lucky, sitting in the flatbed behind him.

Jude and Talal muddled through Sandhurst together as officer cadets and later, after the army and a wealth of bitter experience, attended the same course at the MI6 field operations training centre at Fort Monckton in Hampshire. They are both veterans of the war against extremism.

'Hey buddy,' Talal says. His English is immaculate and shot through with the relaxed idiom of the CIA officers that he spends so much of his time with. Talal has always worn the expectations placed upon him lightly – he is a direct descendant of Jordan's first monarch, and a cousin to the current king.

They hug.

Talal takes his bag and slings it in the bag beside the dog.

'Get in, my friend.'

'Where are we going?' Jude asks as they leave the airport.

'The boss has agreed to see you.'

'Now?'

'Now.'

He hadn't expected to be granted an audience so swiftly.

'How is your friend Camilla?' Talal asks as they drive out of the airport.

A month or so before he'd almost crippled her husband in Soho, Jude and Camilla had spent a weekend on Talal's yacht near

Aqaba on the Red Sea. A few days later, wild camping in Wadi Rum, he'd asked her to leave her husband.

'I just can't,' she'd told him, digging at the red sand with the toe of her hiking boot. 'It would break his heart.'

'She ended the affair,' Jude explains.

Talal shakes his head, wryly. 'Then maybe you had a lucky escape.'

He's convinced that her recent attempt at seduction in Sanjay's loft was deliberately intended to deflect his attention. Which means there's something that's being concealed from him beyond the scandal of Nasruddin's rendition and torture. *But what?*

He'd woken up on the morning after his sister's dinner party to find a message on his yellow burner from Yulia that said:

Enjoy the desert, my darling boy. And good luck with your search for Nasruddin's wife. I wonder what truths you will learn? I shall look forward to an enervating encounter mixing physical pleasure and international relations on your safe return.

He feels unmoored and unbalanced, caught up in events that are spinning out of his control.

The headquarters of the General Intelligence Directorate – the *Mukhabarat* – looms over western Amman like a monstrous white cube. The oldest part of the complex was once one of the most feared prisons in the Middle East, a labyrinth of passageways and underground cells. But there is nothing medieval about its latest above-the-ground facade, no torches on the walls; it's as pristine as a national mausoleum.

It is situated in a district of broad avenues and well-lit stone buildings, with armed military guards at every corner but no signs to identify the buildings. Talal's Land Rover is obviously well known and the guards salute crisply as the vehicle passes. At the main gate, they are stopped briefly at the security checkpoint before being waved through. They drive through an archway to a courtyard with a mature flame tree festooned with long horn-shaped seeds in a circular bed at its centre. The entrance to the building is a modern, multi-storey wall of glass with the flag of Jordan on one side of the door and, on the other, the black flag of the *Mukhabarat* with its motto in Arabic script: 'Justice has come'.

There are two large men in suits wearing earpieces standing waiting for them on the steps. Talal stops the car.

'Come on.'

Jude follows him up the steps and into the building with the guards following. The atrium is dominated by a huge portrait of King Abdullah II in military parade dress and festooned with sashes and medals. Talal leads Jude up a wide marble staircase and along a corridor, lined with oil paintings celebrating the victory of the Arabs over the Ottoman Turks, to a large dimly lit office with oak-panelled walls.

A boy in a shiny suit is standing with his back towards them, looking out across the white and orange pin lights of the night-time city. When he speaks his voice is thin but steely. 'The state has never faced a greater threat than the one we face now. We are looking after more than a million homeless refugees. More and more of them are reporting that there is no food to be had any more in Syria. We want to help them but our pockets are empty.' The boy turns from the window to face them, the light casting shadows under his cheeks and eyes. Jude sees that he is mistaken: the boy is a fully-grown, middle-aged man. He is the Director of the *Mukhabarat*. 'Tensions between Jordanians and Syrians are rising. We don't know who half the people are. Crime is rising. There are agents of Assad and of Islamic State walking amongst us.'

The Director sits down and waves to the chairs at the other side of an expansive leather-topped desk, which dwarfs him. They sit. Talal pushes his chair back a little to withdraw from the conversation. It's up to Jude to explain.

'If I want to find the wife and daughter of Nasruddin al-Raqqah how would I go about it? If I had intelligence that suggested that they were here in Jordan.'

'You would come to me,' he replies.

'And what would you say?'

'I would tell you that they are in the camp that they call the Devil's House.'

'The Devil's House?'

'It's aptly named. It is a chaotic place. The rule of law ends at the camp gates. The older parts of the camp are under the control of a powerful Syrian clan that even Assad would hesitate before taking on. We believe that they are the ones that have control of Nasruddin's wife and daughter. They are fully aware of their value. I warn you, if you go in there we cannot protect you.'

'I have to try and find her,' Jude says.

The Director joins his fingers together to form a steeple. 'I was afraid that you were going to say that.'

'We are concerned that her husband poses a threat to our national security and right now she's the only lead we've got,' Jude explains. 'She may have some knowledge that will lead us to him. It's also possible that he may be looking for her.'

'You want to use her as leverage against him?'

Jude shakes his head. 'No. She's suffered enough. I just want to talk to her.'

'I will go with Jude,' Talal says.

'No,' the Director says. 'You are too valuable to risk inside the camp.'

'We cannot let him go in there alone,' Talal protests.

'And yet we cannot accompany him,' the Director says, firmly. 'However, I am prepared to let you drive Jude to the camp. When you are there you will hand responsibility for him over to the camp administrator. He will take you to meet the man that you seek.'

Jude looks at Talal, who shrugs. 'I can do that,' he says.

The Director looks sceptical. 'Don't even think about disobeying me, Talal.'

Talal answers with his most charming smile.

By daylight, Amman is revealed as a sprawling, unfinished city of cubes and art deco ziggurats built of yellow limestone blocks that are stained by the wind with reddish desert sand. Dirty ochre smog blankets a hodgepodge of hills and dry ravines, and is punctuated, here and there, by the dark green spear-shape of cypress trees.

It is already midday. The delay was caused by Jude's requirement to tip his hat to the team at the British Embassy. It is clear from the beginning that they regard his presence as a mortal threat to their relationship with the Jordanians, or 'Jords' as they casually call them, and they are not willing to offer any assistance. He makes little effort to reassure them and is out of the compound as quickly as possible.

Talal is waiting at the embassy gates in his Land Rover with a .44 Desert Eagle in a holster at his hip and an expansive smile on his face. 'Let's go do some real work,' he says.

'Amen to that,' Jude tells him.

They drive north in the Land Rover and the further they go the larger the spaces grow between the housing blocks until finally there is nothing but jumbled yellow rock and quarries. They begin to descend and it gets steadily hotter the lower they go.

'You must have friends in high places,' Talal tells him.

'Why is that?'

'The Director didn't want you anywhere near the camp. He was over-ruled by the King.'

Is Queen Bee still his friend? It now seems just as likely that she is sending him into danger because she considers him expendable.

'Do you think that Nasruddin is guilty?' Talal asks, after a pause.

Jude glances at him. 'Why do you ask?'

'I've seen nothing that suggests the level of tactical cunning and technical knowledge that would be required for the Basra Ambush.'

'I've seen nothing at all,' Jude tells him. 'His file was deleted over a decade ago.'

'So, what do you know about him?'

'You've seen the video that went out after the ambush. He paraded his guilt to all the world.'

'Okay but what do you know about the circumstances in which the video was filmed?'

'Nothing.'

'Could he have been acting under duress?'

'Possibly,' Jude concedes.

'What else have you got?'

'His fingerprints were on a mobile phone recovered from the firing point.'

'Any witnesses?'

Jude shakes his head, 'None.'

'So, he handled the phone at some point,' Talal shrugs. 'That doesn't necessarily place him at the scene.'

The point has been made to Jude before. 'I know.'

'And your Syrian confession was obtained under torture and as we both know is next to worthless.'

'Agreed.'

'So, what are you going to do?'

'Find out the truth.'

Talal frowns. 'Are you sure that's what's required of you?'

'I'm pretty sure that's not what's required of me,' Jude concedes.

Talal shakes his head and smiles, wryly. 'You haven't changed.'

'Do you think I'm a fool?'

'No. But I think you need to be careful. There are clearly a lot of competing agendas at work here and you're not indispensable.'

'I hear you.'

It is dusk when they reach the border town that is nearest to the refugee camp. As they navigate the dusty streets, Talal points out to him the Saudi-owned hotel where men from across the Gulf come to stay while they negotiate the purchase of child brides from the camp.

'It's a disgrace,' Talal tells him.

They drive over a rise and the vast, sprawling camp is spread out on the plain below them with twists of smoke rising from a thousand campfires. There is a reception committee waiting for them: four large armoured personnel carriers parked outside the entrance to the camp and Jordanian soldiers manning the gate.

'Looks like we'll have to go in through the back door,' Talal tells him and winks. He pulls down on the steering wheel and they veer off the road and rattle across the desert.

25

The boss of the Devil's House

They find Dieter, the camp administrator, in the midst of a crowd of newly arrived refugees sitting amongst bundles of their meagre belongings. They completely surround a fenced complex that is lit up in the darkness of the camp. Behind the chain link fence are rows of empty container-offices for the UN agencies and NGOs that attempt to bring some semblance of order to the camp during the daylight hours. At night, all they can offer are the floodlights.

Dieter looks up as they approach and inclines his head. 'Your Highness.'

'Please. Not here,' Talal looks pained.

'I'm surprised that your friends at the gate let you in,' Dieter tells them. He is wearing a tattered red T-shirt and has a thick white nicotine-stained beard that makes him look like a ragged, somewhat edgy, Father Christmas. 'You should come back in the morning. It's not safe here at night, not outside the lights.'

'We can't wait that long,' Jude says.

'I know you're not frightened to go anywhere in this camp,' Talal says. 'Day or night.'

Dieter smiles and shrugs, 'It's not me that I'm worried about.'

'We'll worry about ourselves,' Jude says.

'Okay then.' Dieter stands. He's tall, at least six foot four. His trousers are through at the knees and his pockets are bulging.

'Come on then.'

They follow him as he picks his way through the mass of upturned faces, stopping now and then to listen to their stories. A woman tells him that her neighbourhood in Damascus was bombed, and people were murdered. Another tells him that her father is in prison and she doesn't know if he's still alive. And another says, 'They told my husband to go to the police station and bring along sweets. He never returned.' To each of them he explains patiently that assistance will arrive in the morning.

'All the people here have seen something horrible,' Dieter tells them, as they approach the edge of the light, 'they have been hiding and running, they have experienced killing and torture, spying and betrayal. These people don't trust anybody any more. Plus, they are traditionally traders and smugglers. They are anti-government. They don't like authority. And your friends in authority don't like them much either, Your Highness. You could ask them to stop firing tear gas into the camp.'

He stops at the dividing line between light and dark and removes two large fist-sized rocks from his pockets. He glances back at them.

'Stay close.'

They plunge into the darkness. It takes a while for Jude's eyes to adapt and only gradually does the shape of the camp become visible by starlight. Dieter follows a dirt road that meanders between blocks of tents packed so tightly together that it is almost impossible to tell them apart.

They smell the latrines before they see them. They pass a low concrete building lit by a single dim bulb.

'This is the most dangerous place,' Dieter tells them, 'especially for women. They've got more chance of being raped here than they do back in Syria. Mind your step.' They circle a pool of foul-smelling water. 'The people who are really in charge here want to keep the camp in a state of chaos so that smuggling continues to be worthwhile. They also want to prevent the aid organisations from installing a power grid, so that they can continue to sell illegally tapped electricity. And they want police to fear entering the camp, so that they can go about their business without interruption.'

Two men step out of the darkness to their right and shadow them as they climb a gradual incline towards the farthest reaches of the camp. Without acknowledging their presence, Dieter says, 'The *Bashar* we are going to see claims that he is the most powerful man in the camp. In the Devil's House, there is a man inside every tent who claims to be the boss, the *Bashar*. Maybe Hussein is lying. Perhaps he was never a fighter. But he understands one thing: the person who makes people believe that he is the strongest man is the *Bashar*.'

Abruptly Dieter turns off the road and they walk carefully along a narrow muddy path that leads through a medieval warren of tents and stacked containers. Here and there they catch glimpses of families around open fires. The two men continue to follow in their footsteps. Around a tent they come in sight of a large trailer with brightly lit windows in the midst of a yard filled with stacks of flour in white-and-blue UN sacks.

'The *Bashar* lives in a trailer that cost three thousand dollars,' Dieter tells them. 'The air conditioner runs with electricity he is tapping from the Italian hospital. The water for his coffee is from canisters provided by UNICEF. He hasn't worked, paid or thanked anyone for any of it. Come on, let's meet him.'

Dieter crosses the yard, climbs the steps and knocks on the door. He pushes it open and steps inside. Jude and Talal follow.

A man with a neatly trimmed beard is sitting on a carpet with a floral pattern. There are two Nokia mobile phones on the carpet by his feet, one red and one pink, a Makarov pistol and a packet of Marlboro Red.

'You are welcome here,' the man says.

Two children and a woman are sitting at the far end of the trailer watching *Teenage Mutant Ninja Turtles* muted on a flatscreen TV.

'I am Hussein. Please sit.'

They sit cross-legged opposite him.

The door opens behind them and the two men who have been following them enter. They cross the trailer and sit either side of Hussein. They are both wearing chequered black-and-white scarves. The woman places ashtrays in front of them on the carpet and Hussein lights a cigarette.

'The first time I saw you walking through the camp at night,' Hussein tells Dieter, 'I have to tell you I thought about having you kidnapped. But then I decided to let you be. You are the only halfway decent one of the whole lot. Will you have coffee?'

Without waiting for a reply, he claps his hands and the woman leaves the trailer.

'If I wanted to, I could have the entire camp burning in five minutes,' he says.

'I know it,' Dieter replies.

'Why have you come to my house and brought these people with you?'

'Because you are the ruler here.'

'The only ruler is Allah.'

'But, Abu Hussein, you have a say here.'

'It is true that I control the streets. My men patrol day and night. I have ten barbers who will give free shaves to anyone who wants one.'

'And what do the people give you in return?'

'Just their love,' he grins, menacingly. 'You know when I first came here a cold wind was blowing and the people were hungry. I went to the UN and said that I wanted food and blankets. A man, I think he was a Jew – he certainly had a ponytail – he told me that someone in Geneva had to make that decision. I said who is sitting in Geneva deciding whether we can eat a piece of bread? I told him that I had killed fifty-two people and that number would reach fifty-three if he didn't give me bread. He gave me bread and cheese and blankets. Everything I asked for. From then on, I was the *Bashar.*'

The woman returns with a tray with small cups of Turkish coffee and offers them around. The coffee is sweet, thick as syrup and full of grounds.

Setting his cup back on the tray, Talal breaks his silence and says, 'We asked to come and speak with you to seek your help.'

Hussein seems reluctant to look at him.

'You think I don't know who you are? The Prince asks for my help in his own kingdom?'

Talal shrugs. 'You are the *Bashar.* You are the man to see.'

'That's right. You are in my house.'

'We are looking for a woman from Dar'a. We believe that she is in your care.'

'And you,' Hussein says, looking at Jude. 'Who are you?'

'No one important,' Jude tells him.

'You are nobody? So maybe I can just shoot you?'

Jude meets his gaze. 'That wouldn't be very hospitable.'

Hussein laughs as though he has told a joke. 'And if I shoot you, your friends will surely send a drone to kill me? You are American? British?' When Jude doesn't reply, he lights another cigarette and smokes thoughtfully for a while. 'Before I was the *Bashar*, I lived in Dar'a.'

'The woman's name is Maryam al-Raqqah,' Talal tells him, leaning forward to engage his attention. 'We want your permission to speak with her.'

Hussein nods gravely. 'And if I know this woman and I bring you to her how do I know that she will be safe?'

'You have my word, *Bashar*.'

'Who am I to doubt the word of a prince?'

Talal shakes his head impatiently. 'Can you take us to her?'

'There is another matter. This woman is a great financial burden on my family. We must provide her with food and lodging. And you are not the only ones looking for her. The others offer me money for her. I am only a poor refugee. I have nothing. What can I do?'

'Perhaps we can help you.'

'How can you help me?'

'You have a nephew,' Talal says. 'He is in the prison in Zarqa?'

Hussein's face takes on a sly cast. 'Unfortunately, this is true. He is my brother's son. He is an innocent man who was wrongly accused by my enemies.'

'Would it please you to have him returned to his family?'

Hussein is delighted by the offer. 'It would.'

He picks up the pistol, stands and tucks it into the waistband of his trousers. The two men either side rise with him.

'Come. I will take you to this woman.'

26

Maryam

It had been as vivid as dreaming. She had sensed the new life forming in the hot, wet dark of her womb first like an apple seed putting out hair-like roots and then a bean with a tentative pulsing heart. The coiling cord pumping life from her into the baby.

They were fugitives in an unfamiliar city in a foreign land with hardly any money. But that didn't matter because they had all they could ever need. They were in love and she was pregnant.

Then the horror.

The terrible blankness that followed the arrest: mummified in black tape and strapped to a stretcher with the baby a sudden, howling absence inside her. Maryam explains that she could not feel anything inside from the time of her arrest in Karachi until her arrival in Damascus.

'I knew she was dead,' she tells the journalist and her interpreter who are sitting cross-legged opposite her on the carpet. 'But still I prayed.'

Kirsty glances at Maryam's daughter sitting there, quietly listening. Safi is pale, small for her age, with a watchful, ethereal quality.

'When I felt her again it was a miracle.' Maryam reaches out and strokes the back of her daughter's hand. She explains that she was detained for a month in a women's prison in Damascus. In a small cell with seven other women who took pity on her and shared their meagre rations with her and let her sleep on the only bed. Then unexpectedly she was released.

She took the bus home to her parents' house in a village in the southern Syrian province of Dar'a and there she gave birth and lived quietly until the uprising began.

'Did you try to find out what happened to your husband?' Kirsty asks.

'How could I?'

It was her misfortune to be born in the province that ignited the uprising against Assad. Fifteen schoolboys were arrested for graffiting walls with revolutionary slogans copied from Tunis and Cairo. Assad had responded to the demonstrations that followed with ruthless violence. He would not make the mistake of other rulers who had lost their positions in the Arab Spring. Tens of thousands lined the streets for the funeral of the dead protestors. Christians threw rice. Security stormed the central mosque and resistance spread to the villages. The arrests and random attacks continued. The army came into the village and it became unsafe for women to leave their houses. The resistance continued and Assad started bombing from the air. Many villages were destroyed. Many left though the men mostly stayed behind.

She remembers the day that they came for her.

She was kneeling beside Safi at the edge of a field. Their heads were just above the wheat as they looked towards the smoke rising from their home.

They were returning from the river where they had been washing clothes.

'Who are they, Mama?' Safi asked.

'Hush,' she murmured, straining to see the shapes moving in the smoke-thickened sky. The armoured personnel carriers were moving across the fields, half a dozen at least, followed by a line of soldiers. One looked straight at where they were kneeling and she crouched down, fearful that she could be seen.

The house was burning like a torch.

'Mama,' said Safi, restlessly, 'can we go home?'

'Hush, child,' Maryam said, holding her close.

She knew then what she must do. This was no chance raid. Assad had sent his men for her. After so many years of shelter, the horror had found her again. She scooped up Safi and ran.

'It took four days to reach the border, travelling by night,' she explains. 'There were no buses and we had to walk. We slept on the ground. If the army had found us they would have killed us. We want to go back but it is too difficult. There's nothing left, our neighbours, our families are not there any more. Every day we hear the names of someone who has died or been abducted. My two brothers, my cousin, my uncle all disappeared and we have not heard from them. Another uncle and cousin were killed.'

'Could you leave if you wanted to?' Kirsty asks.

The answer is self-evident. She is as much a prisoner here as she was in Damascus. Again, she is the pawn of others.

'And now that you know your husband is alive?'

She does not know what to feel. Ten years have passed. Her only priority in that time has been the survival of her daughter and she has learned that for their safety she can only rely on herself. The face on the proof-of-life video that the *Bashar* had shown her was almost unrecognisable. It's not just the physical damage caused by a decade in prison. Everyone has his or her own nightmare. Nasruddin's was solitude; he needed the affirmation of an audience. Without other people, he was nothing. She cannot imagine how ghastly imprisonment must have been for him just as she cannot imagine being reunited with him.

She supposes that she should be angry with him for how foolish and easily led he was, but it was his enthusiasm and his other-worldly charm that had drawn her to him. Looking back, she can hardly believe how feckless she was. He'd driven into her village in a 'borrowed' car and filled her head with nonsense about the life he could offer her outside of Syria. He was beautiful, tall with blue-black hair and dark eyes. And his singing voice: tones as clear as the wind. Her father had advised against the marriage but it wasn't up to him. What a rollercoaster their lives had been. By turns rich and poor: basement apartments to the largest suites in the finest hotels. There were so many dresses, though they often had to go back when his creditors caught up with him.

'Nasruddin was not a terrorist,' she says, in the same incredulous tone she had used when Assad's interrogators had asked her ten years before. But what was he? Before the American invasion he'd played a villain with a moustache in a Baghdad-based soap.

She will never forget his childlike glee when fans recognised him in the street and asked him to repeat the character's catchphrase. Like almost every other actor he had mostly been between roles. To begin with he'd supplemented his income buying and selling mobile telephones for cash out of the back of a van in a central Baghdad market. Later, when the car bombings made that too dangerous, he'd got into more high-end sales via an uncle who ran a business importing televisions. Nasruddin was a natural at sales; chatty, always eager to please, comfortable in any community. But acting was always his first love.

'He didn't write his own lines,' she says. 'Everything was written for him. They put a gun to his head and then they put a gun to my head. He had no choice.'

'Then who is the Engineer?'

She hears voices from the yard and boots on the trailer step, and moments later the door is flung open.

'No more talking,' the *Bashar* snarls.

There are two men with him, neither of them from the camp. One is a foreigner. She hears Kirsty gasp and turns to look at her. She has rarely seen such a rapid transition from shock to anger. She looks from Kirsty to the man in the doorway who appears equally surprised.

They stare at each other in increasingly uncomfortable silence.

'You bastard,' Kirsty says.

'I'm sorry,' Jude replies.

An explosion shakes the trailer and blows in the fly screens. The lights go out and Talal falls on top of her, pinning her to the floor. People are screaming. There is shouting in the yard outside.

Talal climbs to his feet and pulls her up behind him. They run out of the trailer and across the yard through rolling grey smoke that sears her throat. Looking around, she sees Kirsty is running beside her. They make it across the yard before a burst of gunfire cuts through the shrieks of the wounded. They plunge into the nearest tent and Talal jerks her to the ground. She holds her breath while bullets zip through the canvas around them. There are sparks swirling through the tents and she can smell burning. Talal pulls her to her feet again and they stumble onward. She trips over a body but he does not let go of her hand. Ahead of them Jude is leading them from tent to tent away from the trailer. All around them people are screaming.

They are being pursued. She can hear men shouting to each other as they search for them. A man lunges out of the darkness and Jude fells him with a blow to the throat. He picks up the man's rifle and fires in the direction that they have come. The gun jams, and he throws it away. He grabs Kirsty by the hand and all four of them are running again. Many of the tents have collapsed and it's like scrambling across an obstacle course, others are on fire and the flames light up the sky.

They reach an open space with a tap-stand on a concrete dais and a sudden burst of gunfire kicks up dust at their feet. They are surrounded.

A man in a balaclava walks towards them silhouetted by flames. He is pointing a rifle at them. When she hears his voice, she knows who it is. It is the stuff of nightmares: she had hoped not to see him again for as long as she lived.

'On your knees.'

Talal throws his handgun to one side and kneels with his arms raised in surrender. Jude and Kirsty do the same.

The man in the balaclava is standing in front of them.

'Who sent you?' he says, pressing the barrel of the gun to the side of Jude's head.

'Does it matter?' Jude asks, from the ground.

'To me it does. Was it Queen Bee?'

'Who are you?' Jude asks.

'I am the Stranger,' he says. 'Tell her that I am coming.'

Hands grab Maryam from behind. She tries to dig in her heels but they grip her tight by the elbows and half-drag, half-carry her away.

27

Citizen's arrest

'It's not enough to protest,' David says, with all the evangelical fervour of a younger Frank Booth. 'The Trotskyites don't have a monopoly on hope. We need proposals for action that will attract votes from the breadth of the British people.'

There are times when Frank finds his son's enthusiasm and ambition both an inspiration and a source of great pride. Certainly, more inspiring than his youngest daughter Emily's waspish cynicism or his middle daughter Alexandra's conspicuous absence. Elected as a Member of Parliament with an unassailable majority at the age of thirty, David Booth is often talked about as a future leader of the party. Frank is also proud that his son did not have to suffer the uncertainty of his own fragile childhood. David has not had to watch his uncles knock his father's teeth out, up against a wall.

At other times, like now, it's just exhausting. *What is it about younger politicians that they don't have anything else to talk about?* He finds his attention drifting across the room in the direction of a blonde woman dining alone at an adjacent table. She is wearing a wraparound dress with an eye-catching décolletage, her bra lifting and pressing together her plump breasts. He doesn't remember her being there when they arrived. She looks up from her phone and they briefly make eye contact before Frank hurriedly looks away. The restaurant is crowded with diners, despite its hangar-like size, and many of them clearly recognise him. He rarely ventures this far east in London and is constantly surprised by what he sees. Their waiter, with his shaggy beard, tattoos and stretched ear lobes, looks like some kind of Visigoth only recently stampeded off the steppe. Judging by Emily's reaction to him she'd happily be thrown over his shoulder and carried off into captivity. He had told them the building was once a warehouse used to store trams. The centrepiece of the place is a cow in a formaldehyde tank raised above the refectory tables on an industrial plinth. For the life of him, he can't see the point of it.

'Dad, are you even listening?' David asks.

He smiles distractedly. 'You know I'm always happy to make an appearance in your constituency,' he says.

He watches his son and daughter-in-law exchange a meaningful look.

'Maybe when things have calmed down a bit, Frank,' his daughter-in-law says, in her most emollient voice. Once a politician in her own right, the former leader of a Dutch progressive party, Dorinda is renowned for her political acumen. The papers are full of stories about how she wields the real power in his son's marriage.

'Let's face it, Dad, you're an embarrassment,' Emily says.

Ignoring her, Frank catches the eye of the passing sommelier and has his glass promptly filled. 'Are you sure you haven't had enough?' Margaret says.

'I've had a hard day and I deserve a drink,' he tells his wife. 'Several in fact.' He nods to the sommelier, who is giving him a somewhat quizzical look. 'We'll have another bottle.'

The *World at One* had described it as one of the most unorthodox prime minister's questions for years. After the leader of the opposition and the Westminster leader of the Scottish nationalists had asked their allocated questions, the Speaker had recognised a backbench Tory known for an independent streak, who had asked, 'Can the prime minister assure the house that neither this, nor any previous UK government, has been complicit in torture as the former foreign secretary recently felt the need to assert?'

'I have no knowledge of any complicity in torture,' the PM replied, 'but obviously I cannot speak to what individual ministers knew in previous governments. The former foreign secretary has made it clear in recent days that he is perfectly capable of answering for himself.'

Without thinking, Frank had leapt indignantly to his feet and was duly recognised by the Speaker who told the house that, although he suspected that the member did not have a question and it was therefore highly unorthodox, he would, nonetheless, give him the opportunity to deliver a brief statement.

'Mr Speaker, I would like to assure all the honourable and right honourable members of this house that not only do I have nothing to hide but I have nothing to be ashamed of,' Frank thundered, 'and what I said on social media was absolutely true. I have never been complicit in torture.'

The house was in uproar with members on both sides shouting 'liar'. The Speaker promptly stopped the proceedings and threatened to eject anyone using un-parliamentary language.

'No MP may call another a liar in this house,' he shouted above the din.

Frank's phone started ringing the moment he left the chamber and after angrily rejecting several calls from unknown numbers he switched it off and had kept it switched off. It was his wedding anniversary and he was damned if he was going to have it ruined by a pack of journalists digging about in the gutter for dirt on him.

'I think we should raise a glass,' he says, aware out of the corner of his eye that the sommelier and their waiter are having an animated discussion, and frequently looking his way. To hell with them if he wasn't trendy enough for their pretentious bloody restaurant. 'To thirty years of enduring love.'

With a sigh, Margaret raises her glass and Emily, David and Dorinda follow suit.

'Happy anniversary, Mum and Dad,' David says.

Several phones across the restaurant ping simultaneously.

'Oh my God,' Dorinda whispers, looking down at her phone.

'Christ!' David exclaims.

'What is it?' Emily demands.

'Cathy Butcher's released a tape recording.'

'What?' Frank says, barely listening. His wife is right. He has had too much wine and he's feeling suddenly light headed. He notices that the blonde with the perfectly formed breasts on the adjacent table is smiling at him and he returns her smile, tipping his glass towards her.

'It's on the front page of *Mail Online*,' David says, utterly dejected.

'Play it,' Margaret says.

Dorinda reaches out and takes Margaret's hand in hers. 'Are you sure that's a good idea?'

'Play it,' Margaret says firmly.

Dorinda puts the phone on the table and presses play. She's not the only one and the recording takes on an echoing quality as it is played across the restaurant. Frank finds himself the centre of everyone's attention as he listens to his voice from over a decade before:

'I promise you this, Cathy, your sons' suffering will be as nothing to what Nasruddin will experience at the hands of the Syrians. He will pay twenty-five times over what he did and I have the personal assurance of their foreign minister that he will suffer a slow and painful death.'

Silence follows.

Frank barely has time to register the enormity of what it means before all hell breaks loose: the woman in the wraparound dress stands up and throws down her napkin; a paparazzo strides past the maître d' with his telephoto lens pointing like a gun; and, closer to hand, the Visigoth waiter approaches diagonally from between two tables and grabs him in a vicelike grip by the upper arm.

'Frank Booth, I'm performing a citizen's arrest on you,' the waiter says.

'I can't believe this,' David says.

The blonde woman is leaning over the table and holding her phone in Frank's face. 'My name is Tracy Scott and I work for the *Daily Mail*.' She really does have the most astonishing cleavage. 'You have lied to Parliament and to the British people. What do you have to say for yourself?'

Beside him, Margaret has her head in her hands and Emily is comforting her, and his son and daughter-in-law are heading for the exit.

For the first time in his political career, Frank Booth is at a complete loss for words.

28

The distant fortress

Zeina shakes him awake.

'Come on, the Stranger wants you.'

Nasruddin groans and swings his feet off the camp bed. His body's aches have condensed into a general numbness. He gets up and follows her out of the hut. They walk through the ruins of an abandoned village that is on the Syrian side of the border, skirting the bomb craters and piles of rubble, and along the path that leads to the river. There's not a cloud in the sky.

They don't see him at first with the sun behind him. The Stranger is bathing his feet, with his boots and his rifle beside him on the riverbank. The girl is wading with her hands cupped in the water and the dark-haired woman is sitting slightly apart in the shade of a tree, sewing a tear in a dress. Every now and then she looks up towards the river.

She has a worn but attractive face and it isn't until she turns her head, and her eyes meet his, that he recognises her and understands that ten years of prayer in the darkness of a cell have finally been answered.

He stops just short of her, not looking at anything else but her eyes, which seem deeper and more fathomless than the ocean. Then she starts blinking and he can't tell if she is about to start crying. He knows that the Stranger is watching and the girl has stopped in the river. He is afraid to speak. He is still taking it in, the acuteness of the moment. He can see everything with clarity: the glint of the sewing needle, the silver streaks in her hair, the lines etched in her face, the rise and fall of her chest as she breathes.

'I thought you were dead,' she says, and he can see the tears now. They gleam in the sunlight.

He nods but says nothing. He glances at the Stranger, who is watching closely with his feet in the water. He looks at his daughter standing knee deep in the shimmering water, bathed in brightness. She shines like an angel.

Maryam rises to her feet and takes his hand. He feels the firmness of her grip, the warmth of her skin and the urgent pulse of the blood in her veins. He shuts his eyes and then opens them again. It's not a dream.

His daughter is coming towards them. He is filled with love.

'My family,' he finally says.

He watches over them as they sleep, curled up on the camp bed together, his wife's arm shielding his daughter. They have hardly spoken since they were reunited. He cannot bear to describe the years of imprisonment. She seems equally at a loss for words. It is enough to be together again.

He has tried to render the room habitable, sweeping the broken glass into a corner and hanging a blanket over the window. They have had a meal of bread and hard cheese and olives. There is nothing else he can do. He should be sleeping but his mind will not give him rest. He does not know how much time they have left.

He stands up and steps outside.

The Stranger is sitting on a plastic chair in the middle of the street. The parts of his rifle are spread out on a tarpaulin at his feet and he is using a pull-through bristle brush to clean the inside of the barrel.

He looks up as Nasruddin approaches.

'You should have seen your face,' the Stranger says. 'I've never seen anything like it.'

He knows that, in the absence of empathy or any sense of human kinship, the Stranger is endlessly fascinated by other people's emotions.

'What happens now?' Nasruddin asks.

'We're going to take the fight to the enemy. Are you coming?'

It is an illusion, the idea that he has a choice, but it is the Stranger's way.

'What about my family?' he asks.

'As long as you cooperate, I will make sure that they are safe.'

It was foolishness to imagine, as he had done after his release from the basement prison, that he was going to take charge of his life and determine his own future. He is as much of a pawn as he has ever been. There's no escaping it. The only explanation that he has is that it must be God's will. He has never hated God more than at this moment.

'What do want me to do?'

The Stranger puts down the barrel and stands up. He puts his hand on Nasruddin's shoulder and gently squeezes, as one friend might do to another. He's a skilful mimic, but his eyes betray him. They are as cold and unfeeling as stones.

'I want you to do what you've done before, and done so well. I want you to come with me all the way to the end. To say the words that I write for you and strike terror into their hearts.'

He is searching his face for a reaction but Nasruddin is too tired to feel anything other than emptiness. He should refuse but he knows too well that the Stranger feels no mercy. The only way to ensure his wife and daughter's survival is to do the Stranger's bidding.

'When do we leave?'

'You have a few more days.'

He sits facing the camera with the black flag of Khorasan spread against the bullet-marked wall behind him. The white script on the flag – the *shahada* – claims that there is no god but God, and Mohammed is his messenger. Beside the camera on its tripod, Zeina is holding a whiteboard with the words written on them. The Stranger watches from a distance with his back to the wall.

'When you're ready,' Zeina tells him and presses record.

He closes his eyes. He has played a hundred different parts but he knows that this is the one that he will be remembered for, the one that he likes the least. Reluctantly, he summons the ghost of the Engineer. At first nothing, and then he feels a fluttering in his chest and the emotion rising like a tide of bile.

He will only need one take. He has the words memorised.

He opens his eyes and feels them sear the lens.

'My name is Nasruddin and I am the Engineer. I have spent ten years rotting in the darkness of the tyrant's prison. I was lost without purpose but now I am found. I was forgotten but now it is my fate to be remembered. I will never rest again, nor stand still, until I am either dead or have had my revenge. I pledge to you that the British state will taste a full measure of what innocent Muslims taste every day at the hands of the crusaders and Jewish coalition in the lands of al-Sham and the Levant. The duties of Islam are magnificent and arduous. Some of them are terrible. God has spoken and the hour of death is at hand. It will overtake you, even though you are in distant fortresses.'

He lowers his head and raises it again. He is Titus Andronicus. He is vengeance unconstrained by conscience or justice. His mouth is filled with acid.

'Hear me, Samantha Burns. My revenge shall have no bounds. I will burn your flesh and grind your bones to dust. I am Nemesis and I am coming.'

He leans over and vomits.

The Stranger walks towards him, clapping.

PART TWO

NEMESIS

There is no hunting like the hunting of man.

Ernest Hemingway

29

The names

It's raining oil. Thick black gobs of it falling from the sky.

Zeina kneels in the twilight gloom of an abandoned shop. One of the walls is blackened by fire and the other is graffitied with the apocalyptic messages of Islamic State. Opposite there is a row of shops. Aluminium shutters secure a few, but most are ransacked and abandoned with their windows smashed.

She pulls the balaclava down over her head and sprints up the road, towards the locked schoolhouse. Behind it a sheet of orange flames fills the horizon and billowing clouds of smoke obscure the sun.

It looks like Mordor.

The recruiter known as Stork is cowering just inside the vestibule at the entrance to the school. He is terrified that he is not going to escape before the Kurds and their American allies close off the only remaining route out of the city. Already they can hear the rolling thunder of artillery fire. He watches as she unslings her Kalashnikov. 'How much longer?' he asks.

She shrugs and pushes past him. She knocks on the classroom door.

The stench of petrol hangs in the air.

'Who is it?' the Stranger calls.

'Zeina.'

He opens the door and locks it behind her.

There are six young men sitting in a row with their backs to her. As she crosses to the front of the room she sees that, under the grime, they are as eager as pupils waiting for the exam bell to ring. They sit pinned by the tablet arms of school chairs too small for them. In front of each one is a notebook and a freshly sharpened pencil.

They have answered a holy call. They have left their homes in London and travelled in search of the final apocalyptic battle for Islamic State: one flew straight to Gaziantep, the Turkish town on the Syrian border; two of them drove overland across Europe; and three others took more circuitous routes. Three of them arrived within the last week and Stork, who smuggled them over the border, is waiting outside to be paid.

The Stranger crosses to a desk at the head of the class and sits facing them. On the blackboard behind him there is a list of six names written in capital letters in white chalk. The contrast between the darkness and the white is startling.

When Zeina had cleaned her teeth that morning, the toothpaste she spat out was black. She didn't want to think about how much was going into her lungs and her stomach; anybody who had spent more than a couple of days here was suffering from headaches and nausea.

At least the smoke from the burning wells meant that the Americans could not bomb them from the air.

'Thank you, my brothers,' the Stranger tells them, 'and welcome to the final task. Soon we will be finished, I promise you. Thank you to all of you for working so hard to reach this point. You have kindly opened up your lives and your address books to us. In doing so, you have helped us with our plans to take the fight to the enemy. You have joined an endeavour that will strike a deadly blow against the crusaders.'

The names on the blackboard are a result of an exhaustive three-day trawl through their personal history and social media contacts, sifting a web of social, familial, educational, financial and work-related relationships for promising leads.

A bead of sweat trickles down to the side of Zeina's face, trapped between the wool of the balaclava and her skin. Her forehead and her cheeks itch like crazy but she cannot scratch them without taking a hand off her Kalashnikov and she will not do that with the Stranger watching.

'Your final task is to write a letter to the person that we have chosen for you,' the Stranger explains. 'One page only but the very best letter you can. Their names are on the board behind me. You know which one is yours. Remind them of your connection with them. Some of you must stress the bonds of friendship between you. Tell them that they should trust the bearer of this letter. Others of you must highlight their wrongdoing. Tell them that they should fear the bearer of this letter. Either way, they must not doubt the strength and determination of the person who delivers it to them. Pour your heart into the writing. And don't forget to sign your names.'

Zeina watches them composing their letters, the expressions of concentration on their faces. One of them has his eyes closed between sentences and another chews the end of his pencil. The Stranger is clearly pleased that they all seem to understand the seriousness of their task.

Finally, the last one puts down his pencil and they are finished.

The Stranger collects the letters and puts them in a neat pile on the table. Satisfied, he thanks them all and tells them that they will find their reward in paradise.

Zeina cocks her weapon.

She sees the sudden fear on the faces of the men, children really, trapped in their little chairs. It is a shame given the initiative they have shown in making their way here but, as the Stranger explained to her earlier, there must be no evidence of what is planned.

She opens fire.

When she is done and the magazine is empty, the Stranger surges across the room and out the door, chasing Stork who is running towards the fires. The Stranger drops to his knees, takes aim and fells Stork with a single shot.

After that he saunters over to the body and fires two shots into the recruiter's head. He looks across at Fig who has joined Zeina in the black rain.

'Clear this up,' he tells Fig. 'Burn the bodies. Grind their teeth and bones to dust. I don't want anything left behind.'

He takes Zeina by the hand and leads her away from the schoolhouse.

* * *

Fires burn in oil drums on the edges of the town square, illuminating the long line of fighters and their families queuing to board the buses. The Old Man has cut a deal with the Assad regime: free passage for the surviving Syrian fighters and their families in return for handing over the town ahead of the advancing Americans.

Men scramble on the top of the buses calling to each other as they lash luggage to the roof racks. There is a crackle of small arms fire from the perimeter where the foreign fighters that have been told they must remain are holding off the enemy advance.

A few feet away, Nasruddin is saying goodbye to his wife and daughter. They are standing holding each other for dear life, tears streaming down their faces.

A part of Zeina feels sorry for them, for having to say farewell again after so long apart, but tears have always revolted another part of her.

She puts her hand on Nasruddin's shoulder. 'It's time.'

He lowers his head and turns away as his wife leads their daughter towards the nearest bus.

The Stranger is nowhere to be seen.

She finds Jomaa, the Old Man's giant of a bodyguard, sitting in a deck chair at the entrance to the municipal building with a surprised look on his face. There is a neat red entry hole in the middle of his forehead and an extravagant fan of blood spatter on the wall behind him.

It's sad really. He was the only one of the Old Man's bodyguards who hadn't made a move on her. Then again, he was probably impotent from the steroids he was injecting. She steps around him, taking care not to tread in his blood, and climbs the stairs past two more bodies and a scattering of 7.62 cartridges.

The Stranger is sitting on the floor of the mayor's office with his back to the desk and his smoking weapon beside him. The Old Man's corpse is sprawled in his arms. He looks up as she approaches. There is blood on his face and his forearms and his dark eyes shine as bright as marbles.

'He was remarkably calm at the end. He asked me what I thought I'd solve by killing him.' He shakes his head, 'What a strange question. He was like a father to me, or at least that's what he claimed.' He looks at her with curiosity. 'What did you feel when you killed your mother?'

'I felt powerful.'

For the first time in your life.

The intensity of his gaze excites her.

'What did you feel when you killed him?' she asks.

'Me?' He looks surprised by the question.

'You don't feel any emotion for other people, do you?'

He raises an eyebrow. 'Why do you say that?'

'Because I don't either.'

He smiles.

Later, before they leave for the Turkish border, she watches as he lays out his things on a blanket: six handwritten letters, a pile of hundred-dollar bills, a compass, a folding Gerber knife with a four-inch blade and a moulded plastic grip, and an Android smartphone. He slips them separately into clear zip-lock bags and packs them in a money belt that he secures around his waist. It doesn't seem like much to launch an assault on the Western world. She wonders what he has done with his works.

'There are two ways to enter Europe,' he tells her, 'a good way and a bad way. If you want to go the good way, you have to use connections. Guess which way we're going?'

'The good way?'

'The bad way.'

'Why?' she asks.

'So that nobody can see us coming.'

30

Do not pass Go

Totty is waiting in ambush for Jude at arrivals. He is standing at the entrance to a WHSmith by a rack of newspapers. Nasruddin's face stares out from the front page of almost every one.

I am coming.

'Do not pass Go,' Totty says with a smirk on his face. 'Do not collect two hundred pounds. Straight to Queen Bee's office for you, matey.'

Ignoring him, Jude buys a stack of papers and flicks through them as they drive into central London. The inside pages reprise the details of the 2004 Basra Ambush in battlefield infographics and inset witness statements framed by photos of the British dead. Several include photos of an impromptu press statement by a red-faced Frank Booth, standing outside his south London home in a dressing gown, claiming total vindication.

'The Jordanians are apoplectic,' Totty tells him as they drive over London on the flyover, past elevated car showrooms and a big pharma tower. 'They say you recklessly endangered the life of a member of the royal family.'

'Talal's a big boy,' Jude tells him.

They cut down Edgware Road and drive round the back of Buckingham Palace.

'And Queen Bee's not happy,' Totty says.

They cross the Thames on the Vauxhall Bridge Road, approaching the Inca pyramid from the front. The steel gate rolls aside as they approach and closes behind them, sealing them in a narrow blast-wall chicane. A dog on a tight lead trots around the car with a questing nose, and hops in and out of the boot. When its circuit is complete, the barrier is raised and they descend the ramp into the underground car park, one of several subterranean levels that include a hardened bunker and the firearms range where Jude maintains his proficiency with a variety of pistols and semi-automatic weapons.

'She's waiting for you in the temple,' Totty tells him as he parks in a disabled space closest to the elevators. Queen Bee's top-floor office with its expansive view of the Thames is known throughout the rest of the building as 'The Temple of Vesta'.

He finds Camilla standing guard when the elevator doors open. She escorts him along the executive corridor to Queen Bee's office without saying a word.

When he enters, Samantha Burns is standing with her back to him, looking down on the Thames through the curved wall of glass that runs the length of the room. Chuka Odechukwu is there also, perched casually on the edge of a sideboard, beneath a portrait of an imperial adventurer from the Government Art Collection. He looks on curiously as Jude advances across a carpeted expanse to the desk.

Jude resists the urge to stand to attention and waits for the reprimand.

Queen Bee turns to face him. She looks tired.

'When I authorised your trip, I didn't expect to have to placate a prime minister smarting from a dressing down by the king of a friendly nation.'

'I didn't expect to encounter a Brit who made a specific threat against this country.'

If she takes affront at his sudden insubordination she does not show it or he's too distracted to notice. He's remembering kneeling, with the man who'd called himself The Stranger standing over him. His gun pressed to Jude's head, and his softly spoken words, 'Tell her that I am coming.'

'How do you know he was one of ours?' Camilla demands from somewhere behind him.

Jude doesn't take his eyes off Queen Bee. 'His RP accent,' he replies. Received pronunciation or public-school pronunciation: the accent of those with power, money and influence.

'Just because he went to school here doesn't make him a passport holder.'

'It doesn't matter,' Jude replies. 'He'll pass for one of us. You know how dangerous that makes him.'

It has always been the intelligence services' worst nightmare: a homegrown terrorist wearing the casual invulnerability of the ruling class.

'Could you identify him?' Queen Bee asks.

Jude shakes his head, though he thinks that he would recognise the coldness in the man's eyes anywhere. 'He was wearing a balaclava. All I can tell you for sure is that he is tall and broad shouldered. He's a clean skin. That means that Border Force can't stop him because they do not know who to stop, and the police can't arrest him because they don't know who to arrest.'

'And you believe that he's coming here?'

'That's what he said. I think we should take him seriously.'

'What about the journalist?' Queen Bee asked.

'She was there. She heard what he said to me.'

'But she hasn't printed a story.'

'Nasruddin's face is all over the tabloids. His latest video has been watched a million times. You think anyone is going to run a story that suggests that he's innocent? But what if it turns out that The Stranger, the real Engineer, is one of us? And he's threatening to come here and bring chaos with him.'

'That's quite a leap,' Queen Bee says, sceptically. 'You're relying on a single compromised source.'

'We've been to war for less,' he says.

A flicker of exasperation crosses her face.

'You don't have any proof,' Camilla adds. 'Everything you say is wild conjecture. We don't know if this Stranger is of any significance whatsoever.'

'Time out,' Chuka says, making a T sign with his hands. 'It seems to me that proof is the one thing lacking from this entire business. Let's circle back to Nasruddin. I take it you still believe that he is the Engineer?'

Queen Bee is unwavering. 'Until I see conclusive evidence that suggests otherwise, yes, I do. Nasruddin al-Raqqah claimed responsibility for the attack and his fingerprints were recovered from the scene. As you know, the decision to return him to his home country for questioning was explicitly sanctioned by the foreign secretary. And in Damascus, Edward Malik witnessed a confession.'

'If the confession was obtained under torture then it's worthless,' Chuka says. 'It is a shame that we don't have a copy of Ed Malik's report.'

'It is unfortunate,' Queen Bee agrees. 'But as I told you it was overwritten when the files were migrated to the new system.'

'Along with Nasruddin's file.'

'Yes.'

'We're wasting time here,' Camilla says, angrily. 'Nasruddin is out there and we need to concentrate on finding him. What are you doing to find him?'

'I've just got off a plane,' Jude says.

'That's not a good enough answer!'

'Before I left Jordan I was in touch with Joint Task Force HQ in Kuwait. They are tracking remnants of Islamic State. If Nasruddin is still inside Syria then he may be located with one of those groups.'

'Good,' Queen Bee says, 'then you should concentrate on that and not be distracted by anything else.'

'I don't think you're taking this seriously enough.' He looks from Queen Bee to Chuka and back again.

'Of course we are,' Queen Bee says, in her most soothing voice. 'You have all our resources at your disposal. If this man is, as you say, travelling with Nasruddin and if he turns out to be anything more than just an ordinary foot soldier, we'll prioritise his elimination. All the more reason to find Nasruddin, is that clear enough for you?'

'Yes ma'am.'

Jude turns and walks out of her office with Camilla following.

'What do you think you're playing at?' Camilla demands while they wait for the elevator.

'I'm doing my job,' Jude tells her.

'By inventing bogeymen?'

'I met him and you haven't. The only reason I'm here today is because he chose to let me live. He's no bogeyman. He's the real thing.'

The elevator arrives. As they descend, she says, 'You've always had an over-active imagination.'

He wants to ask her what it is that she is so frightened of, what secret she is hiding, but he cannot do it here where the walls have ears.

She gets out on the third floor.

'Find Nasruddin,' she says as the doors close.

31

Ed Malik

In the warren of narrow one-way streets behind the East London Mosque, Jude walks past the site of the old Fieldgate Synagogue and the redbrick tenement block where his grandparents lived after their arrival. Moses Lieb and his wife Esther took a circuitous route to England, fleeing St Petersburg to Montreal in Canada where he struggled and mostly failed as a bootlegger before travelling back across the Atlantic and settling in London's immigrant East End. Back then the Jewish ghetto sat opposite terraced houses full of the Catholic Irish but now both are occupied by Muslims.

The family stories paint Moses, formerly Lieb and then Lyon, as a formidable man given to expansive gestures who kept mistresses in separate houses across the East End. He served in a parachute battalion in the Second World War and was awarded a military medal at Arnhem. He was said to be handy with a Sten gun. After the war, he joined the anti-fascist 43 Group and was questioned by the police in connection with several armed robberies including the 'Battle of Heathrow' in 1948 – a failed raid on a secure warehouse that was thwarted by the Metropolitan Police's Flying Squad. The family stories do not detail the means – a single jackpot or steady incremental acquisition – by which Moses acquired sufficient wealth to escape the ghetto and take up a life of genteel respectability in a picture-box village in the Home Counties, but Jude remembers his father once saying, 'The best crimes are those that remain undetected.' His wife Esther never got to see Surrey. She died in Whitechapel giving birth to their only child, Jude's father, the general.

Tamar is waiting for him in a coffee house with vinyl records on bare brick walls, where the hipsters' beards are barely distinguishable from those of the devout. She is sitting alone nursing a cappuccino.

He sits beside her.

'You want something?' she asks.

He shakes his head. He's had his fill of coffee today.

'I've asked around,' she tells him. 'I've turned over some old stones.'

She has always had their father's taste for the dramatic. 'And what have you found?' Jude asks, his patience tested.

'Edward Malik was dismissed from the intelligence services in 2011 after an assault on the CIA station chief in Kabul. He headbutted him, apparently. What is it with you Vauxhall boys and your love of violence?'

Jude ignores the dig. 'So where is he now?'

'Nobody seems to know but his father lives over there.' She nods in the direction of a front door in the terrace opposite, the one with the green door. The father is a restaurant worker on Brick Lane. This was Ed's registered address after he left MI6. He worked at the logistic company, J & K Travel, that's at the other end of the street. I suggest that you go and have a word with the owner. I don't think anyone has spoken to her recently. Apparently, she sent Ed Malik over to Pakistan to run that end of the business but he disappeared on arrival. Her daughter, Leyla, kicked up a fuss claiming that he'd been abducted by the Pakistani intelligence services, she took off after him and also disappeared.'

'They were a couple?'

Tamar shrugs. 'Maybe. Both are still missing.' She stands up and pushes her empty coffee cup towards him. 'You get to pay for this.'

Sameenah Kassar of J & K Travel is a small woman in a pillar-box red dupatta with a manner that suggests she does not suffer fools gladly. She looks Jude up and down, paying careful consideration to his shoes.

'For four years nothing,' she says. 'And then two of you in as many days.'

Someone else is on the trail of Ed Malik and not the media by the sounds of it.

'I'm very sorry,' Jude replies. 'There must have been some kind of mix up. I wasn't aware that one of my colleagues had been to see you. It would be very helpful if you could repeat to me what you told my colleague. I can make sure you aren't bothered again. Unless we have more news that is.'

'More news?'

'Any news.'

Sameenah Kassar looks at him sceptically. She does not resemble his idea of a woman whose daughter has been missing for years.

'I'd like to see some identification.'

He gives her a card with his name and his green burner's number written on it in felt tip pen. She is incredulous.

'This is it?'

'I'm a friend,' he says. 'If you speak to Ed or Leyla please tell them that I need to talk to them.'

'That's what your colleague said.'

'Did he also tell you that Edward Malik might be in danger?'

Her eyes narrow. 'No, *she* didn't.'

He is sitting in the café waiting for Ed Malik's father to end his restaurant shift when, out of the corner of his eye, Jude sees two men go by on the street outside. There is something about their V-shaped bulk, their dangerous watchfulness and lupine stride that sends a shiver of alarm down his spine and propels him to his feet. He reaches in his pocket for pound coins, slams a handful on the countertop and dodges out the café in time to see the two men enter J & K Travel.

He approaches swiftly, stepping between piles of pink recycling bags on a strip of narrow pavement. At the corner, opposite the shop, he stops and waits. As far as he can tell, there is no one else about. The shop door is closed and the blinds have been pulled down.

He crosses the street quickly and pauses by the door, looking both ways. Carefully he turns the doorknob and pushes but meets resistance. It's locked. He looks around for something to jimmy the lock. There is a broken bedstead and, outside a deserted fried chicken shop, a stack of five-gallon steel drums containing used cooking oil.

When he hears a muffled scream, he does not hesitate. He grabs the nearest drum and lifts it up above his head. He throws it through the shop window and leaps in after it.

Five steps take him across the office floor and between the desks that are sprayed with broken glass, towards the kitchen at the back where the two men are bending Sameenah over a gas cooker. One of them has her left arm pinned behind her back and the other is holding her right hand over the burning gas hob. They react fast, releasing Sameenah and turning to face him, but he is faster and they are in a constricted space. He hits the nearest one under the chin with a palm strike that snaps his head back and then ducks away to avoid the second man's attack before spinning and launching an elbow strike from above, snapping his collar-bone like dried wood. Jude pivots again so that his back is to his attackers and, with his torso bent and his leg parallel to the floor, he kicks backwards, slamming the first one against the wall. He turns again to face the second man who throws a punch at his head with his one good arm. Jude dodges the blow and knocks him off his feet with a sweeping kick. He leaps on him and finishes him with a flurry of hand strikes.

Swiftly he pats down the two unconscious men and removes their wallets. He takes Sameenah by the arm and says, calmly, 'Follow me.' He unlocks the door and leads her out the shop and hurries her along the street in the direction of the mosque. He looks at her hand as they walk. It's swollen and a livid red colour.

'We need to get your hand treated,' he says. They pass Tayyabs restaurant heading east, and on the corner of New Road he flags a cab. He bundles her into the back of the taxi with him and tells the driver to head west towards the city.

'Where's your daughter?' Jude demands, rifling through the men's wallets and removing their driving licences, while she glares at him with her injured hand held clutched against her chest. As soon as he gets a chance he will ring Gretchen and get her to check the names on the licences. 'If you're in danger your daughter is too. Where's your phone?'

'Back in the shop.'

'Good.' He throws the two wallets out the cab window and takes out his green burner. 'Give me her number.'

Jude taps in the numbers.

'Leyla Kassar?'

'Who is this?'

'My name is Jude Lyon. I'm an MI6 officer. I'm with your mother. She's been attacked. She's okay. She's not seriously injured but she needs medical attention.'

She takes it more calmly than he expected. 'Let me talk to my mother.'

He passes the phone to Sameenah and waits as she answers questions in a language that he assumes is Urdu. She passes the phone back to him.

'Are you being followed?' she asks.

'No.'

He can tell from her voice that she doesn't believe him. 'Head east on the Mile End Road,' she says.

He tells the taxi driver to turn around and head back the way they've come.

'Who were the men that attacked my mother?' she asked.

'I'm not sure but they were looking for you and Ed.'

'Why?'

'That's what I'm trying to find out,' he tells her. 'I'm hoping you'll help me.'

'Get out at Bow Road. When you're there call me back.'

Five minutes later they arrive outside the underground station.

He calls Leyla and follows her instructions, along a dusty road between the station building and a high brick wall into a desolate area of shuttered industrial sheds. At the road end, on a narrow promontory between steep banks of littered rock, there is a ramshackle travellers' camp surrounded by a chain link fence.

She tells him to wait at the gate and soon a man emerges from between the caravans. He is grey haired and ravaged with puffy eyes and his trousers are held up with orange string.

'Give him the phone,' she says.

Jude hands it to him through the gate and he holds it to his ear while eyeing Jude, suspiciously. Apparently satisfied, the man opens the gate and gestures for them to enter. He leads them across the camp to a white caravan resting on breezeblocks at the back.

Inside, a young girl of ten or eleven is sitting doing her home-work. The man speaks to her in a language that Jude does not recognise and she gets up from the table and goes to a laminated sideboard. From a drawer, she takes an old biscuit tin with a red cross sellotaped on the lid and carries it back to the table. While they wait the girl dresses Sameenah's wound with antiseptic lotion and a crepe bandage. Soon after she is finished, two people in hoodies run down the bank and roll through a hole in the back of the fence, spring to their feet and approach the caravan. They step inside and sit opposite Jude at the table.

'I'll give you ninety seconds,' Ed Malik says. Beside him, Leyla comforts her mother.

'Why is Queen Bee so desperate to have Nasruddin killed?' Jude asks.

Ed's face gives nothing away. 'Why do you think?'

'He's an embarrassment,' Jude replies. 'She knows that he's not the Engineer.'

'You can tell her that her secret is safe with me.'

'She didn't send me,' Jude tells him, and turns to Leyla. 'But she may have she sent the men that hurt your mother.'

'What do you want?' Ed demands.

'I was there in Karachi when Nasruddin and his wife were arrested,' Jude tells him. 'It left a bad taste in my mouth.'

'And over a decade later you've suddenly developed a conscience?'

'I know that you went down to Damascus to question him. I assume that you got to see his file before it was deleted?'

Leyla and Ed exchange a look. She nods almost imperceptibly.

'Don't make me regret this,' Ed says. 'The first thing you should know is nothing about Nasruddin fitted the usual pattern for terrorists. There were no brushes with the law, no record of violence, no known association with radical groups or even with the Muslim Brotherhood. He was a bit-part actor who specialised in playing villains in Iraqi soaps and sometimes helped out his brother who ran an electronics shop. By the time I got down to Damascus, he'd been so badly beaten it was impossible to get any sense out of him. But the Syrians who'd spoken to him when he first arrived said that he had made repeated reference to a Westerner known as *al-Gharib*. It means the Stranger.'

'Go on,' Jude urges him.

'Nasruddin claimed that he had been coerced. The Stranger kidnapped his wife and the price for ensuring her safety was delivering the 'claim of responsibility' speech that the Stranger wrote for him. He also told his interrogators that he was made to handle electronic components and phones as they were being used to manufacture IEDs. He knew that he was being set up to take the blame but there was nothing he could do. There was no way of escape. He said that even the most hardened al-Qaeda members were frightened of the Stranger.'

'Did he name him?'

Ed shakes his head. 'No.'

'Who is the Stranger?'

'I don't know. But I'm sure that Samantha Burns does. When I got back I started reading through the Basra Ambush file again, looking for anything that might be a clue to the Engineer's true identity. But then my clearance for the operation was revoked and I was re-assigned. Queen Bee brought in a new officer to take over from me.'

'Who was that?'

'Her name was Camilla Church.'

'Time's up,' Leyla says.

Jude's mind is reeling from what he has just been told. Queen Bee and Camilla have been concealing the truth from him from the very beginning. And it's clear from their treatment of Sameenah Kassar that they will act ruthlessly to keep their secret from getting out.

'Read the Basra file again,' Ed tells him. 'If you want the truth that's probably where you'll find it.' He stands up. 'We're out of here.'

Jude watches while Ed, Leyla and Sameenah exit the camp through the hole in the fence. He sits back on the bench and closes his eyes. It's never been more apparent that if he proceeds with this line of investigation he will make an enemy of Queen Bee, and there's no telling what the consequences of that will be. If he had any sense of self-preservation he'd stop now.

He won't though. He's too stubborn and he's come too far to give up now. He's had his loyalty tested to breaking point and he has lost faith in those he once respected.

When he opens his eyes again, the man and the girl are staring at him.

'On your way,' the man says.

Jude leaves the travellers' camp and heads towards the underground station with his green burner pressed to his ear, waiting for Gretchen to answer.

32

Situational awareness

Gretchen is standing waiting for him at the video wall when Jude arrives in the office. She has her tattooed arms folded protectively around her tablet, which she is clutching to her chest.

'Camilla Church is looking for you.'

'I'm sure she is,' he replies, with his best attempt at a sunny smile. Camilla's not the only one. His yellow burner has a message from Yulia:

> My darling, I understand that you are both busy and belea-
> guered. And I am, of course, OVERJOYED that you returned
> unscathed (if unsuccessful!) but I must, regrettably, once
> again, draw your attention to your rather un-gentlemanly
> neglect of me. It's not unreasonable to expect something to
> set the pulse racing: a saucy photo or a secret document?

Even if he was inclined to respond, if only to honour the deal that he struck in the yacht, he fails to see what he can tell Yulia that she does not already seem to know.

He takes off his jacket and hangs it on the back of the nearest chair.

'Not that chair,' Gretchen says with a pained expression on her face.

'Sorry!' He retrieves the jacket and hangs it on a peg on the wall instead.

He wheels a chair from an empty cubicle over to the wall and sits on it. 'What have you got for me?'

'First, I've added the live data from the Joint Task Force to the operations map,' she tells him, tapping on her tablet. 'The dark grey polygons indicate the current known and suspected locations of Islamic State remnants.'

The map on the wall is very different to what it looked like in 2014, when Islamic State had most of the trappings of a nation state, including inhabited land that stretched the length of the Euphrates Valley, from the Turkish border in the north to the outskirts of Baghdad in the south. Now, just a few years later, the final pockets of Islamic State on the map are dispersed like ink-spots in hard-to-reach desert places, often besieged by Russian or American-backed forces, or both.

'How easy would it be for them to break out of any of these areas?' Jude asks.

Gretchen shrugs. 'They say that you can cross any front line or pass through any checkpoint provided that you're prepared to pay. On top of that there are close to a million people on the move inside Syria. It would be easy to lose yourself in the crowd.'

'And Islamic State still has money?'

'Yes, plenty. Their loss of territory has limited their access to oil revenue but they operate a diversified model that still brings in funds from extortion, kidnap and ransom, drug smuggling and antiquities trading. On top of that they are believed to have invested hundreds of millions of dollars in legitimate Iraqi busi-nesses via tribal leaders and businessmen who have clean records and can hide their links to Islamic State. And finally, we believe that they hold tens and possibly hundreds of millions of dollars in blockchain cryptocurrencies like Monero, Bitcoin and Zcash.'

'You're saying that they have the money to fund an interna-tional operation?'

'Definitely,' Gretchen says. 'And the means to move the money without detection.'

'So, I'm right to be concerned?'

'Yes.'

'What about the Stranger?'

She smiles shyly. 'I've found three different intercepts from National Security Agency computers trawling Iraqi and Syrian phone networks that mention *al-Gharib*, the Stranger. The first two are from Iraq and the third is from Syria.'

Jude feels a shiver of excitement. 'Go on,' he says.

'The first is from Anbar province in 2004, the second is from Diyala in 2006 and the most recent is from three years ago, in the Raqqah Governorate in Syria. I'll put the English transcripts up on the wall.'

The first is a conversation between two senior commanders of al-Qaeda in Iraq. The commanders are disagreeing over what to do about a disciplinary matter. A fellow commander named *al-Gharib* has executed a member of the movement who he accused of passing information to the Americans and taken the dead man's wife as his bride. Instead of seeking the permission of the leadership he just went ahead and did it. One of the commanders is in favour of punishment. He says that *al-Gharib* is totally out of control. The other commander is more sanguine. He points out that arrests amongst their ranks have decreased dramatically since the accused man was killed.

'I guess he got the right man,' Jude says.

The second is between a high-level commander known as Fig, who is believed to be a former Ba'ath Party commander and Saddam loyalist named Samir Majid, who joined al-Qaeda in Iraq in 2003. He is speaking to an unnamed acquaintance and saying that although *al-Gharib* can be relied upon to do what they want efficiently and without conscience, the problem is that he also does a lot more of what they don't want and for this reason it is necessary to either execute or imprison him.

In the third an Islamic State foot soldier named Ali is describing to a friend how he helped move a high-value prisoner to a more secure location after he killed two of his guards. Ali says, 'They brought him his food and he killed them with the steel tray. It is said that he remained calm and did not stop smiling even as he was beating them to death.' Ali goes on to describe how the surviving guards used tear gas to subdue the prisoner. Ali's final words are, 'We delivered him to a gang of thieves in the mountains. Nobody knows his real name but they call him *al-Gharib*.'

Jude sits back in his chair.

'That explains why there haven't been any more attacks,' he says. 'They've had him locked up all this time.'

It also explains how Queen Bee could go on maintaining the fiction that Nasruddin was the Engineer. It was all just a tawdry cover-up. Without any further attacks, it was easy for her to argue that the right man had been handed over to the torturers of the Syrian regime. She had sacrificed Nasruddin for the sake of her career.

'But why release the Stranger now?' Gretchen asks.

'Because the circumstances have changed. Islamic State is finished in its current form and they've got nothing to lose. He's their trump card and they've been saving him until last.'

Gretchen is looking uncomfortable.

'What is it?' he asks.

'I checked the driving licences of the two men that you sent me on your way here. They're both fake but I managed to link them to an Increment operation in Iraq last year that was authorised by Samantha Burns.' The Increment was the executive arm of General Support Branch: a group of specialists, often retired special forces working in the private sector, that provided a special operations capability for MI6. 'They both now work for a security company registered in the British Virgin Islands named Apex.'

It was as he had suspected: Samantha Burns had first sent Camilla Church, and then the two thugs to find Ed Malik and silence him.

He hears the click of the deadbolt in the door and familiar footsteps in the corridor.

'There you are.' Camilla, Queen Bee's loyal protégé, marches across the briefing room to his office and stands waiting for him by the open door. He follows and she closes the door behind him.

He crosses behind his desk, aware that Gretchen is standing watching them through the glass. He wonders if she is expecting an explosion. There's a part of him that wants to rage against Camilla for hampering his investigation, for the advantage she has handed to their enemies. But he knows that she is acting under duress. He knows that her husband's career hangs in the balance. He can only guess what else Queen Bee has on her.

'What can I do for you?'

Camilla looks even more harassed. He wonders what it must be costing her emotionally, to maintain Queen Bee's deception. He remembers the way that she tortured herself during their affair: the fits of anger and sorrow, the constant removal and replacement of her wedding ring.

'What have you found out?' she demands.

He shrugs. 'That the threat is credible and Islamic State has the wherewithal to launch an attack in this country. If the Engineer masterminds the attack, I think we can assume that it will be complex and designed to inflict the maximum number of casualties.'

'That's all you've got?'

She's right. It's not much. *But whose fault is that?* He considers telling her that he knows from Ed Malik that Queen Bee assigned her to look for the Stranger, the real Engineer, more than ten years ago. He could demand that she stops lying and reveals the true identity of the Stranger. Then he would have something to work with. But he is cautious; like it or not Camilla is in Queen Bee's camp, and he can't afford to alert Queen Bee to what he knows in case she acts against him.

'What about Islamic State sympathisers in the UK?' Camilla says. 'People who might help him if he gets this far.'

'The National Counter Terrorism Policing Network has three thousand known sympathisers under investigation and only a fraction of them are under active surveillance,' he tells her. 'There are thirty thousand others on a longer watch list. At current capacity, it will take them weeks, maybe months, to check them all out.'

'What about a target?'

'My guess is as good as yours. The distant fortress could mean the MI6 building. That would make sense given that Queen Bee is mentioned in the video, but it could mean something else.'

'We're running out of time,' she tells him. 'What are you going to do now?'

'I'm going home to bed,' he tells her. 'I'm going to take a fresh look at the file in the morning. Maybe there's something I've overlooked.'

She looks angry and frustrated, but there's nothing she can do unless she opens up to him and it's clear that she's not going to do that. She's too terrified of what Queen Bee might do. Deception goes with the job but still he feels diminished, denied respect for himself and for Camilla, and for the whole shitty world.

33

Under the Cat and Mutton

Just before dawn, Jude gives up on the hope of further sleep and goes through to stand naked in front of the wall of windows as grey and indeterminate light creeps across the city. He watches white vans deliver newspapers and fresh bread and sandwiches. A few of the night's revellers are huddled at the bus stop opposite. A police helicopter rattles overhead.

He hadn't known where he was when he opened his eyes. His sleep was haunted by uncommonly vivid nightmares: Jude and Nasruddin dancing a pirouette on puppet's strings in an ancient amphitheatre; the Stranger as Nemesis, striding towards him out of a wall of fire; Yulia's face exultant in orgasm as she stabs him in the chest; the MI6 building an inferno, and friends and family plummeting in flames from its upper floors.

It feels like a steel band is tightening across his skull.

Movement below catches his eye. A morning jogger in black Lycra shorts and a hoodie crosses the road diagonally heading in his direction. When he looks up, Jude recognises Chuka Odechukwu, the lawyer from the Investigatory Powers Tribunal.

A few seconds later, the buzzer goes.

'Get your running kit on,' Chuka says. From the tone of his voice it appears that Jude doesn't have any choice.

'Give me a couple of minutes.' He dresses quickly in his workout clothes and trainers, and five minutes later is out in the street.

'You want to stretch?' Chuka asks. He has a runner's taut hams and thighs.

'I'm good,' Jude replies.

'Lead the way.'

They set off. Jude lopes steadily along. Chuka jogs beside him with neater, swifter strides. Their shadows stretch out in front of them, separating and converging as they swerve to avoid pavement furniture and pedestrians. They head north on the Kingsland Road towards the canal.

'How long has Samantha Burns known that Nasruddin is not the real Engineer?' Chuka asks.

'More than ten years, ever since she sent Ed Malik down to Syria,' Jude replies. 'The Syrians had got the truth out of Nasruddin by then. They knew he was a mouthpiece and a cut-out, a clever disguise for the real bomb-maker.'

'I can see the motive for covering it up,' Chuka says. 'I mean there's no way to row back on what was done, the rendition or the torture. But why maintain it now when it's beginning to unravel? She could confess and let Frank Booth take the fall. After all she has the Intelligence Services Act as cover. Booth must have signed off on the rendition and sending Ed Malik down to Syria.'

'I think it's something to do with the real identity of the bomb-maker.'

'Your mysterious posh-speaking jihadi?'

'They call him the Stranger and I think she knows who he is.'

'But you don't?'

'No.'

'But you're determined to find out?'

It's the question that has been plaguing him all night. If he had any sense the answer should be an emphatic 'No' but caution has never been his strong point. He's made up his mind. He's going to uncover the truth.

'Yes,' he says.

They cross the bridge over the canal at Haggerston and double back on to the towpath. Soon it will be fraught with prams delivering children to schools and nurseries, but at this early hour it's mostly joggers and the occasional cyclist.

'Even at the risk of incurring Samantha Burns' displeasure?'

'I know what she's capable of,' Jude replies. 'And I know the danger that puts me in. But I think that there's a greater danger. If

Nasruddin is the Stranger's proxy and he issues a threat against us I think we have to take it as coming directly from the Stranger. And civilian lives are at stake.'

They run alongside a row of houseboats moored against the bank, with signs advertising tea, woollen hats and tarot readings. The air smells of damp and wood smoke.

'You really think he's coming here?' Chuka says, dodging a cyclist.

'Yes.'

'And he's planning a terrorist attack?'

'You want to take the risk that he's not?'

Chuka runs under the Cat and Mutton Bridge at the bottom of Broadway Market and then stops abruptly on the other side. Jude comes to a halt a few paces beyond him with his chest pounding.

Chuka looks like he's trying to make his mind up about something. 'Would you call yourself a patriot?'

'I suppose so,' Jude replies, with his hands on his knees, struggling to control his breathing. 'I'm not much of a flag waver but this is my home. I believe in it. I want to keep it safe. What about you?'

'I have faith in the potential of this country and its people,' Chuka tells him. 'Even now, in difficult times, but only provided that we are honest with ourselves.'

'What is it that you want, Chuka?'

'I'm told that you're having an affair with the wife of the chief spook at the Russian Embassy?'

'That's right,' he says. 'She's a source of valuable intelligence.'

'I imagine that she says the same thing about you.'

He chooses not to share his growing conviction that Yulia, rather than her husband Valery, is the chief spook at the Russian Embassy.

'Perhaps,' Jude concedes. 'The operation was initiated by Queen Bee.'

'Got that in writing, have you?'

'No.'

A swan is eyeing them suspiciously from the canal.

'And I've been told that you have been socialising with the *Guardian* journalist who broke the rendition story.'

'Information gathering,' Jude replies.

'Is that what you call it?'

Jude shrugs.

Chuka shakes his head. 'That business in Jordan didn't help.'

'If I hadn't gone to Jordan we wouldn't know about the Stranger,' Jude protests. 'What are we doing here?'

'I've decided to help you,' Chuka tells him, after a pause. 'I will assign you as a cooperative witness to the investigation.'

'Okay,' Jude says, unsure of what that means.

'I have control of an investigatory budget and can reimburse reasonable expenses. On top of that I have direct access to Number 10 when the time is right. You'll have to serve two masters, Queen Bee and I, until you can prove conclusively that the Stranger is a credible threat and she's covering it up. Do you think you can handle that?'

'What choice do I have?'

'I believe in the rule of law, Jude. I don't like cover-ups. I think they should be exposed. You know my favourite cover-up quote, apart from the Watergate ones, is by John McCain. He said, "Thank God for our form of government. The media won't let there be any cover-up." Remember that when you're next talking to your journalist friend.'

'You want me to go public?'

'Find the Stranger,' Chuka tells him. 'Uncover the truth. You have my number. Call me if you need any help.'

Chuka turns and sprints away along the towpath. To Jude, it seems as likely that he is being played by Chuka as it is that he is being deceived by Queen Bee.

Back in the Shoreditch loft, Jude peels off his clothes. In the shower, he leans against the polished concrete wall of the stall while clouds of steam rise and engulf him. He feels that he has been outmanoeuvred at every turn. He keeps thinking of the cold steel muzzle of the Stranger's gun pressed against his temple in the refugee camp and the emotions that followed: the certainty of death followed not by fear but by anger, at his own stupidity and richly deserved humiliation. He remembers the Stranger's piercing eyes and the searchlight quality of his gaze, the way that he acted like a centre of gravity, slowing down time and pulling in everyone's attention. And then the softly spoken words and the realisation that Jude was to be spared after all.

I am The Stranger. Tell her that I am coming.

He fears that he is unlikely to be so lucky again.

After ten minutes or so, he puts on a bathrobe and lies flat on his back on the bed with his skin red and hot, feeling dizzy and light headed. He can't tell what his next move should be; follow Chuka's suggestion and speak to Kirsty McIntyre, or confront Camilla and demand the truth.

Jude spends the rest of the day reviewing the Basra Ambush file on his Toughbook, reading the transcripts and looking for clues in the methods and means of attack that might lead to the identity of the attacker. He asks Gretchen to trace everyone who is mentioned in the file.

After lunch, he calls the home of a retired Northern Ireland Police Service officer, Peter Irvine, on his green burner. Irvine was manning the control room that took the tip-off call that launched the Basra operation. Irvine's wife answers the phone and tells him that her husband is out on the golf course but is expected back within the hour.

He spends ninety minutes willing his phone to ring. When it eventually does, he snatches it from his desk.

'Mr Lyon, is it?' the man says with a distinctive Ulster brogue.

'That's right.'

'I hope you'll forgive me but I made a couple of calls and people vouched for you. What can I do for you, Mr Lyon?'

'I'm investigating the circumstances of the Basra Ambush. Am I correct in thinking that you were on duty in the confidential call centre that night?'

'That's right.'

'I'm trying to establish whether British special forces, Task Force Black, were deliberately targeted.'

'Sure. It's possible,' Irvine replies, without hesitation.

'Can you expand on that?'

'Look son, you have to understand what it was like out there. I've seen nothing like it, before or since. It was an utter, fucking shambles! There was no workable vetting system for the call operators on the confidential line. We had no clue who was working for us. So yes, it was perfectly possible for someone inside the call centre to know the Brits were on the quick reaction force list that night and share the information. On top of that, everybody knew the Americans were fed up of wasting their time chasing the old men of Saddam's era. They were after the jihadis. It was obvious that only the Brits would take that task: chasing after some washed-up former Ba'athist who wasn't even on the deck of cards. If someone wanted to deliberately target our boys the chance was there, no doubt about it. Does that answer your question?'

'Yes. Thank you.'

34

Official secrets

The clubroom at Shoreditch House is dark and crowded and it takes a few seconds to locate her. Kirsty is standing by the bar talking intently to an older man and when she sees him, her face hardens. She says something to her companion and they both watch as he approaches.

'Can we talk?' he asks.

Her eyes shine in the bar light.

'Go ahead.'

'Not here.'

'Then I've nothing to say to you.' She turns to the man and whispers something that Jude does not hear. He gives Jude an evaluating gaze.

Jude does not move.

'Are you just going to stand there? If so you might as well meet my editor.' The older man raises his glass. 'This is Jude. He's a spook. He was with me in Jordan and saw what I saw. Perhaps he can persuade you to print my story?'

'I've something to show you,' Jude says. 'It's important.'

She gives him a cool look.

The older man puts his hand on her shoulder. 'Don't go with him.'

That seems to make her mind up. She really doesn't like being told what to do. 'I'm fine. Thanks for the drink.' She downs the glass. 'Come on then.'

Buoyant with relief, he smiles. She shakes her head in exasperation. He feels genuinely happy.

Waiting for the lift, she says, 'Where are we going?'

'A friend's apartment, it's only five minutes away.'

They walk together up Shoreditch High Street. It's risky, taking her to Sanjay's apartment, but he needs privacy for what he is going to show her.

'What did you make of Nasruddin's wife?' he asks.

'I thought she was credible. I believed what she told me.'

'But your editor won't print?'

'That's right. After that video and the tabloids splashing Nasruddin's face across their front pages, he wants verifiable evidence that he's not a terrorist.'

They walk under the railway bridge, and he points at the block that houses Sanjay's apartment. There are no lights on in the building.

'I don't have to do this,' she says.

'No, but you will.'

'Why?'

'Because you want to know who the Stranger is as much as I do.'

He lets them in and they ride the elevator together in silence. Kirsty doesn't speak again until she is standing on the rug at the centre of the living room.

'Fuck me!' she says. 'How on earth did you pay for all this?'

'It belongs to a friend.'

'A Russian friend?'

'He's a Sikh, actually.'

'I don't think they have them in Russia,' Kirsty concedes.

'Why a Russian?' Jude asks.

She walks over to the glass and looks out across the city. 'Someone in Vauxhall Cross is briefing against you, suggesting that you're in the pay of the Russians.'

'It's smear tactics to try and discredit me and deflect from the investigation.'

'That had occurred to me,' she says. 'But why don't they just take you off the investigation?'

Because he's caught in a power struggle between Queen Bee and Chuka Odechukwu. 'Too many competing agendas.'

'That's your answer?'

'I want to show you something.' Jude opens the Toughbook on the zinc counter and logs on to the server. Strictly speaking, what he is doing now is illegal, and possibly treason. He clicks on the folder containing the Basra Ambush file and opens a succession of documents for her to read.

'It's all there,' he says, 'the Basra Ambush file.'

'And how is that going to help me?'

'It's possible that somewhere inside there is a clue to the Stranger's identity.'

He watches as she considers this. She shakes her head and for the first time since he tracked her to Shoreditch House, she smiles. 'You need my help.'

'Maybe,' he concedes. 'You want a drink?'

'Yes.'

He pours her a couple of fingers of Lagavulin and sets it beside the Toughbook on the counter. Then he goes into the bedroom and opens the safe. There are five missed calls from his sister, Tamar, on his red burner.

He calls her back.

'Where are you?' she says.

'Sanjay's place.'

'I'll be there in thirty minutes.'

Before he can protest she cuts the connection.

There's also a fresh message on his yellow burner from Yulia:

Given your ongoing silence, and despite an itch that needs – nay deserves – to be scratched; I decided not to visit you last night. I am beginning to wonder if my husband is right and that I am over-indulging you. As you know, he favours more mechanical means of persuasion (broken limbs, concussions and such). Why are you talking to the press and not me?

He considers responding but he doesn't feel ready to face Yulia's scrutiny yet. Back in the living room, he finds Kirsty sitting cross-legged on the sofa with the laptop in her lap, the screen lighting up her face.

He sits at the island and waits.

'There's nothing written here that seems like a clue to the real identity of the Engineer,' she says, eventually, 'not that I can see, anyway, on a first reading.'

He crosses to the window. 'I spoke to the cop who was on duty at the confidential call line. He retired from the police five years ago with a heart condition. He spends his days playing golf and attending his local church. I don't think he's an accomplice. What he did say was that it was possible for whoever planned the attack to know that Task Force Black, the British special forces unit in Iraq at the time, was on call that night.'

'So, you don't think it was a random target?'

'The guy we're looking for is British and the target was a British special forces unit. I don't believe in coincidences.'

Down in the street, he watches as Tamar drives into the cul-de-sac on her motorbike and dismounts. She removes her helmet and shakes out her hair.

'My sister's here.'

'Which one?'

'The cop.'

The buzzer goes.

'Don't ask me to hide under a bed,' she says.

'That's fine. A cupboard will do.'

She looks at him and he smiles. 'A joke.'

'Ha bloody ha.'

He lets Tamar in and she brushes past him, heading for the living room. 'You took a long time to answer your phone.' She stops mid-stride when she sees Kirsty. 'What is she doing here?'

'She is helping me,' Jude says, feeling somewhat defensive.

'Well then it's hardly surprising that Counter Terrorism Command has been asked to place you under surveillance.'

Jude considers this news. 'Who signed the request?'

'Your friend Camilla Church.'

'How long have I got?'

'Before they have eyes on you? Not long. And they'll be watching me too, because you're my brother.'

'Thanks for warning me.'

'There's something else. The police are looking for a man who matches your description who was involved in an altercation with two intruders in a shop in Whitechapel.'

'Thanks,' he says, again.

'You don't do anything by half do you?' She turns her attention to Kirsty. 'My brother obviously likes you. Please be careful what you print. Don't let his naivety put him behind bars.'

'I'll bear it in mind,' she says.

'You do that.' She looks at Jude. 'Take care, big brother.'

'Understood.'

He walks her back out to the elevator.

'And get yourself some new phones,' she says as the doors close.

Back in the flat, he removes the sim cards from all his phones, dropping them into a Pyrex bowl that he places in the microwave. He gives them ten seconds until they pop. Next, he peels the coloured tape off the back of his phones and attaches the strips to the side of the counter. Then he uses a wooden chopping board and a hammer to smash the phones to pieces. When he is done he retrieves four new fully charged burners and four sim cards still in their packaging from the safe. He attaches a coloured strip to each phone and inserts the new sim cards.

He looks up to see Kirsty staring at him thoughtfully.

'From now on we only communicate via end-to-end encryption,' he tells her. 'And get yourself some burners and change them every few days.'

'Understood. What's the colour coding?'

He looks at his phones. 'Black is work. Yellow is an ongoing operation. Red is private and personal. And green is, well, other.'

'You must have either a good memory for numbers or very few friends.'

He goes back to the safe and retrieves a passport.

'Which number did you give me when we first met?' she asks him, when he returns.

He smiles. 'Do you want another drink?'

'Definitely. When you answer the question.'

Jude takes another tumbler off the shelf and carries the Lagavulin over to where she is sitting. He sits opposite her and pours them both a drink.

'I gave you my red phone number.'

'Interesting.'

'How are you getting on?' he asks her.

'Whoever he is, this Stranger of yours, we can be sure of this: he obviously knows how to set an ambush.'

'There was plenty of opportunity for him to learn that in Iraq.'

'But maybe we trained him?'

'It's possible but we're tracking all former military trained personnel who are known to have travelled to Syria. Most of them are fighting with the Kurds. The ones we know of who joined Islamic State have all been targeted and are believed dead.'

'The ones you know of.'

'We could have missed him,' Jude concedes.

'What can you tell me about Franklin, the warrant officer in charge of the forensic investigation?' she asks.

'He's still serving with 11 Regiment EOD.'

'EOD?'

'Explosive Ordnance Disposal.'

She nods. 'The Stranger must have learned his bomb-making skills somewhere.'

'You think he's EOD?'

'Why not? What better way to learn?'

It makes sense. He kicks himself for not seeing it before. 'Let's go speak to Franklin. Do you have a car?'

'Yes. That said, it's questionable whether it will pass its next MOT.'

'Sounds perfect! Let's go.'

'Now?'

'We'll find somewhere to stay on the way.'

Twenty minutes later they are driving out of London on the Westway flyover in her elderly red Golf, heading for Didcot, the home of 11 Regiment EOD.

'Why are you helping me?' she asks.

'I don't know who else to trust,' he tells her.

'In that case you better tell me the whole story.'

It is reckless, and hard to see how his career will survive it, but given that he is already being accused of collusion with the Russians and soon to be under police surveillance it seems likely his career is already finished; besides he knows that he will feel better for telling her. He begins on the tarmac when Nasruddin and his pregnant, mummified wife are being escorted on to the CIA plane that will take them to Syria. He tells her the information that led to the arrest of Nasruddin was passed directly to him by Samantha Burns. She shakes her head in disgust when he describes the congratulatory phone call from the foreign secretary, Frank Booth. He tells her that Nasruddin's files along with any forensic evidence have been deleted. He tells her about the Dagestani gang that freed Nasruddin and repeats the founding myth of Islamic State and the legend of Old Man of the Mountain. He tells her about the attack on Sameenah Kassar in her shop and repeats his conversation with Ed Malik in the travellers' camp behind Bow Road.

She is silent for a long time.

'You're a dangerous man to know,' she says.

'You can turn back if you want to,' he tells her.

'You know I won't.'

They pull into a service station for toothbrushes and toothpaste, and Jude stays in the car while Kirsty goes in to pay.

'Where are we going to stay?' she asks, when they get going again.

'I know a place.'

Just before ten at night, they stop at an eighteenth-century pub in a picture-box village in the Chiltern Hills. Jude hands over a Belgian passport and pays for two adjacent rooms in cash. The publican tells them that the kitchen is closed but they have an hour before last orders and Kirsty arranges to meet Jude in the bar ten minutes later.

When she arrives in the low-ceilinged bar he notices that something is different about her. There is a shimmer to her cheeks that he did not notice before.

'What will you have?' he asks.

'Hendrick's and tonic.'

'I'll have the same,' he tells the barman.

They carry their drinks out to the beer garden and sit on a bench. Kirsty produces a pack of cigarettes from her bag and lights one.

'Can I have one?' Jude asks.

'I didn't know you smoked,' she says handing him the pack.

'I'm thing of taking it up again,' he says.

He inhales deeply and blows smoke in the air.

'You think that Samantha Burns knows the identity of the Stranger, don't you?'

'Yes.'

'So why is she keeping it hidden?'

'I don't know yet. But I aim to find out.'

'If you do, you'll destroy her career.'

'I realise that. I guess that's why she's so keen to stop me.'

'Can I ask you a personal question?'

'Go ahead.'

'Why are you doing this?'

It is the question that he has been struggling to answer and now seems as good a time as any to try. 'Because I'm angry. At myself as much as anyone. I joined the intelligence services because I believed in keeping this country safe. Because I believed that there were things here worth believing in and protecting. Tolerance and justice. Basic human kindness.' He shakes his head. 'You must think I'm ridiculously naive.'

'No,' she says and he believes her. 'What did your sister mean when she said that you like me?'

He can't bear to meet her eyes and stares at the grass between the picnic tables. He wants to tell her that he is tired of unsatisfying affairs that have no prospect of a future but he is painfully conscious that he has nothing to offer her but the prospect of scandal and possibly prison.

'We should get some sleep,' he says, eventually.

'Sorry I asked,' she says, stubbing out her cigarette. 'I'll see you at breakfast.' He watches while she goes back inside without looking back.

He undresses in his room feeling despondent, realising that he has missed an opportunity that might not come around again. Unable to sleep, he lies awake in bed imagining her just the other side of the wall.

35

Every One's Divorced

The following morning, they drive in hard-to-read silence across the North Wessex Downs and drop down towards the rising clouds of water vapour from the concrete cooling towers of the power station on the plain below. There is a build-up of storm clouds on the horizon that threatens rain.

They pass the military camp and follow a gentle loop through the army quarters, past identical semi-detached houses with freshly mown lawns and redbrick walls that make battlements around them. They park opposite one with a large removal truck parked outside.

A woman holding a crying baby is giving directions to a team of movers who are loading the van with cardboard boxes. She looks tired and harassed.

'I'll handle this,' Kirsty says. She crosses the street with Jude following. 'Mrs Franklin?'

The woman looks at them suspiciously. 'Who's asking?'

'My name is Kirsty McIntyre. Can I speak with you?'

Jude remains silent.

'What's happened?' the woman demands.

'We're looking for your husband.'

'Well you're too late. He's not here.'

'Where is he?'

'He's fucked off back to Iraq or somewhere and now I'm being moved, fuck knows where. I've wasted my whole damn life waiting for him and now he says he's never coming back. You know what EOD stands for? They don't tell you until after it's too late. Every One's Divorced.'

'Do you have an address for him?' Kirsty asks.

'No. He's signed up with some commercial outfit but they won't tell me where he is.'

'Do you know the name of the company?'

'Heliotech.' She shakes her head and seems on the point of tears, 'What the fuck has he got himself tangled up in?'

'I can't say.'

'That's just great. Thank you very much. My husband has served his country for twenty years and this is how we get treated. Fuck! You're not journalists, are you?'

'We're trying to get to the truth of what happened,' Kirsty says.

'Fuck! I thought you were coppers. He warned me not to speak to any journalists.'

'Why did he do that Mrs Franklin?'

Her face twists with rage. 'You fucking vultures!'

Heliotech's website describes them as a full-service company promising innovative solutions focused on water, environment, infrastructure, resource management, energy, and international development. There are links to projects conducted for the US Department of Defense. About delivering explosive ordnance disposal in the Middle East there is not a single reference.

Jude calls Gretchen via WhatsApp on his green burner as they are driving back to London. 'Can you find out what you can about a US company named Heliotech and what they're up to in the Middle East?'

'Sure thing.'

'Thanks.'

'Jude?'

'Yes?'

'Camilla is on the warpath. She wants you to call her.'

Pressing a finger to his lips so that Kirsty knows to be quiet, he dials Camilla's number with his work phone.

'Who is this?'

'Jude.'

'Where the hell are you?' she demands, angrily. 'And why aren't you answering your phones?'

'I'm doing my job. What do you want?'

'The Russian Counsellor has requested a meeting. He says it's urgent. And he says he has vital information for you. He's waiting for you in Kensington Palace Gardens. The minute you're done with him you'll tell me what he said. Have you got that?'

He stares at the phone for almost a minute after Camilla has hung up. Then he realises that Kirsty is watching him.

He looks at her.

'The Russians want to talk.'

'I'll come with you,' she says.

'It's not safe for you. And frankly I'm not sure it's safe for me.'

It seems possible that he's being sent to the meeting as a means of discrediting him by establishing further evidence of collusion.

She looks petulant. 'This is my story now.'

He bites back his frustration. 'This isn't just a story. You have no idea how ruthless the people we are dealing with can be.'

'I'm not a novice at this.'

'I'll do you a deal. Whatever I find out I'll tell you.'

'It's not the same.'

'It's better than being dead.'

'You think they'd do that?'

'To protect their careers? To avoid prison? Of course they would.'

They drive the rest of the way to London in silence. She drops him at the entrance to Kensington Gardens.

'I'll call you,' he tells her.

He gets out of the car and walks briskly down the path towards the palace. On impulse, he stops and looks back. The car hasn't moved. She is sitting looking at him through the open window.

He waves and she drives away.

36

A saucerful of secrets

Yulia is sheltering under a Fox umbrella in front of the iron railings that enclose the gnarled stump of the Elfin Oak. They are just a stone's throw east of the Russian Embassy but there's no sign of her husband.

'It is said that they come alive by moonlight,' Yulia muses when Jude joins her. The nine-hundred-year-old oak is carved with figures of elves, gnomes, squirrels and birds climbing across its knots and burls and peering out of its nooks and crevices. She gives Jude a sideways glance. 'You like Pink Floyd?'

When Jude fails to reply, Yulia smiles, 'My husband likes Pink Floyd. Apparently, the tree is on the inner gatefold of one of their lesser-known albums. It is called *Ummagumma*. According to band lore, it was a failed experiment. You probably think I am making a metaphor? My husband is fond of blunt metaphors and this is one of his favourite places for an amicable parting of ways. If he meets you here it is to say he enjoyed it while it lasted but it didn't work out.'

'Are you chucking me?'

'I am not the sort of lover to demand attention but as affairs have less mutually binding emotional glue than a marriage, one must take care to invest effort into them, otherwise they can rapidly lose their allure. Without regular communication, the whole thing is simply too utilitarian and transactional.' She smiles and passes him the umbrella. 'You should be pleased I haven't arranged to meet you in an abandoned quarry. That's what Valery would have preferred.' They link arms and he grips the umbrella above both their heads. 'Walk with me.'

They head south and towards Kensington Palace as a helicopter from the Royal Flight takes off from the playing fields beside it, carrying a minor royal to a destination unknown.

'How is Queen Bee?' Yulia asks. 'Is she feeling beleaguered?'

'Is that the outcome you are looking for?'

'Do you think that Chuka Odechukwu would make a good replacement for Samantha Burns?'

'I don't know.'

'I can't decide which one I prefer,' she says. 'I like Chuka. He's bright and ambitious, and so handsome too.' He realises that she's teasing him. She knows he's caught between Queen Bee and Chuka. She reaches up and kisses him on the cheek. 'Perhaps I can help him out a little. But then, is that really what I want? Maybe better the devil you know. Samantha Burns is at least reliable in her mediocrity. What do you think?'

'I don't work for you, Yulia.'

She rests her head on his shoulder and says, 'This is a very one-sided relationship, Jude.'

'I don't believe that for a minute. Why did you ask me to come here?'

'All right, all right. But one more question first. How are you getting on with identifying the Stranger?' She stops and looks up at him. 'Ah, I see I have surprised you.'

'You've known all along?'

'Of course.'

It's so bloody obvious that the Syrians informed their Russian allies as soon as the Americans handed Nasruddin over to them. They'd have been the first to know that Nasruddin wasn't the real Engineer.

'What I fail to understand,' she says, 'is why Samantha Burns has maintained the fiction for so long.'

'I should walk away.'

'Come on, Jude. Nobody wants that. Least of all your friend who is following us.'

He looks back to see Camilla Church standing under an umbrella, about fifty metres away, making no effort to conceal her presence.

'Camilla is very keen to find out what we know,' Yulia says. 'And

I expect that she is wondering if she is still on the winning side. You and I both know the top people very rarely go to prison but I think it could go very badly for her. And it's hard to see her husband's career prospering if she takes the fall.' She reaches up and cups Jude's cheeks in her gloved hands. 'My darling, you have such a complicated love life. One woman delivers you to me and when I am done with you I am expected to deliver you to another.' She kisses him on the lips and they resume walking. 'You're waiting for me to tell you my big news.'

'I am.'

'We've found the Old Man of the Mountain.'

'Alive?'

'Sadly not, somebody got there before us, maybe the Stranger, but don't worry, it's not the end of the world, we managed to capture one of his senior advisers. He used to be an intelligence officer in Saddam's army. His name in Samir Majid but he goes by Fig.' Jude recognised the name from the NSA intercepts that Gretchen had found. It was the Iraqi Fig who had warned that with the Stranger you often got more than you bargained for. 'Fig has confirmed that an attack on this country is planned but of the specifics he claims to know nothing. There are signs, though, of planning and preparation that would benefit from closer examination. I think maybe you should take a look.'

'Where?'

'Where do you think?'

'Syria,' Jude replies.

'Correct. An old friend and business associate of mine named Lermontov is waiting there for you. I guess you just have to ask permission? Who is it that you answer to now? Queen Bee or the Black Prince?'

'I'm not entirely sure,' Jude tells her.

Yulia strokes his lapel. 'You must be careful, Jude. Syria is not a safe place.'

She dances out of his reach and heads back the way they came. She pauses briefly to speak to Camilla before heading in the direction of the Russian Embassy.

Jude waits in the rain while Camilla approaches.

'Well?' she says.

'They've found evidence in Syria of planning for an attack here,' Jude explains. 'I need to see it.'

'You want authorisation to go to Syria?'

'I'm not convinced I need your authorisation.'

'Are you planning to defect?'

Under any other circumstances he might have found the question hilarious but it's so wrong-headed that he worries that Camilla is coming apart at the seams. 'I don't think it's my secrets they want,' he says, gently. 'What did Yulia say to you?'

Camilla looks like she might be about to cry.

'She said I need to decide whose side I'm on.'

'She's right,' Jude tells her. He briefly places a consoling hand on her upper arm and squeezes before turning and walking away, dialling Chuka on his green burner.

37

Where the ragged people go

Zeina eases herself watchfully through the mid-afternoon crowd that packs the narrow, cobbled streets of the port town. She is wearing the Stranger's money belt with their remaining cash and the phone inside and has pulled her shirttails out to cover it. Still she is on the lookout for pickpockets. She passes a row of shops advertising ferry services with stacks of buckets in the shop front and cheap-looking orange lifejackets hanging from their awnings.

She stops in the shadows of a crumbling doorway to check that she is not being followed. Satisfied, she continues for a short distance and then dodges down a side street. The Stranger and Nasruddin are in a tiny apartment at the top of five flights of unlit stairs in a dilapidated building where no one asks questions. They have been there for two days now.

Entering the room, her eyes smart at the acrid smell of sweat and vomit. The Stranger is doubled up on the bed in a tangle of sodden sheets. He is shivering and clutching his stomach against the cramps.

She sits on the bed beside him and checks his pulse rate and opens his eyes. He has dilated pupils and a rapid heartbeat. He groans and turns his back on her.

She had first noticed the signs of heroin withdrawal – the restlessness and sweating, the running nose and teary eyes – on the twenty-hour bus ride west to the coast. He hadn't warned her. He'd just done it.

'We have to leave tonight,' she tells Nasruddin. 'There's a storm coming. If we don't go now we'll get stuck here for a week or more.'

Nasruddin is sitting on the other side of the room with his hands on his knees. It does not look as if he has moved since she left the apartment a couple of hours earlier and he seems oblivious to the smell.

She takes three wristbands made from lengths of braided red string from her pocket. They were given to her in return for six thousand dollars by a smuggler who calls himself Jet. 'My work is fast,' he told her. 'That is why my passengers call me Jet. My work is like the speed of a jet.'

She ties one to the Stranger's left wrist and another to her own. She passes the third across to Nasruddin.

'Put that on.'

He doesn't ask why. He seems utterly resigned to his fate.

The Stranger has one arm slung around Nasruddin's shoulders and Zeina has his other arm around hers. His breaths are laboured and rasping, his skin slick with sweat. Together they half-carry him down the pathway that leads from the cliff top to the beach. It is a dark night and they are wearing bulky, polystyrene lifejackets that make it difficult to see where they are putting their feet. The Stranger's foot misses a tread and all three of them nearly tumble.

They can see others moving by torchlight on the pathway ahead. It is getting colder and it has started to spit with rain.

There are several boats on the pebble beach. A teenager with a torch inspects their wristbands and points them to the far end of the beach, where it meets the cliffs. The Stranger's feet are less sure and he is getting heavier. They slip and slide on the pebbles and several times almost fall.

When they reach the boat, they see that people surround it. They are sitting, silently waiting. It is hard to judge but there must be fifty people at least and the boat looks like half that many would be too much.

One of the smugglers checks their wrists and points them in the direction of a clear patch in the midst of the crowd. They sit down and watch as several other families arrive after them. They listen to the sound of the tide rolling in and watch the lines of white foam on the top of the waves.

There is no warning, no message broadcast. Suddenly the entire crowd surges silently towards the boat, pushing it into the water and clambering over the sides and each other in an effort to reach the front. Zeina and Nasruddin drag the Stranger through the water to the boat and roll him over the side before hauling themselves in after him.

The boat rocks from side to side, dangerously overloaded, and then the engine putters into life and the nose turns into the waves and they head out into open water.

The first ones to drown are inside the boat. They pass out from the petrol fumes and sink into the rising slurry of fuel, saltwater and vomit.

Zeina has to keep lifting the Stranger out of the water while beside her Nasruddin bales with a bucket, desperate to keep them afloat. Children are passed hand to hand to the front, which just about keeps above the waves. It is raining harder now and visibility is almost zero. All she knows is that the mainland is somewhere to the north of them. The smugglers are shouting to bale faster and people are screaming.

'Not far!' one of the smugglers shouts. 'Not far!'

Nasruddin has stopped baling and is pointing. He looks terrified. She sees a midnight-blue wave is rising out of the water, growing taller as it rushes towards them.

Then the motor starts coughing and abruptly cuts out.

The next few seconds unravel in slow motion. The wave lifts them out of the boat and they hang suspended in the freezing cold water while the boat sinks into the depths. An instant later time re-asserts itself. They are spun violently around and sucked down. The pressure almost rips them apart but she clings on to the Stranger. Her lungs are screaming. Her eyes are burning. It is impossible to tell up from down. She releases the air in her lungs in an explosion of bubbles.

With all her strength, she surges upwards following the bubbles.

They surface, coughing and spluttering.

A wave smacks her in the face and she kicks her feet to get higher in the water. She kicks off her shoes, then forces her way out of her jeans.

Beside her, the Stranger speaks for the first time in days. 'I'm cold,' he says, his teeth chattering.

Treading water, she turns and sees no one else around them. It has stopped raining and looking upwards she sees a rent in the clouds and the stars above. She sees the Big Dipper and, off to one side, the inverted W of Cassiopeia. Between them the North Star.

She feels a rush of adrenalin. All is not lost.

'This way,' she yells.

She begins to swim, using a sidestroke, pulling water with the right hand and kicking with her legs, while holding the back of the Stranger's lifejacket with her left. She wills them both forward, stroke by stroke. She does not want to die here. To keep her mind busy, she considers her life, the fear and anger that has propelled her, but the details seem meaningless. All that really matters is her purpose. She was put on this earth to deliver the Stranger to his destiny. That is what the Old Man told her when he sent her to release him. He took her hands in his arthritic claws and looked into her eyes.

'I want you to go with him. That is your fate. To be his companion until the very end.'

She is determined that this will not be the end. When she looks behind her, she sees that the sun is starting to rise. A pink line on the horizon. She looks back.

'Land!' she cries, seeing a rocky shoreline and the lights of houses on the hillside.

She kicks her legs with renewed vigour and pulls them through the water towards the shore. Fifteen minutes later they stumble out of the surf and collapse on to the sand. They lie panting on their backs.

The sun is up now.

'It's okay,' she says. 'We're okay.'

She looks around her. There is no sign of Nasruddin.

38

Checkpoint Charlie

The Chinook flies across a blasted landscape lit up by a line of burning oil wells like giant candles on the horizon.

Jude is sitting in the midst of a troop of battle-weary SAS soldiers while across from him a door gunner tracks targets with his machine gun.

Most of the soldiers are asleep, sedated by the helicopter engine's hypnotic vibrations, hunched over their rifles with the barrels pointing at the floor. But the two buckled in either side of him have come instantly and un-fuzzily awake, and are checking their webbing, securing the straps in preparation for deployment. They are Ash and Tommo and they have hitched a ride in with him from Iraq as his personal security detail.

Abruptly, the pilot banks left, drops a hundred feet and then executes a sharp ninety-degree turn. The airframe shudders as he conducts a series of evasive aerial manoeuvres. Anyone who was sleeping is suddenly awake.

The loadmaster holds up three fingers to Jude and his two companions. Three minutes to landing. Now is when they are at their most vulnerable.

The pilot lowers the collective and pushes the cyclic forward and they plummet towards the landing site in a near-vertical cork-screw dive. Jude's head smacks the shoulder of Ash on his right, and he hears an explosion and sees flashes of light, and thinks they are coming under fire for a moment before he realises that it is just the pilot firing counter measures – flares and chaff.

The Chinook's ramp lowers as they approach the ground and the three of them spill out, hit by the scorching blast of the rotor engines. As Jude jumps free, the pilot is already beginning his ascent. He shields his eyes and closes his mouth to avoid a lungful of burning sand as the Chinook roars over them and beats its way across the desert.

An American marine runs up and crouches in the dirt beside him. He is wearing the chevrons and rockers of a gunnery sergeant.

'Mr Lyon, sir?'

'That's me,' Jude replies.

'Welcome to Syria, follow me.' They sprint to the nearest building with Jude's protection detail following. Inside a group of Americans and Kurdish militia are sitting against the walls. They look grimy and exhausted as if they have just survived a battle.

'Hicks?'

'Here, Gunny!'

'Sanchez?'

'Gunny!'

'Ya'll drive the Other Government Agency fellow and his minders over to Checkpoint Charlie.'

The two marines groan and climb painfully to their feet.

'This way, sir.'

Jude follows them out to where two weathered Humvees are waiting with their engines running. He climbs in the first vehicle and eases himself along the bench beside the legs of the top gunner who is manning the .50 calibre machine gun in the turret above him. Ash and Tommo bracket him either side and Sanchez climbs in the front seat ahead of him.

'Let's go,' he says.

They drive through narrow streets beneath a pall of black smoke, zigzagging between rubble and burned-out cars, heading towards the centre of town.

'We've been sitting watching each other across the river for several days now,' Sanchez says, 'ever since the beardies cleared out.'

They roll to a halt in sight of the iron bridge across the river that divides the town. A ranger climbs out of a trench at the approach to the bridge holding an aerial with a white flag attached to it and walks down the road towards them. A tall, red-haired woman joins him from a nearby building. She is wearing jeans and black body armour over a navy-blue polo shirt, and has a pistol in a pancake holster on her belt.

'You have reached your destination,' Sanchez says.

Ash and Tommo dismount and Jude follows.

The woman in the polo shirt shakes Jude's hand and introduces herself as Abby Masters from Anchorage, Alaska. She explains in a relaxed manner that she is an adviser to the Syrian Democratic Forces, a mixed bag of Kurdish and Arab militias who currently control the eastern side of the river.

'The Russians are waiting for us over on the other side,' she says. 'We believe that they are private contractors from Valkyrie, which means they are probably acting on behalf of the GRU, Russian military intelligence, but there's no way to be a hundred per cent sure.'

'Take the magazines out of your weapons and clear them,' the soldier with the flag tells Ash and Tommo. 'And stay real close as we cross the bridge.'

'You understand that once we're over there we're on our own?' Masters says. 'The Kremlin maintains sufficient distance from Valkyrie to be able to deny any involvement if this thing goes south.'

Jude nods. 'You really don't have to come.'

'Hell, I wouldn't miss it for the world,' she says with a broad grin. 'Are you ready?'

'We're ready,' Jude tells her.

It's cooler on the bridge, and the ground is zebra-striped with shadows from the iron girders. They walk slowly, careful not to make any sudden movements.

'You're lucky we're still here,' Masters says. 'Our draft-dodging asshole of a president's been tweeting about pulling us out.'

They are halfway across when they see movement at the other end. A reception committee is waiting with a bald man in an ankle-length black leather coat at its head. Either side of him are two men wearing *telnyashka*, the blue-and-white striped T-shirts worn by Russian airborne troops, and carrying modern-looking AN-94s.

'Hello, Jude,' the man says. He looks to be in his sixties but it's hard to tell given the scars that run laterally across his skull. 'I am Lermontov.'

It's the name of the contact that was given to Jude by Yulia in Kensington Palace Gardens.

'You two know each other?' Masters says, raising an eyebrow.

'Only by reputation,' Lermontov replies. 'Jude is practically one of our own.'

'You've got something to show us?' Jude says, tight-lipped while Masters gives him a searching look.

'This way,' Lermontov says, and leads them past a row of armoured personnel carriers towards an ugly two-storey concrete blockhouse surrounded by concrete blast walls.

Inside it has the sickly-sweet smell of rotting flesh. There is a huge bloated corpse sitting in a deck chair just inside the entrance and more on the stairs behind him.

'They were dead when we found them,' Lermontov explains, in a matter-of-fact tone. If the smell bothers him he does not show it. 'We had our technical people check them for booby traps but they are not dangerous.'

He climbs the stairs and leads them into the mayor's office where the Old Man's corpse is lying on the floor. It resembles a bundle of desiccated rags and sticks.

'The last of the Mighty Men,' Lermontov says. He looks at Jude; 'It is a fitting end, I think. You know, I have received conflicting instructions about you, Jude. Should I listen to the Counsellor or his wife?'

'I think you know the answer to that.'

Lermontov smiles. 'She said you were a cool customer. Follow me.'

He leads them back down the stairs and down the street between collapsed buildings to a single-storey schoolhouse. There is a body lying in the yard.

'We think that's the recruiter known as Stork,' Lermontov explains, nudging the body with his boot and dislodging a swarm of flies. 'He smuggled hundreds of your countrymen here to fight for Islamic State. He was also executed before we arrived.'

Inside the schoolhouse there is a charred and blackened pile of bodies.

'There are six in total. We found the prisoner trying to burn them. All he can tell us is that they were British and they spent two days locked up in here with the Stranger before they were killed. We have people who have managed to extract DNA from their bone marrow and we have dental X-rays. We can share these with you.'

Jude looks around him at the bloodstains and the chairs chewed up by gunfire that are scattered across the floor. Something was planned here, he thinks. Something no one else was supposed to know about. At the far end of the room is a blackboard with six names written on it in chalk. Four men and two women:

Abdul Rahman
Charles Underhill
Mohammed Naser
Safira al-Noury
Steven Turvey
Bakhtawara Wazir

He takes a photo with his phone.

'What sex are the bodies?' he asks.

'All men,' Lermontov replies.

So, the names of the two women on the board, Safira al-Noury and Bakhtawara Wazir, are not a match for the burned bodies in the pile beside him.

'Where's the prisoner?' he asks.

'I'll take you to him.'

Fig is slumped on a chair in a windowless basement. His face looks like a slab of bruised meat and blood is spooling out of his mouth. One eye is closed and the other is scarlet red. The fingers on both hands have been broken and jut out at contorted angles.

Jude pulls up a chair and sits opposite him.

'I'm looking for *al-Gharib*, the Stranger,' he says.

Fig looks up and stares at him with his one red eye. He tries to smile but it makes him groan. 'You won't find him here.'

'Where has he gone?'

235

'You're from England, yes?'

'Yes.'

'That's where he is going.'

'How?'

Fig licks his split lips with his long, pale tongue and bows his head. 'I don't know. Nobody knows but him. And he'll get there. Nothing will stop him. And you should be afraid.'

'Who is he?'

Fig smiles. 'Only the Old Man knew that and he is dead; the Stranger killed him.'

39

The Devil's Garden

Back on the other side of the bridge, Jude picks up a 3G signal from the nearest Turkish cell tower and messages Gretchen in London on his green burner.

'I'm sending you a photo now,' he tells her. 'It's a blackboard with names on it. Run them through the database of known Islamic State sympathisers and their associates in the UK. See what you can find.'

'Roger that. I'll get straight on it. I have something for you too. I've found Jamie Franklin. He's working on a Defense Department-funded project for Heliotech inside Kurdish-controlled Syria. I think he must be somewhere near where you are now.'

'Thanks.'

'Be careful, Jude.'

He ends the call and walks over to Masters and Sanchez who are standing by the Humvee.

'I need to find a commercial outfit called Heliotech.'

Masters gives him a world-weary look. 'They're about fifty klicks south of here in the Devil's Garden.'

'The Devil's Garden?'

'It's booby trap heaven down there,' Sanchez says.

'That's where I need to go.'

'I had a feeling you were going to say that.' Masters raps her knuckles on the driver's window of the Humvee. 'We're heading south boys.'

Jude can hear the answering groan through the glass.

At first the highway runs parallel to the river and then it gradually veers away to the east on a raised dyke that crosses a parched and desolate landscape dotted with the tangled metal of demolished refineries. There is hardly any traffic. When a battered pick-up full of young men approaches from the other direction the top gunners track its passage with the barrels of their .50 cals.

All the culverts are blown and steep ramps have been bulldozed into the sides of the dyke to allow vehicles to drive down on to the sand and then climb up again on the other side. They pass a collection of five elderly buses stranded at the base of one of the ramps. The passengers have rigged up tarpaulins so that it resembles a squatter's camp. The Kurds distribute crates of bottled water out of the back of one of the pick-ups and then they set off again.

After an hour, the lead vehicle turns off the highway and follows a secondary road towards a scattering of palms and flat-roofed buildings in the distance. As they approach the outskirts of the village, they are funnelled down a sandy side street by red hazard tape towards a corral of white Land Cruisers at a control point. Men in flak jackets carrying Kalashnikovs stand watch beside the vehicles.

A short, compact Glaswegian with broad shoulders and a pork pie hat appears from behind one of the vehicles. He has *Heliotech* printed in white lettering on his navy-blue body armour and a paintbrush tucked in its webbing. He waves down the vehicle.

'Hi there, I'm Shug, what can I do for you, gen'lemen and lady?'

'I'm looking for Jamie Franklin,' Jude tells him.

'Then you've come to the righ' place. He's doon the village just now. He'll be back in an hour or so.'

Masters consults her watch. 'We don't have that long. The road's not safe after dark.'

'Can you take us to him?' Jude asks Shug.

'Aye if ya got baws on ya,' he replies and looks at Masters, 'no offence intended, hen.'

Ash and Tommo exchange a look. Masters looks mystified.

'Let's do it,' Jude says and gets out of the vehicle.

'Gather round,' Shug tells them. 'And pay attention to what I'm saying to yous. The area I'm taking you to is full of explosives hazards, IEDs n' aw that. At aw times, you are to follow my instructions. A safe lane is marked with red tape. Don't step outside the red tape. Don't run. Don't pick anything up. Don't throw anything. If something goes bang, stop where you are, inspect yoursel' for injuries and await further instructions. We have a trained paramedic on site. He'll sort you out if you get injured. Where the fuck are you, Tamati?'

A large Maori with facial tattoos and a Red Cross arm patch climbs out of one of the Land Cruisers. 'Here, boss.'

Shug looks at them. 'Any questions? No? Right then, follow me.'

He walks down a narrow sandy path between hazard tape with Jude, Ash, Masters, Tommo and the medic Tamati following in single file.

They cross beneath a power line running perpendicular to the path, and Shug points out to them parallel lines of what look like large molehills following the power line into the distance. The wind has stripped away much of the covering sand, revealing the explosive charges buried beneath. 'You're looking at pressure plate IEDs with a 25-litre main charge in a plastic container. One every couple o' metres for at least three Ks in either direction, that's industrial level production. Roughly one in ten has an anti-lift device, usually a fridge door opener. That's just the first line of defence. After that it's improvised directional fragmentation mines with interlocking arcs to defend against any kind'a assault or flanking manoeuvre.'

The path branches ahead of them, safe lanes winding between houses, alongside stonewalls and through orchards. At the end of each one, a man with a bag of hand tools and a metal detector is on his hands and knees, gently excavating the ground.

Shug sticks to the centre lane and they follow, walking between houses daubed with black Islamic State graffiti.

'The buildings are rigged with radio-controlled demolition devices so they could bring them down on the boys as they approached.'

'Why did they leave and not stay and fight?' Masters asks, looking around her.

'Havenae got a fuckin' clue,' Shug says. He points. 'Jamie's just over there.'

A large man in body armour and a helmet is kneeling at the corner of a concrete building with a snatch block pulley above his head and the end of a pulling line on a drum reel at his feet.

He spots them and gestures for them to join him. They squat down against the wall behind him. He takes a quick look around the corner, at whatever the pulling line is connected to, and then back at them.

'Ready?' he says.

Shug and Tamati stick their fingers in their ears. Jude closes his eyes.

The man reels the line in.

Nothing explodes.

Everyone exhales.

The man stops winding the reel and slumps against the wall. He takes off his helmet and mops his shaven head with a rag from around his neck. He lights a cigarette, takes a drag and stares at the burning end.

'They'll kill you, right?'

'You're Jamie Franklin?'

'That's right.'

'My name is Jude Lyon. I think you know why I'm here.'

Franklin nods and drags hungrily on his cigarette while staring at his boots.

'I'm looking for the man who was responsible for the Basra Ambush,' Jude says, 'I know that it wasn't Nasruddin al-Raqqah and I think you may be able to help me.'

His eyes narrow and the crow's feet around his eyes etch stark white lines in his sunburned face. 'Why would I do that?'

'Because I believe that the real Engineer, the man behind the Basra Ambush, is heading for the UK now and is planning an attack.'

Franklin looks up sharply at that. 'You're sure?'

'About as sure as I can be. I need to find him and stop him before people die.'

Franklin flicks away the finished cigarette and immediately lights another. The reluctance to speak is written on his face.

'Anything you can tell me,' Jude presses him.

Franklin exhales and nods. 'All right, after the attack a rumour went around the regiment that he might be one of ours. He was that far inside our decision cycle it seemed like the obvious answer. He knew where we'd put our incident point and he knew the difference in downward air pressure from an empty helicopter and one filled with casualties. But he also understood our clearance drills, how we'd excavate on to a switch and try to isolate the power source. And then there was the way he attached the detonator to a folded-over length of detonating cord. That's how we teach it and that's what I saw on the devices that didn't go off. It was just a theory, and plenty dismissed it, which is why I didn't include it in the official report. But it kept nagging at me so I put it in a memo as an addendum. I didn't hear anything more about it so I figured that I must be wrong. Then about a year or so later I received a visit from one of your people asking me about the memo.'

'Do you remember the name of the person who came to see you?'

'It was a woman. I think she said her name was Camilla.'

'What was in the memo?'

'You said it, that Nasruddin was a cut-out. A means of disguising the real bomber who might be one of ours.'

'And you had an idea of who the real bomber might be?'

Franklin looks away and looks back again.

'You know when you have that feeling about someone? That there's something not right about them.' He shakes his head and lights a third cigarette. 'You know what the official military definition of a good booby trap layer is? A sick and depraved practical joker. It got me thinking. I met one once, a really good booby trap layer. And he was one of ours. I was a newly promoted sergeant doing the Advanced Manual Techniques course. It was the hardest course I ever did. For the practical test phase at the end of the course, a red team unit from Hereford who were supposed to play the enemy joined us. They were some sort of training cell attached to special forces. As far as I can tell, they were mostly paid to think up new and horrible ways to kill British soldiers. The team leader was an officer. He was Scottish, I think, and privately educated. He was charming but cold, with strange eyes. Word in the mess was that he could turn really ugly if you crossed him. You could tell he had some kind of hold over the rest of his team. It was pretty clear to everyone that they were fucking terrified of him.

'When the testing phase came, he sprung a series of complex ambushes on us that would have wiped us all out if it had been for real. I was shocked. I thought I was better prepared than that. We all did. It was a fucking bad outcome. Several of the guys on the course jacked it in soon after.

'Here's the thing. A few months later I heard that the officer had been discharged for a particularly nasty assault on one of his soldiers. After that, nobody ever heard from him again.'

'What was his name?'

'Fowle. Guy Fowle.'

40

The places only they would know

Woken by a helicopter hovering overhead, Zeina sits at the entrance to the tent and watches the early morning clashes in the muddy field below. Like medieval archers in close order, the police are firing tear gas into the air, the canisters arcing over the battered steel link fence that marks the border and landing amongst the crowd that surges and retreats. Here and there volunteers wearing fluorescent tabards move between huddles of migrants driven back by the gas and in amongst the tents on the hill children wielding pipes, pretending they are guns, mimic the battle going on beneath them.

'Good morning,' the Stranger says, from his sleeping bag.

She looks over her shoulder at him and sees that for the first time since they left Turkey, his eyes are clear and focused.

'Welcome back,' she says.

If he notices her peevish tone he does not acknowledge it.

'Where are we?' he says, looking across the field. The truth is she is too tired to be really angry with him.

'Macedonia.'

'What's the other side of the fence?'

'That's Bulgaria.'

'Where's Nasruddin?'

'He didn't make it.'

The Stranger closes his eyes and opens them again. 'I had plans for him.'

'We need money if we're going to get much further,' she says.

He nods. 'I have to get online.'

'You can get a Wi-Fi signal if you stand next to the Red Cross tent.'

He gets out of the tent. Standing naked in the sun, he reminds her of a statue in a museum – David facing Goliath. He stretches his arms above his head and grins at her.

'We're going to be fine.'

They cross at one of the more remote stretches of border where there is no fence, a long line of them following a local smuggler down into a ravine and across a river that is knee-deep in icy cold water. One of their number is in a wheelchair and they pass her along a chain that stretches across the river and up the far bank.

The smuggler warns them that there are road blocks and roving patrols in a buffer zone that stretches ten kilometres beyond the border and that they should separate and fan out across the countryside to reduce the chances of capture.

Four hours later they board a bus at the centre of a small town and, with the last of their cash, they buy tickets to the capital.

They spend that night in an abandoned warehouse next to the central railway station with water dripping through holes in the roof. It's a haven for migrants, gypsies, prostitutes, and other outcasts.

The following morning the Stranger is waiting outside the offices of Monex when they open. Back in Macedonia, before they crossed, he had sold Zcash to a broker along with a question and answer attachment. There is no requirement to show ID at Monex; he simply hands over the transaction number and the answers to the questions on the attachment, and they release the cash to him in euros. Back at the warehouse they order two Bulgarian passports with Schengen visas for 7,000 euros each and by dusk they are delivered.

That night, they check into a hotel as husband and wife.

While he goes out for clothes and supplies, she runs a hot bath and strips, discarding her muddy clothes in a bundle in the corner of the room. She eases herself into the bath slowly, wincing at the heat. She gradually stretches out in it while the steam rises from the surface of the water. Her tired muscles relax. She can't remember the last time she felt so dirty and tired, or so relieved to be clean again.

She hears the door open and the sound of him moving in the bedroom. Thinking of him she feels a sudden tightness in her nipples and pleasurable warmth spreading across her belly and her inner thighs.

She gets out of the bath and towels herself dry. She puts on one of the hotel's white flannel bathrobes and opens the bathroom door. The Stranger is standing staring out the window at the street below. He looks across at her and she sees the hunger in his eyes. She wonders how long it's been for him, maybe years.

'I'll have a shower,' he says. 'And then we'll dye your hair.'

Ten minutes later, they are both standing at the bathroom mirror while he divides her hair with claw clips and uses cotton wool balls to apply a hydrogen peroxide solution.

'Since the founding days of Islam, the followers of the Prophet have often been forced to disguise their identity,' he tells her. 'The principle of Taqiyah permits the true believer to deny his faith, to drink wine or eat pork, in order to evade capture.'

When he is finished she covers her head with a shower cap and waits thirty minutes before conditioning her hair and rinsing it in cold water.

'I've always wanted to be a blonde,' she says.

'It will take several more goes,' he says. 'You can do me next.'

He carries a chair into the bathroom and sits on it so that she can reach his head. She eases the bathrobe off his shoulders to avoid it getting stained and places her hands on the broad sweep of his collarbones where the tips of the tattooed antlers reach. She feels the strength in him, coiled like a spring.

His hair is too short to be clipped and she applies the peroxide liberally to his scalp and then snaps the shower cap in place.

'Stay there,' she says.

She makes tea and carries him a cup. He is sitting with his eyes closed, with the bathrobe open to the navel, the dark tines of the stag's antlers curling across on his ribs and clavicles. She wants to touch him but she leaves the cup on the sink and retreats to the bedroom where she sits on the bed and waits with a growing sense of excitement while the minutes tick by.

The bathroom door opens and she looks up.

His erection is as magnificent as she imagined: the shaft long and smooth, the head rounded like the unopened bud of a flower. She slips out of the bathrobe and kneels naked before him like a supplicant.

He comes quickly and without warning in her mouth.

Then he picks her up and carries her back to the bed. A few moments later, lying beside him, she asks him his name.

'It's Guy.'

They doze for a while, drifting in and out of sleep with their limbs sliding in and out of contact. When she wakes and lifts herself on to her elbows he is staring intently at her chest and thighs.

He reaches for his knife. 'May I?'

She is sure that he does not mean to kill her, not yet anyway. She nods, excited by what she thinks he is asking for.

He cups one of her breasts in his hands and presses the point of the freshly sharpened blade to the flesh beside the nipple. She feels a brief stinging sensation as he cuts a diagonal line across her skin. Then he puts the knife down quickly and presses his lips to the wound.

'My darling,' she murmurs, holding his head in her hands.

Later, after they have slept some more, she asks him about the Engineer.

He smiles. 'It was a myth; a sleight of hand designed to confound our enemies and disguise our identities. There was no Engineer. We made him up. I designed the ambushes. Nasruddin's job was to play the villain. He handled all the goods and claimed responsibility afterwards.'

'And they never found out?'

'They did, eventually. After they'd captured and questioned Nasruddin.'

'That's when the Old Man cut a deal?'

'Sure. Queen Bee got to maintain the pretence that Nasruddin was a terrorist and not an out-of-work actor and I was kept locked up.'

'And in return, what did the Old Man get?'

'Dollars, of course.'

'So, what changed?'

'Nasruddin was back in play and the Old Man knew his time was up. Dollars had ceased being of much importance to him. He wanted to go out with a bang not a whimper.'

'Did he know that you were going to kill him?'

'He knew.' Guy shrugged. 'That's why he put it off so long.'

'So where do we go next?' she asks.

'Slovakia.'

The taxi drops them outside an apartment block on a dead-end road near some train tracks. Stairs lead down below street level to a shop with camouflage netting hanging from the ceiling. A bottle of schnapps with a picture of Adolf Hitler on the label stands in a glass display cabinet. On the countertop there is a loose-leaf binder with writing in several languages on the cover. In English, it says: *Most of the expansion weapons are originals with minor modifications which disable the shooting with sharp ammunition.* While they are waiting, Guy flicks through the pages of modified pistols and assault rifles.

A slender young man with round wire-framed glasses appears from through a bead curtain and stands at the counter. He seems reluctant to meet their eye.

'I have come to collect an order,' Guy tells him, 'for two Heckler & Koch MP5 sub-machine guns and two Glock 19 9 mm pistols, repurposed as originals with fresh barrels, twelve M85 anti-personnel fragmentation grenade hulls with matching fuse assemblies, and twenty-four PETN electrical detonators.'

He passes a slip of paper with the Zcash transaction number for the deposit across the counter and waits while the young man consults a laptop.

'Most people order Ceskas, Zastavas and Tokarevs,' he says. 'It was not so easy to find HKs and Glocks.'

'But you've got them?' Guy says.

'Sure. You want to try the HKs?'

'Yes.'

'I will take you to the range.'

The young man makes a brief call and then tells them to wait outside. They stand in the street while the man locks up the shop and then all get in a rickety old Volkswagen Golf. They drive through the forest for half an hour on tarmac roads and then turn off on a gravel track that leads to an abandoned quarry. There is a white Mercedes waiting for them in the quarry and a man in a black leather trench coat standing beside it, smoking a cigarette.

He nods at them without speaking and opens the boot of his car where the weapons are laid out on tarpaulin next to several cardboard boxes of 9 mm calibre ammunition.

Zeina watches while Guy charges the magazines with live rounds and the two Slovakians get inside the Mercedes.

Guy gives Zeina one of the machine guns as they walk together to the firing point. There are rows of black silhouette paper targets on wooden posts out to two hundred metres.

Guy spends an hour zeroing the HK machine guns out to a hundred metres with the barrel resting on a pile of sandbags. When he is done, he hands one of the machine guns to Zeina and stands alongside her as she fires three-round bursts from standing, kneeling and prone positions. Several times he adjusts her firing position. After each burst, they walk up to the target and inspect the groupings on the target. They glue fresh targets over the used ones using a paintbrush and glue from a tin can.

Finally, Guy announces that he is satisfied. They return the weapons to the boot of the Mercedes and the young man drives them back to the shop where Guy logs on and transfers the outstanding balance of payment.

'We will send the disassembled weapons in component parts by courier to as many different addresses as you provide us with,' the young man says. 'The likelihood of interception is extremely low.'

He smiles for the first time since they entered the shop. 'It would be like holding back the sea for every parcel to be searched. What do you want me to do with the detonators?'

'We'll take them with us now,' Guy tells him.

The man unlocks a glass cabinet under the counter and removes two olive-drab plastic boxes, one square and one round, with *Detonators Electric, L2A2, Grenade Fuses, L2A2* and corresponding NATO stock numbers printed on them.

That night in Prague, they climb an unlit stairway in a crumbling art-deco housing block and knock on the door of an apartment. Guy is carrying a holdall full of cash and Zeina is wearing a brand new Burberry raincoat. With her blonde hair and sunglasses, she feels like a gangster's moll.

A man wearing a Halloween mask opens the door.

'What's the password?' he says.

'Kill all the lawyers.'

Satisfied, the man leads them down a corridor to a steel door with a Plexiglas window set in it and a sliding metal box like they use in gas stations. The man knocks on the door and the drawer slides open. Guy fills the drawer with bundles of cash and pushes it closed.

They wait while the cash is counted.

The drawer slides open again. Guy reaches inside and takes out a USB drive. He pockets it and winks at Zeina.

Two days later they cross the channel in a rigid-hulled inflatable, leaving a small fishing village near Calais under cover of darkness and landing just before dawn on a secluded stretch of beach at the base of a chalk cliff on the south coast of England.

Guy jumps clear of the boat and wades forward through the surf before falling on his hands and knees on the pebbles and kissing the ground.

41

Without conscience

Jude walks through the quiet streets of Pimlico and approaches the redbrick 1930s monolith that is Dolphin Square, traditional home to retired and serving MPs, peers and civil servants, including spies. It's the kind of sharp-edged Fascist-era architecture that usually provokes a rebellious anti-establishment response in him. He walks through an archway beneath its martial ranks of white-framed windows into the courtyard beyond.

He crosses the gardens in the square, passing pensioners sitting in pairs on park benches in the late summer sun, and enters Raleigh House on the south side.

He rides an elevator as narrow as a coffin to the ninth floor.

Baroness Fowle is a small, steely-eyed woman with a bluish sheen to her skin. She is wearing an Alice band, a cashmere sweater, a string of pearls and a navy corduroy skirt. She stares coolly up at him from the doorway.

'My name is Jude Lyon,' he says and shows her his Foreign Office pass.

'Of the Bowes-Lyons?'

'I'm afraid not,' he replies. He is tempted to say 'of the Jew Lyons'.

If she is disappointed she chooses to hide it. 'What can I do for you, Mr Lyon?' she asks, politely.

'I'd like to talk to you about your son, Guy.'

The reaction is barely perceptible, a narrowing of her eyes and a tightening of her gnarled, liver-spotted grip on a silver-topped walking stick.

'Have you found his body?'

'I believe that your son is alive,' Jude tells her.

'You had better come in,' she says.

The sitting room is tiny and stuffed with furniture that is too large for it, the remnants of a collection that looks like it used to grace a Highland castle. The largest item is a portrait of the Baroness's father, a kilted Brigadier in service dress and a black glengarry, with a stern and disapproving expression on his face.

'Please sit down.'

She perches stiffly on the edge of chair upholstered in a hunting tartan and he sits opposite her. She grips the walking stick and does not take her eyes off him. She is as alert as a bird of prey. 'I've lost count of the hours I spent asking myself, what next? Then for ten years I dared to believe that he might be gone. I can't tell you how relieved that made me feel. What news do you have, Mr Lyon?'

'I believe that he is on his way to this country.'

This does not appear to surprise her. 'What more can you tell me?'

'Hardly anything,' Jude admits. It's astonishing really, in this age of data, that someone could be so invisible. 'That's why I'm here. Your son's school, medical, dental and army records are all either missing or destroyed. He doesn't have a valid driving licence, national insurance number or a passport. No bank account or credit cards.'

'Have you spoken to my former husband?'

'Not yet.'

'And what do you know about me?'

'That you are a prominent physician and academic. That you were made a life peer in 2004.'

'So, you'll appreciate the bitter irony of it. I spent my entire career in the National Health Service in Scotland, Mr Lyon, as a practitioner, a manager, and an academic. I worked in the Hebrides and then across Argyll and the nation. I have devoted my life to curing people, irrespective of class or behaviour. But I could not cure my son.'

'I simply want to understand.'

'You will never understand my son, Mr Lyon.'

'I need to know more about him,' Jude replies. 'If I am to stop him.'

'Very well.' She closes her eyes and then opens them again. 'From very early Guy was wilful, aggressive and deceitful. All children are deceitful and manipulative to a degree, but we were painfully aware that it was more than that. We knew something was wrong before he started school. By the age of five he believed that he could get away with almost anything. We thought his sister Katherine had a problem with her tummy, but it turned out that he was punching her in the stomach at night. We had to lock her door. After that it was the cat. I caught him trying to flush it down the toilet. He wasn't bothered at all about being caught. When I told my husband and he asked him about it, Guy calmly denied that anything had happened. The cat lasted another two weeks. We found her staked to a tree with her stomach hanging out. There were a lot more animals after that, frogs and rabbits to begin with. Then family pets began to disappear across the island that we were living on. The authorities never linked him to it but I knew.

'By the age of twelve he was procuring girls, including Katherine, for sexual favours for the older children. We had no choice but to send him off the island to a boarding school. He lasted a year before the headmaster asked that he be removed. He said that Guy was a cold and self-sufficient child who lived by his own rules and would not respect the rules of the school. The headmaster told me that these factors had played a part in the school's decision, but the real reason for the expulsion was that he was an accomplished thief. Another school took him and another after that. As long as we were prepared to pay we secured a few months at each new school. I used to dread the school holidays. I couldn't leave him alone with Katherine.

'By the time he was fifteen we had tried everything: punishment, family arguments, threats, pleas, none of it made the slightest difference. I even referred him to one of my more discreet colleagues, a psychiatrist with a reputation for working with troubled teenagers. My colleague committed suicide not long after. I suppose that was the last straw. And so, I left. I took Katherine with me and moved away. I ceased all contact with my son.

'And then he changed, or at least that's what my ex-husband told me via my solicitor. I suppose that, for a short time, I hoped that it might be true. But no, he was perfecting his act. He stopped getting caught and he started covering his tracks. From then on, he was careful, with a clear eye for the consequences. I believe that, on at least one occasion, he evaded a drug smuggling charge by implicating one of his fellow pupils. I know that there are many others whose lives were ruined by my son, Mr Lyon. He was bright enough to get through his final years of school and then university without drawing the attention of the police. I heard that he sailed through the Regular Commissions Board of the army. Either he falsified his school records or he destroyed them. I believe that the first boarding school that we sent him to was destroyed in a fire. Then again maybe the army didn't check. He can be very convincing when he wants to be.'

'And you didn't try and warn the army?'

Her pupils constrict and he glimpses something cold and ruthless beneath the mask of politeness. 'Are you a parent?'

'No.'

'Then you have no right to judge me.'

He chooses to ignore her response. 'When did you last see him?'

She is silent for a while, as if deciding whether to terminate the discussion.

'The same year we invaded Iraq,' she says, eventually. 'Guy had finally been thrown out of the army. He showed up at my door demanding money. He seemed aggrieved that he wasn't going to war. In those days, I carried a can of Mace in my bag. I used it on him.'

'Has he tried to communicate with you since then?'

'No.'

After a pause, Jude says. 'Thank you for your time.'

'Before you go, Mr Lyon, tell me this: is it true what Ms Camilla Church told me, that my son is a traitor responsible for the death of all those soldiers?'

'I believe so.'

She looks away. 'I wish I had smothered him at birth.'

42

First post

You'd miss it if you weren't looking for it: an over-stuffed architectural salvage shop with a narrow frontage, hidden behind vendors' stalls selling handbags and imported Japanese phone cases, on Leather Lane, one of the city's winding medieval streets. Zeina looks through the smeary glass past the 'Closed' sign and sees items both large and small, from ostrich eggs and Victorian pith helmets to Edwardian dressers and coat racks, as well as a menagerie of taxidermy, including a snarling stoat in a tank on a writing bureau and a plunging white owl with its claws outstretched.

Beside her, Guy pulls a lever and an old bell jangles loudly somewhere inside. After a while, an elderly man in black shuffles out of the depths of the shop. The crown of his head is bald but he has a fringe of grey hair from ear to ear that hangs down to his shoulders.

'Can't you read the sign?' he says through the glass and coughs. 'I don't take kindly to visitors.'

'I've got a message for you, Mr Underhill,' Guy says. He takes the first of the letters out of its envelope and presses it up to the glass. The man plucks at several pairs of glasses and a jeweller's loupe that are hanging around his neck before settling on a pair of tortoiseshell frames and propping them on his nose. He reads the letter carefully through the glass and then glances up at them both over the top of his frames.

'Zahir was very complimentary about your skills,' Guy says, folding the letter and returning it to his pocket.

Underhill reaches down and pulls back a bolt at the foot of the door and reaches up to pull one back at the top of the door before turning a key in the lock and letting them in.

'Close it behind you,' Underhill says. He shuffles back down a narrow path, only wide enough for one person at a time, between vertically stacked fireplaces and church pews piled to the ceiling. 'And bring the key with you.'

Zeina throws the bolts and locks the door. Pocketing the key, she sets off after Guy and the old man towards the back of the shop.

'I liked Zahir,' Underhill says, pausing at an intersection. In one direction, there is a row of metal-finned radiators and, in the other, silvered mirrors and wood-panelled window shutters. 'He had an eye for it, the differences in brightness and contrast.' He sets off down a trench between ranks of shutters. Several times they have to step over shoeboxes full of door handles and other bric-a-brac. 'He could tell which way a crease should run in plastic. He had a neat hand and he was patient with glue.'

Eventually Underhill stops at a large Chinese cabinet beside a smiling blackamoor holding a tasselled lamp and produces another key. He unlocks the cabinet and the doors swing open. Behind it there is a brick wall with a metal door inset in it.

'It pays to be cautious in this business,' Underhill says. 'I expect it's the same for you?'

Guy does not reply and Underhill shrugs and uses another key to open the door. Inside there is a small, brightly lit room with floor-to-ceiling industrial cabinets with labelled drawers covering two walls and open galvanized steel shelving on the other two packed with electronics and rolls of plastic. In one corner, there is a stool in front of a rigged-up sheet with a camera on a tripod facing it. At a green baize-topped desk there is a black plastic chopping board, a neat row of scalpels, an angle-poise lamp and an up-to-date Mac desktop computer with several different printers and a laminating machine stacked on shelves beside it.

Underhill sits behind the desk. The only other place to sit is the stool in front of the camera and so Zeina sits there. Guy stands. His presence fills the room with menace.

'What's in the bag?' Underhill asks, considering the holdall in Guy's hand.

'Cash.'

'Is it genuine?'

'Check for yourself.'

Guy puts the holdall on the desk on top of the chopping board. Underhill continues to stare at it without making a move towards it.

'I'd like to see the letter again,' he says.

'Of course.'

Guy takes it out of his pocket and puts it on the table beside the bag. Underhill opens a drawer in the desk and retrieves a pair of latex gloves, which he snaps on his wrists. He unfolds the letter, puts on one of the pairs of glasses around his neck and switches on the angle-poise lamp, lowering it to within a few inches of the paper. He reads it again, more slowly this time. 'It's not like him to use a pencil but I'd recognise his handwriting anywhere,' he says. 'He had a beautiful hand. He used to do calligraphy for that place he worshipped at. I told him don't ever do anything you're not getting paid for. He'd laugh at that. I was disappointed when he left. We could have made some good money. But he got political. I'm not political.'

'Neither are we,' Guy says, with a smile. 'We're just ordinary decent criminals.'

'What do you want?' Underhill asks, eventually.

'I need five clean credit profiles including ready-to-use credit cards,' Guy tells him, 'MasterCard or Visa, I don't care which, but they must have at least a £10,000 limit on each of them and five separate billing addresses. I'll be making a number of retail and wholesale purchases online. They need to be good for at least seven days. I also need a clean driving licence to match each of the profiles. And I need it all today.'

Underhill nods as if the requirement is not unusual. 'You want paper evidence: wage slips, council tax receipts, gas or electricity bills, that kind of stuff?'

'For one of them,' Guy says, 'enough to lease a commercial unit. For the others, as long as the credit histories stand up to scrutiny that will be sufficient.'

'What about passports?'

'No.'

Underhill reaches forward, unzips the holdall and considers the contents. He takes out ten bundles of fifty twenty-pound notes and stacks them side by side on the desk. He slips off the rubber band holding together the first bundle, breaks it like a deck of cards and runs the upward note under a desktop UV scanner. He does this several times for each bundle, scanning the notes randomly, until he is satisfied.

'As you can see, I am prepared to pay generously for speed, quality and discretion,' Guy says.

'Whose face goes on the licences?' Underhill asks.

'Mine.'

Underhill glances at Zeina and back to Guy again. 'Just you?'

'That's right.'

'You better go and get yourself cleaned up for the photos,' he says. 'You look like you slept under a hedge.' It's not so far from the truth. 'There's a sink out there. Turn right by the radiators. There are also some clothes on a rack.'

After he is gone, Underhill looks at Zeina. 'Would you like a cup of tea?'

When she nods he produces a Thermos flask from under his desk and two paper cups from a drawer.

'How is Zahir?' he asks, casually, as he fills the cups.

'He's fine,' she says. The tea is strong and sweet with barely any milk. 'He's happy with his work.'

'You can give me the front door key back now,' Underhill says.

'Sorry.' She passes it to him. He pockets it.

'Your friend makes quite an impression,' Underhill says, 'and not a favourable one. How long have you been together?'

'Not long,' she says.

'I met people like him when I was in prison. I tried to steer clear of them.'

She doesn't reply.

'What I don't understand is why Zahir didn't do this work for you wherever you came from?'

'We were on the move,' Guy adds from the doorway. Zeina is always surprised at how silently he moves. His face is clean and his dyed blonde hair is swept back from his face. He has changed his hoodie for a white shirt and a double-breasted suit jacket. 'We didn't want to cross an international border with multiple identities for fear of raising suspicion.' He smiles at Underhill. 'Does that answer your question?'

Underhill nods. 'Of course.' He looks at Zeina. 'You'll need to give up that seat for your friend.'

She stands and Guy takes her place at the stool.

'Stare straight at the camera,' Underhill says. 'Don't smile.'

He takes several shots and then removes the memory card from the camera and slots it into a port on the desktop. 'This is going to take a few hours. I need to buy the numbers on a carder site and test them before I manufacture the actual cards. Only once the cards are done will I go ahead with the driving licences and the other items. You don't need to stay.'

'I have things to do,' Guy says, taking off the jacket. 'But my friend here will remain with you.'

'Of course,' Underhill says. 'You don't trust me. I get it.'

43

Mr Kurtz

'I said to him what use is an accountant in Syria.' Abdul shakes his head, sorrowfully. 'He wouldn't listen. I blame his late father for filling his head full of nonsense.'

They are sitting beside each other on the cream leather upholstery of Abdul Rahman's Mercedes outside the largest of his eponymous cash and carry stores in one of the narrow side streets behind Brick Lane. Guy is wearing a hoodie and a black beanie hat with a pair of wraparound sunglasses. Abdul's bulky Sikh driver is eyeing Guy suspiciously in the rear-view mirror.

'Tell me this. Why shouldn't I just tear this up?' Abdul says, waving the letter from his nephew in his hand.

Guy shrugs and removes his sunglasses. 'It's not the letter that counts it's the information that it contains. One call to the taxman with the account numbers and you're in a world of pain.'

Abdul continues shaking his head. 'Why did he give you this information?'

'I told him that it was necessary to grab your attention.'

'You have my attention.'

'Good.'

Guy takes the black holdall from between his feet and places it on the seat between them.

'Go on, open it,' he says.

Abdul unzips the bag with shaking hands and looks at the bundles of cash inside with a mixture of horror and confusion.

'What do you want?'

'I need a range of different shipping addresses for products that I order. You have a sufficient number of shop premises across London for my purposes. The parcel deliveries will start tomorrow and continue for a few days. Most will be national but there will be some international deliveries. All will be addressed to you personally but with the word 'Kurtz' in brackets after your name. You need to warn your workforce to set them aside for you and not to open them. When the deliveries are complete, you will bring them together and deliver them in a single consignment to me in a van that you will drive. No passengers and no followers. And believe me, I'll know if there are.'

Abdul nods.

'What are you buying?' he asks.

'Chemicals and lab equipment, and some protective clothing.'

'You're cooking meth.'

It's not a question; it's a statement. Guy doesn't bother to correct him. Cooking meth seems to be pretty low on the list of bad things Abdul thinks Guy might be up to. In fact, he looks pathetically grateful that it's only drugs.

'There's a phone in the bag with the money,' Guy explains. 'When the time comes I'll let you know when to centralise the parcels and then I'll the send you an address for the delivery.'

'I understand. Everything will happen as you have determined,' Abdul says enthusiastically. He seems to imagine that there is now some kind of kinship between them. 'There is something else though.'

Guy stares at him.

Abdul is trembling and smiling at the same time, 'I don't want you selling it in my community.'

'We'll talk about that when it's cooked,' Guy says.

'How is my nephew?' Abdul blurts out.

'He's dead.'

Guy opens the car door but pauses and looks back before getting out. 'Releasing the information in this letter is the least of what will happen to you if you cross me. Do you understand?'

'I understand,' Abdul says.

Guy walks across Spitalfields, Shoreditch and Clerkenwell with his sunglasses on and his beanie hat pulled down over his ears.

When he rings the bell to Underhill's shop, Zeina comes to answer. She kisses him passionately on the mouth in the narrow corridor between the stacks of salvage. He surprises himself by returning her kiss with equal passion. He usually tires quickly of women but there is an unusual quality about Zeina that retains his interest.

'He's finished. It all looks good,' Zeina tells him. She takes him by the hand and leads him to the back of the shop to Underhill's hidden office where he has the credit cards and licences fanned out on the green felt.

He looks up at Guy with sly satisfaction on his face.

'All you need to do now is sign them and start using them.' He scoops up the cards and licences and puts them in a brown manila envelope, which he offers across the desk. 'Even though I say it myself, I think I've done you a hell of a job.'

Guy nods. 'Good.'

'Now fuck off out of my life.'

'There's no need to be rude,' Guy says. There's no overt threat in the words. His tone seems pleasant enough. But she can see the signs that Underhill doesn't seem to notice: the reasoned words, the deadened voice and the sudden slight tension of a body rising to critical mass. 'I can't abide that.'

Guy grabs him by the wrist and with his other hand sticks his knife in Underhill's scrawny neck. He twists the blade and cuts the artery. Underhill's head snaps backwards and as his hands clutch at the air, bright red arterial blood sprays across the walls and equipment.

While Zeina stands watching Underhill bleed out, Guy goes out into the shop and returns a minute or so later with an old cricket bat which he places on the table beside the keyboard. He pushes Underhill out of his chair on to the floor and sits at the monitor. Zeina passes him a tissue, which he uses to clean the blood off the screen. He opens a VPN link and accesses a series of websites which he uses to purchase goods using the range of credit cards, including retort bottles and glass beakers from a laboratory equipment site, hexamine blocks for camping, chest webbing and gasmasks with charcoal filters from an army surplus store site, potassium nitrate fertiliser for waterlogged lawns from Amazon, and police uniforms and tactical gear from www.policeforce supply.co.uk. In each case he pays for the swiftest possible delivery. He sends a WhatsApp message to the shop in Slovakia that is holding the gun parts and grenade hulls providing the consignee and delivery details across Abdul's range of cash and carry shops. He books a rental van for pick up later that day at Southend Airport. Finally, he places a three-month deposit with Network Rail on a storage unit in an unlined railway arch in Shadwell, arranging to collect the keys the following day.

When he is done he uses the cricket bat to utterly destroy the computer, hard drives and the other equipment while Zeina watches. He feels the same atavistic desire to set fire to the place that he has always felt when covering his tracks but he needs more time than that would give him. Locking the old man's corpse inside his office means that it is unlikely to be found for days, weeks even.

'Get his keys,' he tells Zeina. 'Lock every door behind you. I'll meet you outside.'

Riding on the top deck of a bus, less than an hour later, with Guy beside her, Zeina thinks that the East End is no longer familiar. Around them there are shiny new tower blocks that were not there before and on the Bow flyover she catches glimpses of the Olympic Park. She had fled the country before the Games were held but she remembers the day in 2005 that the city was awarded them, or rather she remembers the day after – the 7/7 London bombings. An experience that should have been horrifying but one that drew her to it like a strange compulsion: within hours she was standing on Tavistock Square staring across the police barriers at the remains of the bus that had been covered in tarpaulin. People were talking about a man exploding and the back of the bus flying through the air, that and the three other bombs on the underground. She remembers feeling a rush of excitement and a stab of something like jealousy. Even then the desire for self-destruction was strong in her.

'Okay?' Guy asks her.

'I was thinking about 7/7.'

'We'll do better than that,' he says. 'I promise.'

She believes him.

They take a train from Stratford and arrive at Southend Airport at dusk. Guy uses one of his recently acquired identities to hire a white mini-van that they drive out of the airport.

Fifteen minutes later Guy parks outside a pebble-dashed semi-detached house on a crescent of identical homes on a housing estate on the outskirts of Southend. He hands Zeina a letter.

'Your turn.'

She gets out of the van and walks up the driveway past a child's tricycle to the front door. She presses the buzzer and listens to the commotion inside.

A large man with a bushy beard and a small child peeping out from between his knees opens the door.

'Salaam, brother Mohammed,' she says. 'I bring news of Hasib.'

His eyes widen.

'What is it Daddy?' the child says.

'Nothing,' he says.

'Can I come in?'

He steps aside to let her in. She glimpses a woman in hijab looking up from a stove in a kitchen at the end of the corridor.

'Go to your mother,' the man tells the child. He opens the door to the nearest room and ushers Zeina in. It is a small sitting room with leather armchairs, a television and framed calligraphy on the walls.

She gives him the letter and watches while he reads it twice. When he is done he seems reluctant to meet her gaze.

'How much do you want?'

'Four twenty-five litre bottles.'

'I'm opening up the factory tomorrow,' Mohammed tells her. 'Come to the loading bay at 8 a.m. I'll have it for you then.'

'Thank you,' she says.

The moon has come up over the horizon, a full shamanic moon that illuminates the Essex marshlands. In its light, they park in a deserted layby beside a muddy creek feeding into one of the lesser tributaries of the River Thames. Guy gets out of the van and Zeina follows him to the edge of the creek where she watches him urinate with his eyes closed. The air smells of mud and rotting vegetation.

'We'll sleep in the back of the van tonight,' he says. 'Tomorrow we'll have somewhere to stay.'

They spoon beneath their coats in the back of the van. Her dreams, which follow one after another, are filled with violence: her mother with a knife in her hands and a burning building behind her; something about a crazy mullah and a Koran with blood on it; something terrifying rising from the mud. When she wakes, she feels like weeping.

He orders two teas and a bacon-and-egg roll from a roadside caravan.

'Want one?'

She shakes her head.

'We're hiding amongst the heathens,' he says. He winks and bites. She watches a dribble of bright yellow egg yolk run down his chin.

'Fuck, I missed bacon,' he says, between mouthfuls.

He pulls her to him. She is revolted and excited by the taste of pork on his breath.

'You're going to heaven,' he tells her and kisses her.

At 8 a.m. they are parked outside a single-storey brick building that houses a factory that manufactures car batteries in a nondescript business park on the edge of the Thames Estuary. They sit and wait, staring out across the reed beds and winding channels of the marsh. Five minutes later, Mohammed Naser emerges from a loading bay carrying two black containers marked *H2SO4 (sulphuric acid)*. She gets out and opens the rear door of the van. He places them on the plywood floor beside their rolled up sleeping bags and goes back for two more. When all four containers are in the van, he walks away without speaking or acknowledging her presence.

44

Born not made

It's a forty-minute flight from Glasgow. The tiny plane crosses the water and flies in over the craggy, densely wooded eastern coast on the leeward side of the island, and across the barren moorland and beaches of the windward side.

The plane lands and taxies to a halt on the island's runway. A round man with a clipboard is waiting on the tarmac beneath an oyster coloured sky. He walks Jude to the nearest car and makes him sign the rental agreement in triplicate.

'You'll know where you're going?' he says, in a soft Hebridean accent.

'Breothadh.'

The man looks at him strangely and seems on the point of saying something but then thinks better of it.

'It's at the end of the county road,' he says, handing over the keys. 'Just keep on until there's nowhere else to go.'

'Right,' Jude says. He looks in the car's rear-view mirror as he is leaving the car park and sees the man talking to someone on his mobile phone.

The road south across the island is straight as a compass needle. The surrounding moor is marked at intervals by black peat cuttings like knife slashes.

The moor ends at a village with a ferry port and a crescent of cottages strung along a broad bay. From the village a single-track road follows the coastline, climbing and descending through heavily wooded inlets, the last remnants of a primeval forest. Twice he passes white painted customs sheds and glimpses the maltings towers of whisky distilleries between the trees. It begins to spit with rain.

The only car he sees after the village is a red postal van parked in a passing place at the side of the road. The postie gets out as Jude approaches and waves him down.

Jude lowers the car window and the postie leans in.

'I hear you're going to Breothadh?'

He knows now who the man in the car park was talking to as he left. 'That's right.'

'Have you been there before?'

'No.'

'Do they know you're coming?'

'No.'

'You might get a better reception if you take the post.'

'Okay.'

The postie looks relieved. He fetches a Royal Mail pouch from the back of his van and passes it through the window.

'I haven't been up here for a few days,' he says. 'The house is down beyond the castle. If he agrees to talk to you, tell him his granddaughter needs new shoes.'

Jude continues driving along the road until the tarmac runs out at two lichen-stained granite gateposts that mark the entrance to the estate. Each one is topped with whale vertebrae with the silvery patina of driftwood. A wooden sign reads:

Breothadh Estate
KEEP OUT

Jude decides to leave the car and continue on foot. Glancing at his phone he sees that there is no longer a signal.

He advances down a rutted gravel drive beneath dripping beech trees that are draped in moss. The sides of the track are thick with cushioning moss and bright green ferns and in several places the track is divided by streams. Abruptly, the track enters a broad area of grass, the remnants of parkland dotted with old oaks. There are two grazing roe deer that look up as he approaches and take flight.

The track leads up to the ruins of a castle destroyed by fire. It's five storeys high and has a tower and small windows set well above the ground. It's the sort of fortified house that was necessary back in the time when being the head of a clan meant defending yourself. Now it is charred and roofless.

Jude walks up the steps, ducking his head as he enters the low doorway set in walls several feet thick. He stands at the centre of what must once have been a large hall that is now overgrown with brambles and stares up through the blackened timbers towards the sky.

When he looks down again there is a young woman pointing a rifle at him. He raises his arms in surrender.

'Who are you?' she demands.

'My name is Jude Lyon. I work for the Foreign Office.'

'What do you want?'

'I want to speak to you and your father.' When she doesn't reply he says, 'It's Katherine, isn't it?'

'Put the bag down and move back.'

He backs up five paces.

She advances towards him slowly and nudges the pouch with her foot. Her eyes flick down and up again. She is wearing a beanie hat with strands of blonde hair poking out.

'What's in it?'

'Your mail,' he tells her. 'Can I put my hands down now?'

'Turn around and lift your jacket,' she says.

He obeys. 'I'm not carrying a weapon.'

'You can pick the bag up again.'

She steps back out of reach and allows him to pass.

'You can go on,' she says. 'I'll follow.'

He leaves the ruins of the castle and proceeds down the track with the woman walking a few steps behind him. Soon they are walking through a wood of overgrown exotics that give off a resinous smell: swamp cypress, eucalyptus and Douglas firs. They pass a grove of giant redwoods. He glances back at her and sees that she has lowered the barrel of the rifle a few degrees.

'When was the fire?' he asks.

'When I was twelve,' she says.

'How old was Guy then?'

'Fifteen.' She raises the barrel again. 'Stop speaking.'

The track leads out on to a promontory where an old coach house and stables form a muddy courtyard. There are elderly Land Rovers parked in the yard, two of them up on blocks. As they approach a door opens on the other side of the yard, and a large wolfhound lopes towards them. Jude stops and lets the dog sniff his fingers.

Angus Fowle appears in the doorway. He is tall and rangy with a full head of swept-back grey hair, overgrown eyebrows and a thicket in each nostril. He is wearing a weathered Barbour jacket and muddy wellingtons, and holding a shotgun levelled at Jude.

'I'm Jude Lyon.'

'He says he's with the Foreign Office,' Katherine adds.

'Did Samantha Burns send you?' There is a sneering quality to his voice and something strange and mesmeric about his eyes.

'No.'

'What do you want?'

'I want to know about your son, Guy.'

'And how will that benefit us?'

'It might help me catch him.'

Fowle lowers the shotgun, breaks it open and returns the shells to his pockets. 'If you catch my son, Mr Lyon, it will be because he wants to get caught.'

Inside, it smells of damp and dog, garbage and chimney soot. There are piles of newspapers and dirty plates on every surface. A pair of lumpy wingback chairs with the stuffing coming out in tufts are arranged either side of a peat fire. They sit facing each other and Katherine brings them tea in chipped mugs. She stands by a window that is too dirty to see through.

'There's no money for the boiler,' Angus says. He's sorting through his mail. Most of it goes on the fire unopened. A couple of letters he tucks down the side of the chair until all that he is holding is a postcard that Jude is not close enough to see.

'The postie asked me to tell you that your granddaughter needs new shoes.'

'Look around you,' Angus says. 'Does it look like I'm in a position to carry the numerous bastards my son spawned on this island? Is Guy coming here?'

'I don't know. Will he?'

'If he comes, we're ready for him. We've got enough ammunition and food to withstand a siege. You can tell Samantha Burns that. And I've learned better than to expect any help from your lot, so don't bother pretending.'

'I spoke to your former wife.'

His face twists with sudden rage and his voice rises, 'And I suppose she blamed me? Nobody made Guy what he is. No amount of torment could have produced that outcome. Nothing happened to him. He happened to us. He's evil.'

'Evil?'

'He has Satan in him!'

Jude glances at Katherine in the window to gauge her response to the outburst, but her face remains impassive.

'I see that you don't you believe me,' Angus says, calmer now. 'You don't know him very well, then.'

'I believe that your son is a very dangerous man, Mr Fowle. And I believe that he is planning a terrorist attack in this country.'

'What do you expect me to do about that?'

'I'd like you to look at a video clip.' Jude offers his black phone. 'Will you look at it?'

'Get me my glasses,' Angus says. Katherine opens a bureau and digs about until she locates a pair of reading glasses.

Jude watches as he puts them on and looks at the screen. Katherine has crossed to stand behind him. She reaches over his shoulder and taps the screen. Together they watch Nasruddin's latest speech.

'I believe that Nasruddin al-Raqqah is a proxy,' Jude tells them, when it is done. 'Your son uses him to make threats.'

'It's Guy, all right,' Angus says. 'He could never resist bragging.'

'What does he mean by the distant fortress?'

Angus hands the postcard to Katherine who gives it to Jude.

It's a photo of the MI6 building lit up at night viewed from the other side of the Thames. Jude turns it over. *X marks the spot* is written in black felt tip alongside the address. The stamp is Bulgarian, a double decker tram. It was posted five days ago.

'That monstrosity is a big enough target for his ego,' Angus says. 'But don't underestimate his cunning. It may be a diversion designed to draw you away from the real target.'

'Do you have any idea what the real target might be?' Jude asks.

'We should show him the others,' Katherine says.

'Go on then.'

From one of the pigeonholes in the bureau, she retrieves a bundle of postcards tied with a rubber band.

'Give them to me,' Angus says. He rifles through them and starts passing them to Jude. 'They are all much the same.'

A collection of London landmarks with Dutch stamps on them, and messages scrawled in felt tip pen. One of the Houses of Parliament postmarked 2005 that has *I know where to find the Bitch* written on it.

'This one,' Katherine says, passing another to him. It's a post-card of trooping the colour postmarked 2004 with ranks of guardsmen in red coats and bearskin hats on Horse Guards Parade. The message says: *You should be proud papa: I've found a vocation. I've become an engineer.* 'We showed that to Camilla Church when she came to see us.'

'You think that any one of these could be the target?'

'Don't you?'

'Can I keep them?' Jude asks.

'Take them,' Angus tells him. 'We have no use for them.'

'Thank you,' Jude says. He stands up. Suddenly, he's feeling the lack of a phone signal acutely.

Angus remains seated. 'If you see my ex-wife again, tell her to send money. There's no money here.'

Katherine picks up her rifle and walks him out with the wolf-hound at her side.

He stops for a moment in the courtyard. He wants to say something, to offer some sympathy, but when he looks at her he sees that there's no life in her eyes.

'You need to catch him soon,' she says. 'And kill him.'

45

In the wind's singing

Jude is sitting in the departure lounge at the island's airport taking photos of the postcards on his green burner and sending them to Gretchen, when his red burner vibrates. A WhatsApp message from an unknown number:

Call me. Big news! Kirsty

He calls her back immediately.

'You okay?' he asks.

'I'm fine,' she says. 'Where are you?'

'A Scottish island.'

'What are you doing there?'

'I'll tell you when I see you. What's your big news?'

'I've found Nasruddin.'

He's impressed. 'Where?'

'On a Greek island, he called me.'

'He called you?'

'I gave his wife my business card in Jordan. She must have passed it to him in Syria. He persuaded a journalist to let him use her phone. He wants to talk.'

'Where are you?'

'Athens, waiting for a connection.'

'Okay, I'm coming.'

He starts browsing for onward flights from Glasgow.

They meet in a café on the edge of the square at the centre of the island's main town. The park in the square is a bivouac camp with families that Kirsty tells him have fled the fighting between Arabs and Afghans in the migrant camp up the road. It's eleven in the morning, Jude has flown overnight and Kirsty is drinking ouzo.

'The Greek riot police tried to drive them back into the camp but there were too many of them,' she says, angrily. 'They kept them in the midday sun for four hours before letting them through.'

A paramedic wearing a white tabard with the red logo of Médecins Sans Frontières is bandaging a child's head under a nearby tarpaulin.

'It's a fucking disgrace,' she says.

'Where's Nasruddin?' Jude asks, gently.

'He's safe for now,' she tells him. 'But he's scared. Can you guarantee his safety?'

'I've had an idea about that. I think so.'

'Come on then,' she says, leaving some euros on the table.

They walk out of town on the only road running north. After a couple of kilometres, they come across a contingent of bored-looking riot police sitting in a field with their riot shields lying on the parched grass beside them. An entrepreneurial Syrian has set up a stall selling water and soda cans opposite them. Kirsty buys a couple of litre bottles of water and gives one to Jude.

'There are six thousand people inside the wire, which is three times as many as it was designed for and another thousand, mostly men, in an overflow camp beside it they call the Castle. The aid workers pulled out when the fighting began so no one really knows what's going on inside. And the worst thing is this mess is no accident. It's a deliberate message of deterrence. The European Union has created a buffer zone of island camps so bad that they hope people will stop coming. And when the winter comes people are going to start freezing to death.'

After another couple of kilometres, they come over the top of a rise and catch sight of the camp in a natural bowl at the base of a mountain. Kirsty approaches the gates of the camp, which are open, but just before she reaches the entrance she turns off on a path that runs alongside the barbed wire fence and through the overflow camp, and then climbs the wooded mountainside.

It takes them about an hour to reach the top.

Nasruddin's hideaway is in a glade that is partially concealed by trees and bushes. The view from the mountaintop is stunning – white cliffs, black-pebble beaches, and a sparkling azure sea. On one of the trees there is a painted wooden sign that reads in English: 'this place is not exclusively for one person. It is a home for every person in need. Please do not use filthy words and don't live without manners. You have to be a real person even in the most difficult situations.'

Kirsty leads him to a tent at the edge of the glade where a man is sitting beside a fire with a blackened kettle on it.

In the flesh, Nasruddin doesn't look the scary villain of the video messages. Without the hair and beard, he is slight, dwarfed by a sweater that is several sizes too large for him.

Jude sits down on the ground beside him with the fire between them.

'This is the man that I told you about,' Kirsty says, sitting beside Jude. 'He says that he can help you.'

'You look tired,' Nasruddin says. He has soulful eyes and a world-weary expression. 'Would you like some tea?'

'Yes please,' Jude replies.

Nasruddin pours tea into three glasses.

'I'm sorry but there's no sugar,' he says, handing them a glass each.

'I prefer it that way,' Kirsty says.

Jude sips his tea. 'Thank you,' he says. 'My name is Jude Lyon and I work for the British government. But I am not your enemy. My aim is to uncover the truth about what happened to you. I know that you're not the Engineer. I understand that you were forced against your will to say the things that you did.'

Nasruddin closes his eyes and opens them again. 'Thank you.'

'I can help you,' Jude tells him, 'but I need to know how you got here and who you were with, where you were going and what were you going to do there.'

Nasruddin nods, gravely. 'Of course.' When he speaks it is with a quiet dignity that seems extraordinary for all that he has suffered. 'I'm sorry that I cannot tell you the details of the attack. The Stranger would not trust me with that kind of information. But I can tell you that it is coming and your country is the target. He will use explosives and other means. As for my role, the Stranger has an aversion to cameras but he wants, or rather needs, someone to speak for him. I was to be the face of the attack.'

He goes on to describe the overnight hike through the mine-fields that marked the Syrian border and the bus journey across Turkey that felt like it would never end. The days spent waiting in the port town, while vomiting and diarrhoea wracked the Stranger, the terrifying night journey across the sea that ended in disaster. How he passed out after the boat sank and came to on a beach at dawn surrounded by the corpses of the drowned. He describes how the woman Zeina had cared for the Stranger with a tenderness that suggested intimacy.

'What can you tell me about her?' Jude asks.

'She was English but from Pakistan or India, I think.' He closes his eyes and describes her from memory, her height and weight and her glossy black hair, the mole on her face and the marks of self-harm on her forearms. He shakes his head, sorrowfully. 'There was something not right about her.'

'What do you mean by that?'

'To survive in the company of the Stranger it is necessary to observe certain rules. Anyone who lasts more than a few days with him knows that: he tires of people easily so it's best to keep your distance. You should never touch him. The most important rule is not to make eye contact. He has killed men for less.'

'But she'd look him in eye?' Kirsty asks.

Nasruddin nods his head. 'That's right. I wouldn't say that she was without fear. She was frightened. You could see her trembling. But there was this ... excitement ... as well. Anticipation. Eagerness. Like a bride on her wedding night. And he didn't seem to mind. In fact, he seemed genuinely interested in her. I couldn't understand why but then I heard them talking by the fire. He knew some things about her. That she had been a policewoman in London. That she lived at home with her mother. And then I understood why he was so interested. He knew that she had used a baton to kill her mother. You know, I think he envied her for that.'

'Excuse me,' Jude tells him. He stands up and walks across the clearing. With Kirsty beside him, he calls Gretchen. 'We're looking for a South Asian woman in her mid-twenties. She served in the police. She is probably wanted in connection with the death of her mother.'

'Hang on.'

He listens to Gretchen's fingers on the keyboard.

The reply is almost immediate. 'Her name is Zeinab Hussein, known as Zeina. She fled the country six years ago and is wanted for questioning in connection with the death of her mother, Benazir Hussein. She was beaten to death with a police-issue baton. Zeinab's prints were found on it. She is believed to be in Pakistan.'

'Not any more. She's on her way home. Find a photo and circulate it to Counter Terrorism Command and the Border Force. And get them to put out an Interpol Red Notice.'

'Sure thing.'

He cuts the connection and immediately dials Chuka.

'Hang on,' Chuka tells him. 'I need to step out of a meeting.'

Jude waits patiently.

'Shoot,' Chuka tells him, a few moments later.

'I'm putting you on speaker phone,' Jude tells him. 'I'm with Kirsty McIntyre.'

'Okay,' Chuka replies, cautiously. 'Why is she on the call?'

'I want a witness.'

'This is not the way we do things, Jude.'

'I know the real identity of the Stranger,' Jude tells him, making eye contact with Kirsty whose eyes widen in surprise.

'Okay,' Chuka says.

'But before I tell you who he is, I need you to do something for me.'

'Go on.'

'We're with Nasruddin. He's prepared to talk. I want you to offer him and his family witness protection and resettlement in the UK.'

There is a pause.

'It's not easy for Syrians,' Chuka replies, eventually.

'We owe him that at least!'

'Alright. I hear you.' He sighs. 'I'll talk to NCA and the PM's office.'

Jude glances at Kirsty. 'You got that?'

'I got that,' Kirsty confirms.

'The Stranger's name is Guy Fowle,' Jude tells Chuka. 'He's an ex-British army officer and his mother is in the House of Lords, Baroness Fowle.'

'Christ!'

'Fowle entered Greece by boat and he's definitely heading for the UK.'

'Where are you?'

'Greece, but I'm heading back to London.'

'Call me as soon as you land. I have to get back to the cabinet secretary.'

He cuts the connection.

Jude walks back to where Nasruddin is sitting and squats down beside them.

'I need to leave now,' he tells Nasruddin. 'I have to try and stop the Stranger. I will arrange for you to be taken into protective custody. The Greek police will come for you but they will treat you well. I'll make sure of that. And they'll keep you safe until we find you a more permanent home. Are you going to be okay here for a few more days?'

Nasruddin shrugs. 'What choice do I have?'

'I'm truly sorry for what happened to you,' Jude tells him. 'I promise you I will do everything in my power to keep you safe and if I can I will reunite you with your wife and daughter. I can't promise you where yet but you won't be going back to Syria.'

'I will never find a place more beautiful than my country,' Nasruddin tells him. 'But Syria is gone, there is no more Syria.'

Jude stands up and nods to Kirsty before walking away. She catches up with him halfway across the clearing and grabs him by the arm. He turns and she kisses him on the lips. He can taste the ouzo on her breath but it's not unpleasant. He feels something unfurl inside himself and he eagerly returns her kiss.

When they are done she cups his head in her hands and smiles.

'You've done the right thing.'

46

Cuckoos

Stevie is hunched on a square of cardboard outside the station with a guitar in his hands and a cap on the pavement in front of him. He looks older than his years, whittled down to skin and bone. In between badly played Oasis covers he wipes his nose and scratches at the back of his hands.

Zeina has been watching him for half an hour from the anonymity of a bus shelter on the other side of the road. Takings are meagre. She has only seen a couple of coins added to the cap. Most people move to the edge of the pavement to avoid him.

A young man with a Staffordshire bull terrier on a lead stops and talks to him for a few minutes, shifting restlessly from foot to foot. He gives him a cigarette and Stevie smiles at him, revealing the gaps in his teeth. The young man moves on.

Zeina takes it as her prompt. After two nights sleeping on the hard floor of the van she is desperate for a shower and a bed. She tucks her greasy, unwashed hair behind her ears and crosses the road towards him. She squats down beside him and he looks up at her with a wary expression on his face. There are dark smudges under his eyes and a cluster of sores on his lips and round his nostrils.

She smiles and speaks softly in a reassuring tone.

'Stevie?'

He looks down at his feet. 'Yes.'

'I'm Zeina. I'm a friend of Sim Card.'

He looks confused. 'Sim Card?'

'From Mrs Bingham's home,' Zeina says. 'He said you were fostered together, ages ago. You stayed in touch. You put him up a bit last year when he was passing through. Remember that, Stevie?'

He nods and smiles sadly. 'Mrs Bingham was nice.'

'He asked me to find you. He wrote a letter. I've got it here.'

She takes the envelope that she has brought from Syria from her pocket and gives it to him. She watches as he turns it over in his dirty fingers with a bewildered expression on his face.

'Open it,' she urges.

He shakes his head and passes it back to her. 'You do it. Please.'

She carefully lifts the flap with the edge of her thumbnail and tears it open. She takes out the folded sheet of paper inside and hands it to him.

She waits patiently, a Good Samaritan ministering to a damaged young man, while pedestrians pass by without giving them more than a moment's thought.

He finishes reading and looks up at her.

'You need somewhere to stay.'

'Just a few days until I get my head straight, Stevie.' She suppresses a shiver of disgust and places her hand on his arm. 'I've got a little bit of money that'll keep us going. Are you hurting, Stevie?'

He nods his head miserably.

'I can pay for a fix,' she says, 'if I can stay with you. Sim Card says you're a good man, Stevie. I need somewhere to stay. It's not safe on the streets for a girl like me.'

Stevie nods in agreement and considers the letter. 'Sim Card says you can be trusted. He says you're a good friend.'

'I can be your friend too,' she says, caressing his arm. 'Shall we go find someone who can help you, Stevie? Then we can get some provisions and go home. Is that okay, Stevie?'

Stevie's flat is at the end of a corridor on the eleventh floor of a high rise on an estate known as the Dead Flats. There is hardly any furniture and no carpet, just rough concrete covered in flattened cardboard boxes to protect against the cold. The walls are daubed with graffiti left behind by a Romanian gang who took it over and held Stevie captive for six months while they dealt drugs in the stairwells. There is a devil on the wall in the sitting room. It has red eyes, horns and bat wings, and a huge erect penis. It's convincing enough to be terrifying.

It is secure though. The Romanians left behind a smooth front door leaf of brushed steel with a spy hole. There is no visible leaf frame and three dead bolts.

It is perfect.

She puts coins in a dusty electricity meter that looks long neglected and realises that she will have to go out for light bulbs. She fills a kettle with bottled water.

Stevie is sitting in the only chair at the kitchen table with his works spread out on the scratched wooden surface. She watches with her back to the countertop while he cooks the heroin and a little water in a spoon with his lighter. He ties off his arm with his belt and goes in to the vein on the inside of his elbow. When he shoots, a cloud of bright red fills the syringe before he presses the plunger.

'Shit,' he says, with a smile.

There is a knock at the door.

She glances at Stevie but he is oblivious. She leaves the kitchen and goes to the door, pressing her eye to the spy hole. Guy is standing in the corridor, wearing a hoodie. She throws the bolts and lets him in. He strides past her and systematically checks each room, ending in the kitchen.

'Stevie?' Zeina says.

Eventually Stevie's eyes focus and he looks up in stoned terror at Guy looming over him.

'This is Guy,' Zeina says. 'He's a friend of mine. He needs somewhere to stay too. I've told him you're our saviour, Stevie.'

'You live here alone, Stevie?' Guy asks.

'Yes.'

'Are you expecting any visitors?'

'No.'

Guy looks pleased. He takes Zeina in his arms and kisses her hungrily on the lips while Stevie is watching.

★   ★   ★

They begin by cleaning the kitchen using bleach and disinfectant to scour every surface. They chip away the burned food enamelled to the cooker, unblock the build-up of cooking fat in the drains and wash away the mildewed inside of the fridge-freezer. The grease-stained pizza boxes and polystyrene containers and the curling flypapers crusted with the summer kill go in black bags that they stack in the hallway.

Next, they clean the bathroom with bleach and mildew remover; the porcelain, tiles and grout. They work side by side, standing and kneeling, and she has never felt more at ease and less in need of filling silence than she does with him. They sweep the living room and the bedroom and bag the detritus. They turn over the mattress and strip the filthy bedclothes. When they are done the hallway is stacked to the ceiling with garbage bags.

Guy goes out leaving Zeina with Stevie who is chained to a radiator in the living room, lost in a drug induced haze. She runs a bath by candlelight in the newly cleaned bathroom to prepare herself for her lover's return.

She strips naked. Uncovered there is hardly any part of her chest or thighs that does not have cuts on it. The newer ones are dark ridges of scab. In the candlelight, they shine like polished tortoiseshell.

47

Cooking

Guy parks the rental van at the front of a line of similarly unbranded white vans outside a shuttered Bengali meat bazaar in Shadwell and switches off the engine. The shop sits at the entrance to a one-way street that runs alongside the dirty brick viaduct that carries the railway tracks through east London towards the heart of the City. On one side of the single-lane street is a row of enclosed railway arches occupied by commercial units and on the other a wooden fence that marks the boundary of a low-rise housing estate. From where he is sitting in the darkness of the cab, he can see any vehicle approach the arch that he has rented, a former automotive workshop that is still advertising 'part worn and new tyres'. It's midway down the street and sits between a carpet bazaar on one side and a fish bazaar on the other. It's close to midnight and the street is deserted.

He has already texted Abdul to warn him to be ready to deliver the goods. After watching closely for fifteen minutes, he gets out of the van and walks the length of the street and back, sticking to the shadows with his woollen hat pulled low over his forehead, confirming what he believed from careful study of Google Street View when he hired the unit at the forger Charles Underhill's office – that there are no CCTV cameras.

Back in the van he texts the address of the arch to Abdul and sits and waits. Less than half an hour later, he watches impassively as a van marked *Abdul's Cash and Carry* passes him on the street with Abdul at the wheel. It pulls up outside the former tyre shop.

Guy's phone pings.

I'm here

Guy replies:

Wait

He watches as a black BMW turns into the street and parks within sight of the arch and just ahead of where he is sitting. After a couple of minutes, the flame of a lighter inside the car illuminates Abdul's driver's face and turban. The driver winds down the window and taps ash in the street. Guy smiles.

Only one.

The Sikh is keeping half an eye on Abdul's van while smoking and surreptitiously flicking through Tinder profiles on the phone in his lap when Guy reaches in and cuts his throat. Guy steps back into the shadows and watches as the man falls sideways into the passenger seat. When he is satisfied that he is dead, Guy approaches and opens the driver's side door. He cleans his Gerber blade on the man's sleeve, relieves him of his phone, winds the window up and pockets the car keys.

Back in the van he starts the engine and briefly checks his face in the mirror. There's a crimson streak of arterial blood on his left cheek. He wipes it off with his sleeve.

It's time to take delivery of the goods.

He indicates and pulls into the street. He accelerates rapidly for a few seconds and then stamps on the brake pedal as he comes up close behind Abdul's van. He gets out, strides the length of the van ahead and, without acknowledging Abdul, crosses its headlight beams, which are lighting up the entrance to the arch. He unlocks the metal shutter and rolls it up. Then he waves Abdul in, pointing him to a space alongside the inspection pit at the back of the shop. Next, he reverses the rental van in so that the tailgates of the two vans face each other. He pulls down the shutter and flips the switch on the circuit breaker. The blackened brick interior of the arch is lit up. He walks around to the back of the rental van and opens the doors and waits expectantly. The phone of the man he has just killed pings in his pocket.

Seconds later, Abdul gets out of his van and approaches.

'I have done as you wished,' he says, looking about him nervously. 'I have your packages.'

'Good. Let's get on with it.'

Abdul unlocks the rear doors and opens them. Inside there are stacks of cardboard boxes and plastic-wrapped packages. They spend ten minutes transferring them from one van to the other. When they are done, Guy fetches the holdall from the passenger seat of the rental and offers it to Abdul.

'There's the rest of your money,' he says.

When Abdul reaches out, taking hold of the grip so that they are knuckle-to-knuckle, Guy pulls the knife out of his pocket with his free hand and sticks it in Abdul's throat. It's not such a clean kill this time and he only partially severs the artery. Abdul staggers back and forth for a bit, spraying blood and pawing at his throat, before Guy kicks him into the inspection pit.

He goes out on to the street and walks back to the parked BMW. He lifts the Sikh's legs out of the foot well and heaves the corpse fully into the passenger seat. He then drives the BMW into the arch and parks beside the rental van. The corpse goes into the inspection pit along with Abdul's.

He stands above it looking down at their contorted bodies and again he feels the deep desire for conflagration. It feels sloppy to leave so much forensic evidence and there's enough fuel in the car and Abdul's van to destroy the site, but he must contain his desire for fire to buy a few extra hours preparation.

He drives the rental van out of the arch, and then returns to turn off the lights and close the shutter. He has everything he needs for the attack that he is planning.

Guy parks the van close to the entrance to the tower block. They spend an hour transferring the parcels and boxes from the van to the flat. When they are done they open a soft parcel containing camping gear and shake out the sleeping bags inside. They zip two together and sleep for a few hours.

She feels him wake suddenly beside her. The room is dark and cool, but he cannot rest. She aches for more sleep but instinct takes over. She rolls up her T-shirt and exposes her breasts. He bends over her body. She feels the cold tip of the knife and gasps as he cuts her.

She breathes the coppery smell of her own blood until he

presses his mouth to her wound. His lips make soft, suckling noises.

Her fingers play with his hair and she murmurs, 'My darling . . .'

Her mind reels, filled with lurid images of butchery, blood everywhere, blood spilling from her mother's body and soaking her trousers, Guy's bloody seed in her mouth, blood oozing from her breasts.

Exhausted, they sleep again.

Zeina wakes at ten and stretches lazily in the down sleeping bags. Beside her, Guy does not stir. For the first time in her life, and despite the bloody marks on her T-shirt, she feels that everything is right.

She rises quietly and goes to the bathroom. After a long shower, she wraps herself in a towel and wakes him with a mug of tea.

'Good morning, handsome,' she says.

They begin cooking at midday, dressed in white paper suits and gas masks. First, they mix sulphuric acid and granular potassium nitrate fertiliser in a spherical glass retort bottle on a retort stand. Heating the mixture with a Bunsen burner produces red fuming nitric acid that condenses and flows along the retort's long neck to a spherical glass beaker nestling in an ice water bath.

They continue heating until no more acid collects in the neck of the retort and it stops dripping out of the neck into the beaker. While Guy checks the temperature in the beaker with a glass thermometer, Zeina uses a mortar and pestle to grind fuel tablets from a box marked *hexamine blocks for camping stoves* into a fine powder. When the acid has cooled sufficiently, she starts adding the powder to the beaker to create the explosive slurry, RDX.

He has warned her that the mixture is now at its most volatile and as the temperature immediately starts to rise, she swiftly pours salt and ice into the water bath to bring it down to zero. Guy carefully stirs the mixture and it begins to crystallise. He continues stirring, keeping the temperature at zero degrees.

After thirty minutes, Guy pours the mixture into a large bowl of crushed ice that she has prepared. He shakes and stirs the mixture. Once it has melted, he passes it through a coffee filter to retain the crystals and she pours the corrosive liquid residue down the toilet. Next, he adds the crystals to a beaker filled with boiling distilled water and filters them again. They repeat the process several times until a strip of litmus paper held against the crystals remains blue and Guy declares the crystals stable and safe. They spread them out across baking trays and store them in the fridge.

Guy removes his gas mask and runs a hand through the hair that is plastered against his scalp. 'We're done for now,' he says, 'but you have another letter to deliver.'

'I know,' she says.

'Clean yourself up first and bring back something to eat.'

48

Tell me you wouldn't have done the same?

Guy's postcards to his father are displayed as a mosaic on the video wall.

'The postcards were all printed before 2003,' Gretchen explains to Chuka who is seated in front of the wall. 'With the exception of the most recent one they were posted in the centre of Amsterdam.'

'Given that we believe that he was held captive in Iraq and Syria during the period when they were delivered, I think it's fair to assume that he used a re-mailing service,' Jude adds, from the back of the room. He's come straight from the airport, and he's desperately in need of a shower and a change of clothes.

'There are twelve potential targets on the cards,' Gretchen continues. By rights she should be even more tired than he is. As far as he is aware, she hasn't left the building since he left for Greece. 'The MI6 building, Horse Guards, the Gherkin, 10 Downing Street, Kensington Palace, Harrods, Broadcasting House, St Paul's, Parliament, the Barbican, the London Eye and the Stock Exchange.'

'From what you're saying any one of them could be it,' Chuka says, 'or it could be something else entirely?'

'He wants to make a big statement,' Jude replies, 'so it will be a high-profile target.'

'But not necessarily one of these?'

'He could be trying to steer us away from the real target,' Jude acknowledges.

'So, what do we know for sure?'

'I think we can say with some confidence that it will be a complex attack. He knows how we respond and we should expect him to exploit our vulnerabilities.'

'If it's a complex attack, surely that suggests accomplices and logistical support,' Chuka counters. 'More than Zeinab Hussein can provide.'

'Yes,' Jude concedes. 'He'll have help but probably not from anyone on our radar. He's too smart for that. He'll favour black-mail and intimidation over ideological fervour.'

The door clicks open.

It's Camilla Church.

They stare at her without speaking. It's the first time that Jude has seen her since Kensington Palace Gardens and he is shocked. She looks pale and exhausted. She is also wearing glasses, which she hates because she thinks they make her look vulnerable, which he takes to mean that she hasn't been home for as long as it has taken her to run out of the stashes of daily lenses that she carries with her for emergencies.

Has your husband's patience finally run out?

She's right about the glasses. Jude thinks that she has never looked more vulnerable.

'I wish to make a statement,' she says.

'It wasn't long after Ed Malik had returned from Syria. Queen Bee, I mean Samantha Burns, was contacted via an intermediary in Dubai who explained that he understood her difficulty and he was in contact with someone who could ensure that any further attacks like the Basra Ambush were prevented. You have to under-stand the situation she was in. Ed Malik's report was unequivocal. Nasruddin wasn't the Engineer. Which meant the wrong man had been rendered and tortured and she was responsible. On top of that she was terrified that there would be another attack. The war was unpopular enough as it was without further loss of life on that scale.'

'So, you cut a deal?' Jude says.

They are sitting across from each other, with Chuka at Jude's side and his phone on the desk between them, recording their conversation. It's not the only recording device in the room. Soon Queen Bee will know that her most loyal servant has betrayed her.

'Samantha Burns sent me to Dubai where I met up with the intermediary. He claimed to represent a senior commander in al-Qaeda in Iraq, who went by the name *Sheikh al-Jabal*, the Old Man of the Mountain. The Old Man outlined the terms of an agreement, in which we paid a monthly stipend into a numbered Swiss account and in return the real Engineer would be kept locked up. As long as we continued to pay there would be no further attacks.'

'So, you paid?'

'Yes.'

'Just like that?'

'Don't treat me like I'm a fool, Jude. Samantha Burns made it absolutely clear that any negotiation would be dependent on them revealing the identity of the Engineer. I honestly think at that stage, she had no thought of paying. She just wanted to know who the real Engineer was.'

'And the Old Man told you?'

'Yes. And it was worse than any of us could have imagined: a highly intelligent psychopath with first-world military skills and all the resources of an extremely successful terrorist organisation. The thought of him on the loose was unbearable.'

'So, Queen Bee paid?'

'Tell me you wouldn't have done the same?'

'I wouldn't have done the same,' Chuka says. 'For a start, paying protection money to a terrorist organisation or one of its representatives is in direct contravention of the Terrorism Act 2000 and the Proceeds of Crime Act 2002.'

'It was approved by the foreign secretary.'

Chuka is aghast. 'Frank Booth knew about this?'

'Of course he did.'

'How was the money paid?'

'A direct transfer from the unofficial reserve.'

'I thought that was closed down decades ago?' Chuka says.

'Queen Bee asked the Americans to replenish it.'

'The CIA paid for this?' Chuka says.

'Yes,' she replies. 'They're not squeamish about paying protection money.'

Jude remembers the un-named American at Queen Bee's farm-house in the hidden valley, the day before *The Guardian* story broke, and his parting remark to her, 'I hope you survive this . . .'

'How much?' Jude asks.

'Fifty thousand dollars a month.'

They both do the mental arithmetic. Chuka gets there first.

'At least eight million dollars.'

Camilla nods miserably.

'And nobody gave a moment's thought to the fact that an inno-cent man was kidnapped, locked up and tortured?' Jude says, barely containing his fury. 'And what about his wife? She was pregnant, for Christ's sake.'

'We were fighting a war,' Camilla says.

'Even wars have rules,' Chuka says.

'You've brought Fowle here,' Jude tells her.

'You're going to have to give a statement to the National Crime Agency,' Chuka says. 'You'd better hope that disclosing informa-tion to them helps you with your defence.' He picks up his phone and ends the recording. 'I need to phone the PM's office. Neither of you are to leave this room until I tell you otherwise.'

He leaves Jude's office, strides across the operations room past Gretchen and out the door.

Camilla looks at Jude.

'Forgive me,' she says.

49

Between the desire and the spasm

It's the end of anther working shift and Zeina watches from the shadows as the staff stream out of Palestra House, the eleven-story blue glass slab with distinctive cantilevered upper floors that houses the London Streets Traffic Control Centre. A part of her is relieved to be away from the flat with its noxious chemical fumes, but a greater part of her wants to return to Guy as soon as possible. He needs her beside him, she is sure of that.

She watches as a woman in a pale brown hijab with a pass on a red lanyard around her neck comes down the steps. Zeina crosses the road with her head down and falls into step beside the woman as she heads south towards the tube station.

'You're Tawara,' Zeina greets her, 'I thought it was you.'

The woman glances uncertainly at her through thick-lensed glasses. She has a round face and prominent front teeth. A pear-shaped body. 'Do I know you?'

'I recognise you from the photos.'

'What photos?'

'I need to talk to you,' Zeina tells her, and leans in to speak softly in her ear. 'Please, it's important. It's about your family.'

Tawara looks alarmed. 'My family?'

Zeina steers her into the adjacent park. She points to a nearby bench, 'Let's sit down.'

They sit beside each other. Tawara clutches her handbag tightly to her chest.

'Thank you so much for speaking to me,' Zeina says with a friendly smile. 'Your name is Pashto, isn't it? It means luck, yes?'

'That's right.'

'And your family is originally from Waziristan in the tribal areas? But they live in Karachi now?'

'I still don't understand what this is about,' Tawara says. 'Are my family alright?'

'I'm so sorry,' Zeina says, 'you must think me very rude. I can assure you that your family are fine. Your mother and father and brothers are all in good health. I asked you to come here because it is a delicate matter and I thought it was best to talk somewhere private but informal.'

'I have to get home,' Tawara says, 'so please hurry up.'

'Of course,' Zeina says. 'Jasmin will be waiting for you.'

Alarm turns to fear on Tawara's face.

'I'll be as brief as I can,' Zeina says, briskly. 'You see I work for a company that helps other companies to gain a competitive edge. We're researchers really. And I expect you know that the Traffic Control Centre is the envy of the world. Karachi wants something similar. I can see you know what I am talking about. The traffic there is chaos. If you can help my client to win a bid then you would be doing your home town a great favour.'

'I'm sure I can introduce you to my line manager if you'd like,' Tawara says, in a panicked tone.

'That's very kind but I'm afraid the proprietary software is simply beyond the means of my client. We need the source code.'

'I don't think I can help you with that,' Tawara says.

'Of course you can,' Zeina says and passes her the buff A4 envelope that has been sitting beside her on the bench. 'Have a look.'

Tawara draws out the stack of photographs and gasps. Naked, with her face scrunched up in orgasm, she looks a bit like a hamster. Several of the photos are stuck together and she has to peel them apart.

'I have a nasty feeling that they are held together by sperm,' Zeina adds, solicitously.

It's as if Tawara's body caves in: shrinking in size while wracked with sobs. Zeina puts a protective arm around her shoulders and with her other hand deftly retrieves the photos. She rests her chin on the crown of Tawara's forehead.

'Love in any form is beautiful,' Zeina says, 'and that between two women especially so. You are lucky to live in a city that is so tolerant, so blind to disgrace and dishonour. You are also lucky that your lover's brother, who professes to be devout, was obviously more excited than offended. He carried them in his backpack for months. I think at times he felt guilty. He even wrote you a letter in which he apologised for stealing them from his sister's computer. But what good is an apology in these circumstances? I tore it up. And I promise you that I can do the same for these photos.'

'You can?'

'I must,' Zeina tells her. 'If your family saw them I know they would kill you. They are traditional people who live by a code. What choice would they have?'

'What do you want me to do?'

'Something very simple.'

'I'm not brave,' she whimpers.

'You don't have to be brave,' Zeina says. She takes the USB drive containing the zero-day malware from her pocket and presses it into the young woman's hand. 'When you go to work tomorrow morning, I want you to plug this into one of the computers. Not yours, someone else's. It will download automatically. Give it ten seconds and then remove the drive. Take it out of the building immediately and throw it away.'

'Okay,' she says.

Zeina hugs her again. 'Now wipe away the tears and be strong.'

Back at the Dead Flats, she finds Guy sitting at the kitchen table. He is assembling one of the pistols, fitting the metal slide to the polymer body. The two MP5 carbines are already assembled and hanging by nylon slings from nails on the wall.

'How was it?' he asks.

'No problem at all.'

She loves it when he smiles, even if his gaze will never thaw.

'I brought you Chinese,' she says, setting the bag on the counter, and unpacking the paper cartons.

He nods and wipes the grease from his hands with a cloth.

They eat in companionable silence. Guy wields chopsticks with surgical speed. Watching the precision of his movement, she is reminded again, yet again, that he is an apex predator at the peak of fitness. Looking at the guns on the wall, she feels awed by what is to come.

After dinner, they mix the RDX with Vaseline and knead the mixture in a large aluminium bowl to create a malleable paste. Guy rolls the paste into cylinders that will fit the pouches on the chest webbing and vests, while Zeina makes balls that will fit in the grenade hulls. When he is done he returns them to the fridge in waterproof bags.

'What next?' she says, eager to help.

'Dressing up time.'

They unpack the police tactical uniforms purchased from the internet: black cargo pants and navy-blue polo shirts, black HG1/KR1 body armour, black Protec tactical vests with CS and Taser pouches, black Bates 7-inch Gore-Tex boots, black Velcro belts with baton and torch holders, and black needle-resistant gloves. There are even black-and-white Velcro union jack patches. They strip down and put the uniforms on to see how they fit.

Fully dressed, she stares at herself in the bathroom mirror and is surprised by how at ease she feels back in a police uniform again. More than she ever felt as an actual police constable. She has never been this powerful.

She makes a gun of her index finger and stares down the sight at the tip of her thumb.

'Kapow!'

'Come here,' Guy calls out.

He is standing on the mattress, naked with a stick of artist's charcoal in his hand. His police uniform is on a hanger on a nail.

'Take you uniform off,' he tells her. 'You don't want to get it dirty.'

While she undresses, he starts to draw a diagram on the wall above the bed, beginning with a rhombus and sketching straight lines from it at angles, like spokes. She sits, cross-legged at the foot of the mattress while he continues to build a map of the target. It doesn't take her long to recognise it and, when she does, she feels another rush of adrenalin.

'You'll have a helluva Wikipedia entry,' he tells her and begins to outline the plan, choreographing their moves with swift strokes of the charcoal.

X marks the spot where she will die.

Afterwards, they lie on the mattress in their zipped-together sleeping bags and load magazines with 9 mm cartridges.

'Are you going to record a last message?' she asks him.

'That was Nasruddin's job,' he tells her. 'I wrote it for him. The suicide bomber's final soliloquy: his fierce hatred of the state, his disgust at the heedless entitlement of the rich and the mindless prejudice of the herd. He'd have done it with feeling.'

'You could still do it.'

'I don't like cameras.' He looks at the wall and then in her direction. 'Do you want to say something?'

She wonders what she would say. That she is glad that her mother is dead. That she is in love and would rather die than be there when it ended.

'No,' she says.

When they are finished, she cuts herself again.

'What happens in the morning?' she asks, cradling his head in her arms.

He looks up with blood running down his chin.

'We collect the child.'

50

COBRA

Just before midnight, Jude enters via the Cabinet Office entrance on Whitehall and is escorted down a long corridor with a plum carpet to Briefing Room A.

The Downing Street Head of Communications separates himself from a knot of people at the door that includes the Assistant Commissioner of Specialist Operations at the Metropolitan Police and the Permanent Secretary at the Home Office, and advances on Jude. He has his hand pressed to his slowly shaking, freshly-shaven head. 'Absolutely not,' he says, into the phone. 'Wait.'

He barks at Jude. 'How fucking bad is this?'

'Potentially very bad,' Chuka replies. He has materialised at Jude's side holding a bound folder marked with yellow post-it notes.

Inside the room people are helping themselves to tea and coffee and ducking in and out of the room to take calls. Jude sees that Samantha Burns and Evan Calthorp, the Head of the Security Service, MI5, are already sitting in the cramped leather-backed chairs that surround the blond wood table. There is an apparent ease at the table, and Jude realises that most of them are university contemporaries or schoolmates.

It's Jude and Chuka that are the interlopers.

Chuka sits opposite Queen Bee as if to mirror her. It is abundantly clear to Jude that their fates are entwined. It is equally clear which camp he is now in. He helps himself to a black coffee and sits beside Chuka.

Queen Bee rewards him with her blandest stare.

Behind him they can hear the approach of the PM's entourage. The cabinet secretary, the prime minister's fastidious gatekeeper, steps in the room. He is a tall stoop-shouldered man with a chilly stare and the rigour of a Victorian schoolmaster. He sits at the head of the table opposite the video wall and briskly calls the table to order.

'I have called you here because whatever course of action we choose to take, it demands your immediate and personal attention, and the full resources of all the agencies represented here may be required in the coming days.'

He pauses and down the table heads are nodding. At the centre of the table Samantha Burns stares at the place setting in front of her with the trace of a smile on her face.

'You have all read the report from Chuka Odechukwu. In response, I have to advise the PM on whether or not to invoke the Civil Contingencies Act. To begin with I want to hear from the intelligence officer who has led the investigation. Jude Lyon, what can you tell us about the man that you claim poses such a threat to us?'

Jude is aware of curious eyes assessing him as he looks up from his notes.

'His name is Guy Fowle. He is a British citizen, a former British Army officer who served with the Royal Engineers and subsequently the Intelligence Corps. His last posting was to a Hereford-based training team that played the "enemy" for special forces exercises. He was an instructor on the All Arms Penetration Course, designing scenarios to defeat our tactics. According to the only surviving psychiatric evaluation, which was conducted on him when he was still at school, he is a psychopath of extraordinary versatility.'

'Why wasn't this picked up when he joined the army?' the cabinet secretary asks. The kilted major general in command of counter terrorism for the army looks pained.

'We are very rigorous in our recruitment processes, Cabinet Secretary.'

'Not rigorous enough, clearly.'

'His medical records were destroyed in a fire and it's possible that he falsified his school records,' the general explains. 'The investigation that led to his dismissal from the army cast doubt on the testimony of contemporaries from school and university who were interviewed during the vetting process for the Intelligence Corps.'

'He is a convincing liar and he's learned how to cover his tracks by means of blackmail and intimidation,' Jude explains. 'It's important for everyone in this room to understand that he does not show any of the signs of distress that characterise mental illness. Unlike psychotics, psychopaths are rational and aware of their actions. He is capable of fooling people and institutions. I believe that soon after he was discharged from the army he travelled to the Middle East and offered his skills to our enemies. We believe that he came under the influence of *Sheikh al-Jabal,* the Old Man of the Mountain, a senior commander in al-Qaeda in Iraq. He was subsequently responsible for the ambush in Basra that caused the loss of life of twenty-five British servicemen. You know him as the Engineer, though in Iraq they called him *al-Gharib,* the Stranger.'

'So, who was Nasruddin al-Raqqah?' demands Evan Calthorp, head of MI5.

'Nasruddin was a proxy for Fowle,' Jude replies, 'a means of claiming responsibility without revealing his true identity. It also played to his sense of superiority. We thought Nasruddin was the enemy but he knew better.'

'If I understand correctly,' the cabinet secretary says, 'what you are asserting is that a previous British government captured and, with the assistance of the Americans, transported the wrong man to Syria?'

'Yes.'

The cabinet secretary turns his attention to Samantha Burns. 'Were you aware of this?'

'Not at the time.'

'But subsequently?'

She raises her chin. 'Yes.'

'And you chose to do nothing about that?'

'I acted on the instructions of the foreign secretary. By the time we became aware that Nasruddin was not the terrorist known as the Engineer we believed that he had died in Syrian custody.'

The cabinet secretary and Chuka Odechukwu exchange a look. 'If Nasruddin was not the Engineer and the attacks stopped when he was captured why are we are only now talking about a fresh threat when he is released? Can you answer me that?'

'I came to an arrangement,' Samantha Burns says.

'With who?'

'With a senior commander in al-Qaeda.'

'The *Sheikh al-Jabal*,' Jude says.

'And what form did the arrangement take?' the cabinet secretary demands.

'An annual stipend,' Samantha Burns replies.

'You're telling us that for more than ten years you paid protection money to our greatest enemies?'

'What I did, with the blessing of the foreign secretary, and in the full knowledge of our American allies, was necessary to keep this nation safe from Guy Fowle.'

'And are we safe now? Jesus Christ, Samantha! How many other terrorist attacks has your generosity financed?'

Samantha Burns does not reply. The trace of a smile on her face has become a rictus.

'I'll expect your resignation on the PM's desk within the hour,' the cabinet secretary tells her. 'You're excused.'

They stare uncomfortably at the table while she considers the pile of papers in front of her. She decides to leave them in place and taking nothing, she rises from her seat and walks around the table. She pauses at the door and glances back at Jude as if she has something to say, but thinks better of it and departs.

The cabinet secretary contemplates the assembly and his disapproving gaze lands on Jude. 'Where is Guy Fowle?'

'We know that he left Syria more than a week ago,' Jude replies. 'He travelled by bus west across Turkey in the company of Nasruddin al-Raqqah and a woman, a UK citizen named Zeinab Hussein. She is a former police constable who is wanted in connection with the murder of her mother. They were smuggled by boat into Greece alongside a group of migrants fleeing conflict. Nasruddin was separated from them when the boat sank.'

'I thought that we had a fucking agreement with Turkey to prevent this sort of thing?' the head of communications snarls.

'The numbers taking the sea crossing have decreased but substantial quantities are still getting through,' the permanent secretary at the Home Office explains to the obvious irritation of the cabinet secretary. 'And there are plenty of other migrant routes. We face the largest migrant crisis since the Second World War. It's a booming trade and law enforcement is struggling to contain it, particularly in the face of a massive increase in social media use and money exchanges that allow a pay-as-you-go system.'

'So, he's in Europe?' the cabinet secretary snaps.

'We believe that he sent a postcard to his father from Bulgaria five days ago,' Jude replies.

'He sent a postcard?'

'A picture of the MI6 building with a message on it that says *X marks the spot.*'

'Is he taking the piss?' the head of communications demands.

'He's taunting us,' Jude replies.

'And you're convinced that he is planning an attack? Is MI6 therefore the target?'

'We can't say that for certain. It may be a ruse. He has been sending threatening postcards to his father for nearly two decades. All of them London landmarks.'

'What are we doing to find him?'

'We've issued an Interpol Red Notice and warned the Border Force at points of entry,' the assistant commissioner from the Met explains. 'If he tries to come in via an official route we stand a good chance to stop him.'

'And if he is as intelligent as you say he is and he's found some other means of entry? He sent a postcard five days ago. What if he is already here?'

'We're not hearing any chatter from our sources within the communities that shelter Islamic State sympathisers,' Evan Calthorp says.

'And we shouldn't expect to,' Jude says. 'If he has help it will come from unexpected sources. I think it's likely that he's here already.'

Exasperated, the cabinet secretary looks up and down the length of the table. 'Can someone help me?'

'We have the names of six people who I believe may be accomplices, either willing or coerced,' Jude says.

'We're searching for them now,' the assistant commissioner adds.

'How long is that going to take?'

'There are thousands of people across the country with names that match those found on a blackboard in Syria. We're checking them now; prioritising London addresses because that's where we think the threat is greatest. But this isn't just a matter of cross-referencing data. We need more boots on the ground, police officers knocking on doors and asking questions.'

The cabinet secretary makes his decision. 'I'm going to advise the PM to invoke the Civil Contingencies Act. I want the threat level raised to critical and I want extra police officers pulled in from across the country to help with the search and to protect potential targets in London.'

He looks at Jude. 'Whatever support you need, you have it.'

Finally, he turns to the head of communications. 'I want photos of Guy Fowle and the woman travelling with him released to the press. The PM will issue a public statement within the hour.'

51

Falls the shadow

It's 2 a.m. before Jude crosses back over the river to the Situational Awareness Group offices. Entering, he finds Gretchen sitting at her workstation. She tells him that they have a match on the DNA recovered by the Russians from one of the six bodies found in the Syrian town.

'It's on the national database,' she tells him and pulls a face. 'His name is Asim Jaffer, also known as "Sim Card". He was convicted of section 20 GBH for knowingly engaging in sexual intercourse with two women after being found to be HIV positive. He didn't notify the women of the risks or inform them that he was carrying the disease. He was sentenced to five years and served half his sentence in prison and the rest under licence in the community.'

'A nasty piece of work,' Jude says.

'He's been stopped and questioned twice by counter terrorism officials since then. The first time was following a trip to Tanzania: he claimed he was going on safari. On landing in Dar es Salaam, he was detained along with two others, fellow members of an east London amateur football club. They were kept overnight and then deported. According to Tanzanian officials they were detained because they were drunk and abusive. Asim was interviewed at Heathrow on his return because it was thought that he might have been trying to travel to Somalia. At that point, he was put on the watch list. The second time he was attempting to travel to Kuwait. He was blocked because of an email that he sent four months earlier to a friend in which he expressed sympathy for an al-Qaeda operative who had just been convicted in a US federal court for attempted murder. Six months ago, he disappeared. Several of his friends and associates have been interviewed under caution. They all agreed that he was desperate to leave the country.'

She taps her tablet and the video wall displays a rocky landscape dotted with concrete homes and a fire smouldering on the horizon.

'War is hell,' someone says in London English. 'I had one guy die in my arms and I had to help one guy tie a tourniquet around his leg to stop the bleeding. That's it so far. I'm sure there will be more to come.'

'This was uploaded two months ago,' Gretchen explains. 'Voice recognition confirms that it is Asim.'

The camera focuses on a rifle in the narrator's lap. 'I got my AK all ready,' he says. The clip ends.

'There's one more,' Gretchen explains. She taps another icon and Asim Jaffer's haunted face fills the screen. 'This is only twenty days old.'

'I've been separated from my squad. I've been hit by shrapnel,' Asim says, as gunfire crackles in the background. 'I came in this old building. I don't know if this is going to be my last fucking video or not. I'm getting blasted at in here. I got three full clips left and a grenade, so . . .'

His eyes widen at the sound of a metal door being kicked open.

'Fuck,' he says. 'Bye.'

The clip ends.

'At that point he was presumed dead,' Gretchen says.

'But he survived?'

'Yes, long enough to be shot along with five others inside the schoolhouse.'

'Have you found a link to one of the names on the blackboard?'

She shakes her head. 'I've checked the names of friends and associates. I've cross-referenced with the prisons database. Nothing.'

'What else do we know about him? Family, upbringing, etc.?'

'He was born in Kuwait to Iraqi parents of Bedouin origin. When the Kuwaiti government rejected their application for citizenship the family moved back to Iraq and from there to England. They settled in in east London, in Tower Hamlets and Newham. His father died not long after their arrival and Asim was taken into care at the age of five. According to the reports, his mother was sectioned after a violent confrontation in the street. Asim entered the foster care system and by the time he reached eighteen and left school he was thoroughly maladjusted with a string of convictions for petty crimes.'

'Check everything and everyone that he might have interacted with: schools, care homes, football teams.'

'I'm on it,' she says. 'And you should get some rest.'

She's right. He's exhausted.

'Where do you sleep?' he asks her.

'Under my desk.'

He nods at her and goes through into his office. He makes a pillow of his jacket and curls up on the floor.

A few hours later he is woken by a call from his sister.

'Welcome to my patch, big brother,' Tamar says, as they duck under the police incident tape and head away from the crowd towards the railway bridge at the bottom of the street. They are both wearing white paper suits with surgical gloves and blue plastic bags on their feet. 'Abdul Rahman runs a cash and carry chain with five outlets across east London. His wife didn't report him missing until twenty-four hours after she last saw him. Apparently, it's not unusual for him to stay out overnight. According to the CCTV footage from the car park of one of his shops, he left at 11.30 p.m. two nights ago, driving one of his own vans. He was accompanied by his personal driver who was at the wheel of a black BMW, also owned by Abdul Rahman. We tracked them on traffic camera footage driving east on Commercial Road at midnight that night and turning south towards Shadwell on this street. There was no footage of them joining the Highway, which is beyond the railway bridge ahead of us, and so we searched the arches.'

There is a police BMW blocking one of the side streets that runs alongside the railway viaduct. Jude recognises it as a Trojan, an armed response vehicle from SCO19, the Metropolitan Police's Specialist Firearms Command.

'We evacuated everyone within a two hundred metre radius,' Tamar explains. 'We've collapsed the inner cordon but the outer one is still up.'

They turn right into the street beside a shop advertising halal meat and walk between the railway arches on one side and a row of white vans parked nose-to-tail on the other. There is a transit van blocking the street marked *Explosive Ordnance Disposal*. It has its back doors open and a uniformed soldier is manoeuvring a tracked robot up the ramp into the back of the vehicle. There are further police cars with their lights spinning at the other end of the street.

'The arch was rented with a six-month deposit paid by credit card. An individual carrying the correct identification, including a driving licence and council tax records, picked up the keys yesterday. The card and the ID are professionally made fakes. They used the identity of a child that died of meningitis thirty years ago. No other purchases recorded on the card.'

The assault team are standing around outside the arch with their helmets off. Some of them are smoking. One of them nods to Tamar as they pass.

She leads him inside the arch to where the van and the BMW are parked beside a vehicle inspection pit. A white-suited scenes of crime officer is taking photos of the pit.

'We have identified tyre marks from a third vehicle,' Tamar says. 'Another van.'

She stops at the edge of the pit. Beside it, there are two black body bags waiting to be used. The air above the pit is heavy and still and smells of meat.

'It's Abdul and his driver,' she says, looking down at the bodies in the bottom of the pit. 'It seems that you were right about the names on the blackboard.'

Jude looks across at the van with its rear doors open.

'Fowle cross-loaded goods and drove away,' he says. 'You should track recent deliveries to Abdul's cash and carry shops.'

'We're already on it,' she says.

'What about the van he was driving? Do you have any camera footage?'

Tamar shrugs. 'There isn't any better camouflage than a white van around here. They're everywhere.'

'Come on, it was late at night. The nearby roads must have been quiet?'

'Yes,' she replies, 'and we've got a white van turning on to the Highway.'

'So?'

'He stole the number plates from one of the other vans in the street and switched several others over. People have been driving around with the wrong plates on for more than twenty-four hours.'

'Shit! What about the driver?'

'Black hat and sunglasses.'

'How far did you track the van?'

'Not far. My guess is he switched plates again somewhere within a mile or so of here. We're reviewing all the local camera footage but if he waited for a while for the traffic to pick up then there's no way for us to identify him.'

Jude walks back to the entrance and stares down the street. 'We have to assume that he has all the equipment and supplies that he needs to mount an attack.'

'Are you any closer to identifying the target?' Tamar asks.

Jude shakes his head.

Already, the news channels are showing images of armoured personnel carriers parked outside the MI6 building and Broadcasting House, and armed police at all major London landmarks.

'What if it's outside London?' he says.

'Come on,' she says, 'crazies always head for the capital. It's crazy catnip.'

'He's not crazy!' Jude says, more forcefully than he intended.

Tamar gives him a look that suggests that she thinks the pressure is getting to him. 'So, what is he?'

'Do you believe in evil?'

'Like Holocaust evil?'

'Not institutional like the Nazis, evil concentrated in an individual.'

'I've seen some fucked up stuff,' she says, taking off her suit, 'but that kind of evil? I don't know. Maybe that's new.'

Jude is sitting having a coffee in a corner shop café near the crime scene when his red burner rings. It's Kirsty.

'Where are you?' he asks.

'I'm in Scotland. You were right about old man Fowle. I'm lucky I didn't get an arse full of lead pellets.'

He smiles at the image.

'Where are you?' she asks.

'East London. We found one of the names on the board.'

'Is he talking?'

'He's dead. He ran a chain of cash and carry shops. They've been taking delivery of parcels addressed to a Mr Kurtz for three days now. We think Fowle has been equipping himself for an attack.'

'Any luck with any of the other names?'

'No but we've identified one of the bodies found in Syria and we're searching for a link.'

Tamar taps on the window.

'I've got to go,' Jude tells Kirsty.

'Be safe,' she says.

He hurries out into the street after Tamar.

'What is it?'

'We've had a distress call from police following up on one of the names.' She hands him a helmet. 'Safira al-Noury.'

52

The moon-faced boy

Before he became a suicide bomber, he was just a chubby little boy named Asad. The day he was born his mother, Safira, was seventeen. She gave her baby a name meaning 'lion', believing that it would make him strong and invincible.

Asad's father was a soldier who came one day to the small Syrian village where Safira had lived since she was born. A small village surrounded by fields of wheat, sitting off the highway, and nothing else around for miles except an ancient Roman ruin. The soldiers set up a checkpoint on the edge of town. Asad's father's name was Fouad and he was handsome and softly spoken. He told Safira how pretty she was, how he loved her shiny, black hair and hazel eyes and slender wrists. He said it in a way that sounded like he meant it, not the way the boys from the village said it. He was an officer and he wore a smartly pressed uniform and carried a clipboard. He drove a jeep that his soldiers kept polished. She fell in love with him. But the soldiers moved on after a few weeks and she never saw him again. When she told her father what had happened, he went after Fouad, to make him face up to his responsibilities. But Fouad was related to someone close to the ruling family and her father was detained by the secret police and beaten half to death in a shipping container.

When she began to show, they were forced to leave the village. They packed up their few belongings and moved to the city to stay in a cramped apartment with relatives. It was okay except for the way her father's brother touched her when no one else was around.

Pregnancy was easy until the end. The delivery was terrifying and painful but over quickly. The baby came in the spring. A boy just like she had hoped for with a round smiling face. Safira fed, cradled and changed him. No matter how tired she was she was always there. It didn't take her long to notice the differences in him. He had eyes that slanted upwards and outwards and a small mouth with a tongue that stuck out. At times, he meowed like a cat. The back of his head was flat. He only ever learned a handful of words.

When Asad was four, Safira's father died of a heart attack. He hadn't been the same since the beating. He was walking to the café that he spent each day in with the other old, unemployed men. He fell over in the street and died.

After that, there was very little money and the drought came. Her uncle often shouted at Asad and occasionally beat him. He made Safira pregnant and forced her to have an abortion. There were complications. The doctor told her that she couldn't have children after that.

Things became even more difficult. The demonstrations paralysed the city. One day she got swept up in a crowd and surprised herself by chanting along with her fellow demonstrators. Then the bombing began and they were forced to spend hours in the basement.

She remembers it as a bright morning when the men of Islamic State arrived in pick-ups waving their black flags. They were as hungry and sleek as wolves. She married one of the foreign fighters, a Uighur with Chinese eyes, who liked to joke that Asad was his own. He dealt with her uncle by denouncing him as a foreign spy and they were allowed to keep the apartment after his execution. The Uighur took Safira to see the Old Man, the *Sheikh al-Jabal*, who had such wisdom and compassion in his eyes. He told her that little Asad had been chosen for a special purpose that would guarantee him a place in heaven where his defects would be healed. She wanted that more than anything.

She agreed to the special training and was reconciled to die on the front lines of the final battle where the men with the black flags would defeat the crusaders.

In the event, the Uighur and all the other men of Islamic State fled at night leaving Safira and her son behind. At dawn, she disconnected the battery and removed the detonator from the vest that Asad was wearing. She helped him out of it and left it in the bottom of the trench. Together they walked out through the mine-field and greeted the advancing army.

They were moved to a camp in Turkey. The weather was harsh in the winter but people were nice to her. Everyone agreed that little Asad with his perpetual smile of vacant sweetness was special. She knew in her heart that his destiny was yet to be filled.

Asad smiled on the plane that carried them to England and smiled at the uniformed guards in the asylum centre. It was at the centre that she met the young man Zahir whose job it was to help her assimilate in a foreign land. He secretly warned her against letting her guard down in the lands of the *kuffar* – the unbelievers.

'Do not trust them,' he told her. 'They are your enemies.'

He shared with her his ambition to travel to the Islamic State and give his life fighting the crusaders and in return she shared with him the words of the Old Man and her ambition to secure a place for Asad in heaven.

The crusaders in black uniforms with batons and handcuffs on their belts sit opposite her, filling the tiny living room of the coun-cil flat. Beside them, the woman in the hijab with the painted nails shows her two photographs and asks her in Arabic if she recog-nises the man and the woman. She squints at the pictures to show that she is concentrating. The man looks much younger in the photo but it is unmistakably the man who brought her the letter from Zahir. He has the same unsettling eyes. The woman's photo is more recent. Her hair is different but it's her. She has been warned this might happen. She widens her eyes and stares sorrow-fully at the interpreter.

'I'm sorry. I've never seen them before.'

The older policeman says something.

'Do you mind if he has a look around?' the woman asks.

It's not a good idea but she shrugs. What will happen will happen, *inshallah*, it is God's will.

He stands up and goes out into the corridor. She hugs little Asad close.

Guy is pressed against the wall behind the bedroom door with the knife in his hand. He listens to the sound of the policeman's footsteps in the corridor, the opening and closing of doors. He watches as the door handle rotates beside him and the door swings open.

Two steps and he plunges the knife in the policeman's neck. Arterial blood sprays across the walls. The policeman, clutching at his throat, staggers and collapses, hitting the carpet with a thud.

Guy steps over him and out into the corridor.

When he reaches the living room five steps later, the other policeman is already out of his seat and has pressed the orange panic button on his radio. The interpreter screams when she sees the blood spatter on Guy's clothes and the grin on his face.

Guy steps inside the swing of the policeman's baton and slides the knife under his flak jacket and into his abdomen. He pulls it out and stabs again, this time in the policeman's neck. He shoves him against the wall, turns and advances on the interpreter.

He puts his hand over her mouth and slides the blade between two ribs into a lung. He holds her with the tenderness of a lover while the blood bubbles up out of her mouth and she drowns.

Carefully he lowers her to the floor.

He looks up at Safira and her son. The boy has blood on his cheek. While Guy is watching, the boy touches it and then licks the blood from his fingers.

'We have to leave now,' Guy tells them, in Arabic.

'We're ready,' Safira replies.

As they walk across the pavement away from the estate and towards the white van, they can hear the sirens of the police cars approaching from every direction.

53

Between the essence and the descent

Jude follows Tamar from the incident control point to the low-rise apartment block, where Safira al-Noury lived. They are both back in white paper suits.

'She arrived here last year under the Vulnerable Person Resettlement Programme,' Tamar explains, as they climb the stairs to the second floor. 'We're waiting on social services to release her files and running sheets but one of my colleagues just spoke to her care worker who says that she was held captive by Islamic State and used as a sex slave. She doesn't speak English, hence the need for an interpreter.'

She nods to the firearms officer guarding the door and they enter the apartment. They immediately have to stand back against the wall as a SOCO passes.

Tamar points to the bedroom on her left, where the constable is lying. 'Judging by the blood spatter, Fowle stepped out from behind the door and cut his throat with a knife. It was the same with Abdul Rahman and his driver. And the other constable and the interpreter.' She walks forward to the living room where two more bodies are sprawled on the carpet. 'Is it too much to hope that he doesn't have access to firearms?'

'He'll have found a way to get the weapons he wants,' Jude tells her.

He tries not to look at the bodies or the blood on the walls but focus instead on the contents of the room. The furniture looks second hand. It's clean but scuffed and chipped. The most striking thing is the lack of any personal belongings. There are no photos. No knick-knacks. Nothing that suggests a life.

'The child's bedroom is at the end of the corridor.'

'There was a child?'

Jude opens the door and steps into the room. It's not much bigger than a cupboard.

'A little boy with Down's syndrome,' Tamar tells him. When she sees the expression on his face, she says, 'What is it?'

He's remembering the details of the Basra Ambush. The child running out of the house carrying what the assault teams in the circling helicopters assumed was a baby in a blanket.

'The child will carry the first bomb.'

Jude's phone rings. It's Gretchen.

Tamar watches intently while he listens.

'We've got a link to a Steven Turvey,' Jude says. 'He spent a year in the same foster home as Asim Jaffer, aka Sim Card.'

Back in the Dead Flats, with the boy sitting beside him, Guy carefully slides the cylinders of explosives into the pockets of the police tactical vests and the pouches of a small-size set of black chest webbing. Next, he snips the corner of a sealed plastic pouch filled with steel ball bearings and, using a plastic funnel, pours them into the pockets and pouches so that they fill the air gaps around the explosives.

Across the table, Zeina fills the grenade hulls and attaches them to the igniter assemblies. She works quickly, worried that their hideout may not be safe for much longer, trying not to think about the enormity of what will soon be expected of her. At the same time, she marvels at Guy's lack of anxiety; he seems utterly focused, unburdened by doubt or fear or the nagging voice of the self.

Asad's mother makes black tea and the boy watches intently while Guy uses a pencil to create an indentation in the top of each cylinder of explosives where the detonators will fit when the devices are armed. Next, he tapes a simple phone to the shoulder strap on the harness of one of the vests and another on to the webbing. He connects them via a relay circuit to each bomb's wiring. For the remaining police vest he uses a longer length of wire that will run down Zeina's arm and links it to a red toggle switch, which he shows her how to tape to her wrist.

When he is done, he picks up the chest webbing.

'Let's see if it fits.'

He raises his arms over his head and Asad copies him. Guy lowers the harness over the boy's head and secures it at the waist. He adjusts the strap to tighten it and then steps back to observe the effect.

The boy smiles innocently.

'Fetch his coat and hat,' Guy tells the boy's mother in Arabic.

They watch while Asad promenades up and down the corridor beside the stacks of garbage bags. He is wearing a duffel coat with the suicide vest beneath. With the hat on he looks like Paddington Bear.

'That'll do,' Guy says. He looks at Zeina. 'You're next. Put your uniform on.'

She strips down to her underwear in the kitchen and dresses for the attack. When she is done, he zips up her vest and steps back. She has the MP5 in her hands, held by a sling around her neck, and the pistol in a holster on her hip.

'Stand up straight,' he tells her and she snaps to attention at his command.

'That's right,' he says with an indulgent smile, 'now put the guns and the vest in the bag with six of the grenades.'

She unzips one of the black holdalls and carefully places the guns, grenades and spare magazines in first and after them the vest and gloves. He tears opens the final parcel and hands her a trench coat, which she puts on over her police uniform. Again, she marvels at the detail of his planning. There's nothing he hasn't prepared for.

'Put your sunglasses on and walk up and down.'

She picks up the heavy bag and slings it over her shoulder, glad of the strength in her arms and upper body. Holding her head up high, she practises walking without revealing the weight that she is carrying. With her blonde hair and shades, she feels like a catwalk model.

Guy nods, apparently satisfied.

Next, they prepare Safira. Zeina removes her hijab, and undresses her while Guy speaks words of encouragement to her in

Arabic. She puts on Zeina's black leggings and her Ramones T-shirt. Zeina uses eyeliner to accentuate her eyes and backcombs her hair. When they are finished, she looks like an Egyptian goth.

Finally, Guy prepares himself. Minutes later, he is standing before them, dressed as a police firearms officer. From his pocket, he takes a narrow strip of red rubber, which he stretches before attaching it to a red handheld helium canister, and blowing it up. He ties a length of string to the balloon and offers it to the boy, whose eyes light up.

He looks each of them in the eyes, and Zeina feels the pride swell in her to have been given such an honour. Her earlier anxiety is forgotten.

'Are you ready?' he says in English and Arabic.

The grown-ups nod their heads. The boy smiles sweetly.

'Let's go.'

54

The Dead Flats

Jude climbs after Tamar into the back of a surveillance van on an east London housing estate.

'Look what the cat dragged in,' the silver commander greets them. It's Patrick, the rugby-playing DCI from the North East Counter Terrorism Unit, who Jude last saw in Yorkshire.

'Nice to see you too, Paddy,' Tamar replies. 'You're a long way from Kansas.'

'We've all been pulled in for this one,' he says. 'Let's hope no one commits any crimes up north for the next few days.'

They are parked about a hundred and fifty metres from the entrance to a block of flats with ugly grey cement cladding, metal framed windows with dirty net curtains, and no balconies.

'Steven Turvey lives in one of the corner flats on the eleventh floor,' Patrick explains. 'He's a heroin addict and according to the local police his flat was taken over by a Romanian gang last year. They used it as a shop for selling drugs. They moved on after a few months but while they were there we believe that they forti-fied it. We're going to have to blow our way in.'

The inside of the van has a floor plan of the flats blu-tacked to one carpeted wall and a bank of monitors beside it.

'The flat looks down on us here at the front,' Patrick says, 'so the tactical firearms team have assembled at the back and will come around the front in single file.' He looks across at Tamar. 'We already have two of your undercover officers in the living room of the flat directly above. They're inserting a fibre-optic cable. We should have eyes on the inside of the flat any minute now.'

Jude imagines Tamar's colleagues lying prone on the floor trying to make as little noise as possible while using a specially adapted drill with a suction device to prevent plaster falling from the ceiling of Stevie's flat.

One of the monitors crackles and flickers into life. The first thing they see is the red-eyed devil with the bat wings and the huge penis on the wall.

'Charming,' Tamar says.

The camera pans across the room, taking in a long trestle table with laboratory apparatus on it and discarded cardboard boxes and packing material strewn around it. A stack of empty plastic sacks catches Jude's eye. 'Can you zoom in on that?'

Patrick speaks into his radio and the topmost sack jumps into focus: it's labelled *potassium nitrate fertiliser*.

'It's a bomb factory,' Jude says.

'Gold, this is Silver,' Patrick says into his microphone. 'You've seen the confirmation. We're still waiting on the bomb squad.'

'Wait out,' Gold responds from the Scotland Yard control room.

'We need to evacuate the building,' Tamar says.

'You think there's time?' Jude asks.

Patrick silences them with a swift hand gesture. 'There's movement on the other side of the room.'

The picture pans 180 degrees to where a ragged man, who until that point had been standing motionless in the corner of the room, lurches forward several steps with a clanking sound and emits a barely human groan.

'There's someone in there,' Tamar says. 'What's he saying?'

'Help me!' the man shouts. He reaches the limit of the chain shackled to his ankle and jerks to halt.

'Where's the bomb squad?' Tamar demands.

'Gold this is Silver, where's the bomb squad?'

'This is Gold, Traffic Control Centre are reporting lane closures as a result of collisions in both directions on the Mile End Road and Commercial Road.'

'Shit!' Tamar shakes her head.

Jude watches through the eyepiece of the periscope as the tactical firearms officers from the assault team appear from around the side of the building and approach the entrance in single file.

'Silver this is Spartan One, we're entering the building,' the assault team commander informs them. On one of the monitors, the man in the flat is prowling back and forth like an animal in a cage.

'All stations, this is Gold. Traffic Control Centre is reporting unusual congestion as a result of multiple collisions on red corridors across London. The traffic light system has failed.'

Jude watches via a head-cam on one of the monitors as the assault team climbs the stairs. Through the walls of the van they can hear the sound of car horns in the streets surrounding them.

'All stations, this is Gold. Traffic Control Centre is compromised. London is under attack. I repeat, London is under attack.'

'It's started,' Jude says.

The team is assembled outside the steel door to Turvey's flat.

'We need to get in there,' Jude says. 'It's our only chance of finding the target.'

'Not without the bomb squad,' Tamar says.

'Agreed,' Patrick says. 'Gold, this is Silver. The assault team is in place but we do not have EOD on the scene. I repeat we do not have EOD.'

'Silver, this is Gold. We cannot wait.'

Patrick bangs his meaty fist against the side of the van in frustration and then shouts into his microphone: 'Spartan One this is Silver. Go! Go! Go!'

They watch while one of the assault team members places a linear breaching charge against the hinged side of the door and they all withdraw to the stairwell and hurriedly put on their gas masks and switch on the torches below the barrels of their carbines.

'Firing now!'

The detonation blows the door inward off its hinges and fills the corridor outside with smoke. A few moments later, the monitor lights up with the flash of stun grenades.

'We're in!'

There is garbage everywhere and shreds of floating black plastic. One of the assault team stumbles and falls and another team member pushes past him, and kicks open the first door.

'Room clear!'

It's a bedroom. Through the swirling smoke on the monitor, Jude glimpses a mattress and beyond it a black line drawing that looks like a diagram on the wall.

'There's something there,' he says.

The team has moved on.

'Room clear!'

'I need to see what was on the wall,' Jude tells Patrick.

All of the monitors go black.

The bomb punches a hole in the block of flats and rains masonry and glass on the car park below.

Jude is out of the back of the van and running towards the building before he has time to think. Smoke is pouring out the hole in its side. All around him there are wailing car alarms and the distant sound of sirens.

He barrels through the entrance and sprints up the stairs. By the time he reaches the eleventh floor his lungs are screaming and he is forced to stop to catch his breath. Ahead of him, most of the smoke and dust has been sucked out of the flat and he can see one of the surviving assault team members crawling through the debris towards him. There's no time to stop and help. He steps over him and enters the flat. He sees his first dead body. The force of the blast has stripped the police officer naked, scorched his body and torn away his legs. Another is slumped at the end of the corridor, naked but for his helmet, his chest and thighs scorched meat.

The smell makes Jude want to retch.

The entire wall of the living room is open to the sky and the floor and remaining walls are blackened and bloody. Whoever was in there at the time of the explosion, there's no way to distinguish them now. Flames are shooting out from a gas pipe and water is running down one of the remaining walls and pouring out through the hole. Disorientated, Jude realises that he has come too far. He turns and struggles back along the corridor through the debris and plaster dust. He pushes aside the splintered remains of the bedroom door and enters the room.

There's a charcoal drawing of a building on the wall above the mattress. The unmistakable rhombus of the central hall, with the courts, chambers, corridors and lobbies spread out horizontally and above them, at a slight angle, the rectangle of the great hall.

He staggers back out into the corridor and out on to the landing where the surviving police officer is sitting staring at nothing with blood coming out of his ears.

Jude grabs his radio.

'Tamar?'

'Yes, send!'

'It's Westminster,' he says, 'the target is the Houses of Parliament. Get your bike.'

He heads down the stairs, pausing for a few seconds between each flight. By the time he reaches the bottom, Tamar is waiting outside the entrance on her Triumph. He climbs on the back and grabs her around the waist. She guns the engine and accelerates across the car park through burning debris.

55

This is the way the world ends

Zeina rides the escalators up the deep concrete shaft from the Jubilee Line. She is wearing the trench coat and has the black holdall slung over her shoulder. Her peroxide blonde hair tumbles to her shoulders and she sees the world darkly through wrap-around shades.

Not far behind her Safira and Asad are following with the red balloon bobbing above their heads. The boy is holding the balloon's string tightly in his fist.

Zeina reaches the ticket hall and battles against the influx of commuters. She passes through the barrier and climbs the steps towards Big Ben. Outside there is a cacophony of horns and distant sirens. The traffic is backed up over Westminster Bridge and across Lambeth and Vauxhall. Parliament Square is at a standstill and people are beginning to get out of their cars. She stops at the very top of the stairs by the entrance to the station and presses herself against the wall to allow others to pass. Looking back at the crowd, she is in time to see the boy lose his grip on the balloon. It floats upwards towards the ceiling.

She takes the phone out of her pocket and steps away from the entrance and to one side, pressing herself against the granite wall in the covered walkway. She looks down at the glowing screen. There is only one number saved in her contacts.

It is time.

Now. She presses the green button.

Inside the crowded concourse, the boy's vest detonates. The sound is immense. Hundreds of steel ball bearings shred the crowd and the blast wave propels people out of the cave-like mouth of the underground station. Smoke pours out after and rolls across the road towards Big Ben. She discards the coat revealing the police uniform beneath. She kneels beside the wall and unzips the holdall, removing the tactical vest containing the suicide bomb. She quickly puts it on over her body armour and runs the wire, with the toggle switch at its end, out to her wrist where she tapes it in place using black gaffer tape that she tears with her mouth. Next, she reaches for the pistol and the machine gun. She holsters the pistol and pulls the carbine's sling over her head and across her back. She makes ready and lets the gun fall to her side. Finally, she extracts six grenades and distributes them across the remaining empty pockets of her vest.

She walks out from under the covered walkway and down the steps on to the street, stepping amongst the injured and dying. She eases herself between two buses and drops to her knee by the front wheel of a car. All around her people are running and screaming. The air is full of drifting acrid smoke. She pulls the pin from one of the grenades and throws it high in the direction of Parliament Square. She flattens herself against the wheel of the car, her head to the rubber.

After the thump of the detonation, she dashes forward between two cars, pulls the pin from the second grenade and lobs it in the other direction, behind her towards Westminster Bridge. Again, she flattens herself against the nearest car.

'Misdirection is the key,' Guy had told her. 'You have six grenades. Throw them two-at-a-time away from each other. Make them think there are multiple attackers approaching from multiple directions.'

After the second grenade goes off she stands up and advances into the smoke with her machine gun raised.

'Kill as many as you can,' he had told her, on the mattress of Turvey's flat, with the barrel of his Glock pressed between her scarred breasts. 'And then blow yourself to bits.'

On the far side of Parliament Square, Guy is striding through gridlocked traffic on Abingdon Street when the bomb in the underground concourse explodes. He has the barrel of the machine gun raised and the butt snug against his shoulder.

He is wholly present in his will, choice and movement.

You have become death, the destroyer of worlds.

He hurdles the black metal chicane with the statue of Richard the Lionheart on his left and the Queen's entrance on his right. As expected, the defence of the building has been concentrated at St Stephen's Gate and there are only two weapons-carrying police officers, standing side by side at the guard post, at the discreet, often-overlooked entrance to the House of Lords.

He drops them before they have a chance to react with a scything burst aimed at the groin and upper legs so that they fall into his arc of fire. He finishes them, one after the other, with a head shot at close range. He pauses long enough to strip the bodies of a radio, a canister of mace and two spare magazines, and barges through the swivel door into the vestibule.

He shoots the doorkeeper at the desk and the two unarmed security guards at the metal detector.

Then he is advancing down the corridor between wooden coat racks laden with jackets, heading towards the stairs. To his left a baroness comes out of the toilets and he drops her with a single shot. To his right a young woman wearing a visitor's pass emerges from the Family Room and he shoots her in the chest. On the Peers' Staircase, he kills a former chief of the defence staff and a bishop. When he reaches the top of the stairs he stops, attaches one of the grenades to the wall at ankle-height with a strip of black gaffer's tape hanging from his vest, and runs a trip wire across the corridor from the pin. He advances into the blue-carpeted Victoria Hall at the back of the House of Lords Chamber and shoots two clerks and a former chancellor of the exchequer who is fleeing down the Bishops' Corridor. He scans right to the Royal Gallery, which is empty, and turns left, entering the Chamber via one of the rear doors. He emerges alongside the golden dais and the Royal Throne, beneath the high windows and the statues of barons who forced Bad King John to sign the Magna Carta. There are too many targets to count. The debate has just been suspended and many of the peers are standing in front of the red leather benches or filing down the stairs towards the brass gates at the main entrance. Guy strafes the government and opposition benches with gunfire.

Peers die like flies.

When his magazine is empty he lets go of his rifle and it drops to his thigh on its sling. He kneels by the Woolsack, retrieves a grenade from his webbing, pulls the pin, and throws it in a high arc to land at the packed entrance just as armed police officers are pushing their way forward through the evacuating peers. He folds himself tight against the bench beside the corpse of the Speaker, and swiftly changes his magazine.

The detonation reverberates around the Chamber.

Guy jumps up out of cover and fires two three-round bursts into the rolling grey smoke. He retreats to the Victoria Hall. To his right, there is another detonation as the wire is tripped at the top of the stairs. More carnage.

He charges down the red-carpeted Bishops' Corridor heading east and turns left on to the book-lined Peers' Library Corridor. He shoots an armed policeman, who is running towards him, in the chest. The policeman lands on his back, firing his magazine into the ceiling until it is empty. Guy tips the barrel of his gun down, presses it to the man's forehead and gently squeezes the trigger.

The man's face caves in.

Guy throws a grenade through the door of the Bishops' Bar on his right and the Peers' Dining Room on his left.

Seconds later, he enters the Peers' Guest Room Bar.

It's a frozen tableau. Many are standing but an equal number are still sitting. He shoots the waiting staff first and then peers and their guests, methodically moving between the tables, first with his machine gun and then with his pistol, until there is only one person left. She looks up at him from the back of the room, beside the lead glass windows that look out on the Thames. She has an unfinished glass of champagne on the table in front of her and the expression on her face is one of profound disappointment.

'Why?' she says.

He pauses to change magazine and then puts the machine gun to her head.

'I am disgraced, impeach'd and baffled here,' he says. 'Pierced to the soul with slander's venom'd spear, the which no balm can cure but her heart-blood which breathed this poison.'

'Spare me your theatrics,' his mother says. 'Just get on with it.'

'I would like to kill you, mother,' he tells her. 'I really would. But I think it will cause you more pain if I let you live.'

He turns and strides out the bar into the corridor turning right towards the House of Commons, where the carpets are green.

56

The screaming pope

The motorbike races along the Embankment on the pavement straight towards a crowd of people fleeing the attack. Tamar accelerates further and pedestrians press themselves flat against the plane trees or leap out of the way. Over her shoulder, Jude can see the smoke and dust from the tube station explosion rising in a billowing cloud above Big Ben and he can hear the distinctive crackle of gunfire followed by the deafening thump of grenades going off.

Tamar skids to a halt beside the statue of Boadicea at the end of Westminster Bridge and they both jump clear. Tamar has her Glock out of its holster and is advancing diagonally across the front of the tube station, dodging between cars and vans peppered with shrapnel. Jude remembers that he is unarmed and stays close beside her. They can hear bursts of gunfire from the direction of Parliament Square and from inside the Palace of Westminster. They see a firearms officer slumped beside the wheel of a car with blood leaking out from beneath his flak vest.

Tamar kneels beside him.

'How many of them are there?' she asks.

He shakes his head, 'Lots. I don't know. They're everywhere. They're inside and outside the building. They're wearing police uniforms.'

Jude extracts the policeman's pistol from its holster, pumps a round into the chamber, and dashes forward with Tamar following. They run west between Big Ben on one side and Portcullis House on the other. They run into the smoke still pouring out of the tube station entrance, dodging to avoid people stumbling in the other direction. Sound is muted inside the smoke and seems to swell and recede. Jude runs between two double decker buses and alongside a high-sided truck with a huddle of wounded people sheltering silently beneath it.

He hears a burst of gunfire and the shotgun-pop of car tyres exploding ahead of him and to his left, and runs towards it. Through a rent in the smoke he sees the distinctive over-sized egg shape of a grenade flying overhead.

'Grenade!' he dives to the ground.

Immediately after the detonation he hears the sounds of shrapnel spattering the surrounding cars and buses. Powdered glass from shattered windscreens falls like hail.

Right behind him he hears a grunt of pain. He crabs around, low to the ground, and sees Tamar rolling back and forth with a hand clamped over her arm and blood leaking out.

'Dammit!' she says. 'That hurts!'

He crawls to her. 'How bad is it?'

She pulls a face. 'Better than a family get together.'

'Show me.'

She releases the pressure, and he watches as the blood oozes rather than spurts. 'The artery is okay.'

He looks around him. There's a man in a T-shirt lying face down beside them. Jude tears the T-shirt off his back, balls up the cloth and presses it against Tamar's wound.

Another grenade goes off.

'I'll catch up with you,' Tamar says, pressing her hand to the makeshift bandage. 'Go!'

He nods and turns, springing to his feet. Another burst of gunfire guides him left. He sprints diagonally and rolls across the bonnet of a silver car that has piled into the back of a white van at the intersection on the edge of Parliament Square. He glimpses someone in police uniform shooting at people spilling out of Parliament's main gateway. He ducks down against a driver's side door in time to see another grenade thrown.

After the detonation, he rushes forward again, using cars as cover. Someone at the gate is returning fire and the shooter ahead of him ducks down before looking his way.

for what happened to their client and his family, and compensation for their wrongful arrest and torture. Vandals have defaced the door to Baroness Fowle's Dolphin Square apartment and she is believed to be in hiding. Armed police officers are shown outside the gates of Fowle's father's estate on a Hebridean island and a reporter delivers a live broadcast from the police checkpoint by the gibbet at the entrance to the coomb, less than a mile away.

'How is she?' Jude asks.

Chuka shrugs. He's been with a team of lawyers questioning Samantha Burns all afternoon. 'I think she really believes, despite all this, that what she did made our country safer.'

'Perhaps the opposite is too difficult to admit, even to herself.'

'Do you still think that Fowle is coming here?' Chuka asks.

'It is unfinished business,' Jude replies.

'Then why not go after the father?'

'For the same reason that he let his mother live. Their lives will be hell for evermore.'

In breaking news, the presenter informs them that the body of a female employee of the London Traffic Control Centre has been found dead in her apartment, suspected of taking her own life.

'GCHQ are saying the malware used in the attack probably originated in North Korea,' Chuka tells him. 'Let's hope it didn't for all our sakes.'

The news switches to the latest Twitter spat between the mayor of London and the US president, who has blamed the attacks on lax immigration policies.

'I'm going home,' Chuka tells him, wearily. Jude wonders what kind of home life Chuka has. Maybe someone back in the city is waiting for him but there's no ring on his finger.

'I'll see you in the morning,' Chuka says.

Stepping outside on to the stone patio, Jude sees that someone is already there, standing smoking a cigarette. It's the young major named Howell who commands the SAS squadron manning the cordon that runs along the escarpment around the coomb.

Jude lights up and says, 'Is everything okay?'

'I've just walked the perimeter,' Howell says. 'If he comes we're ready.'

Jude wishes he shared the SAS officer's confidence.

A helicopter flies the length of the ridgeline, its searchlight roving across the gorse-studded downs and briefly lighting up a dense copse of trees.

'You're the one who shot the woman in the square before she could detonate her vest?' Howell says.

'Yes,' Jude admits. He feels lucky that the story put out in the aftermath of the attack that he was a police firearms officer has not been challenged.

'That was good marksmanship.'

'I didn't stop to think,' he replies, truthfully. He remembers it with absolute clarity though. Time slowed down: the martyr's expression on Zeina's face as she spread her arms wide, the thump of the helicopter blades, the thud of his heart, the fire-extinguisher red of the switch in her hand, the tightening of his finger on the pistol's trigger.

The shot.

'I just wanted to stop her.'

'I suppose you're wishing that's the last shot you'd fired?' Howell says.

'Yes.'

His recollection of events in the Chamber, emptying a magazine into the screaming man in the Speaker's chair and the subsequent detonation are, by contrast, cloudy, as if blurred by a primitive, numbing effect.

'It's a messy business,' Howell says. 'You do what you think is the right thing. There's nothing to be gained by beating yourself up about it.'

And there's nothing to say in response to that.

'Go get some sleep,' Howell tells him. 'We've got this.'

Jude drops the cigarette butt to the stone flags and grinds it out with his heel. 'Good night,' he says.

In the kitchen, he finds Samantha Burns in a Japanese print dressing gown, filling a kettle from the tap. She looks up from the sink and out into the darkness of the garden.

'I used to have a double,' she says, 'someone who could be me when I was somewhere else. But I lost the use of her when I resigned. I wonder how I would have responded if they'd told me that she could be the bait in a trap instead of me.' She glances at Jude. 'I'm having camomile tea. I find it helps me sleep. Would you like one?'

'Please.'

Together, they watch the kettle on the Aga top.

'I always liked you,' she says, eventually. 'You knew how to get a job done and you were never intimidated by complexity. The same could not be said for Camilla.' She sighs. They both know that if it wasn't for Camilla's confession, the news that the Secret Intelligence Service had been paying protection money to Islamic State might never have got out. 'How is she?'

He shakes his head. 'I haven't heard from her.'

'I've asked them to go easy on her,' Queen Bee says. 'She was simply following instructions.'

Jude doubts that Samantha Burns' word counts for much any more.

'Are you still in touch with Yulia?' she asks.

Jude has been receiving and ignoring sympathetic messages from Yulia since the attack.

When he doesn't respond, she says, 'What about the journalist?'

The kettle starts to sing and he is relieved not to have to answer.

She fills two mugs.

'You really need to find someone more suitable,' Queen Bee says, handing him a mug.

At 3.30 a.m., Jude wakes to the sound of gunfire on the ridgeline and an ear-splitting collision as a recently stolen 32-tonne tipper truck smashes through the police cordon, the grab-bucket on its Hiab crane dragging one of the Trojan armed response vehicles behind it into the narrow lane that leads into the village.

Jude drops off the couch on to the carpet, and kicks himself out of the sleeping bag. He puts on his boots, hurriedly lacing them.

He wishes that he had a weapon to hand – but there was no way, after he'd killed a government minister, that they were going to let him near one again.

He hears shouting in the corridor that runs the length of the house and the sound of heavy boots on the floorboards. He steps out of the room and two armed men in camouflage run past him and out the front door into the darkness. He can hear Howell, the SAS major, shouting into a radio, 'All call signs this is Control, pull back to the house!'

He continues to the end of the unlit corridor and stands in the shadow of the doorway to the living room. Howell is hunched over a Bowman HF radio on a desk with the silver commander standing beside him.

'A vehicle has broken through the east barrier,' the silver commander is saying into a phone held to his ear. 'He's inside the cordon. He's seconds away. I need the helicopter on the house now.'

There is gunfire outside, tyres screech and an engine roars. The room is lit up with blinding white light. The truck crashes into the room, sweeping ahead of it a bow wave of shattered glass, bricks and flint, and lathe and plaster. Howell and the silver commander are picked up off their feet and slammed against the back wall. Jude reels backwards into the darkness of the corridor and dives to the floorboards in a cloud of dust and falling debris.

Seconds later, all the lights in the house go out.

A scything burst of gunfire shatters the remaining windows the length of the building. It is so close that Jude curls up as tight as a ball and rolls into the space under the stairs. Somewhere in the ruins of the living room, the radio is still functioning and broadcasts a high-pitched scream. Someone empties an entire magazine in a single burst.

The helicopter rattles overhead, its searchlight in the hedgerows and ditches. The pilot's voice cuts across the screaming. 'This is India 99. I have multiple targets on the infrared. Control this is India 99, over?'

The helicopter is hovering overhead, the downdraft causing a tornado of plaster dust in the ground floor, its searchlight lighting up the garden and the driveway, throwing grotesque shadows across the interior walls.

'Control this is India 99, over?'

Jude hears someone on the stairs above him. He catches a glimpse of a moving shadow on the opposite wall. Ahead of him, at the end of the corridor, the front door crashes open and a soldier charges in. He is cut down by a burst of gunfire from the landing halfway up the stairs. His rifle with its under-slung torch rattles across the floorboards.

Jude rolls out from under the stairs and eases himself forward to the edge of the oak bannister at the foot of the stairs. The dead man's gun is within reach but out of cover. He cranes his neck, trying to see what is above him.

Then Samantha Burns screams.

Jude dashes forward and scoops up the gun, turning as he does so, pulling the arc of the barrel upwards towards the landing, expecting to die. There's no one there. He runs up the stairs to the landing, staying close to the wall. The stairs head up at a right angle from the landing to a low-ceilinged corridor with rooms off it in either direction. He snatches a quick look down the corridor. Queen Bee's room is at one end. The door is open and he can hear a struggle.

He advances down the corridor with the gun raised and the torch a spear into the darkness.

Guy Fowle is standing on the far side of the bed, silhouetted by the helicopter's searchlight, his face covered in blood. He has an arm around Queen Bee's waist and a gun to her head.

'Do you want me to kill her?'

He is grinning, his teeth bright white by torchlight.

'No,' Jude replies.

'Then get that light off me!'

Jude lowers the barrel of the gun, the light travelling down the front of Queen Bee's white nightdress and creating a circle of light at her feet.

'Back up,' Fowle tells him. 'We're going outside.'

Jude walks backwards out of the room and down the corridor with Fowle and Queen Bee following.

'When we get to the bottom of the stairs,' Fowle tells him, 'you're going to tell the people outside not to fire. Tell them we're coming out. Tell them I'm going to surrender and no one else will get hurt.'

Jude backs down the stairs, one step at a time, the barrel pointed at their feet as they come down after him.

'I remember you from the camp in Jordan,' Fowle tells him as they reach the landing. 'Your name is Jude, isn't it? You're a tenacious fucker.'

At the bottom of the stairs, Jude turns his back on them and approaches the front door, which is open. The gravel driveway is lit up like a stadium. He puts the gun down on the floor.

'It's Jude Lyon,' he shouts, 'I'm coming out! Don't shoot!'

He steps out into the downdraft with his arms raised.

'Get down!' someone yells.

He drops to his knees.

'He's got a hostage!' Jude shouts. 'Don't shoot!'

Fowle pushes past him with the gun held to Queen Bee's head. 'I surrender!'

He throws the pistol away and releases Queen Bee. She staggers towards the edge of the light. Fowle raises his hands and a bloody knife falls at his feet. He battles forward against the wind. A figure in black charges out of the darkness and rugby tackles him to the ground. Others pile in after him.

The last thing that Jude sees before his face hits the gravel is the look of astonishment on Queen Bee's face as she stares at her bloody hands and a red stain spreads across the front of her nightdress.

58

The end of intervention

For a woman who consistently and adroitly sidestepped the lime-light, Queen Bee's funeral service is a surprisingly public event. From where he is standing, beneath a loudspeaker attached to a stone buttress on the south aisle, Jude can see the entire tableau: the prime minister in the transept, flanked by three former prime ministers who counted Samantha Burns amongst their closest advisers. In the row behind them are several former foreign secretaries who were equally reliant on her softly spoken counsel. Only Frank Booth is notable by his absence.

Chuka Odechukwu, the newly appointed head of MI6, has secured a place for himself in the front row of the nave with his head held high. Jude had learned of the appointment hours before it was officially announced, by message from Yulia. It was followed a day later by a further message:

> All fun aside, I do hope the Prince continues to respect
> the mutual value of our liaison.

Scanning the crowd, with Elgar's 'Nimrod' issuing from the speaker above him, Jude spots Camilla standing beside her husband. She is in black with her head bowed like a penitent. Her husband, Roger Church, looks up and, for a moment, he stares accusingly at Jude.

The eulogy is delivered from the pulpit by the serving head of MI5 who describes Tracy Samantha Burns' twinkly-eyed rise from modest beginnings in Glasgow, via Hutchesons' Grammar school (affectionately known as Hutchie), the Glasgow University Debating Society and Her Majesty's Treasury to the higher eche-lons of the intelligence services, the National Security Council and MI6. He acknowledges the seismic effect of the cataclysm that was September 11th, 2001 and how it shaped her worldview and determined her actions. He does not shy away from the catastrophic intelligence failure that provided a dubious pretext for the Iraq invasion, or the disastrous civil war that followed. He pays tribute to her indomitable defence of her beloved British Isles and salutes her contribution to deterring a major attack on British soil every year for more than a decade. He describes her as a bulwark against unreason and chaos, and he repeats the often repeated saying that crisis never disturbed her bonhomie.

Of her killer, the homegrown terrorist, who is currently remanded in custody in the high security unit at Belmarsh Prison, there is no mention. It's too soon after the Westminster attack for agonising reappraisal. There are too many other funerals to attend and families to console. But Guy Fowle's shadow is long and those in the congregation cannot help but think of him when reference is made to her untimely death.

From the priest, her confessor, Jude learns that she was a recent convert to Catholicism.

It's her husband, a stoop-shouldered Oxford don, who speaks last. He forgoes the pulpit for a position standing alongside her coffin that is draped in white lilies. His voice is brittle with anger and suppressed grief.

'It's not true to say that she was unmoved,' he says, 'that she was without feeling or gentleness. She felt the burden of office more keenly than anyone I know, including many of you who dined at our table.' He stares at his feet and then looks up at the politicians and public servants that have closed ranks around one of their own. He blinks to fight off the tears. 'The last time I spoke to Samantha we argued. I told her that the simplest solution to any problem is rarely the best one. I told her that again and again governments create dependency and then renege on their responsibilities. She did not disagree. I told her that violent revolutions never result in something better and revolutionaries always become what they despise. Again, she did not disagree. And then, because my blood was up, I told her that when you destroy autocratic and barbarous regimes you inevitably cause more death and suffering than the regime itself. She turned her back on me for saying that. Whether in fury or shame I could not tell. I was too angry, too pig-headed to apologise. And now I will never ever get the chance.'

He shakes his head, too distraught to continue.

The priest steps smoothly forward to lead the gathering in the final hymn, 'I Vow To Thee My Country', as the coffin containing Samantha Burns is carried out into the rain.